This **Large** Print Book carries the
Seal **of** Approval of N.A.V.H.

SECRETS of
BELLA TERR

Cente
Large

SECRETS *of* BELLA TERRA

A SCARLET DECEPTION NOVEL

CHRISTINA DODD

CENTER POINT PUBLISHING
THORNDIKE, MAINE

This Center Point Large Print edition
is published in the year 2011 by arrangement with
NAL Signet, a member of Penguin Group (USA) Inc.

The text of this Large Print edition is unabridged.
In other aspects, this book may vary
from the original edition.
Printed in the United States of America
on permanent paper.
Set in 16-point Times New Roman type.

ISBN: 978-1-61173-225-2

Library of Congress Cataloging-in-Publication Data

Dodd, Christina.
  Secrets of Bella Terra : a Scarlet Deception novel / Christina Dodd. — Center Point
large print ed.
    p. cm.
  ISBN 978-1-61173-225-2 (library binding : alk. paper)
  1. Private investigators—Fiction. 2. Hotelkeepers—Fiction. 3. Large type books.
    I. Title.
PS3554.O3175S43 2011
813′.54—dc22
                                                                        2011030279

Thank you to the family and staff at Seghesio Family Vineyards for their kindness and patience as I asked questions and stuck my nose into the operations at the winery and vineyards, for guiding me through tastings and most of all for teaching me that "fruit forward with a spicy finish" is not as risqué as it sounds.

A special thank-you to Rachel Ann Seghesio for graciously sharing your stories and histories, and giving me a sense of the family and community that I tried to infuse into the Scarlet Deception series.

Acknowledgments

Leslie Gelbman, Kara Welsh, and Kerry Donovan, my appreciation for your constant support. More appreciation to NAL's art department led by Anthony Ramondo. To Rick Pascocello, head of marketing, and the publicity department with my special people, Craig Burke and Jodi Rosoff, thank you. My thanks to the production department and, of course, a special thank-you to the spectacular Penguin sales department: Norman Lidofsky, Don Redpath, Sharon Gamboa, Don Rieck, and Trish Weyenberg. You are the best!

SECRETS of BELLA TERRA

Prologue

With the precision of a surgeon, he sank the screw into the aged cork, curling it around and around; his experience had taught him to go so far and no farther. Then, working meticulously, he eased the cork out of the plain green glass bottle.

Like so many things in life, these matters took planning and attention to detail; anything worth having was worth waiting for.

This was worth waiting for.

Although in this case, he had waited almost too long. . . . He was robust, yes, but not a young man. Still, at last, victory was in his grasp. And the victory, he now knew, would be so much more than he'd ever anticipated.

The wet end of the cork was dyed almost black and when he sniffed it, his nose wrinkled in dismay. This bottle on which he'd spent so much time and money was probably like all the rest he had collected throughout the years—so far past its prime as to be undrinkable. Yet tenderly he poured a few sips into the bottom of the stemmed glass and raised it to the light.

He had hoped to see a rich plum color; instead it was a faded, muddy red.

He swirled the wine in the glass, lifted it to his nose, and sniffed.

Not good. Not good at all. There should be fruit and spice. Instead there was cork taint and vinegar.

Still he persisted, filling his glass, sipping the wine, and rolling it across his tongue.

He shuddered at the taste; his eyes filled with disappointed tears.

Yes, people feared him. Yes, people tiptoed around him. Yes, rumors of treachery swirled around him. But really, he had the heart of an artist, and this . . . this setback almost broke that heart.

Another bottle, so rare as to be legendary, and it was spoiled by age and neglect. With great care, he poured the wine down the drain, watching as the liquid stained the white porcelain a reddish brown.

The phone rang, his second line . . . his secret line. He looked at the caller ID with distaste, but answered it anyway.

"Hey! Listen. There's news I thought you should hear." Ah, that voice. Brash, confident, a little too loud, like a cheap wine in a handsome bottle.

Lowering his voice to a whisper, he said, "Tell me."

"Flores got shot dead."

"Interesting." His voice rasped.

"He's out of the picture."

"Interesting," he repeated.

"That's what happens when you go out of town for your talent."

"Interesting," he said again, but what he meant was, *Insolent.*

"You want me to take over now?"

He played with the cork, crumbling it between his fingers, watching as the old wine and tannins stained his fingers purple and black. And he thought.

He'd never seen his caller. No need. He knew the type, and he knew the details on this specific tool: ambitious, cruel, easily led with money and flattery. Perfect, if not for the prison time—but that was served in a foreign country under an alias, and, should it become necessary, was easily expunged.

At the silence, the tool's confidence slipped. "I can do it. I promise. I don't have to move into place. I'm right here on top of the action. You might as well take advantage of that. C'mon. C'mon. Give me a chance."

There was so much at stake here. His family's honor, stained as his fingers. And, of course, the promise of wealth that put his current fortune to shame.

He made his decision, and whispered, "Same terms."

"Yes! Good! I like the terms."

"Punishment for failure."

For the first time the tool paused. "Punishment? What kind of punishment?"

"Punishment," he whispered again.

13

"Okay. Okay, sure. I'll do it. No need to worry about punishment. I can do it. When do you want me to start?"

"Now." He drew the word out, caressing each sound with his husky whisper.

Then he hung up.

He got out a clean glass, pulled out another bottle of wine, and tried again.

Chapter 1

Bella Valley, California

As Sarah Di Luca drove along the winding road out of town and back to the home ranch, she heard the whisper of new leaves struggling to be born from the grapevines. The wind that blew through her open window smelled like fresh-turned earth and sunshine on newly mown grass, and the cool air slid around her neck like a luxurious fur. The rows of vivid green vegetation made her smile; another year, another spring, another day. At her age, all of that carried a weight and a joy nothing else could ever replace.

She pulled up to the house, the hundred-ten-year-old homestead that stood on a rise at the far end of Bella Valley, and climbed out of her Ford Mustang convertible. She'd bought the car new in 1967. The official color was "playboy pink"; her grandsons called it "titty pink." She laughed, figured boys would be boys, and drove more slowly every year. Reflexes, you know.

Old age was not for sissies.

She and her sisters-in-law said that every time they spoke on the phone. If only it weren't so true.

She put her purse over one arm, fished her grocery bags out of the passenger seat, and looked up the stairs at the wide, white-painted front porch. The treads were narrow and steep, not up to the current building codes, but when the house was built, there were no codes, only tough immigrants carving out places in the heat of California's central valleys. This house, with its tall ceilings, narrow windows, ornate trim, and root cellar, had been the epitome of the stylish farmhouse.

Now—Sarah climbed to the porch, dropped her purse and bags before the front door, and sank into the big rocking chair—she looked over the valley that stretched sinuously through the wooded foothills of central California. In the lush bottomlands, robust orchards nestled into the layers of thick soil brought down from the mountains. But up here, on the edges of the valley, jutting black stones, the bones of the earth, broke through and challenged the grapevines planted so precariously in the thin soil. Those tough vines grew the best grapes, and those grapes created the wine that in the early part of the twentieth century had made the Di Luca name famous.

Then Prohibition arrived, with the revenuers who smashed their wine barrels and destroyed their chance at prosperity.

As Sarah rocked, the floorboard moaned and complained as if it felt the ache in her back and the tremble in her legs.

In 1921, in a desperate venture, the Di Lucas opened the Bella Terra resort, a place for the wealthy from San Francisco, Sacramento, and, in the thirties, from burgeoning Hollywood. There they rested, relaxed, and were pampered. Now the resort stretched like a jewel among the rows of grapes, the cornerstone of the Di Luca family's wealth and influence.

It made Sarah's heart swell with pride to see how thoroughly the Di Luca family had sunk their roots into this valley, to know how the famous and affluent flocked to Bella Terra to vacation.

At the same time, she missed the early days when the wine country was rural, quiet, homey.

But that kind of nostalgia was another sign of old age, wasn't it? Just like this weariness that plagued her after a mere trip to the grocery store.

Trouble was, she couldn't let the store deliver, and she couldn't ask one of the kids who worked at the resort to meet her here and carry her groceries in. She'd done that once and her grandsons, all three of them, had found out within an hour and called to see if she was dying of some dreadful disease.

She *was* dying, but from old age, and death would take its own sweet time. In fact, these days, eighty wasn't so old.

She groaned and stretched out her legs.

Of course, it wasn't so young, either.

But she'd always been an active woman, and she was still in pretty good shape. If only . . . She glared at her shoes, ugly, sturdy things with all the proper supports. Some days, she was in the mood to put on heels and dance.

The bunions had taken care of that.

Still, there was no use complaining. There were people in worse shape, and if she slacked off on going to the grocery store and driving herself to church, her grandsons would soon have her wrapped so tight in protective gauze she'd be good for nothing. With renewed determination, she focused on putting the groceries away before the ice cream and frozen peas melted in the heat.

Pushing herself out of her chair, she gathered her bags, opened the front door, and walked down the dim hall, past the parlor on the left and the bedroom on the right, past the bathroom and the second bedroom, and into the big, old-fashioned kitchen. The appliances were new, state-of-the-art, but when the boys had wanted to do a complete remodel, tear out the counters and the cabinets, change the flowered wallpaper, she'd said no. Because, of course, they would have wanted her to move to the resort to avoid the mess and fuss.

She visited the resort occasionally: swam in the hotel pool, enjoyed the occasional massage at the spa, visited with the guests. But she knew that a woman of her age couldn't move out of her house for a month without pining for the peace and quiet of her own company.

The boys said she was isolated.

She told them she was content.

Dropping her purse and her bags on the table, she briefly noted the cellar door was open—odd, she didn't remember leaving it ajar—and went to the sink. She adjusted the faucet to line up with the center of the sink—she must have been in a real hurry this morning; she usually left it in its proper position—then looked out the window at her yard.

The boys were always fussing about something. They wanted to bring the driveway around to the back door so she didn't have to tote her groceries so far, but to do that they'd have to pull out the live oak in the backyard.

The wide, long-branched, evergreen oak had been planted in 1902 by the first Mrs. Di Luca the year she married Ippolito Di Luca and moved into the house as his bride.

Like the house, like the valley, like Sarah herself, the tree had survived storms, fires, droughts, years of prosperity, and years of famine to grow old and strong. Its dappled shade had protected generations of Di Lucas as they played and worked. She wouldn't have it removed. Not it, nor the rosebushes, now scraggly with age, sent from England in 1940 by young Joseph Di Luca . . . her husband's cousin.

He hadn't survived that war. Old grief, but still grief. Oh, and not the amaryllis the boys grew in pots every Christmas and then had planted outside . . .

A cool draft wafted across her cheek.

Cold realization struck her.

The cellar door was open.

She turned to look. Yes, it was open, a dark, gaping mouth with a gullet that led to the windowless basement.

Why was the cellar door open?

She had not left it ajar. She knew she hadn't. She'd raised one son and three active grandsons in this old house, and the entire time, that steep stairway and the cold concrete at the bottom had scared her half to death. One tumble and they would have cracked their little skulls. But she didn't tell them that. They would have viewed it as a challenge. Instead she told the boys that she kept her wine down there and the bottles needed the dark and the cool temperature to age. They understood. If there was one thing the Di Luca family took seriously, it was wine.

Her wine . . . bottles of wine . . .

Her heart leaped.

She hadn't left the faucet catawampus, either. She remembered finishing the dishes, wiping the sink with a damp dish towel, and placing the faucet correctly.

Her blood pressure peaked, a nasty feeling that made her light-headed. With her gaze fixed on that open door, she pushed herself away from the sink.

Someone had been in her house. Might still be in her house.

She looked around. Saw nothing else out of place. Saw no one.

She needed to get out.

Her purse and keys were on the table.

Whoever it was, was gone. Surely they were gone.

She walked briskly, quietly to the table and gathered her stuff.

Amazing how the aches and tiredness vanished under the impetus to *get out*.

She turned toward the back door, intent on removing herself from the scene. She opened her purse as she walked, fumbled for her cell phone. She glanced down long enough to locate it, heard the cellar door creak. She half turned to see the door swaying.

A man ran toward her, a tire iron in his hand. He swung at her skull.

She flung her arm up.

The bar connected.

Pain, bleak and bitter, exploded through her nerves.

Ramming her from the side, he knocked her into the wall.

Luckily, the plaster beneath the flower-patterned paper was old and it crumbled under the impact of her head. Luckily . . .

Sarah woke with the sun shining in her face. For a moment, she couldn't remember what had happened: why she was on the floor in the kitchen, why she could see through only one eye.

Then she did remember.

An intruder. Get out!

She sat up. Her forearm flopped uselessly at her side. Agony struck her in waves. She wanted to vomit, but she didn't dare. She was afraid to move. She was afraid to stay. She listened to the house, to the familiar silence, and realized the hot breeze was blowing in her face. Little by little she turned her head to look.

The back door was open.

He was gone.

Slowly, slowly, each inch a new torture, she withered back onto the floor, an old, hurt woman who didn't want to face what would happen next.

She lay there, eyes closed, fighting the nausea, grappling with the reality of her situation.

If he was still hanging around, she was in trouble. But he could have finished her off while she was unconscious, so probably he'd hit her and left.

She wondered if he had instructions to hurt her, as a warning, or if that had been panic on his part. She hoped it was panic; she hated to think of the state of a man's soul when he willingly sabotaged and attacked an old woman.

She hated even worse to think of the man who must have ordered the attack. But then, his soul had been damned years ago.

No matter how much it hurt, she had to get up, get to the phone, call . . . Oh, God, her grandsons were going to have a fit when they heard what had happened.

But she had no choice. There was blood on the floor and she was pretty sure she had a concussion, so gradually she opened her eyes—no, her eye—again.

Huh. By some instinct, she'd managed to hang on to her cell phone. *Good job, Sarah.*

Squinting at the numbers on the touch screen, she dialed 911 and talked to the dispatcher—a dispatcher who knew her, of course. Almost everybody in Bella Valley did. By the time the conversation was over, Sarah knew she didn't have to worry about calling the boys. They'd find out through the grapevine. They'd be here in no time.

Instead she went through the painstaking process of making a conference call to her sisters-in-law, one on Far Island and one on the Washington coast.

She didn't waste time with a greeting. She simply said what needed to be said. "It's started again."

Chapter 2

Tradition.

Tradition had governed the Di Luca family for an eternity.

Tradition had governed Bella Valley for one hundred and twenty years.

Until Brooke Petersson moved to Bella Valley, she'd never seen that kind of tradition at work.

Oh, she understood tradition. Until she was eleven, she was an Air Force brat, and if there was one thing the military did well, it was traditions. But family traditions . . . not so much.

Her father, Captain Kenneth Petersson, was a fighter pilot, born in Minnesota, tall, tanned, blond, blue eyed, and broad shouldered, with a mother who made lutefisk and a father who ate it. Brooke had lived with her grandparents while her parents were both deployed to various hot spots in the world, and while she didn't enjoy that—she was nine; she missed her daddy and mama—she discovered what it meant to be half Swedish. That gave her the sense of having roots, which, since the family moved about once a year, she really didn't.

But Brooke's mother, Kathy, was from Oklahoma, straight black hair, striking blue eyes, curvaceous figure, with pale skin that burned unless she was wearing SPF 50. So the next year, when her mother was back from her assignment in the Middle East and the two of them were living on the base in San Antonio, Brooke made a friend who was red-haired and freckled, who sounded like Enya when she sang, and whose parents were from Ireland and spoke with a brogue. The McBrians were Catholic, had six kids and another on the way, and were even poorer than most of the Air Force families. But Brooke ignored their lack of furniture and bare walls and focused on the family, so loud, so vital, so wrapped up in religion and their tales of the Old Country, so unlike her own with its comings and goings and long stretches of loneliness. . . .

So the next time she visited her grandmother in Oklahoma, she asked in a hopeful voice if they were Irish. Her grandmother, a formidable woman who had raised three kids with no help from anybody, turned on Brooke, put her finger in her face, and said, "We're not Irish, we're not Mexican, we're not French, we're not any of those nationalities. We're Americans, and don't you ever forget it."

It wasn't the answer Brooke was looking for, but she wasn't dumb enough to complain. She shut her mouth and looked for something else to concentrate on—and found it in her parents' bitter divorce.

That broke every tradition and vow she'd ever imagined.

That had broken her life and her heart.

In Bella Valley, Brooke had quickly learned from the Di Lucas that their kind of family traditions were different. The Di Luca family was American, sure. Ippolito Di Luca had immigrated to California in the late nineteenth century, married an Italian girl whose father owned a swath of land and vineyards in Bella Valley, and every child born to the family since had been born in the United States and spoke English as their native tongue.

But the Di Lucas had hung on to the essence of being Italian. They gestured when they talked. They drank wine. They corresponded with the family in the Old Country. They ate Italian. Northern Italian, to be specific. Not that the Di Lucas never got Chinese takeout or made a turkey for Thanksgiving, but every one of them knew their way around a pot of golden, slowly simmering polenta—and God forbid some well-intentioned fool should mention instant polenta. The Di Lucas flirted. . . . Brooke didn't understand how flirting could be passed down as an Italian tradition, but it was. Every one of the Di Luca men and women used charm like a condiment, to bring flavor and pleasure to a relationship.

The Di Luca traditions meant that when they liked someone, they adopted that person into their family. Brooke knew that firsthand; she had been a part of the family almost from her first day in Bella Valley, and no matter what happened in her life, she was still one of them, almost a daughter, completely a friend.

The Di Luca traditions also meant that when someone got hurt, cards, flowers, and phone calls flooded in and the nearest and dearest gathered close.

So when Rafe Di Luca strode through the door into Sarah's hospital room, Brooke had been expecting him. Waiting for him . . .

But neither knowledge nor foresight could ease the sweet, familiar shock of recognition. That long stride, that stern profile, that carved body displayed so pleasantly in blue denim and black leather . . .

He nodded at his two brothers.

At thirty-four, Eli was the oldest, the tallest, the least likely to shoot off his mouth and get in a fight—and the most likely to win if he did.

At twenty-eight, Noah was three years younger than Rafe, with the Di Luca family head of curly black hair and a pair of green eyes that had turned many women's heads.

The resemblance between the brothers was strong, but Rafe was the son who looked most like his father—heart-stoppingly handsome—and acted least like him, for the dangers he faced every day were not the fevered imaginings of some scriptwriter, but real and terrifying.

Brooke braced herself for the moment when his heated gaze touched her.

He didn't seem to notice her sitting in the corner. Didn't even glance in her direction.

Even so, the room grew smaller, the air warmer and more concentrated, Brooke's heartbeat slower, stronger, each throb spreading heat and life and pleasure.

So many years had passed since she'd seen him for the first time, on her beginning day of the new school, when he plucked her out of the crowd and summoned her with a jerk of his head, and she giggled like . . . like the prepubescent girl she had been and tagged after him like a love-starved puppy.

Even so many years later, the memory made her wince.

Today, all the Rafe Di Luca charm was bent on his grandmother.

"Raffaello, I have been waiting for you." A trembling smile broke across Sarah's face, and she extended her good hand.

Rafe stopped a few feet from the bed and assessed her—the broken arm, the battered face, the IV in her arm—and shook his head with mocking reproval. "Nonna, how many times have I told you not to get in bar fights?"

For the first time since she'd been attacked, Sarah chuckled. "I learned everything I know about getting in trouble from my grandsons."

He lowered the silver rail and leaned close, put his cheek against hers and closed his eyes. "You scared me half to death," he murmured.

Sentiment clogged Brooke's throat.

No matter what she thought of Rafe, she knew his adoration for his grandmother ran deep and true.

As he straightened, he smiled at Sarah. "Now—tell me the truth. Why were you in a bar fight?"

"You should see the other guy." Sarah smiled back, but no eighty-year-old could have her head bandaged and a cast on her arm without some wear and tear, and the flush of happiness Rafe's arrival brought quickly faded.

Rafe saw it, of course. He saw everything. Cradling her hand, he turned to his brothers. "What do we know about the perp?"

"Not a damned thing." Noah bit off his words. "Nonna was unconscious probably a half hour, which gave him plenty of time to get away. We think she arrived right after he broke in—or rather, walked in, since she never locks her doors—"

"Don't need to," she said.

Like male versions of the Fates, the three brothers turned in unison and glared at her.

"This proves you do, Nonna," Rafe said.

She snorted.

Brooke hid a grin.

To Noah, Rafe said, "Go on."

"We couldn't see that the perp disturbed anything," Noah said. "He hid in the cellar, then rushed out, attacked her, and ran away."

Rafe's expression became cold interest. "So he was panicked . . . or he was sent there to attack her."

"Who's going to attack an elderly woman?" Eli ran the winery. He called himself just a farmer. Yes, maybe. But he had also proved to have the Di Luca way with wines, creating reds that consistently ranked in the top ten percent of the reviews. Neither of the other two Di Luca brothers had the nose, the art, the sensibility, and in the circle of the larger Di Luca family, Eli was venerated.

In this bleak hospital room, of course, he was merely one of the brothers.

"People do all kinds of heinous things for money, for fun." All too obviously, Rafe knew what he was talking about. "Did you see him, Nonna?"

She shook her head, and winced. "No. Ski mask. But definitely a big man, white, tall, fit, young. Of course, at my age I think everyone's young."

"At your height, you think everyone's tall, too," Eli said.

"Eliseo, come over here so I can swat you." But Sarah was smiling again, and when Eli

30

leaned over the other side of the bed, she gave him a mocking sock to the chin.

"Good point, Eli. Was he as tall as me, Nonna?" Rafe asked.

"No." She sighed. "I'd say six-foot or a little below."

"Oh, good. That narrows it down to about five thousand guys here in Bella Terra." Rafe smiled his crooked smile.

Brooke told herself that when he smiled like that, he looked like Novocain was working on one side of his mouth.

But that wasn't true. Instead, in his jeans and black leather jacket, he resembled a tough, half-amused, world-weary Gerard Butler. She'd seen that expression work magic on women from around the world. She'd felt the impact herself.

She felt it now, and it wasn't even aimed at her.

"The police said the burglar might be a vagrant," Noah said.

"Everybody always wants to think it's a vagrant rather than someone who lives in their nice little town." Rafe's cynicism grated on Brooke's nerves.

And on Sarah's, for she stirred restlessly, and winced.

He turned to her right away. "Don't worry, Nonna. We'll keep you safe. No one's going to hurt you again."

At once, Sarah recognized her chance to get

her way. "At home. Promise me I can stay at my home."

The brothers exchanged exasperated, helpless glances.

"Nonna, it would be so much easier if you'd stay at the resort," Noah said.

"Or with me. You know you love my house." Eli had finished his new home on Gunfighter Ridge overlooking the glimmer of Bella Creek. "I've got a guest cottage. You can be alone as much as you like."

"In my own house," Sarah said stubbornly, but her voice trembled and a single tear slid down the soft wrinkled cheek.

Sarah never cried, and that one tear broke the guys.

"I'll keep you safe in your house," Rafe promised.

"I know. I trust you." She smiled, but her lips trembled. "I'm not afraid for myself. But if something happened to one of my boys, I couldn't live with myself."

Real amusement lit Rafe's face. "I'll take care of my feeble brothers."

"Yeah, Nonna, Rafe'll take care of us." Eli used sarcasm like a weapon. "Nothing can happen to him. As long as the mugger hits him on the head, Rafe'll be fine."

"They have knives. They have guns," Sarah said fretfully. "Even after all these years, he's so angry. . . ."

Brooke came slowly to her feet.

The brothers all leaned forward, intent on their grandmother's face.

"Who, Nonna?" Rafe's voice was the soft rasp of velvet. "Who are you afraid of?"

"What?" Sarah looked puzzled. "I'm not afraid of anybody. I just want you to be careful."

The brothers exchanged glances, and nodded. Brooke could almost see the communication between them—*Later*.

"I'm going to have to have someone stay with you," Rafe said firmly.

"Someone's going to have to stay with her anyway," Noah said. "That concussion—"

Sarah broke in. "The arm hurts worse than anything."

"I'll take care of security for you, Nonna. I need to talk to someone who knows a lot of people, and for that, Brooke will help me. Won't you, Brooke?" For the first time, he turned his head, the deliberate motion of a predator viewing its prey.

Of course. The man was in the security business. He cased a room as soon as he walked in.

He had always known she was there. He had known she was observing him. And the iciness in his eyes made her want to cower.

But she didn't. She knew men like him, men who stayed at the resort for rest and relaxation, who carried with them a chill that froze the marrow in her bones. It was her policy to never, ever let them know how much they scared her.

And Rafe scared her more than any of them.

Because no matter how much she hated it, he still made her want him.

Chapter 3

Brooke walked to the bedside and did the one thing the guys were afraid to do—she stroked Sarah's head, smiled into her eyes. "I'm going to help Rafe find the person who did this, and bring him to justice. You know I can do it, too."

Sarah relaxed and looked like the Sarah they all knew: kind, happy, optimistic. She smiled back at Brooke. "I know. I have absolute faith in you." She turned to Rafe. "You, too, dear. All of you boys are so good to me. The best children . . . I don't deserve you. . . ." Tears welled again.

Brooke turned on the grandsons. "Sarah's had enough. Why don't we leave her alone so she can rest?"

It wasn't really a suggestion, but an order, and the guys weren't about to argue. They had those looks on their faces, the panicked expressions men got when they recognized the onset of a tearful storm.

They nodded, backed toward the door, and exited in a rush.

Brooke leaned over the bed and pushed the call button. "We'll ask the nurse for your pain medication."

With her good hand, Sarah caught Brooke's arm. "It's my fault you have to do this. I'm sorry."

"You mean work with Rafe?" Brooke smiled

and shook her head. "What happened, happened a lot of years ago. It's not important anymore. And anyway, it's no more your fault for getting hit than it's mine for becoming the resort concierge. Neither one of us could foresee these kinds of events, could we?"

Sarah's eyes went out of focus, dreamy and sad. "Not foresee, but I always thought . . . feared . . . it wasn't over."

Brooke hit the call button again, harder. "What do you mean? What wasn't over?"

"The feuds drag on and on, one generation to the next. . . ." Sarah's sad voice petered out.

"Nonna?" Brooke leaned close to see if she was breathing.

The nurse, Kayla Garcia—she and Brooke had gone to high school together—huffed as she came through the door. "I came as quickly as I could. What's the problem?"

Brooke straightened. "She's in a lot of pain, but . . . she was talking and not making sense."

Kayla, short and plump and kindhearted, shed her irritation. Leaning over Sarah, she used that professional nurse voice to ask, "Mrs. Di Luca, how are you feeling?"

Sarah focused on her face. "Fine. Why?"

"Brooke thinks you'd like your pain meds," Kayla said.

"I would, yes. I'd like to sleep, but I'm uncomfortable."

Kayla glanced at the chart. "Then let's do it." She added the meds to the IV, glanced toward the closed door, and her eyes shone with the gleam women always got around the Di Luca men. "Was that Rafe Di Luca I saw?"

"Yes. All the brothers are here now."

"I'm surprised you had room to breathe with all those broad male shoulders in here."

Brooke grinned. "They are a little overwhelming. But nice guys."

"As long as they get their own way." Kayla checked Sarah's pulse and ran her blood pressure.

"All men are like that," Sarah said, her voice slurred from the drugs.

Kayla and Brooke laughed, and watched Sarah fall asleep.

Kayla nodded. "Sleep's the best thing for her." She looked up at Brooke. "She's eighty years old, she was attacked, and she's got a concussion. She's going to have moments of confusion. That's just the way it is."

"Will she be okay?" Brooke needed the reassurance.

"You mean will she be as sharp as she was before the attack? I don't know. I wouldn't know if she was twenty years old—concussions are tricky things. But she's in good health, has lots of friends, keeps busy. There's no reason to think anything except that she's going to be fine."

"Thank God." Brooke leaned over Sarah again to brush her hair away from her face. "I don't know what they'd do without her." If someone was trying to threaten the Di Lucas, they'd picked the right way to do it.

And the stuff Sarah had said . . . it sounded as if she knew something, as if she'd been threatened before.

But Kayla hadn't heard the discussion in here, or Sarah's ramblings. Thank God, because she loved to gossip, and that wasn't the kind of gossip Brooke wanted to encourage.

Instead Kayla headed right for the possibility of juicy Di Luca brothers rumors. Sighing gustily, she said, "That Rafe. I had such a crush on him when I was a kid. Remember that movie he did? The one with the dragon who was his best friend when he was little and then he grew up and forgot about him?"

"I remember." Like Brooke could forget. Wandering to the window, she looked out over the cars in the parking lot, over the roofs of the houses, the small businesses on the outskirts of downtown, the larger hotels and shops set around the square. She could see the thin, silver line of the river, and beyond that, the pre–World War II homes of the longtime residents. She could pick out her mother's house, tucked onto a tiny lot on a short block in an old neighborhood. Beyond that, the plots of land grew grander, and in the midst of each one was a mansion owned by someone who had recently discovered the charms of Bella Terra. And beyond that were the vineyards that created the valley's affluence.

Bella Terra was a mix of old and new, poverty and prosperity, and Brooke loved it all.

"Rafe was such a handsome boy even then." Kayla whistled softly, then sensibly said, "Well, look at his parents."

Brooke did not want to talk about Rafe or his parents or how gorgeous he was. She had experience with nosy reporters and nosy guests; she could have shut Kayla down. But she liked Kayla, and better this than speculation about the attack on Sarah Di Luca, especially when it sounded as if . . . as if it wasn't a random event.

Kayla chatted on. "You don't see people who are more beautiful than Gavino Di Luca and Francesca Pastore, and when they got together and made Rafe—I mean, the Di Lucas have always been hot stuff, but he takes it to a whole new level. That tanned skin. Those blue eyes. Those long, black lashes. Whew!" She waved her hands at her face.

"Yeah. Whew." Brooke picked up her purse.

"I remember when you two used to hang together. You were so close, we all thought you'd get married."

Ah, the small-town high school, a germ factory of scandal. Prosaically, Brooke said, "I wanted a career. He wanted to go in the military. So we waved good-bye."

"I knew it! I told the girls you were still friends, but they didn't believe it."

Brooke leaped on the opportunity to spread the right kind of rumors. "Every time we see each other, we fall right back into that friendship. Now I'm going to help him set up security for Mrs. Di Luca. You know—because I know everybody in town and can help him figure stuff out."

"Oh. Good. Makes sense." Kayla nodded, but she didn't care about something as dull as friendship when there was Hollywood and glamour to discuss. "I wonder why he quit making movies."

"I think because he wanted to live with his grandmother." Brooke eased toward the door.

"Really?" Kayla sounded surprised. "I heard it was because he was always in so much trouble his mother gave up on him."

"Maybe you're right." Kayla was so right.

"Well, you'd know. You know the family and Rafe better than anyone."

Brooke stopped easing and looked Kayla right in the face. "I know the resort. That's all. That's my job."

"Sure." Kayla didn't believe her, but she didn't press the matter. Instead, in a reflective voice she said, "About six months ago, I showed that

40

dragon movie to my kids and cried so hard the DH went out and bought me ice cream. That's a lot of talent Rafe abandoned for some dangerous job fighting bad guys. I mean, the combat job— that's really real."

Brooke walked toward the entrance again. "I'll tell the Di Luca boys what you said about Mrs. Di Luca. I'm sure they'll appreciate the news."

Chapter 4

The three brothers spilled out of Nonna's room into the bright, green, glaring hospital corridor. As the door swung closed behind them, they drew simultaneous breaths of relief. Then Eli and Noah turned on Rafe.

"Where have you been, man?" Eli asked.

"Nonna's been fretting about you," Noah said.

They both punched Rafe in the arms, Eli on the left and Noah on the right.

"Hey!" Rafe rubbed his biceps. They were bruised for sure—but he figured he deserved it.

Besides, next thing Eli got his arm around Rafe's neck and gave him a noogie, while Noah kissed him on both cheeks, Mafia-style. Rafe fought, of course—it was required. But he didn't fight very hard, and when Eli released him, they were all grinning.

So were the nurses at the desk.

Knowing how fast rumors spread in this town, Rafe kept his voice low. "I was in Kyrgyzstan. No quick way out. Anyway, I had to get someone to take my place first or that woman was going to get—" He took a breath. "Well. I got here as fast as I could."

"I thought you were done taking that kind of security job." Eli was the oldest by three years, from Gavino Di Luca's first marriage to a

Chilean beauty queen and actress who, when she found out about Gavino's affair with Rafe's mother, had first tried to kill Gavino with a kitchen knife—the publicity had been great for Gavino's movie career—and then, five years later, when she got out of prison, kidnapped her son from Nonna's house. For years, no one had known where he was. . . .

Eli never spoke of those missing years. Never.

"Friend of mine from the military called," Rafe said briefly. "His daughter's an Air Force helicopter pilot. She went down close to the Chinese border. Rebels. Religious zealots. The Chinese. They were all after her. I do favors when I can."

His two brothers nodded; then the three of them stepped out of the way as Kayla Garcia brushed past them, scowling, and entered Nonna's room.

As the door swung open, Rafe caught a glimpse of Brooke leaning over the bed, talking to Nonna, brushing her hair back.

All Rafe's life, Nonna had been his bulwark, the one thing that he could depend on to be there, to support him, to love him. Now someone had attacked her.

Seeing Nonna resting in the bed, seeing Brooke beside her . . . they were everything he'd ever cared about.

If only he didn't feel so guilty for being gone . . .

and for never really being here when he was here.

The door swung closed, cutting off his view, and the now sober Di Luca boys headed for the empty waiting room at the end of the corridor.

They stopped and stared at the old-fashioned coffee machine in dismay.

Eli sighed. "There's better coffee in the cafeteria."

"Can't leave. I need to wait for Brooke." When Rafe had entered Nonna's room, he had noted Brooke sitting quietly in the corner. He had noted she looked tired. He had noted she wore a pair of jeans, a white button-up shirt, and faded pink tennis shoes. But he hadn't really looked at her. His grandmother had commanded his attention. His grandmother deserved his comfort and his kindness.

But now he moved on to other priorities: finding Nonna's attacker, and then . . . then spending time with Brooke, listening to her voice, breathing the same air, wishing that things could be different, and knowing that was impossible.

Because all those years ago she'd told him she wouldn't have a man who made danger his business. She wouldn't travel the world with him. She wouldn't wait and worry about him as she had about her parents.

She knew what she did and didn't want. He had accepted that years ago . . . and yet, every time he saw her, he knew—she was the only one for him.

She had put down roots in Bella Valley, and those roots grew deep.

"How bad was Nonna?" he asked his brothers. When he'd gotten the news, up there in the Kokshaal-Too Mountains, he had been incredulous. During all his travels around the world, Nonna's home, this valley, had glowed in his mind like a warm coal of reassurance.

"We thought we were going to lose her." Noah's hand shook as he picked up the pot and poured a cup of coffee, then another, then another and handed them around.

Now some bastard had ripped his grandmother's security away from her, and at the same time stolen Rafe's comforting delusion of Nonna's immortality and a home that waited for him forever.

Rafe was going to make that bastard sorry he had ever been born. He clutched the cup, taking comfort from its warmth. "What haven't you told me about the attack?"

"Nothing, damn it. Not a damned thing." Eli took a sip and shuddered at the flavor.

"We don't get that much violence here." Noah was the director of Bella Terra Resort, in touch with city and state officials. "Drunk tourists, of course, some drugs and shoplifting, but not this kind of random stuff, and the cops haven't got the personnel and equipment to deal with it."

"Get me the police report." Then, remembering these were his brothers and not someone who worked for him, Rafe said, "Please, can you get me the police report?"

Eli pulled out his smartphone, punched a few buttons, and said, "I've forwarded it. Will you review it right away?"

"No." Most definitely no. "I want to make my own observations untainted by what anyone else has decided."

"Bryan DuPey was the one who said it was a vagrant," Noah said, "and he's the chief of police."

"Dopey is the chief of police?" Rafe couldn't believe it.

Eli laughed at the reminder of their high school taunts. "Yeah, but we pronounce it DuPey now."

"Why? He was always an idiot." Rafe dismissed DuPey without a second thought.

"Yeah, but he loves Nonna's cookies," Noah said. "He really tried, Rafe, but the thief, or whatever he was, didn't do anything to the house. They even tried fingerprinting and didn't get anywhere."

"So the perp wore gloves. That's not your usual drug addict, 'I've got to get enough cash for my next fix' thief." Rafe looked at his brothers, who were both slouched against the wall and grimacing about the coffee.

He took a sip and reflected that it wasn't so bad. Bitter and grainy, but at least it was hot.

But what did he know? Kyrgyzstan didn't boast a lot of Starbucks.

"What if Bryan is right? What if it was just a vagrant?" Noah sounded relaxed, and looked as if he'd been worried every minute of the last two days.

"Then Nonna wouldn't be troubled about us." Rafe remembered what she'd said: *They have knives. They have guns. Even after all these years, he's so angry.* "Who's so angry? The Marinos?"

"They're wild men, but even they draw the line at beating up old ladies," Noah said. "Joseph Bianchin is a mean old bully, but he's the last of his line, and I don't know why he'd start a gang now."

"Then who's she talking about?" Rafe insisted.

Chapter 5

Nonna's got a concussion. She's . . . been rambling." Eli threw his unfinished coffee in the garbage.

Rafe's chest grew tight. "She is going to be okay, right?"

"Yeah. Sure." But Eli didn't look at him.

And Rafe knew about concussions. He'd seen enough of them in combat; he probably knew as much as the doctors. Touchy things. He didn't even know why he was asking except that he desperately needed reassurance. Desperately needed to know his grandmother would be back in her place on the home ranch, there to welcome him when he came home. "Have there been any other attacks like this one? Any attacks in Bella Valley or Sonoma or Napa?" he asked.

Both Rafe's brothers shook their heads.

"All right." So it was probably a targeted attack. "What details does Nonna give about the attack?"

"She isn't talking much about what happened this week." Noah sat on one of the plastic chairs. "But she's crystal clear about what happened fifty-nine years ago."

"What happened fifty-nine years ago?" Rafe asked.

"She got married." Noah stretched out his legs.

48

"Got pregnant on her wedding night. Worse luck," Rafe said.

"Nine months later produced our father." Eli had that look on his face, the one he got when he tasted bad wine.

"Any other disasters you know of?" Rafe asked.

His two brothers shook their heads.

Noah said what they were all thinking. "Isn't that enough?"

Gavino Di Luca was Nonna's only son, and at fifty-eight still too handsome for his own good.

The questions had to be asked, so Rafe asked them. "Where is the old man? Why isn't he here?"

"He's filming in Thailand. He was on the phone all the time until she was out of danger, but he can't come home because of the schedule." Noah's cynicism felt like shards of glass. "Also, he's got a new—"

"Wife?" Rafe snapped.

"Girlfriend," Noah said.

With a cynicism to match Noah's, Rafe said, "Let me guess. She's twenty."

"No, this is an older woman. She's twenty-seven." Noah smiled without humor. "He puts the *dys* in dysfunctional."

"Don't we all," Rafe muttered.

"Exactly." Noah spoke firmly—Rafe's younger brother didn't lack for confidence. "The fruit doesn't fall far from the tree. We're the proof of that."

"Speak for yourself," Eli said. "I keep my affairs private and I never get in over my head."

"You're the sensible one, all right," Noah allowed. By that he meant Rafe was not.

So Rafe changed the subject. "Has the Di Luca family thought about donating one of those fancy 'make everything' coffeemakers to the hospital?"

"It has to go through the hospital board first," Eli said ominously.

"So?" Rafe wasn't following.

"One of the Marinos heads the hospital board, and Joseph Bianchin's involved, so . . ." Eli shrugged.

The rivalry between the three families had originated long ago, and the three families had stubbornly carried it to America and through more than a century.

"Why isn't Joseph Bianchin dead yet?" Rafe asked.

"If life was fair, he would be, but the old fart is still puttering along in his mansion, yelling at the kids when they steal his oranges." Noah had been one of those kids, and Nonna had received a nasty phone call about that.

"And the Marinos?" Rafe already knew the answer to that.

"They're still stealing Bianchin's oranges." Eli shook his head, half in admiration and half in disgust. "They're stealing our grapes. They're having parties that only break up when the cops arrive. They're drag racing on the county roads. And that's just the parents."

Rafe laughed, but Noah said, "It's like having our own California Italian rednecks right next door."

"At least they're consistent," Rafe said.

The Bianchins and the Di Lucas had been respectable families when they'd come across from the Old Country.

Not the Marinos. They had been tossed out by the Italian authorities. They still had a chip on their shoulders about that, and about the fact they'd made their money during Prohibition making moonshine, running the cathouses, and owning dive bars.

They still owned the bars. The other stuff had gone by the wayside. At least, as far as Rafe knew, it had.

Noah poured another cup of coffee, sipped again, and groaned pitifully.

"Maybe if we say we want to donate a coffee machine, they'll do it?" Rafe suggested.

"Maybe. Right now, the Marinos are pissed because the Di Luca Miele Cabernet Port beat them out of the gold at all the wine festivals." Noah grinned at Rafe, then at Eli.

"Nice." Rafe nodded at Eli. "Been kicking ass, have you?"

"I've done okay." The words were modest. Eli's tone was smug.

"He's been kicking ass all over California and Washington with his cabs and zins." Noah didn't mind bragging on his brother.

Rafe glanced again at the hospital room door.

It remained stubbornly closed.

He wondered if Brooke was stalling, not wanting to see him, talk to him.

But no. Not Brooke. Even as a scared kid that first day of school, she had set her chin and done what had to be done without flinching.

For her, he knew, he was a task to be faced without flinching.

Noah stepped right in front of Rafe. "So listen to me. About Brooke."

Rafe wasn't proud of himself, but he wanted to snarl like a wolf protecting his mate, a visceral reaction, unbidden and instinctual. "What about her?"

"She's the best. She knows everybody in this town, everybody at the resort." Noah met Rafe's gaze head-on. "But she works for me."

"And?"

"I'll let you use her to find the perp, but I don't want you to mess with her."

Noah was right. Rafe knew it. So he reined himself in, put on his civilized face, and said, "I'm not going to mess with her. All she's got to do is cooperate and everything'll be fine."

If only she didn't look like Brooke—five-foot-nine, tanned, with dark brown hair as sleek as sable and an athletic build that made him think of hard matches on a sunny tennis court, cold Cokes from the convenience store, and the slow bead of sweat sliding down her cleavage. . . .

"Cooperate with you? That doesn't sound good." Noah viewed him with suspicion.

"I mean cooperate in helping me find the perp," Rafe said patiently. "Look. Brooke's not a stupid woman. She's not going to sleep with me again." Unfortunately.

"I don't care if she sleeps with you," Noah said scornfully.

Good. Because that means you aren't sleeping with her.

"I care whether she gets involved with you." Noah came to his feet. "I remember the last time that happened. When you left, she looked like someone ripped out her heart."

Eli joined Noah. They stood shoulder-to-shoulder facing their outcast brother, and Eli said, "With what happened this month, she's not going to be able to deal with you and your prima donna ways."

"A prima donna. For God's sake, I just spent two weeks in the mountains in Kyrgyzstan freezing my gonads; how does that qualify me as a—Wait." Rafe zeroed in on the important phrase, and repeated, "With what happened?"

Noah turned on Eli and glared.

"What happened?" Rafe insisted.

"He's going to find out soon enough," Eli said to Noah. "The gossip's barely died down."

Rafe damn well needed to have all the facts before he plunged into this investigation, even if they pertained to his former girlfriend. Especially if they pertained to his former girlfriend. "What gossip?" He could barely open his jaws, his teeth were clenched so hard.

Noah gestured at Eli: *You started this,* the gesture clearly said.

"Three weeks ago, she shot an intruder at the hotel." Noah held up a hand as if to stop Rafe before he said a word. "Cruz Flores was an illegal immigrant, had served prison time in Mexico and in the U.S., and six months ago his wife and daughter disappeared. Their blood was all over their house. The cops believe Flores killed them and stashed the bodies somewhere. He posted bail, disappeared, then turned up at the resort, cornered Brooke, and she shot and killed him. End of story."

"So tell me the rest of the story," Rafe said.

"Brooke was completely exonerated." Noah looked like he was ready to go toe-to-toe with Rafe.

Eli stepped between them. "Idiot or not, Bryan DuPey said it was a clear-cut case of self-defense. Flores had a knife in his hand and a

Glock in his belt. He was coming at Brooke and she shot to kill. He's dead. I'm glad."

Rafe had traveled the world. He had seen the worst acts men could perform. He'd suffered torture. He'd seen bloody death. He thought nothing could shake him—but the idea of Brooke, in this safe little town, facing death, made his breath stop. "How did she learn to shoot?" he asked.

"I don't know, Rafe. She's the daughter of an Air Force pilot and a retired Air Force officer. How do you think she learned to shoot?" Noah barely kept his sarcasm under control. "It's one of the reasons I hired her. On a resort that sprawls over twenty-five acres, with wealthy guests and two hundred and thirty employees, a familiarity with firearms is a valuable skill to have."

Brooke should never have been threatened. If things had been different, Rafe would have been here to protect her.

If he had been strong enough, he would have been.

Then Nonna would never have been hurt either.

"When this manhunt is over, you'll leave again, right?" Noah asked.

"My work isn't here." Obviously. And more obviously, Noah wanted him out of here. Why? Did Noah want to put a claim on Brooke?

It didn't matter if he did. Rafe had no right to

55

bellyache if she wanted another man, even if that man was his brother.

But saying that didn't make it the truth.

"Quiet." Eli indicated Nonna's door.

Brooke came out in a rush, her face calm. But she held her purse like a shield, as if she'd been under attack.

"What's wrong?" Rafe asked. "Is it Nonna?"

"Nothing's wrong. Kayla says Nonna's okay and going to get better." She spoke to them all, then turned on Rafe. "Come on. I'm ready."

"Nonna's car is in the parking lot." Eli tossed him the keys. "Figured you'd want to drive it."

For the first time since he arrived, Rafe smiled with true humor. "Nothing says home like a titty-pink Mustang with a two eighty-nine V-eight. C'mon, Brooke. Let's go check out the scene of the crime."

Chapter 6

Brooke had known the Di Luca brothers since she'd arrived in Bella Terra. They were all extraordinary, all handsome, all so wounded by their careless actor father and his various wives that Brooke knew Sarah despaired that any of them would marry and give her the great-grandchildren she craved.

But although Brooke was friends with Noah and Eli, it was Rafe she understood. It was Rafe with whom she bonded.

She didn't want to.

They just had so much in common: crummy fathers and enough childhood trauma that they had made it to adulthood only because they had found each other.

Then they had lost each other . . . found each other . . . lost each other. . . .

Their relationship had been a boomerang of exhilarating highs and ghastly lows, and looking back, all she could do was shake her head at her youthful self.

Never again.

Yet at times like these, as they sat side by side on the factory-original Mustang sport seats . . . she still knew Rafe Di Luca better than any person on earth. She knew that as they drove through Bella Terra's busy streets, he would be on edge, relearning the feel of his grandmother's Mustang, surveying the town where he'd spent his high school years, looking for changes, for old friends, for the perp. Then, as they reached the narrow, winding road that led to the home ranch, he would open up, punch the accelerator, drive the car as it was meant to be driven, quickly, smoothly.

He did all that. Of course he did.

As they blasted down the highway, she rolled down her window—the car lacked anything automatic, and that was fine with her—and the wind rushed in, blowing memories into her face.

She'd arrived in Bella Terra on the eve of her thirteenth birthday. She had been used to first days and new schools . . .

But that day was different, because her mother had divorced Brooke's father, quit the military, and declared Bella Terra would be their home for the rest of their lives.

And why? That was what Brooke hadn't understood. Why?

Well. She'd sort of understood why her mother had divorced her father. He was an Air Force pilot, glamorous and handsome. Lots of women thought so. Lots of women.

When Brooke thought about him, and how he had another wife in Japan . . . it hurt too much. So she didn't think about him.

Yet . . . Bella Terra. *Geez*. As far as Brooke

could see, her mother's choice was arbitrary, not close to Oklahoma or even Minnesota, where their families lived. Bella Terra was this random little town north of San Francisco and east of nowhere.

Everything Brooke knew had changed, and even her body had betrayed her, growing in the last year to a freakish height of five feet, nine inches. She was taller than every other kid in seventh grade. She hunched her shoulders and wouldn't look at anyone, sure they were laughing at her.

For sure they were staring.

Until Rafe strolled in. He was taller than her, topping every boy by at least six inches. He was older than all of them, held back because his schooling had been hit-or-miss. He was darkly tanned, extravagantly handsome, with black curly hair, darkly lashed blue eyes, and the most amazingly effective sneer Brooke had ever seen. As he swaggered down the corridor, she stared— all the girls stared—mesmerized. The local girls told her he was from one of the premier families in the valley, the Di Lucas, and it was clear that meant more in this town than the fact that he had already been a movie star before the age of nine.

Brooke was impressed.

Man. What a fool she'd been. What a sucker she'd been.

Now, turning her head away from the open

window, Brooke looked at Rafe: at his sharp profile silhouetted against the blue sky, the bold jawline, the black, curly hair swept back from his forehead, the broken, flattened nose so out of place on his noble face, the lips that every straight woman on the planet wanted to kiss. . . .

As she stared, she saw his expression shift from blissful thoughtlessness to sharp curiosity, and she didn't like it . . . but once again she knew what his next move would be.

The Mustang slowed. Rafe's attention moved from the road . . . to his investigation. He pulled into a turnout, put the car in first gear, cut the engine.

Silently she counted down . . . *Three, two, one.*

He turned to face her, slung his arm over the back of her seat. "Who do you suspect attacked my grandmother?"

Good to see you again, Brooke. I dream about you every day I'm not holding you in my arms. "I don't know," she said.

"You know everyone in town. You must have some ideas."

I've been remembering every moment we ever spent together. "I don't suspect anyone and I'm not accusing someone simply for points with the local law enforcement—or you," she said.

"So you agree with Bryan DuPey? You think it was a vagrant?"

You look better than ever, and I've missed you

more than life itself. My darling, I'm so sorry for the horrible way I've treated you. I am nothing without you, and all I want is to come home . . . to you. "I don't think anything. I don't think Bryan DuPey is a moron. I don't think it was a vagrant. I don't think it was one of the winery workers or one of my employees. I'm as bewildered as anyone." She focused on his chill, still expression. "Tell me who you think did it."

He waved her question away. Obviously, he intended to do the interrogation. "Who discovered Nonna?"

She sighed. "Didn't your brothers tell you?"

"No. Who got to her first?"

He wasn't going to like this. "I did."

Those lushly lashed eyes narrowed. "After she'd called emergency."

"Yes."

"But not much after."

"I heard she was hurt and started up to the house ahead of the ambulance."

"Where did you get that information?" He shot words at her like bullets.

"I didn't exactly get the information. One of my gardeners looked miserable and when I asked him what was wrong, he told me how much he enjoyed working on old Mrs. Di Luca's yard because she gave them lemonade in the summer and hot chocolate in the winter. . . ." She wanted to gesture nervously, but forced herself to remain motionless. "Part of my job is hearing what people aren't saying."

"You heard him not say that he had hurt her." Rafe put just the right note of disbelief into his tone.

Her hackles rose. "No. I heard him not say he knew she'd been hurt."

Rafe's blue eyes held all the warmth of an iceberg. "I want to interview him."

"He's gone."

"Where?"

"When I came back from the hospital, he'd left town. No one's seen him since."

Rafe's teeth snapped like a wolf's on the attack. "How very convenient."

People who lost their tempers easily were ill suited to the job of concierge, and Brooke's early life with her parents had taught her the advantages of a placid disposition. Yet every time Rafe came into town—every time—she found herself riding a series of highs and lows best suited to a drama queen. Now, although she knew better, she got mad. "Are you accusing me of being behind the attack on your grandmother? Or perhaps even attacking your grandmother?" She was pleased to note her tone remained even.

A beat. "No."

"Generous of you." She smiled faintly, and looked him right in the eyes, challenging him.

"Yes." He seemed serious. "What was this gardener's name?"

"Luis Hernández."

"I'll get his Social Security number from the office. See if I can track him down. He's got to be somewhere." Turning back to the wheel, Rafe put the car in gear and drove on up the road toward the home ranch.

Brooke turned her face back to the breeze, let the wind cool her cheeks, and tried to be glad of the reminder of Rafe's suspicious temperament before she tumbled back in love once again.

Chapter 7

Bella Terra was just a place.

Ever since he could remember, Rafe had been making this drive up to the home ranch. Before he was five, he had strained to see past the sides of the car seat, uncaring of the vineyards and the olive trees, the signs advertising little wineries and the long driveways leading into them. He had longed for that first glimpse of Nonna's house, decorated for Christmas with its lights like beacons leading him home. Even in the chilliest weather—and the hills of central California got occasional blasts of cold—she was always there on the porch, waiting for them to drive up so she could unhook his seat belt and carry him inside. His grandfather had a deep, gruff voice. His brothers were whirling dervishes. The smells had flooded Rafe's senses: evergreen, cinnamon, and Nonna's warm scent, like flowers dipped in vanilla. The tastes had been glorious: ham, turkey and dressing, fruit salad with whipped cream, cranberry apple pie, and fruitcake bursting with dried fruits and walnuts.

It had been a horrible shock the day he'd eagerly accepted a piece of fruitcake from a friend's mother and discovered it was nothing like Nonna's.

But then, no one was like Nonna.

He glanced at Brooke, who stared pensively out the window.

Brooke was just a woman.

On the first day of school in the first year he'd returned from Italy, fresh from his movie career, hating himself and everyone else, Brooke had been standing in the corridor, hunching her shoulders and clutching her books. Something about the way she had looked—wretched, depressed, and terrified—appealed to him. After all, misery loved company.

He had been two years older than the rest of his classmates because he hadn't gone to school, not consistently, and the schools he had attended had been Italian or Indonesian or Australian. Wherever his mother filmed, he went to schools or had a tutor.

So Bella Terra didn't know where to place him. He was miles ahead in logic and math; he read and spoke English perfectly—and about five other languages—but didn't understand a speck of English grammar. He didn't play baseball or football, not the American kind, or basketball, and he refused to have anything more to do with acting. And he had a surly attitude, one developed during all the years of listening to his parents and their shouting matches, then of watching his mother conduct her flamboyant love affairs and constantly profitable marriages.

She'd finally given up and sent him to live with his Nonna, his half brother Noah and his half brother Eli, who was back from Argentina and closed up tighter than a drum.

But Nonna always made everything better.

Brooke was the same personality type. Loving, generous, understanding. He'd been attracted to her not because she was like his Nonna but because . . . well, because she was tall with a nice rack and good legs. Not admirable reasons, Rafe now admitted, but hell—he'd only been fourteen. At that age, higher aspirations were beyond him.

So he'd hauled her along in his wake as he swaggered and sneered his way through seventh grade.

By eighth grade she was a habit.

By the time they reached high school, she had grown into her awkward beauty and every guy envied him. Not that he laid a hand on her. She was too young, too innocent, too adoring of him, and he was by God determined not to be the jerk his father was, grabbing at every young woman bowled over by his looks. So he kept her at arm's length, and kept all the other guys there, too, and he was pretty proud of his restraint right up to the time when her crap-ass father came for graduation. When he left, she told Rafe every-thing went well.

He snorted.

She looked at him, blue eyes wide and

unblinking, and even he, dumb, insensitive guy that he was, saw the anguish she concealed. What was he supposed to do? Leave her to suffer alone?

He wasn't inexperienced sexually, hadn't been since his earliest adolescence. He knew better than to sleep with her, but my God! They were best friends . . . who fell so wildly in love.

First love, bright and clean. Forever.

Except, of course, it wasn't forever.

His own fault, he guessed. Because ever since Rafe figured out his own father was far from the hero he portrayed on the screen, since Rafe had done his role in that dragon movie and realized people expected him to be who he had pretended to be—Rafe had been determined to become the real thing. Not some silly on-screen superman, but a brave man. A man of integrity. A true hero.

At the end of that magical summer, he had followed his dream and joined the military.

When Brooke found out, she had thrown a fit unlike anything he had ever imagined from the cool, composed girl. She said he should have consulted her.

Now, looking back, he knew why she'd thought that. They had a relationship.

And she talked. She talked about going to college and what she was going to study. She discussed her mother's puzzling behavior in moving them here, and how it was fate that

Kathy Petersson had chosen Bella Terra and he'd moved in with his grandmother at the same time. She speculated about their future, painting mental pictures of their lives entwined together forever.

But it never occurred to him that his plans mattered to her, or that she'd consider his determination to join Special Forces a clear sign that he would turn into a jerk like her father. She hadn't understood that his decision had nothing to do with her father and everything to do with his.

In the annals of arguments, theirs had been epic, and by the time he boarded that plane to go to basic training, their relationship was over and she vowed never to speak to him again.

That hadn't worked out so well. Her senior year in college . . .

He sighed.

"What?" she said.

"Nothing." They were like two planets circling each other, and each time it was a cosmic event filled with light and heat and always, always a colossal explosion.

They pulled up to Nonna's house and Rafe had a choice—get right down to business or have a frank and open discussion about their relationship.

He got down to business. Not because he was a coward, but because his priority was Nonna's safety. He told Brooke, "I want you to follow me through the house. I'm looking for something, anything that strikes you as odd. Anything out of place. Anything . . . anything."

"You want a second pair of eyes," she said.

"I want a feminine perspective. You taught me early on that women look at things differently."

"Not differently. Women look at things properly." She grinned.

"Hm." He didn't grin back, but not because he wasn't amused. Because when he saw that impish smile light her whole face, it tugged at his heart, his memories, his . . . *Damn it.* At his groin.

He needed to get this mystery solved, and soon, so he could clear out.

At his lack of response, her pleasure faded and she got out to stand beside the car.

He got out, too, and listened. It was quiet up here. A light breeze ruffled the leaves on the trees and brought the scent of spring from the orchards and vineyards. Nonna was a sharp old lady. If it had been this quiet up here that day, she would have heard an accomplice moving around outside. So probably there was the one guy in the cellar.

Rafe looked up and down the driveway, then up at the house. At the steep steps, clean of any betraying footprints. At the wide covered porch with the swing that hung from chains from the ceiling, Nonna's rocking chair and table beside it, the hanging baskets filled with fluorescent orange impatiens. He gazed thoughtfully at the tall blue-flowered hydrangeas that flourished on either side of the steps and down the sides of the house.

"I don't see anything," Brooke said.

He walked into the flower bed, pushed aside first one hydrangea, then another, until he found what he was looking for. "Here." He pointed at the track of the single wide tire. "Did DuPey note this? That the perp arrived by motorcycle and hid it in the bushes?"

"No." Brooke looked at Rafe with a renewed respect.

Stupid to want to preen.

Plunging deeper into the foliage, he found the marks made by shoes with a distinctive tread, and came out satisfied that he'd made a start. He headed up the steps—listening to them creak, he made a note to replace and paint them while he was here—and onto the porch.

Brooke followed.

Up here, everything looked routine, including the condition of the lock on the front door. There were no scratches, no sign of forced entry. As he knew and his brothers had said, if the intruder had come from this direction, he'd have walked right in.

Rafe unsuccessfully tried the door. At least now it was locked.

Gazing out over the yard, over the valley, he saw the familiar vista and yet . . . how different things were now, knowing as he did that somewhere out there, a predator lurked and, perhaps, a plot to harm his grandmother. Why, he didn't yet understand. But he would. He would.

"If you don't have the keys, I do." Brooke fished them out of her purse.

Well, of course she did. In the years since he'd lived in Bella Terra, Brooke had received the key to every Di Luca lock.

Opening the door, she gestured for him to precede her.

He entered the house, and stopped just inside to listen and observe.

The dim hallway went straight back to the kitchen. To the left, a wide arch opened into the old-fashioned parlor complete with crocheted doilies on the arms of the chairs and the couch, and . . . "When did Nonna get a flat-screen TV?" he asked.

"When she realized she could watch football in HD."

"Of course." His Nonna had always been an outstanding athlete, as competitive in badminton as she was in softball, and that translated to a fierce love of pro sports.

Brooke smiled fondly at the massive television that covered most of the wall over the fireplace. "She's into Australian football now."

"What's so great about Australian football?"

"She says it's faster, more exciting, and since the guys don't wear pads, she can really see their tushies."

Rafe rounded on Brooke.

She held up her hands. "Hey, I'm just repeating what she said."

Women. He turned back to his examination of the room.

"But she's right," Brooke said reflectively.

"You've been up here to watch with her?" He kept his tone noncommittal.

"Yes. It's fun. I bring hors d'oeuvres, she serves champagne, and we shout at the TV."

"Aren't hors d'oeuvres and champagne contrary to the spirit of Australian football?"

"Probably. Does that kind of nefarious activity make me even more of a suspect?"

He fully faced her. "Yes."

"Which part?" Brooke's eyes sparked with ire. "The hors d'oeuvres and champagne, the tushies, or enjoying an evening with the matriarch whose grandsons don't spend enough time with her?"

Chapter 8

Rafe winced. Brooke never hesitated to make her opinion known, at least not to him, and he should have seen that reproach coming. "What makes you a suspect? All of your activities. None of them. I may not have been here for Nonna when she needed me, but I'm not going to fail her now."

"She worries about you."

"No need."

"You're not Teflon. You already proved that once."

"Nonna knows I'm fine."

"Avoiding the issue. I guess you're not as brave as the military medals might signify."

Brooke could always talk rings around him.

He turned to the bedroom on the right, Nonna's bedroom. He pushed the door open, stepped inside, and breathed in Nonna's perfume, flowers dipped in vanilla. The flowered comforter was spread precisely over the queen-size bed; the dust ruffle brushed the off-white carpet; the pillow shams were arranged against the headboard. Family photos covered the walls and the cedar chest, and Nonna's collection of glass perfume bottles was arrayed on the dresser. Everything looked exactly as it had every morning when Nonna left it.

He was lucky. Nonna kept her house habitually and with precision. If she'd been a different woman, this investigation would be a lot more difficult.

Beside him, Brooke said, "It's amazing how this house makes me feel like all the generations of Di Lucas have worked to create a safe haven."

Because she had said exactly what he was thinking, he curtly answered, "Somehow this generation blew it, since a few days ago the heart of the family was hurt. See anything out of place?"

"No."

He moved on to the dining room, a good-size room where a dozen chairs of various shapes and sizes surrounded a long, battered walnut table. Cabinets were built into the far wall. All were constructed in the forties by Palmiro Di Luca, a carpenter. The top row of doors was glass, displaying Nonna's heirloom china and cut glass. Nothing expensive, just stuff that had been passed down through the generations and was precious to the whole family.

He scanned the shelves. Eventually, he'd look in the cupboards, but right now, everything looked as it had looked all the years of his life.

Yet here in the dining room, something was out of place. . . .

He narrowed his eyes, putting the room out of focus.

"The candles," Brooke said uncertainly. "They're . . . sort of . . ."

"Yeah." Ever since he could remember, Nonna had lit the dining room table with tapers inserted into empty Di Luca wine bottles. Now instead of lining the center of the table, the six bottles and their candles were lined up before the master's chair.

Brooke started to walk forward, but he gestured her back, flipped on the overhead, and walked in a slow circuit around the table, examining the floor.

"What are you looking for?" Her voice, always low and throaty, was quieter than normal, as if she feared being overheard.

"A man's dirty footprint." He barked out a laugh that mocked his expectations. "The driver's license he dropped."

"I already looked for that."

She spoke so solemnly he looked to see if she was serious. Only when he realized her expression was deadpan did he sigh and shake his head reprovingly. He donned a pair of latex gloves. "Don't touch anything," he warned, and walked to the table.

She followed. "Nonna could have been cleaning the bottles."

He pointed at the wax drippings that dusted the

table, then lifted one candle out of its base. It easily came free. "He removed all the candles, looking for . . . what?"

"More important, he replaced all the candles when he was done. Why would a thief care enough to tidy up after himself?"

Of course Brooke would observe the fact that most interested him. "We'll see if Dopey can lift a fingerprint off any of these," he said.

"Don't be childish, Rafe. His name is DuPey."

Her sharp tone was a slap to his pride. "Dating him, are you?"

"I would, but his wife has access to his guns."

Is that where you got the pistol with which you shot and killed a man?

But he didn't ask. Not yet.

He glanced around one more time, then gestured her back into the hallway. They checked the bathroom and second bedroom, but all was in order there.

They entered the kitchen. He saw the dent in the plaster wall Nonna's head had created, the splotch of blood on the floor where she'd lain unconscious. His cold, clear anger grew, and for that he was grateful. That icy rage gave him the edge that had made him the best tracker in his unit.

Out of respect for Nonna's wine collection, someone had shut the cellar door her attacker had left open.

Still, it smelled off in here, and Brooke gave an exclamation of dismay. "Honestly. You men. Couldn't you have cleaned up the groceries?"

He looked. A puddle of ice cream had leaked from the cloth bag and dried on the table and the floor. "I wasn't one of the men who . . ." He shut up. He wasn't going to win that one.

Brooke went to the counter to collect paper towels.

"Leave it," he said. "We'll get someone up here to clean it up. One of the maids from the resort."

"No. I want to do it." Brooke pulled a swath off the roll and used it to wipe up the worst of the mess. "Nonna wouldn't like it to sit here on her table and floor."

He wanted to tell her no, he didn't want her fingerprints muddying the crime scene. But that ship had sailed; the EMTs had been in here, and the cops, and Brooke had been here, too, on the day his grandmother had been attacked. Besides, the slight quaver in Brooke's voice alerted him. She'd seen the bloodstain, too, and she wasn't as callous as he was.

Or maybe she was guilty.

Or maybe she knew his grandmother's wishes better than he liked to admit.

"Make yourself happy," he said, and made a tour of the kitchen, studying everything. The condition of the back door—it had been forcefully yanked open, so the guy was definitely fleeing. The faucet—it was centered on the sink, and Nonna was a tyrant about that. And finally, most important, the area around the cellar door—still no footprints, no dirt from the flower beds. "So the perp was wearing latex gloves and maybe shoe protection," Rafe mused aloud. He would have to follow the trail out the back door, to the bushes where the guy had stashed the motorcycle, and photograph the marks left by the tires. If they were original to the bike, the tread could be traced to a specific manufacturer, and then Rafe could check public records for everyone who owned that kind of motorcycle. But first . . . "Are you done? C'mon. I'm going down to the cellar. I could use your keen eye."

"No. No, when I finish here, I'm going outside." Going to the sink, she wet a dish towel. "I'll meet you there."

He watched her as she returned to the table and swabbed the sticky ice cream away, then knelt on the floor and did it again. "That's right. You don't like the basement."

She didn't answer for a long moment. Then, "No. No, I don't like the basement. It's silly, I know. No good reason for it, and I do go down, because every time Nonna goes to get potatoes or garlic or a bottle of wine, I worry. To tell you the truth, that was the phone call I was afraid to get—that she'd fallen down those steps and broken her arm or—" Brooke took a quavering breath. "I didn't expect her to get mugged in her own house. That's all."

"You're upset."

"This is the first time I've been back since I was here with the ambulance." Pale with cold sweat, she sat down heavily on one of the kitchen chairs.

Opening a drawer, he pulled out a kitchen towel, ran it under the cool water, and laid it around her neck. "Do you know where Nonna's flashlight is?"

She didn't ask why he needed it, simply pressed the towel closer and gestured toward the cupboard beside the sink.

"Better to put your head between your knees than to fall on the floor," he instructed, then opened the cupboard.

The flashlight was the one he'd given Nonna for Christmas, with three LEDs that gave a strong, white, directed light. Remembering her enthusiasm, and satisfied he'd given her a cool gift that she could truly use, he took it and headed down the stairs into the cellar.

The cellar probably looked like every other cellar constructed in the late nineteenth century—a hole in the ground, twenty by thirty, with a high ceiling, rough cement walls, tiny windows up at ground level covered by outdoor vegetation and indoor grime. Not even Nonna, who so carefully tended her home, would climb up to wash those windows.

Sometime in the early twentieth century, someone had run an electric wire to a bare bulb in the middle of the room, turned on and off by a good long stretch and a chain. Not long after her grandsons arrived, Nonna had an electrician in to bring the electricity up to code. A fluorescent fixture replaced the bulb, which still dangled, useless, from the ceiling.

Rafe flipped the switch, and with a flicker, blaring white light illuminated the cellar.

A slow, constant shower of dust from the ceiling coated the floor. A couple of paths ran through it, created by his grandmother as she trekked to the shelves where she kept her winter vegetables and to the wall filled with wines.

Men's footprints tracked across the floor, not too many, all with their own tread.

The cops had been down here, of course.

But none of those footprints matched the motorcyclist's, and none had that distinctive lack of tread that shoe covers would have provided.

So Nonna's attacker had been down here looking at the same stuff she did. The vegetables? Not likely. The wine? For sure. She had some valuable bottles, but hell, who came all this way to steal a few bottles of wine when half the households in Bella Valley had great wine sitting around in unprotected wine cellars? Add that to the fact that no similar break-ins or attacks had happened, the candles were out of the wine bottles on the table, and there were no fingerprints, and Rafe had a mystery on his hands.

Turning off the fluorescent lights, he flicked on the flashlight and shone it around the basement, using its bright focused illumination to spot anything out of place. There was nothing. Except . . . He shone it in the slots where the bottles of wine rested. The dust in each slot had been disturbed and—he pulled out the bottles one by one—the labels had been wiped off. For a better look?

Yes, the perp had been searching for something specific, and doing it with subtlety. If Nonna hadn't come home and interrupted him, she would never have known he was there.

On the other hand, she'd said he hit her with a tire iron, and she had the broken arm to prove it. So the perp had come prepared for trouble.

Rafe put the bottles back and shone the flashlight around one last time, then turned it off.

What bottle was the perp searching for? Did Nonna know? Did she hide a secret?

And why had the trouble started now?

Chapter 9

Rafe came around the house to the front to find Brooke reclined on the stairs, her feet braced against the bottommost step, her long legs stretched out straight, her head and shoulders resting on the porch. Her eyes were closed. Her face was turned up to the sun.

She had her father's fair skin. "You'll burn," he said.

"SPF forty at all times," she answered, and never stirred a muscle.

He nodded, climbed the stairs, and sat down on the top step, his elbows resting on his knees, his hands clasped loosely between his legs. "You killed a man."

Still she didn't open her eyes. Or move. "It didn't take long for you to garner that information."

"I didn't *garner* that information." He'd forgotten how irritating she could be. "It was given to me by my brothers as a reason why I should catch the perp and get out of town."

"They were trying to scare you away?"

"They were telling me I shouldn't screw with you."

She smirked. "Because I would kill you, too?"

"No, because you're fragile from your ordeal."

Her smile disappeared. "I'm really not."

"So you killed that guy and haven't thought twice about it?"

"He deserved it."

The silence stretched. Usually when he saw Brooke, she was dressed in a black suit with a skirt and heels. Usually she had her hair carefully controlled and her cosmetics were perfectly applied.

He liked to look at her like this, in faded denim jeans and an oversize white button-up shirt tucked into the waistband. Her pink running shoes were scuffed, her hair had been styled by the wind as they drove, and if she was wearing makeup, it was damned little.

Right now, the way she looked reminded him of high school. High school and first love . . .

"Where did the crime occur?" he asked.

"My crime, or his?" Still cool. Still calm.

"Where did he find you?"

"In building A, in the housekeeping closet on the north end of the property. He trapped me there, so I shot him."

"You just happened to have a gun on you." He put hard disbelief in his tone.

"I had been uneasy for several days. My people had reported a man skulking on the grounds, and Noah made it clear that if I found myself in a situation, I should defend myself." Her voice didn't rise in volume or tone. Her eyes never bothered to open, not even a flicker.

"How did you know this skulking man was a threat?"

"Didn't your brothers tell you? The guy pulled a knife."

"And you shot him."

"I shot him."

"Because he pulled a knife."

"The leather, the boots, the tats, and the piercings seemed less than reassuring, too." Still not a twinge of guilt or distress in her voice.

"So you shot him," Rafe repeated, trying to make her react the way he knew she should. "Once? Twice?"

"I emptied the gun."

"Six shots?" He hadn't expected that. "Surely one shot brought him down."

"I didn't hit him the first time."

"But you were defending yourself, and you were trained to shoot."

She opened her eyes. She pushed herself up on her elbows. She looked up at him in annoyance. "If you know everything, why are you questioning me?"

"When two acts of violence occur so closely together, both of them concerning people I care about, I want to know all the details."

Brooke sighed and sat all the way up. "I was supervising one of the maids. Madelyn is fairly new, so I'm keeping an eye on her. She was cleaning the rooms and I was following behind her, checking her performance and giving her corrections, and she ran out of wood soap. So I went to the supply room to get her some, and he followed me in. He was grinning and holding a knife. I tried talking to him, but he lunged at me. So I shot him."

"What happened when you missed the first time?"

"I panicked. I shot again. And again. I shot him until I knew he was dead and I had no more bullets."

Rafe didn't believe a word of it. Not a word. Not with that calm recital. But he nodded as if he did. "You must have nightmares."

"Nightmares?" For the first time, she seemed to realize she should be not merely telling the story, but displaying some emotion—the kind of emotion she'd shown in the kitchen when she once more faced the crime scene where Nonna had been attacked.

"The first time I killed a man . . . well. I can still see his face at the moment of his death." Rafe scooted down to sit beside her. "The blood spurting from his chest, his neck, splashing me as he collapsed, knowing he would never stand on this earth again . . ."

"Better him than you," she said. "And better this guy than me."

"Of course. But for all that your parents are soldiers, you are not." He slid his arm along the step behind her back, lifted her to him, brought her close. Leaning back against the steps, he placed her body across his. "When you think about committing bloody murder, no matter how justified—you need comfort."

"Sure." She tugged against him, but halfheartedly as if she didn't quite know how to react. "But not yours."

"Mine more than anyone's. Mine because I know you better than any man on earth." He was trying to tell her he knew she was lying.

Did she comprehend?

He thought so, because she looked into his eyes and her blue gaze weighed him and her next move.

No. None of that.

He pulled her as close as he could, wrapped one hand on the back of her head, and held her still for his kiss.

A cautious press to the corner of her mouth. To the other corner. Then full on, opening her with his tongue and tasting her for the first time and knowing this was homecoming.

Yeah. Homecoming.

Brooke was the woman he dreamed of every day of his life.

Brooke was the woman he denied himself for her own good, because she wanted Bella Terra and he wanted the world.

But for his own good, he had to kiss her.

Because touching her brought back memories of necking at the far end of the orchard alongside an irrigation canal. And because she smelled like wine flowers and fertile earth, and youth and passion and true love.

"Rafe . . ." she murmured against his lips. Lifting her head, she tried to push away.

Yes, because this Brooke was cooler. Calmer. With none of the hero worship she'd shown him in high school. And none of the helpless compassion that had moved her in college. She was in face and form still Brooke . . . but she wasn't his Brooke. Not anymore.

And he, like the beast he was, wanted to break through her serenity and see for himself whether the young, exuberant Brooke still existed beneath the mask . . . or if she had become the woman she pretended to be.

He slid one hand down to her butt and one up to the back of her neck, and with his fingertips he stroked her ear.

She stilled.

She was the same, at least in that respect. A caress to her earlobe hypnotized her with pleasure.

He kissed her again, and the taste of her . . . ah, that blocked everything but the passion and sweetness and glory that was Brooke.

She was cautious. God, so cautious. In some rational part of his brain, he completely understood why she held back. But the lustful, animal part of his brain—okay, not his brain, his dick—didn't care. He held her with his arm across her back, her body so close against his that the layers of clothing between them were nothing but a hindrance. He knew her shape, sensed the changes that seven years had wrought, exulted in them. He probed her mouth with his tongue, swept away her cool control, brought all their old, dusty feelings into the sunshine and the new day.

She was still motionless, as if waiting. . . .

But he knew he'd won when she slid her fingers into his hair and kissed him back, deftly giving him as much delight as he offered, amplifying his need for possession into a thing that relentlessly clawed at him, making him imagine all the ways he could take her, here, in the sunshine on his grandmother's front steps overlooking Bella Terra.

He knew her so well.

But she knew him, too, and it didn't take psychic ability to know where his mind had gone, not as close as they were.

So when she got her elbow between them close to his throat and pressed with increasing force, he knew no amount of ear rubbing was going to change her mind.

"My pager's vibrating," she said.

"Is that what that is?" He smiled at her. "I was hoping for something . . . different."

"I'll bet. If they're paging me now, when I've told them not to, it's important. So . . . ?" She was polite and unflustered, considering he had a hard-on approximately the height and girth of a sequoia pressed into her belly. Or maybe she was unimpressed.

"Sure." He let her go.

He let her go. Again.

Chapter 10

Rafe on her heels, Brooke strode from the public parking lot, packed with springtime tourists, up the side street and past the cars stacked up under Bella Terra's portico.

The resort's main building had been constructed in the twenties in the old California Spanish style: thick golden stucco walls to keep out the summer's heat, a clay tile roof, and green-painted shutters. The family had added on until it included three wings with one hundred guest rooms. Each generation had remodeled until the merest remnants remained of the original building, and within the last fifty years, cottages had been scattered throughout the vineyards and among the trees.

Always the Di Lucas had treasured the feel of California's history, intertwined with theirs, the ups and downs, the grapes and the land, the heat and the glory.

The front door led onto First Street and the bustle of downtown. The back door of the main building led to the check-in area. There the valets took control of the cars, golf carts waited to take the guests to their cottages . . . and it was there Brooke headed. She nodded to the bellmen, 'young men and women casually dressed in dark golf shirts and khaki chinos, pushing carts of luggage toward the bell desk.

She paused and critically observed as the server for their winery of the day, Folderol Winery, poured for their incoming guests from their selection of four wines, discussed their merits, and handed out information.

The resort kept a large beverage server full of lemonade to offer to their guests; someone had spilled a glass on the polished concrete floor. One of their housekeepers was on her knees cleaning it up.

Brooke walked to her side and placed her hand on Madelyn's shoulder.

Predictably, Madelyn jumped. She looked like a street fighter: short and thin, with blond hair shaved close to her head, a snake tattoo around one wrist, and a scar on the side of her neck. The housekeeping staff complained that she was freaky, but because Madelyn worked hard, took their shifts if they wanted to slack off, and took double time if they were shorthanded, they usually forgave the freaky.

Brooke lifted a brow to the manager behind the desk and got a nod in return. Although the afternoon check-in rush was ongoing, he and his staff had everything under control.

She took her first deep breath since the moment Rafe had walked into Sarah's hospital room, and felt herself relax. She was back in her element, in charge of making sure the visitors to Bella Terra

Resort were happy, at ease, well fed, and entertained—and she had the personnel to handle that task.

Turning to the concierge desk, she waited while her second in command, Victor Ruíz, laid out a wine country map for an older couple and circled suggested destinations.

"How does he decide where to send them?" Rafe asked.

"If they know the kinds of wines they enjoy, we have something to go by. But a lot of the time people haven't got a clue about whether they like cabernets or carignans, whites or reds, or if they like wine at all. Then it's tricky. Restaurants are easier. Everyone knows what kind of food they like—although sometimes they lie about it so they sound sophisticated." The line in front of the desk took a sudden jump as a group of four couples stepped up to the desk and a very young couple stepped off the elevator looking confused and concerned. "Will you excuse me?" she said to Rafe, but didn't wait for a reply. At this time of the day, the staff all performed double duty, whatever needed to be done, and if that inconvenienced Rafe, well . . . good.

She got behind the desk and dealt with the couples first, setting them up on a wine country tour bus for the following day. She helped two elderly ladies get a reservation at Speak-Easy's Cajun Restaurant, directed two already inebriated young men to the pool with instructions to introduce themselves to the female lifeguard, looked around for the confused young couple—and saw Rafe speaking with them. They were laughing and nodding, less concerned, more relaxed.

Good. After all, it was his family's resort. In a crunch, he could pitch in.

She watched as he walked them through the lobby and out the front door onto Bella Terra's main street, then stood and gestured as he told them how to get to their destination.

He came back in as the rush died a sudden death, leaving Victor, Rafe, and Brooke looking at one another in relief.

The men moved toward each other, two fellows confident in who they were.

Brooke introduced them. "Rafe, this is Victor Ruíz, my second in command, and lately, my very overworked right-hand man. Since Sarah's been in the hospital and I've been with her, he's been picking up the slack." She watched as the two men shook hands, then told Rafe, "Victor is originally from Paraguay, has trained and worked in the best hotels all over South America, and when I vacationed in Buenos Aires, I watched him. He knew celebrities, always said the right thing, handled his employees with tact and discretion. So I seduced him into coming to the U.S."

Eyes twinkling, Victor bowed toward her. "I was very willing to be seduced, especially to work with a concierge of such international fame."

"You are too good." She was aware that Rafe watched them without smiling. "Victor, why did you page me?"

"I didn't page you," Victor said.

"Really?" She pulled out her pager and looked. "Someone did. I assumed since I instructed that only you—"

"No, but as long as you're here . . ." Victor launched into a litany of problems that cropped up every day at the resort, matters he was completely able to handle.

Brooke frowned as she listened. If he hadn't paged her, who had? Only a few people had access to her number, and those few people had been given strict orders to leave her alone so she could be with Sarah. She interrupted. "Is there anything here that requires my attention?"

"There is. You have a guest who is asking to speak to you. No one else will do." The words were severe, but Victor's eyes were twinkling as he spoke, and he indicated the lobby.

Brooke stepped around the corner into the generous room Noah had transformed into their lobby.

Three walls were glass reaching twenty feet in the air, with views of gardens and foliage so thick and rich and colorful, every table and chair had a view of paradise. The fourth wall was a wide, floor-to-ceiling fireplace with openings on either side that led to the elevators and the check-in area. A small bar occupied the center of the room, and there they served a continental breakfast in the morning and drinks at night. Each seat had been chosen for comfort. Every guest was made welcome with offers of salted edamame served in small blue and white porcelain Asian bowls, and bottled springwater. This was, after all, California, home of holistic foods, environmental correctness, and fierce snobbery.

Victor gestured widely. "Your Italian friend has returned."

"My Italian friend?" Brooke scanned the lobby until she found that distinctive head of fiery red, curly hair. "Francesca? Francesca's here?"

"Francesca? The only Francesca I know is . . . Oh, my God!" For the first time since he'd arrived, Rafe looked as if he had had the feet knocked out from under him. Before Brooke could hurry into the lobby, he grabbed her arm. "My mother? My mother is here?"

Chapter 11

She frequently vacations here. Now if you'll excuse me"—Brooke plucked Rafe's hand away—"I'm going to greet my guest."

She stalked into the lobby.

My God, he was irritating. Irritating, handsome, and far too dangerous to her . . . in every way. With him, she had to be careful about what she said and did, because he always, always watched her far too closely.

As she neared the table, she softly called, "Francesca!"

With the polished motion of a dancer, Francesca swiveled in her chair. Her face, so fabulously shaped, lit up. She stood, perfectly clothed in cream slacks, a black V-necked sweater that hugged her every curve, and, of course, black heels so high Brooke would have teetered and fallen. Francesca moved as if the shoes were an extension of her feet. She enveloped Brooke in a perfumed embrace, and in a rich Italian accent said, "Brooke! Darling girl, at last I see you. I have been asking for you, but your dear friend Victor tells me you're busy with Sarah." Francesca pulled back and looked into Brooke's eyes, her own swimming with tears. "Such a tragedy, and to such a sweet woman. She was one of only two good things I got out of my marriage to that *bastardo*, Gavino Di Luca."

"I can't imagine what the other is," Brooke said drily.

Francesca looked over Brooke's shoulder. "Raffaello! My darling boy, you are here. I had hoped so. It has been so long since I've seen you." She flung her arms around Rafe's stiff form.

Rafe grimaced and rolled his eyes.

But everyone in the lobby was staring, and Rafe hated scenes. "Let's sit down," he said.

"Of course, darling. We should stop making spectacles of ourselves." Francesca turned her face to Brooke and winked.

As he pulled out Francesca's chair, then hers, Brooke hid a smile.

If he knew Brooke too well, Francesca knew him, too. She thrived on scenes, used them to manipulate the situation to her advantage, to make Rafe behave like a properly affectionate son.

The three arranged themselves around the table where a tiny cup held the dregs of an espresso. Francesca, her eyes, large and exotically tilted, beamed on the two of them. "How good to see you together again! So young, so perfect for each other. The passion, it still burns as hot as ever?"

Oh, God. Brooke had forgotten how horribly blunt Francesca could be. And the waiter, on his way to pour water and take orders, stopped so suddenly and looked so enthralled, clearly he had heard Francesca's exclamation. "My palate has matured," Brooke said. Remembering the kiss on Nonna's porch, she didn't dare look at Rafe. But she wouldn't let Francesca rattle her composure. "Trent!"

The waiter's attention snapped to Brooke. Hurrying forward, he poured ice water into their glasses.

"Francesca, would you like another espresso?" Brooke offered, "or perhaps some wine?"

Francesca lavished a smile on the young man. "Children, will you share a bottle of that lovely Di Luca sangiovese with me?"

Brooke wanted to say no. She'd been getting along on too little sleep, and to deal with Rafe, she needed to stay sharp. But Francesca showed signs of wear: Her smile quivered at the corners and she had shadows under her eyes. Something was very wrong, so Brooke told Trent, "We'll have a bottle of the 2004 Dragon Fire Sangiovese and three glasses." She waited until he scurried off, then turned to Francesca. "Now tell me what brings you to Bella Terra."

"I heard about the attack on Sarah and I wanted to make sure she was all right. . . ." Francesca cast her gaze to the floor, looking so guilty Brooke wondered how she had ever won that Academy Award for best actress.

"What else?" Rafe's forbidding tone made his disbelief clear.

The silence stretched a moment too long, Francesca frowned miserably, and Brooke ventured, "I think perhaps Francesca had some marital problems."

Trent arrived with the bottle of wine and glasses, showed the label, got approval, uncorked and poured in record time. And when Francesca tasted it and smiled at him, he staggered backward as if he'd been shot by the arrow of love.

Francesca had that effect on men.

Brooke waved him away. "I'll call you when we need you again."

He nodded, a handsome young man who'd just met the woman of his dreams—and she was older than his mother.

Francesca took another sip of wine, and sighed as if her heart were broken. "The divorce wasn't my fault."

"It never is," Rafe muttered.

Francesca continued. "It was his. He gave me a disease."

Brooke didn't know if she could remember a time when Rafe's mouth dropped open in surprise. "God, Mama, are you okay?"

"Yes, antibiotics cleared it up, but it was that which informed me—Raimund slept with other women. Many other women. Not attractive, either. Not like me." Francesca's nose wrinkled in fastidious disgust. "Unwashed women with tattoos on their hands and on their noses."

"And diseases," Rafe said.

"Shut up, Rafe." Brooke took Francesca's hand. "Did you ask him why?"

"I'm sure she did." Rafe produced his crooked smile. "At the top of her lungs."

"Shut up, Rafe," Francesca said, then turned to Brooke. "Yes, I asked. He said I was old, losing my looks."

Both Rafe and Brooke stared, dumbfounded, at her: at the long, curly auburn hair, the smooth skin with only the finest wrinkles, the startling blue eyes, and the face to launch a thousand ships.

"You're kidding," Rafe said. "Even I can see you're gorgeous."

"Ah, thank you, son." Francesca patted his arm. "But the breasts—they point south."

"You're fifty," he said flatly. "A little southern exposure is to be expected."

"Shut up, Rafe." Brooke turned back to Francesca. "It sounds to me as if Raimund was weak and abusive. I'm so glad you got away from him."

"Yes." Francesca picked up her glass, saluted them, and took a sip.

Rafe knew his mother. He recognized that mischievous expression. Slowly he placed his glass on the table. "What did you do to him, Mama?"

Francesca chuckled, warm and deep. "Did you not hear the scandal? It was all over the news."

"We've been a little distracted here," he told her.

"I saw something about the divorce, but not any reason for it," Brooke said.

With a flourish, Francesca announced, "The cameras caught Raimund kissing his male lover."

"He's homosexual?" Brooke sounded shocked—and disappointed.

"Why the surprise, Brooke?" Rafe realized he'd been a little too sharp, and moderated his tone. "A lot of gigolos go with the paying customer."

"On the screen, he seems so sexually intent on his female leads. . . ." Brooke blushed. She actually blushed as if she lusted after this guy.

"Oh, he is." Francesca used both hands to fluff her mass of hair. "He has no interest in men. In fact, he hated all my gay friends, avoided them, made loud, rude comments about them. So it was no trouble at all to ask dear Neville if he would involve Raimund in a scandal, and Neville agreed at once. In fact, he said he'd always wanted to plant one on Raimund, and when Raimund came out of the nightclub and posed for the cameras, Neville had already given his interview confessing that their love was the reason for our breakup."

For the first time, Brooke realized that Rafe's crooked smile was the exact copy of his mother's.

Francesca continued. "The paparazzi were enthralled. They almost carried Neville to Raimund's side. Neville threw his arms around him and called him darling. Neville's a former rugby player, you know, and although Raimund struggled, he never had a chance to get away. . . ." Francesca's laugh was long, low, constrained. "There's even a photo of Neville's hand squeezing Raimund's shapely rear end. He's still going to get offers for leading roles, of course . . . but I think the films will have a different focus than before."

Rafe leaned back in his chair and chortled.

"So I came here to see Sarah, because she always is so lovely to me, makes me feel as if she's not Gavino's mother, but mine, and I find she is in the hospital!" Francesca's eyes filled with tears, and Rafe thought—wanted to believe—that she suffered for Sarah's pain. "I wish to go down and visit her, but at the desk they tell me no one but family is allowed. Am I allowed?"

"She would be delighted to see you." Brooke summoned Trent to the table. "Please go to the desk and confirm Miss Pastore's suite for this evening and in the immediate future."

Trent nodded, his eyes shining, and backed away as if Francesca were royalty.

The kid was infatuated.

"I'll stay for a few weeks. I am not putting you out, am I, my dear girl? You won't have conflicts with guests who need a room?" Francesca looked distressed.

"It's the off-season, and you require one of the expensive rooms, so I'll place you in Millionaire's Row, and when you come back from the hospital, we'll check you in and take you to your cottage." Brooke stood, her glass of wine virtually untouched. "Having you visit Sarah now is so helpful to us. Please assure her I'll be back this evening"—she turned her gaze to Rafe—"as will the boys?"

"Of course." He helped his mother out of her chair.

Brooke said, "I'll go tell the doorman to call a car to take you to the hospital."

"And then we'll go to introduce me to the resort's heads of staff?" Rafe asked.

Her expression cooled, became indecipherable. "As you wish."

Rafe watched her walk off, tall, aloof, desirable, and so very much not his.

Francesca cupped his cheek and turned his face to hers. "You'll come to spend time with your mama?"

"I will." He was caught, but oh, how he

abhorred the constant wildly thrashing tornado of emotions that swirled around Francesca at all times.

"Good." She smiled the brilliant smile that men around the world were willing to die for. "In return, I'll help you acquire your heart's desire."

Not just no. Hell, no. In Italian, he said, "Mama, please. I have everything I need."

"Not true!" she said decisively. "I say it is time you stopped living a half life. It is time you had everything you *want*."

Chapter 12

Miss Pastore?" Victor interrupted them with a bow, his brown eyes warm and deferential as they rested on Francesca. "If you would come with me, your car is at the door."

Francesca placed her hand on his arm. "Victor, you are so handsome, so debonair. How have you managed to remain single?"

"I run very fast," Victor said earnestly.

As they walked away from Rafe, he heard his mother's distinctive, throaty laughter.

Damn it. Like there wasn't trouble enough with his grandmother attacked, Dopey as sheriff, and Brooke Petersson as Rafe's contact. Now his mother was here. When he remembered his early years—the screaming fights between his parents, his mother's copious tears every time his father slept with another girl, their touching reconciliations, and then another round of wild emotion and anguish—he couldn't stand it. When his parents had divorced, he'd lived with Francesca as she bounded between the highs and lows of affairs and marriages so passionate they had set the paparazzi on fire.

Francesca loved scenes. She thrived on drama. And when Rafe got the role in his movie and won the accolades of the world, the world expected him to be like his mother.

He was not. That was why he had finally come to live with his grandmother. At the age of fourteen, and with the brutality of youth, he had made himself clear. He told Francesca that acting was the same as lying, and he would never again be a liar. Like her. Like his father.

She had cried.

He hadn't cared. Because he no longer believed in her laughter and her tears. To him, every movement looked like acting. Every word sounded like acting. Like lying.

He had been determined to be the real thing—and that determination had almost gotten him killed. Worse, it had almost destroyed him.

Only one thing had saved him, one person. . . .

With the stillness he'd learned from years in the field, he waited for Brooke to return. She should have been back by now.

Perhaps Francesca had detained her. Perhaps she'd been caught by a guest or a staff member. Most likely she was simply unwilling to cater to him and what she considered his unreasonable demands.

But he was on an investigation. She might make him wait, but he could make good use of his time. Turning, he walked back toward the check-in area. He intended to look at the map of the guest cottages, pick out the one he wanted to use as a base, and pick up the key card. He would bring his bag in from his rental car—he didn't trust it to the curious hands of any of the bell personnel—and at some point today, he'd get into his cottage and set up his technology.

When he neared the concierge desk, a tall blonde with a bouncing ponytail, a carefully tended tan, and legs up to her ass turned toward him. She was the typical California beauty in the resort's regulation dark golf shirt and light chinos. At the sight of him, her big blue eyes lit up and she bounded over like a tennis player retrieving a drop shot. "Hi, Rafe, it's been a while."

"Hi . . ." He lifted an eyebrow at her, trying to decide whether she was one of those women who had seen the movie he'd made when he was a kid and pretended to know him, or if she was someone he had genuinely forgotten.

Either was possible.

"Jenna. Jenna Campbell." She offered her hand and a wide, white beauty-queen smile. "Remember? We had calculus together, and I was awful, and you helped me with it? At the library? Remember? After school? You and me in the dusty old stacks?"

"Of course." He didn't have a clue, but at least now he was pretty sure she was someone he'd forgotten. "You were on the pep squad, right?"

She reared back in incredulity. "The pep squad?"

Apparently he'd insulted her.

"Our senior year, I was the *head cheerleader*."
For sure he'd insulted her.

"I was the only one who could do a backflip all the way down the field. You know." She half turned as if to prove her prowess by allowing him to view her ass.

He didn't object. It was a fine ass. But she seemed a little manic and way too impressed with herself.

When he didn't answer, she insisted, "I dated Eric Wright, the quarterback. Remember?"

"I do remember." Something about her stirred his demon, and he asked, "Did Eric ever come out of the closet?"

"What?" The pleasant tone was gone, given over to the snap of an insulted female.

Rafe didn't care. "Did Eric ever come out of the closet?" he repeated.

"You mean, like, out of the closet?"

"Yes. Did he announce he was gay? I expected he would as soon as he got to college."

"No! Don't be silly. He wasn't gay; he was . . . Well, he wasn't!"

"Okay." He stuck his hands in his pockets and tried to look peaceable. "I must have been wrong."

She smiled, all sharp, shiny white teeth. "Why are we talking about Eric? What have you been up to?"

"Traveling."

"I love to travel! Where have you been?"

"Here and there." He waited for her to declare she loved here and there.

She wasn't as dumb as she pretended, or maybe she was too self-centered to notice his evasion. "I'm the manager of the spa here at Bella Terra. If you'd like a service—a hot-stone massage or a French body polish, let me know and I'll see to it personally."

What was he supposed to say to that? Really, only two words would do, and the first ones that popped into his mind seemed inappropriate. So instead he said, "Thank you."

"That sounded provocative, didn't it?" Like a cat in heat, she rubbed her shoulder against him and giggled.

"Not at all." He was starting to remember this chick; she'd been like a high-class groupie, making it clear she would do whatever it took to take possession of one of the Di Luca sons. Jenna was a social climber, his grandmother had declared, and none too subtle about it. Cocking his head, he studied her. "You know, I was lousy in calculus."

She giggled. "Maybe *I* tutored *you?*"

"Maybe you did." He took a step away. "I imagine I'll be too busy with my family to have time for any spa treatments, but thank you for the offer." Looking across the lobby, he saw Brooke making her way toward him. "Excuse me," he said, and walked away, forgetting all about Jenna, her spa services, and her readily available ass.

Her ass, after all, might have been good for a grope in high school, but he wasn't a desperate, horny kid anymore. At least, not when he looked at Jenna Campbell.

He saved all his desperation for Brooke.

Rafe Di Luca didn't remember her.

Jenna Campbell stared at him as he walked to the check-in desk with Brooke Petersson.

Rafe Di Luca didn't remember her.

Jenna recalled that conversation in the library, their laughter together, the way he'd looked, the way she'd bent over him, thrusting her cleavage in his face. . . . Like a starving man, he'd grabbed her, drove her against the wall, fondled her tits, thrust his tongue in her mouth over and over, as if he were desperate for a good piece of hot ass instead of his cold bitch of a girlfriend. Then he broke off and fled, as if he were too scared to do Jenna in the library.

And now Rafe Di Luca didn't remember her at all. He had barely tried to pretend.

Humiliation curled through her.

She recalled luring him to the library with the promise of help in calculus—not that she'd had to lure very hard. She recalled every detail of the kiss, of the groping. He had been the best she'd ever had, wild, forceful, out of control. At night, she'd imagined what it would be like, a man like that, his cock big and hot, his hips pumping. He'd be able to do it more than once a night. He'd be in her all the time.

She bit her lower lip hard enough to hurt.

All her life, she'd expected Rafe would come back and finish what he started.

But he didn't remember her.

He remembered that bitch Brooke Petersson.

Brooke Petersson.

Jenna's boss.

Right now, he was looking at Brooke as if he were ice cream and she was hot fudge with a cherry on top.

In high school, Jenna had despised Brooke for being so droopy, so hurt by life, such a wimp. But right from the first moment, Brooke had snagged the best-looking Di Luca, becoming his boon companion. Everyone had known nothing was going on between them, because little Brookie was a virgin and too scared to do him.

Then, all of a sudden, they were an item, so hot the air around them scorched the skin. The kids all whispered about them: They were so absorbed in each other they held each other's hands, breathed each other's air, had eyes for only each other.

It was nauseating, and Jenna couldn't stand it. She had convinced her daddy she needed to leave early for college so she could get to know the campus.

And when she found out Rafe and Brooke had broken up almost as soon as she left town, and she hadn't been there to pick up the pieces, she was pissed.

After that, Jenna had waited for years for her chance to convince Rafe he wanted to fuck a real woman.

And he didn't remember her.

Jenna's pager went off. She checked it, expecting it would be the spa with some stupid towel-folding emergency.

Instead . . . it was *him*. Not some stupid teenage fantasy like Rafe.

Sure, *he* wasn't rich. Yeah, he scared her sometimes. Okay, he had a mean streak that could get them both in trouble.

But he was a man, an honest-to-God man.

She stared at the number, angry that he'd contacted her here, where the danger was so great . . . and thrilled that he couldn't keep away from her. That first night, she had been alone in the spa cleaning up after one of the stupid masseuses threw a tantrum and a bottle of oil and quit. Jenna should have had housekeeping handle it, but that housekeeping supervisor had an attitude, and while nobody much scared Jenna, Ebrillwen did.

The first time Ebrillwen realized that Jenna had

been closing the spa and signing off on the cleaning before the crew was finished, she'd threatened to tell Noah and Brooke. Jenna had skated a little too close to the edge too many times; she was already on probation . . . so she had stayed to clean up the masseuse's mess. When he broke in, she was finally done scrubbing. She'd stripped off her clothes, hopped into the shower, turned—and there he was, watching her and grinning. She'd screamed and kicked. He'd dragged her to the massage table, bent her over, and poured into her. His cock had been hot and hard and real, and he had rubbed her clit with hot stones while he did her.

That night, he'd fucked her three times. Three. Until she was sore, and each time was better than the first.

Bet you couldn't do that, Rafe I-am-so-cool Di Luca.

Victor walked behind the concierge desk. "What can I do for you, Jenna?"

She stared at him, trying to remember, while excitement rolled off her in waves. She pressed her thighs together, trying to contain herself. But that caused a bigger ripple. So she made an executive decision: She'd take her break right now, find her guy, get laid, then teach him a few things in return. What could go wrong?

She tossed a scornful glance at Rafe and Brooke as they looked at the map of the resort.

The really important people were busy.

"Victor, I wanted to talk to Brooke, but I don't want to interrupt her. I've got to leave for a couple of hours." She made her patented embarrassed expression. "Female problems, you know."

Victor stepped back as if she were contagious. "I'll tell her."

"And let the spa know so they know to call Brooke if they need help?"

"I'll tell them, too."

"Thank you, Victor." Jenna fluttered her fingers. "I'll be back as soon as I can." She walked to the door and stopped. Turning, she looked at Brooke, all prissy-ass and authoritative. She looked at Rafe, leaning over Brooke and smoldering with sexuality.

God damn them. She was going to make them sorry they were born.

Chapter 13

G*reat.* Without even knowing where Brooke was living, Rafe had picked the cottage next to hers. She'd tried to convince him he needed bigger accommodations, but he wanted that location for the same reason she liked it—it was central to everything on the premises.

So they were neighbors. No big deal. She could handle knowing he was skulking around in the bushes. After all, his only interest in her was whether or not she'd hit his grandmother with a tire iron. That was it. He seemed much more interested in chatting up Jenna Campbell, whom he'd managed to find while Brooke was outside with his mother.

Brooke rubbed her forehead. She must be getting cranky, because she knew Jenna pretty well, and without a doubt Jenna had found him. Frankly, it was of no concern to Brooke whether he flirted with every scaggy female in town, as long as he stayed out of her bushes. So to speak.

"I'm glad that's settled." With expertly false sincerity—she was, after all, a concierge— Brooke smiled at Rafe. "Now, if you'll excuse me, I need to relieve Victor for a while, so I'll go change."

"Get into uniform?" Rafe asked.

"Exactly."

"Wait here. I'll get my bag and walk with you."

"Get your bag and the bell staff will bring around a golf cart to take you to your cottage."

"Why bother the bell staff when you can take me?"

"I can change without your help."

"I want to reacquaint myself with the grounds, meet more of the employees."

Irritated beyond reason, she snapped, "Why don't I call a conference, line them up for you, and you can interrogate them all?"

"Casual meetings are more likely to produce results." He seemed oblivious to her sarcasm.

She knew better. But she wasn't going to shake him, and she was pretty sure he wanted to see where she lived, whether she had neglected to wash Nonna's bloodstains off her bathroom vanity. "Get your bag, then. I'll wait for you here." She watched him stroll out the door, toyed with the idea of running the other direction, figured that was immature and silly . . . and anyway, she couldn't run far enough or fast enough.

Besides, as soon as he walked away, a mob of guests arrived at check-in, and she moved behind the desk to help. The rush continued for the next half hour, and the only time she thought of Rafe was when she caught sight of him and Noah passing out cups of lemonade and water to the people in line, soothing male tempers and flirting

116

expertly with the women. More of that Di Luca charm, used like a condiment to give flavor to everyday life.

When the rush subsided again, she came around to find the brothers arguing about whether Rafe should reside with Noah or Eli or on resort property. She didn't even disagree when Rafe said, "I want to act like a guest, listen to the locals who come in for a drink, see if the maids or the gardeners know anything they're not telling. The sooner we get this solved, Noah, the sooner I'm out of here."

The way Noah looked at her, as if he were worried about how she would handle the situation, made her step between the brothers. "We'll be okay, Noah; it's not high season for the tourists, and we don't need the cottage. I'll take him out there. I need to talk to the staff anyway, make sure everything's running smoothly, then get back to the hospital to check on Nonna before lights-out."

"When do you sleep?" Rafe asked. "Seems as if you're working overtime."

Do not. Punch him. In full view. Of the lobby.

Turning on her heel, she started down a narrow corridor into the depths of the hotel. "It's not work to go see your grandmother. I'm glad to do it."

Rafe and Noah followed.

"You're tired," Rafe said.

Noah stopped her with a hand on her shoulder and looked at her worriedly. "Have we been driving you too hard? How about you take a couple of extra days off?"

To be at Rafe's beck and call? Not a chance. "I'm off at ten," she snapped, then took a calming breath and turned to Rafe. "The night staff has instructions to call Noah if there are problems, and during this emergency, Victor has truly been a godsend. As has Mrs. Jones."

Noah shivered.

Rafe looked between them. "Who's Mrs. Jones?"

"Our housekeeping Nazi," Noah said.

Brooke stopped before a wide, plain door with a plaque that read, HOUSEKEEPING. "*Shh.* She'll hear you."

Noah shivered again in great exaggeration. "You two are on your own. Let me know if you need anything, Rafe. Brooke, take tomorrow off. We'll cover for you. I'm going back to the hospital." For a moment, the youngest Di Luca brother looked weary and worn. "I can't stand to see Nonna in pain, but I have to keep checking on her. If I'd checked on her more often, this might not have happened."

Brooke put her hand on his arm. "If you were always checking on Nonna, she'd slap you on the side of the head and tell you to get a life. You know that. What happened . . . happened. All we

118

can do now is make sure it doesn't happen again."

Both brothers spoke in unison. "It won't."

These two Di Lucas were the ones most likely to go head-to-head on any subject, but on this, they were in agreement.

"I know. And she knows, too." She shoved Noah. "Take Nonna something from the restaurant. The hospital food is not good and she's losing weight."

"Good idea." Noah headed down the corridor.

Turning to Rafe, Brooke said, "Noah requires that we hire half our staff locally, but a great many of the privileged young ladies from Bella Terra have never cleaned their own room, much less anyone else's, and our former head of housekeeping had a difficult time training and maintaining discipline." Opening the door, she led them into a room filled with buckets, bottles, and towels. A tall, thin, cold-eyed woman dressed in a blue starched maid's uniform stood by a desk. "Rafe, this is our head of housekeeping, Ebrillwen Jones. She's originally from Wales, the housekeeper for a large estate, but when visiting the castle and seeing her exemplary work, I lured her away with the promise of sunshine."

"You have delivered. I swim every day." Ebrillwen shook Rafe's hand firmly. "I've heard a lot about you, Mr. Di Luca." *None of it favorable,* her tone implied, and her eyes did not warm.

Not that he expected every woman to fawn over him.

But they usually did.

So he made a judgment: Miss Jones had broad shoulders and a narrow waist that gave her an inverted-triangle shape, and all she needed was jodhpurs and a riding crop to be the caricature of a British boarding school principal. This woman would respond to straight talk from him. "Mrs. Jones, during my stay, I'll be working in town and here at the resort, looking for clues about what happened to my grandmother, Sarah Di Luca. I imagine you know your staff better than anyone, and if you can offer me any assistance, if you've seen anything suspicious, I'd be grateful for your guidance."

Ebrillwen's dark eyes narrowed on him. "When I arrived, we had many hooligans here."

He got the feeling she was including him in her condemnation.

She continued. "But I cleared out the staff and rehired to my taste, and for the most part I would stake my reputation on their trustworthiness. My young men and women are reliable."

"Thank you, Mrs. Jones," Brooke said, and started to turn away.

"However." Mrs. Jones stopped them with a single, sharply intoned word. "I see sloppiness in other areas in the resort. If Miss Petersson would give me a free hand over the spa staff and the gardening staff, I could whip them into shape."

Brooke stood straight, looked her right in the eyes, and said, "Ebrillwen, when I need someone to take over the supervision of the spa and the garden, you'll be the first to know."

Mrs. Jones nodded stiffly. "Miss Petersson, I hope I didn't offend."

Brooke's smile was nothing short of snappish. "I take stock of my employees on a regular basis and do occasionally revise my opinion of their competence. Keep that in mind, please."

It was a threat . . . and a promise of retribution. He had no idea his Brooke could command with such authority—or frighten a woman as intimidating as Ebrillwen Jones.

"Of course." Mrs. Jones inclined her head.

Brooke walked out of the room, leaving Rafe staring after her in amazement.

"Mr. Di Luca?" Mrs. Jones said. "I will contact you if I recognize any problem with my staff."

By that she meant she'd have to see someone wiping their bloody switchblade on a corpse before she'd report any discrepancies to him. "As Miss Petersson just pointed out to me, it would be more appropriate if you report to her."

"Yes, I believe that's correct." Frost dripped from every word.

He hurried after Brooke, catching up with her

as she strode out the door and into the gardens. "You're a formidable woman," he said.

"I'd appreciate it if you wouldn't undermine my authority among the staff that I supervise. I realize you're on the hunt, and I have the greatest sympathy and desire that you succeed in finding Sarah's attacker. At the same time, I require the staff to report to me, not you. In the case of the gardening crew, which is predominantly men, there's already a tendency to want to dismiss my authority." Brooke stopped, turned to face him, and pointed her finger in his face. "I do not have the time to complete my duties at Bella Terra, call my mother every day, and spend time making sure your grandmother has everything she needs at the hospital if I have to follow around after you and reestablish my authority here!"

Man. He hadn't faced a woman so coldly angry since basic training and his first smart-ass remark to a female drill sergeant. "I'll make sure that anyone I speak to knows I'm doing so with your permission."

"Good idea. And don't countermand my command while I'm standing there." Swinging on her heel, she strode up the path again.

As he followed, he mused that he should be ashamed for being more concerned with the shape of her ass than the weight of her authority.

Chapter 14

Yet Rafe followed Brooke, watched the way her shoulders took on the erect posture he associated with the military.

Yep. She was mad.

He supposed she had the right.

So he let the spring air cool her cheeks, and watched the dappled sunlight as it slid golden fingers over her dark hair and down her back. When the path widened and he judged she'd had a moment to regain her composure, he caught up with her. "You don't need to spend all your extra time taking care of my family. I can go back to the hospital tonight and take care of my grandmother."

"No, you can't." Brooke glanced at him and shook her head as if he were nothing but a big, bumbling idiot. "Because of the concussion, they don't want her standing on her own yet. You can't help her to the bathroom when she wants to go. You can't help her keep her cast dry while she showers."

"I'm a tough guy," he said with a full helping of irony. "I can do it."

"She'd hate it. Whether you like it or not, she needs me."

"It's not that I don't like it. It's that I don't like taking advantage of you." In the sunlight,

Brooke looked weary and a little sad, as if recent events and resort duties were taking their toll.

She shrugged off his concern. "I choose to do what I do. It's only for a little while, only until Nonna is out of the hospital. Then Noah will hire a private nurse and I'll visit less frequently."

"Why don't the nurses at the hospital do this stuff?"

Incredulous, Brooke asked, "Do you have any idea how overworked and understaffed they are at that hospital? They'll give her care, sure, and they're good at what they do, but there are so many patients and so few nurses." Taking a long breath, she turned to face him. "Look. Every time I walk in there and she's not in her bed—the nurses have her sitting on the sunporch, or she's up in X-ray, or someone has helped her to the bathroom—my heart skips a beat. I know I'm overreacting, but my God, Rafe. If you could have seen her on the floor of the kitchen, blood oozing out of her scalp and her arm shattered. And she was on the phone! Somehow she had thought to call your aunts and they were talking to her, encouraging her to hang in there. When I see families like yours, taking care of one another, it's, well, it's cool. You know that. I've thought that forever."

"Yes. I remember." He remembered far too well.

"Your grandmother always made me feel part

your family, and I don't want her to have to wait for her bath or to get ready for bed. So I do what I can. That's all. Don't get hung up on thinking the reason I'm doing it is that I'm guilty, or the reason I'm doing it is that I'm a saint. It makes me feel good, like I'm repaying someone who has gone out of her way to be kind to me."

"Hm." This he believed. But he was a man who dealt in solutions. He knew how to ease Brooke's fears and take the burden off her shoulders.

She must have heard something in his voice, for she asked, "What? Rafe?" But before she could pin him down, they broke out of the well-tended jungle of native plants and into the pool area.

The complex had been Noah's idea, to build a recreational center that consisted of three interconnected pools with waterslides, rocky waterfalls shadowed by exotic vegetation, and a river that wound around the perimeter. A retractable roof covered two of the pools, making them an attraction in the winter, and the atmosphere was more like Hawaii than central California.

Rafe stopped at the edge of the first pool and took a deep breath. It smelled tropical, warm, welcoming.

His little brother was some smart son of a bitch. He knew what worked, what made people shake their troubles off their shoulders and relax.

Brooke was oblivious. "Part of the gardening crew is always working in the pool area. With children visiting the resort, we have vegetation emergencies on a regular basis."

"Vegetation emergencies?" Rafe lifted his brows.

"Kids falling in bushes, kids eating leaves and berries, and parents freaking out and threatening to sue."

"Shouldn't the parents watch their children?"

"What a revolutionary idea." Brooke had perfected her deadpan delivery. "But since that doesn't always happen, we have gardeners here who extricate the children, and explain that we have no poisonous flora at the resort while dialing our on-staff nurse. In their spare time, the gardeners work on the planters." She glanced around until she located a group of three men dressed in dark khaki uniforms. "I'll introduce you."

The man giving orders was about fifty, with black skin, long, curly hair, colorful tattoos up and down his arms and neck, broad, deep shoulders, and a barrel chest. He nodded as they approached, held up one finger to indicate patience, and continued speaking to his men in a slow, deep, Southern-accented voice. When he had finished giving his instructions, he ambled over and said, "What can I do for you, Ms. Petersson?"

"Rafe, this is Zachary Adams. He's in charge

of keeping our grounds groomed."

Zachary removed his glove and offered a broad hand, cracked and rough with calluses. "You're the Di Luca who's in security. I imagine you're here to investigate the attack on the elderly Mrs. Di Luca."

"That's right." Rafe knew more than a few people would speculate correctly, and the shrewd expression in Zachary's eyes proved he'd put all the pieces together. "How many people do you have working for you?"

"Full-time, twenty men, five women. Right now, springtime, I add another five hands temporarily to try to keep up with the weeds."

"And the gophers," Brooke added.

"It's a constant running battle with the gophers. We clean out one nest and ten more pop up." Zachary looked disgusted. "Worst spring we've had. I've got the exterminators in to take care of the fuzzy little bastards."

"I understand one of your gardeners disappeared the day my grandmother was hit."

"Luis Hernández. Yeah. But he didn't have it in him to strike an elderly woman, especially not that one. That guy was not too bright, but he was a good gardener who liked his plants. I always put him on the crew to go up to Mrs. Di Luca's and work on her yard. He was amiable. He was religious, Catholic. She liked him, and she has a good gut about people."

Yeah, she did. "What'd he look like?" Rafe asked.

"Hispanic, six-foot, a little overweight."

"Family?"

"No one around here. Had a mama in L.A. Maybe he went back home." But Zachary frowned as if he didn't believe his own theory.

"He was worried about something," Brooke said.

Zachary shook his head. "Maybe. I don't know. I don't babysit my people. I expect them to do the work and handle their own lives."

"Anybody else you'd suspect?" Rafe asked.

"Most of the guys I hire have a record." Zachary met Rafe's eyes. "Hell, I have a record. But I pick out my workers pretty carefully, stay away from the violent types, stick with the petty thieves and marijuana smokers. I figure we all deserve a second chance."

A guy dressed in the gardeners' dark khaki came up the walk. He hesitated when he saw the group, but Zachary gestured him over. "What is it, Josh?"

"Excuse me, Mr. Adams, Miss Petersson." Josh's gaze skimmed Rafe in acknowledgment. "The gophers have made it into the planter between the kiddie pool and the playground equipment." He was young, lightly tanned, blond with blue eyes, as sober as if he'd announced the return of the black plague.

"Damn it!" Zachary's voice was virulent, but quiet. "We'll have to shut the area, go in at night, and clean them out." To Rafe, he said, "We can't kill gophers in front of the kids."

"Right." Rafe nodded.

"Do you want me to stay late tonight to help?" Josh asked. "I can always use the overtime."

"Good. You're on," Zachary said.

Rafe watched him walk away. "Why does he need the overtime?"

"Josh Hoffman is one of our local hires," Brooke said. "After high school, he was in and out of college. Worked around the country a little, and now he's saving to go back. Figures he'll have enough by next fall."

"Too bad, really. He works hard, doesn't squirm at the tough stuff. I would have never thought it. Most of the locals don't like to get their hands dirty." Zachary glanced at the guys weeding the flower bed and bellowed, "Not those! We just planted those marigolds."

The guys froze.

Zachary turned back to Rafe and Brooke. "Listen, I'll keep an eye out for you, an ear cocked for conversations. If I stumble on anything suspicious, I'll let you know. Now I've got to go before my temps take out everything we planted last week."

After Zachary walked away, Rafe said, "I like him."

"I like him, too." Brooke started up a different path.

"Straightforward. Smart." Rafe followed and made his educated guess. "Did time for a murder, right?"

Her step faltered. "Maybe."

"That's an answer in itself, Brooke. Don't sweat it. I work with guys like him—the ones who learn their lesson, pay their penance, and go forward with their lives. We fight the ones who discover they like violence, and go out to kill again."

She stopped by a small stucco cottage set off the path, with marigolds in the window box and a sturdy black door with a lock. "You've met the supervisors and a few of the workers. Do you think anyone is violent?"

"If it were that easy, I'd be out of a job. I know Nonna said her attacker was a white man about six feet tall. I also know that almost every person, male and female, that I've met today, was white and about six feet tall."

Brooke viewed him as if he'd lost his mind. "Zachary is not white."

"It's easy to buy a pale mask and gloves. And your Ebrillwen Jones could easily dress the part of a man."

"The criminal could be, as DuPey said, a drifter."

"Do you believe that?"

"It could be."

"That's also an answer in itself, Brooke." Deliberately, he loomed over her. "I wish you would tell me what you know."

Naturally, she wasn't intimidated at all. "Believe me or not, I don't care. But I don't know anything about the attack on your grandmother."

He couldn't believe that she did, and yet—something was wrong. Something was off. Brooke was lying to him, daring his disbelief. And why?

She stopped in front of the narrow cottage isolated by lush vegetation, with window boxes where bright golden marigolds grew. "Here we are—Millionaire's Row, home to the priciest places on the property—and me. And now you. Yours is the next cottage on the left. Is there anything else that you need from me?"

Yeah, but you're not going to give it to me. "No. Go rest." He stripped off his leather biker jacket, revealing for the first time his white T-shirt stained at the pits, grimy at the neck—the red, healing line of his newest scar slicing up his arm and over his elbow. "I'm going to get cleaned up, and I've got work to do." He walked down the path and out of sight, knowing she was watching him . . . and wondering. Wondering what work he would do. Wondering why he hadn't muscled his way into her cottage to look the place over, and maybe to look her over, too.

She was smart and wary and curious.

And that was fine with him.

Chapter 15

At seven that evening, Brooke walked into Sarah's room wearing a smile and carrying a bouquet of wildflowers Zachary had sent.

She stopped short.

Nonna wasn't in the bed.

Her heart skipped a beat.

Then the bathroom door opened, and a strange woman helped Sarah out.

Sarah looked good, dressed in her robe with her hair damp.

The stranger was a brunette, diminutive, and supporting Sarah with her arm around Sarah's thin waist.

"You're stronger than you look," Sarah was saying.

"I work out a lot," was the reply.

Brooke noted a few things: Sarah looked tired, but she looked happy, too.

And the stranger resembled an Asian martial arts instructor, with beautiful, smooth, tanned skin. With a single pass, her eyes cataloged everything about Brooke and dismissed her as unimportant.

No, not unimportant. Nonthreatening.

"Brooke, dear, how good to see you!" Sarah called as the stranger maneuvered her toward the bed. "This is Bao. Rafe sent her over to help me so you and the nurses don't have to."

Brooke came over, put the flowers on the table, and helped Bao ease Sarah onto the mattress. "Nonna, I like to help you." She was, she realized, calling Sarah "Nonna" to emphasize their warm relationship. But it stung, being replaced so easily.

"I know you do, dear, and I love having you." Sarah settled on the pillows, then took Brooke's hand. "But you're running yourself ragged with everything you've got to do."

"Did Rafe tell you that?"

"No. But I could read between the lines. He's worried about you. He's so thoughtful, my Rafe."

Brooke contained a burst of explosive laughter.

Bao did not. She laughed long and hard. In perfect English, she said, "Thoughtful he isn't." She spoke to Sarah, but met Brooke's gaze, sending her a wordless message. "He wants to make sure you remain safe and secure, Mrs. Di Luca, and you don't suffer any setbacks in your recovery."

Brooke made the leap of logic.

Rafe had sent Bao to be Sarah's bodyguard.

She looked at Bao again.

Bao was a dangerous woman. She had calluses on her hands, the kind a martial arts expert developed from breaking bricks. Even in here, in the confines of a California hospital room, she wore close-fitting jeans, boots, a dark button-up shirt, and a jacket, and somewhere underneath those clothes she hid weapons, and knew how to use them.

Brooke had two choices: Be resentful. Or recognize the good sense of having someone to help and protect Sarah here at all times.

Brooke was, above all things, reasonable— even when she didn't want to be. "I understand. Rafe really is very thoughtful." She picked up the vase with its wilted flowers. "Let me throw these away and replace them with the new bouquet."

Bao took the vase away. "I'll do this. You sit down and chat with Mrs. Di Luca. She's been waiting for you to come."

So while Bao arranged the flowers in the vase, Brooke sat and talked to Sarah, who looked better tonight than she had since the attack, alert and in some nebulous way herself again. Brooke told herself it was Rafe's arrival that made the difference, but when she got ready to leave and leaned over Sarah to kiss her cheek, Sarah caught her shoulder in her good hand and held her still. With a grin that looked like the old, mischievous Sarah, she said, "I'm so glad not to be a burden on you, Brooke, and I hope you'll visit even when you don't have to help me pee."

"Next time I come, maybe we can find some Australian football on TV," Brooke said.

"I'd like that. I'd like that a lot." Her grip tightened. "Today I've been talking to Annie and June."

June Di Luca lived at the family's southern California beach resort. Annie Di Luca lived at the family's resort on the wild Washington coast. The three women were very different, but for as long as Brooke could remember, Sarah and her sisters-in-law had always formed a little female cadre of support known as "the girls."

"What have you been saying?" Brooke asked.

"The girls think I should tell you what happened."

Brooke's nerves grew taut. "What happened . . . you mean when you were attacked?"

"No. What happened a long time ago. I don't want to. I'd thought we've moved beyond it. I'd rather hide my head in the sand." For the first time that evening, Sarah got that soft, out-of-focus expression. "But they're right. When Rafe has a moment, bring him up to visit me."

"He always has a moment for you, Nonna."

"Eli and Noah, too, I suppose. Everyone needs to know." Sarah let her go. "But not tonight. I'm tired. Bring them tomorrow. In the afternoon. I feel sharpest in the afternoon."

"Tomorrow afternoon for sure."

With a sigh, Sarah settled back and closed her eyes. "Good night, dear."

"Good night, Nonna." Brooke pressed a kiss to her cheek, then lingered over the bed.

Yes, Sarah was better, but that moment of confusion when she mentioned the past . . . it worried Brooke. What was so awful that Sarah herself said she wanted to hide her head in the sand? That her sisters-in-law had to insist she tell them?

Bao leaned against the wall by the door, her sleepy appearance at odds with the nod she gave as Brooke passed.

As Brooke headed for the parking lot, she pulled out her cell phone and called Rafe. "Nonna wants to see you and your brothers tomorrow afternoon."

"We'll be there," he said.

"She wants me to be with you."

"Is she matchmaking?" Like the jerk he was, he laughed.

Brooke was not amused. In fact, she thought she'd completely lost her sense of humor. "No. It's moral support. For her. And while we're talking, who's Bao?"

"You didn't figure it out?" His voice was deep, warm, soft.

The sound sent an unexpected shiver up her spine. "You couldn't have warned me before I went over?"

"I thought you'd want to meet her, assure yourself that Nonna was in good hands." However many times Brooke talked to Rafe, she was always aware of that undercurrent that

137

flowed between them, like foreplay for the mind, like verbal sex.

But she could ignore that; right now, the words were more important. "Nonna seems to think Bao is a nurse-companion."

"My original intention was to send one of my men in to keep her safe, but when you told me she needed help only a female could give, I called Bao and asked if she was up-to-date on her aide license. She is, so she went in to take care of Nonna."

Brooke heard it in his voice; he liked Bao, and he was proud of himself. "You have a bodyguard who's a nursing aide?"

"Most of the people who work for me can at least fake their way through a couple of jobs," Rafe said patiently. "Don't worry about Bao doing anything to accidentally hurt Nonna. Bao's grandfather was the South Vietnamese karate champion, fought for our side in the war, survived five years in one of their prisons. Her father was born on a beach over there while the family was boarding a boat into the South China Sea. The whole bunch of them is tougher than nails, but I'd trust Bao with my most precious possession—and in fact I am."

That smartly put Brooke in her place.

He continued. "Bao doesn't have the creds to take care of Nonna when she goes home. Then we'll have to hire a real nurse, but Nonna will know Bao, so she won't fret when she sees Bao hanging around."

"Providing security."

"Exactly. Until we find our perp, she's going to have round-the-clock security." His voice changed, got stern. "In the meantime, you can visit Nonna and not worry about whether she's going to want a shower or needs to go to the bathroom. Now go see your mom. I'm sure she'd like a little more time with you."

He was right. But that didn't make her happy about his high-handedness. Snidely, she asked, "What are you going to do?"

"I'm going to have a drink with my brothers."

Chapter 16

Like three old-time gunfighters, the Di Luca brothers hunched over the bar in the Luna Grande Lounge in the main building of the Bella Terra resort.

Unlike old-time gunfighters, they each selected a bottle of the family wine to sample and share.

The wall behind the wine bar rose two stories to the ceiling, a gleaming display of fine wines, each one chosen by Eli or their bartender, Tom Chan. The series of glass panels covered the gleaming bottles, red, white, and rosés, and each variety was cooled to the correct temperature. The bar's computer kept track of the location of each bottle and, when the right code was entered, unlocked the necessary panel. The most expensive reds were high on the wall, and watching Chan roll the library ladder into place, slowly ascend, and with a flourish retrieve a bottle endlessly entertained the patrons, leading to more wine sales and more profit.

Now Tom opened and decanted the reds, and set out nine glasses before them. A genial man, part of the extensive Chan family, Tom had tended this bar since it had opened twenty years ago. He was a veteran of the Gulf War who'd lost part of his left foot on a mine, he was the man who gave a second opinion when Eli asked about blending his wines, and he had been Eli's best friend for many years.

The Di Lucas paid Tom very well to keep their bar and restaurant among the top in rankings and awards online and in print in the United States.

Rafe swirled their Bella Terra Zinfandel, sniffed and swirled again, then tasted it and leaned back with a sigh of pleasure. "Eli, you are a genius."

"Our basic zin, retails for less than twenty dollars a bottle, and it's had a rating of ninety or above for the past three years." Noah lifted the bottle in front of him and poured a little into three clean glasses. "Try the Luna Rosso Meritage. It's brilliant. I've never had better in my life."

Rafe swirled, sniffed, swirled, and tasted. "What's the undernote?"

"He doesn't care for this one as much," Eli said solemnly. "He doesn't like licorice."

As soon as Eli said that, Rafe identified the flavor. "That's it! Licorice. You're right; it's not my favorite, but still—a very good wine. Warm and rich."

Tom leaned across the bar and murmured, "Fan approaching on your left."

The brothers turned to face the flushed young woman standing beside Rafe. She stood wringing her hands, staring at Rafe adoringly, and her voice quavered. "Excuse me, I hate to interrupt, but I just had to say, Mr. Di Luca, how much I loved your movie. The one with the dragon?"

"Yes, that's the only one I did." Rafe nodded.

"When I was a kid, I watched it over and over, and I pretended I had a dragon, too, but that I never grew up. Even during my teenage years, when I was all . . . stupid and pimply, I watched that movie because it made me feel like I would make it through without just, you know, killing myself." She was really flushed now, feeling foolish but unable to stop babbling.

"Thank you. The story was wonderful, truly magical, and it means a lot to me to know you liked it." Rafe knew the right thing to say—he'd said it hundreds of times. He glanced at the piece of paper she clutched. "Would you like me to sign that for you?"

She glanced down at the cocktail napkin she'd crumpled in her nervousness. "Oh, I'm so stupid! I was nervous. I was afraid you would, you know, snap at me."

"As long as he's well fed, he never snaps," Noah said.

She looked at Noah, so taken aback by his interruption he might have been Rafe's dragon.

"We've got lots of napkins." Eli plucked one off the stack and slid it in Rafe's direction.

As Rafe signed the napkin, the girl shifted her gaze back to him and stared adoringly.

He handed her the napkin, she thanked him and hurried back to her table, and, knowing full well what was about to happen, Rafe turned to face his brothers. His damned, smart-ass brothers.

In a falsetto whisper, Eli said, "Oh, Rafe, you're so big and tall and handsome."

"You make me swoon, you hunk of a man." Noah's voice was as high and as quiet as Eli's.

"I hate you both." Rafe turned to Tom. "Aren't you going to talk in a girly tone, too?"

"No way. They're jealous. Besides, you're some kind of big fighter guy. You can rip off a man's pair of family jewels with a flick of your wrist." Tom grinned at the other brothers' chagrin. "Drink your wine, guys. Not everyone can be a movie star and the real James Bond all wrapped into one." He wandered down the bar to pour a drink.

"Yeah, fine. I'm jealous," Eli said.

"When I'm around you, it's the only time I feel invisible," Noah said.

Rafe shrugged. "It's not about me. It's movie magic."

"It would help if you'd get a paunch," Noah said.

"I'll work on that." Rafe grabbed a handful of nuts from the bowl in front of him and ate them one by one.

Eli poured the last bottle. "Okay, movie star, this will be your favorite."

"What is it?" Rafe asked.

"You tell me." Eli waited.

"You know I haven't got your palate." But Rafe swirled and sniffed, swirled and tasted—and smiled. "Sangiovese." He tasted. "Primarily sangiovese. But cabernet, too." He sipped again, and rolled it across his tongue. "Fruit forward—black cherry and plum. Nice spice, and a kick of pepper." He sighed with pleasure. "You're right. It's my favorite."

The brothers each filled the glass of their favorite, sipped and smiled, and shared a rare moment of accord.

"Good thing we have you, Eli, to make the family fortune." Rafe grinned at his brother, and was surprised when Eli didn't grin back.

Uh-oh. Had there been a bad harvest? Was that why Eli looked as if he had indigestion?

"What wines have you got coming up?" Rafe asked.

"I've got a pinot noir that's going to do great things, and I've put together another wine from those old vines on the hill behind Nonna's house." Eli smiled faintly. "That could turn out to be interesting."

"What kind of grapes are they?" Rafe asked.

"Red."

Rafe rolled his fingers, urging Eli to explain.

"I don't know. We've always flung some into the mix when we create our table wine, but it

144

occurred to me that the grapes could stand on their own." Eli shrugged. "I could be wrong."

"But you're not," Rafe said.

"But I could be."

"But you're not," Noah said.

Tom returned and leaned across the bar. "Fan approaching from behind."

Eyes shining with anticipation, an older woman waited for Rafe to turn around. "Young man, I have to tell you how much my family and I loved that dragon movie you did when you were a little boy. I showed it to my grandchildren when they were little."

"Thank you, ma'am. It's good to be remembered so many years later," Rafe said.

"Won't you ever do another movie?" she asked. "A sequel? All your fans would come to see it!"

"I would, but the dragon has retired from show business," Rafe said solemnly.

As she was supposed to, she laughed. "You scamp! I'll tell you what—I don't want your signature. I want a hug and a kiss!"

"I always like to smooch a pretty lady. It's one of the perks of the job." Leaning down, Rafe embraced her and kissed her cheek, then watched her walk away.

He turned back to his brothers.

"You scamp!" they said in unison.

"Shut. Up." Rafe wanted to kill them both.

Tom ominously cleared his throat. "That did it. Every female in here and the gay guys in the corner are getting ready to rush the bar. You might want to evacuate before you're kissing every tourist who ever dreamed of owning a dragon."

As the brothers scrambled to leave, Noah told Tom, "Pour the wines for the wedding party in the corner, Rafe's treat. If you need us, we're going to the Beaver Inn for pizza and beer."

"The Beaver Inn, huh?" Tom watched them walk out the door and shook his head. "Those boys are looking for trouble tonight."

Chapter 17

Brooke juggled a bouquet and a vegetable plate, tapped on her mother's door, then opened it and called, "Mom! You home?"

Kathy Petersson stuck her head around the corner. "I'm back here getting ready. It's bunco night!"

"I remember." Brooke walked through the living room to the kitchen. "When's everybody getting here?"

"At eight. Sylvia will be late, of course, so we'll snack a little and gossip a little, and when she shows up, we'll start."

"And play until, ooh, ten thirty?"

"Don't make fun of us, young lady. I'm sure we'll be here until eleven, and all of us yawning tomorrow."

Her mother's house was a cozy 1950s bungalow set on a narrow lot with an alley in the back, a white picket fence all around—and a handicapped ramp beside the front steps. "Zachary sent you a bouquet for the dining table," Brooke said. "The cook at the resort put together an appetizer for you. I had a heck of a time convincing him you didn't need any cheese or chocolate."

Kathy laughed. "Is he crazy? He buys the cheese for the restaurant from me."

"He thinks veggies are second-class citizens." Brooke slid everything onto the counter, and turned to hug her mother.

Neither of them let the metal bars of Kathy's walker get in the way.

Kathy Petersson had once been as tall as Brooke, with a swift step and a strong grip. She had given orders to her soldiers in a tone that cracked the whip, and if they didn't respond quickly enough, she pounced and they learned to pay attention.

She still applied her makeup and tended her sweep of dark hair with the care of a model. But time and rheumatoid arthritis had shrunk her frame and robbed her of the ability to dance or fight; the disease had twisted her bones until she moved at a painful snail's pace. Last year's hip replacement had eased her misery, but slowed her further, and now on bunco night, when Brooke could make it, she helped her arrange the food and set up the card tables.

"I didn't think you'd be here, honey," Kathy said. "I thought you'd be at the hospital with Mrs. Di Luca."

"I got relieved of most of my duties." Brooke got the dice and notepads out of the drawer. "Rafe arranged for a bodyguard-slash-nurse to stay with Sarah and take care of her. I'm to visit, but the responsibility is off my shoulders."

"That's good."

If Brooke hadn't been listening, she wouldn't have heard that off note in her mother's voice. But she was, and she did, and she knew what was coming.

Kathy continued. "I know you're fond of Sarah—I am, too—but I thought you were overdoing it."

"I guess."

Long pause. "So Rafe is back in town."

"This afternoon."

"It took him long enough to get here. Where was he?"

"I don't know, Mom, but I imagine he was in, as you have so aptly put it, one of the shitholes of the world."

"So he's still touring the shitholes, hm?"

"I don't know that, either. He doesn't check in with me."

"No, thank God. That's over." Another pause, more significant this time. "You won't have to see him much while he's here, will you?"

Now this conversation was going to get tricky. "I'm working with him to find Sarah's attacker."

Kathy turned on Brooke with fire in her eyes. "Why?"

Brooke put the lacy paper napkins on the table and fanned them out. "Because he thinks the attacker is probably someone in town, maybe at the resort, and I know everybody."

"Let him work with Brian DuPey!"

"He doesn't think the sheriff is good for much more than traffic tickets."

"I don't care. Rafe shouldn't be hanging around with you."

"Mom, I've heard you say it a hundred times. You don't think Brian DuPey is good for much more than traffic tickets. And you ought to know. You used to be in charge of all kinds of stuff in the Air Force, stuff you won't even tell me about." Facing her mother, she said, "To quote you, 'Don't piss on my shoes and tell me it's raining.' In this case, DuPey isn't good enough; we both know it, and I don't want some guy running around town bashing helpless women with a tire iron."

"Especially when you're related to a helpless woman." Kathy didn't get bitter about her condition very often, but this was one of those times. "Sometimes I wish we'd never come to this town."

"I used to wish that, too."

"I never understood why you were so unhappy when we moved here."

Of course she didn't. Kathy had been a military officer in charge of a whole gob of people doing secret government stuff. For a woman to thrive in the service, she had to let her grasp of the subtleties of human emotion slip away. So when she said she didn't understand, she meant it.

"Mom, when we moved here, you didn't tell me what was going on. If I'd known about the arthritis, that you needed a dry climate and a big medical center close by, I might not have been so bewildered."

"I didn't want you to worry that I wouldn't be able to take care of you."

"I can truthfully say it's never crossed my mind that you would be anything but a success." Even now, bent and crumpled, Kathy Petersson carried in herself a valiant spirit, and her cheese shop was the model of how to find a niche that needed filling. Brooke continued. "I wasn't worried about starving. I was worried about being unlovable."

"But why?"

"Daddy didn't love me. Or at least he didn't love me enough not to take another wife."

"Your daddy doesn't love anybody but himself. But I'm not sorry I married him. If I hadn't, I would never have had you, and you have always been the light of my life." Kathy brushed a hand across her eyes. "That's why I hate to see Rafe Di Luca in your life again. He's the worst thing that ever happened to you."

"Oh, no. He wasn't. Sometimes I think he was the best thing." Brooke went to the closet in the second bedroom, her old room, brought out two of the card tables, and put them up in the living room.

Kathy followed. "Rafe broke up your engagement to that nice man!"

"What nice man? Dylan? Mom, I broke off that engagement." Brooke moved the recliner back against the wall to make room for the last table. "Rafe didn't make me. He cleared my mind."

"By screwing you out of it!"

When Brooke was a teenager, she'd wished Kathy's speaking weren't quite so blunt and to the point. But she was over that now—most of the time. "No. By making me realize I couldn't spend my life with a man as good and kind and completely, horribly boring as Dylan Roper."

"It's better than being married to a . . . womanizing adventure addict."

"I was never married to Rafe, and while I admit he seems to thrive on adventure, he isn't a womanizer."

Kathy scoffed. "How do you know?"

"You always said you could tell when Dad was having an affair."

"I don't know if that was really true," Kathy said reflectively, "since he was having an affair all the time."

"You can say a lot of things about Rafe, about what he did wrong and how that ended our relationship. But I wasn't exactly the figurehead of maturity myself." Remembering, Brooke chuckled. "Actually, considering we were in high school the first time, I suppose we could both get a pass on the maturity thing."

"And the second time?"

"I knew exactly what I was doing, and why, and what was going to happen afterward. So back off, Mom." Brooke had never been so forthright with her mother before. "When Rafe's with me, he's with me. He can't stay, that's all. He's not Dad, and I'm not you. You know that. You even like him."

"When he's not messing with you." Kathy leaned away as Brooke marched to the coat closet and dug out the folding chairs.

"He doesn't mess with me. I'm an intelligent woman. When I'm with him, I'm perfectly aware what I'm doing isn't smart." Brooke put out the chairs, and she smirked. "But it is fun."

"How can you joke about this?" Kathy asked quietly. "After the last time?"

Brooke's smile faded. "He needed me, Mom."

"And you went running to him."

It was true. "The first time, I needed him. The second time, he needed me. If all of our relationships are based on need, then here, now—nothing will happen because neither one of us needs the other."

As if Brooke's words pained her, Kathy put her hand to her heart. "Honey, I don't want you to get hurt, and he always seems to do just that."

"I won't let him hurt me." Brooke was desperately earnest.

"You say that, and yet you won't even date seriously."

This was new territory. Brooke hadn't realized Kathy knew or cared about her social life. "I haven't found anybody."

"You work at a resort! Men come through there every day. Politicians. Rock stars. Movie stars. Wine barons. Millionaires. Billionaires. You even said you have a con man who vacations at Bella Terra. Gagnon, I believe you said his name was." Obviously, Kathy had given this some thought.

"You want me to date a con man?"

"He sounds charming."

Brooke recalled Gagnon's dark hair, tanned skin, his towering height . . . the slash of scar across his cheek, the way he smiled as if he knew all too well what she wore under her clothes . . . "He's French. Of course he's charming." She also remembered the bodyguards never left his side and the unrelenting watchfulness in his dark eyes. "He's dangerous, too."

"You're too sedentary. A little danger would do you good."

Brooke couldn't decide whether she should be amused or appalled. "Mother, how desperate are you to get rid of me?"

"It simply seems as if you should give at least one of those men a whirl."

"They're not bicycles!"

"Rafe Di Luca has been back less than twenty-four hours and he's already mesmerized you."

"No, he hasn't," Brooke answered a little too quickly.

"Has he kissed you?"

"You mean like . . . today?"

Kathy saw right through that evasion. "Oh, Brooke. Not again."

"It was just a kiss." . . . His lips smoothing hers. His body pressing her onto the sun-warmed front steps until Brooke felt each tread against her spine, until the smell of the old boards and old paint had been a newfound pleasure . . .

"Find a man," Kathy said. "Settle down. Have some kids."

Now, that was insulting. "I am not having kids to distract me from Rafe."

Kathy narrowed her eyes at Brooke. "I'm going to pray the next time you have sex, the condom breaks."

"Vibrators don't wear condoms, Mom." Brooke thought that would put an end to the conversation.

Instead, Kathy said, "Don't I know it."

It took Brooke a second before she caught on. Then she groaned, "Oh, Mom. Gross me out."

Kathy laughed.

"Ew. I'm scarred for life." She heard women's voices on the walk, and saw her chance to

155

escape. "Everything's set up." She kissed her mother on the cheek. "I'm going out the back. I'm going home. I'm going to take a bath—alone—and read a book—alone—and I'm going to pretend I never heard you say that."

Kathy caught a strand of Brooke's hair. "When you get out of the bath, why don't you get online and book your next trip? Go someplace civilized. Someplace romantic."

"Someplace Rafe would never go?"

"Exactly." Kathy's expression reflected her satisfaction. "Go to France or Spain or Italy. Or Scandinavia! You've never been to Scandinavia."

"That would be different." Brooke warmed to the idea.

"Yes! Find someplace you like. Get a job in a hotel there. Don't come back."

"Mom!" Brooke couldn't believe she was talking that way.

"I'll get along without you, and so will the Di Lucas. It's time you went out into the world and lived your own life." The bell rang. Kathy went to the door and looked back at her daughter. "Go on. Get going."

She didn't mean get out of this house.

She meant get out of town.

And for the first time, Brooke entertained the idea.

Because maybe Mom was right.

Chapter 18

In the fifties, when the Marinos built it, the Beaver Inn had been a cramped, crummy bar across the river, and in the twenty-first century, it was still a cramped, crummy bar. But now it was run-down, too. It boasted the original girly calendars—thus the Beaver Inn—the original fixtures, the original pool tables. . . . Rafe supposed the chairs were new, but "new" was a relative term. Every one of the metal-framed chairs had a black, cracked, padded plastic seat and at least one short leg. The place smelled like beer and piss, not necessarily in that order, and the lit Budweiser sign in the window flickered in an annoying offbeat rhythm.

Despite the name, when the Di Luca brothers stepped in the door, there was not a single woman in the place. It was, however, full of men who spent more on their tattoos than on soap and had the body odor to prove it.

Rafe gave a sigh of relief. As a general rule, guys who hung around in places like this—field laborers, truck drivers, linemen—were good with fists and knives, but they never watched movies about a kid with an imaginary dragon. If they did, they for sure never admitted it.

"No Marinos," Rafe observed.

"Good. I don't feel like beating the shit out of someone tonight," Eli said.

"Liar," Noah said.

"Yeah. You're right. I'd like to beat the shit out of a lot of people tonight." Eli didn't fight often, but when he did, he was bare knuckles and balls to the wall. "They all deserve it."

Rafe looked sharply at his brother.

Not that he didn't understand the sentiment. This attack on Nonna left him frustrated and angry.

But Eli sounded bitter, ready to take out his anger on anyone who stepped in his way. Eli met Rafe's gaze, held it, then shook his head. He wasn't going to talk.

Okay. If there was one thing Rafe understood, it was that a man had a right to his privacy, and Eli was more private than any man Rafe had ever met.

Rafe was pretty sure that here in the Beaver Inn, if they played it right, they'd find someone with a similar urge to use his fists. "Let's see what we can do for you."

The Di Luca brothers wandered up to the bar and ordered shots: Maker's Mark for Rafe, Stolichnaya for Noah, Hornitos for Eli.

The bartender, a burly, unshaven guy with that sneer that mocked their clean clothes and white teeth, said, "You gotta pay first."

"Of course we do." Rafe grinned back at him, knowing full well the nasty little prick recognized them. "First round's on me." Getting out his wallet, he put the bills down.

The bartender lined the drinks up in front of them.

The brothers clinked the glasses, slammed down the shots.

Rafe coughed.

Behind them, someone seated at a table laughed.

Rafe coughed again, a high little sound as if he'd just swallowed his first liquor, and whimpered.

Eli turned to him. In a voice meant to carry, he said, "Don't worry; you'll get used to it."

"I don't know. That tasted really harsh," Rafe answered.

More laughter behind them.

The three brothers swapped grins.

The bartender picked up the phone and made a call, glancing at them occasionally as he spoke.

The Di Lucas settled down to continue the conversation cut short at the resort.

"I've found a home nurse for Nonna," Noah said.

"Who is she?" Eli asked in his normal tone. "Does Nonna know her?"

"No, but that's a good thing." Noah indicated that they needed another round. "Olivia's not from here, got nothing invested in the case or impressing one of us. She'll be all about Nonna."

Rafe and Eli nodded.

"She's got great refs as a nurse," Noah

continued, "plus she's got some creds in self-defense."

"I already had my man install a security system in the house," Rafe told them, "and when Nonna goes home, the place will have guards, but I'm always in favor of everyone having a little knowledge of self-defense."

"But will Nonna like her?" Eli asked.

"I think so." A smile tugged at Noah's mouth. "She's smart and funny, knows a lot about history, and isn't afraid to live up there alone with Nonna."

The smile tripped an alarm in Rafe.

Maybe in Eli, too, because he asked, "How did you find her?"

"She was in the hospital cafeteria, filling out an application, and her pen went dry. She asked me if she could borrow one, and we got to talking." Noah wore a fond and distant expression.

An expression Rafe didn't trust. "Why Bella Valley?"

"What?" Noah stared at him.

"If she's not from here, why is she moving to Bella Valley?" Rafe asked.

That snapped Noah out of his stupor. "Are you suspicious of everything? Bella Valley has a good rep among people looking for a more laid-back lifestyle."

"She's young and pretty—and she craves a laid-back lifestyle?" Rafe insisted.

"I didn't say she was young and pretty," Noah answered quickly.

"You didn't have to," Rafe said.

"Why don't you investigate her?" Noah's brown eyes grew icy. "I mean, my God, if you don't trust Brooke, you don't trust anyone. Have you had Eli and me investigated?"

"Not yet." Rafe's irritation rose to meet Noah's. "But you haven't told me everything that happened when Nonna was attacked. How the hell do you expect me to find Nonna's attacker when you haven't told me everything?"

Noah looked him right in the eyes. "We called you because we thought Nonna might die and she'd want to see you first. We didn't call you so you could fix all our problems, turn us all into the perfect example of humanity you are."

"Sarcasm's not going to bring Nonna's attacker to justice." By some miracle, Rafe kept his voice down.

"I don't know what it is we're supposed to tell you that's going to lead you to some revelation about the vagrant who broke into her house, attacked her, and ran away." Eli put his hand on Noah's shoulder, but Noah shrugged it off.

Rafe could not shrug off his responsibilities; nor could he let Noah get away with his offenses and his resistance. "Did you know whoever it was drove a motorcycle up there and hid it in the bushes?"

Noah's expression changed from resentment to suspicion to wary curiosity. "DuPey didn't mention that."

"Did you know this guy wore shoe coverings as well as gloves?" Rafe demanded.

Eli got it. "So he planned it. It wasn't a random thing."

Noah got it, too, but he didn't like it. "Are you sure?"

"Did you know he went into the dining room and lifted the candles out of the wine bottles on the table?" Rafe drove his point home with words like bullets.

Noah's color rose. "Why would he do that?"

"I don't know. I just know the more we find out, the better chance we have of catching him." Rafe was breathing hard.

So was Noah. They faced each other like boxers in the ring, brothers who should have been allies and found themselves at odds.

Rafe wanted to rage with frustration. At these small-town cops with their small-town minds, at his brothers, so determined to believe them, at his father for being out of touch, at his mother for being here. At this crime that had hurt Nonna and pulled any sense of security out from underneath him.

If something didn't happen soon to relieve the tension, there was going to be a—

Someone flung the bar door open. A man's

voice called, "Hey, look. It's the three Di Luca boys. Eliseo the winemaker, young Genoah, and our movie star, Raffaello." Stefano Marino sauntered in, hands on his hips, grinning in challenging amusement.

His brother, Greg, stood beside him. Their cousin, Primo, six-foot-seven, two hundred and fifty pounds, and a former running back for UCLA, stood behind and towered over them both.

Each of them was one year younger than each of the Di Luca brothers. It was almost as if, Eli had once said, it never occurred to any of the Marino parents to screw unless someone else proved they'd done it first.

"We are so honored." Primo's voice was a deep rumble.

"Slumming, boys?" Greg's smirk was as insulting as Stefano's.

"We thought we'd come down to the Beaver Inn for a little beaver." Eli pretended to look around. "Hey, Primo, is your sister here?"

Chairs scraped across the linoleum as the barflies pushed their chairs back.

"Why?" Primo bunched his huge fists. "You want to get beat up by a girl?"

The bartender hurriedly took the liquor bottles off the shelf and stashed them below the counter.

"Not a problem. You're here, girly-boy." Rafe couldn't believe he was talking like a teenager. And enjoying it.

"I hear your father's getting married again," Stefano mocked. "How old is this one?"

"Old enough to vote, but not old enough to drink, huh, Noah?" Greg swaggered forward.

Noah met him. For all that Noah looked like the ultimate smooth businessman, he was tough, with a whipcord speed that surprised the unwary bully who dared pick a fight. He'd had to be—he was the youngest.

Greg knew that, though. Starting in preschool, they'd kicked each other's ass on a regular basis, and now they stood, ready to go at it again.

So to even the odds, Rafe kicked Primo's legs out from under him.

Primo landed with a thud so jarring that empty glasses rattled and dust sifted out of the yellowed tile ceiling. Rafe jumped him while he was down—it was the only chance he had against Primo—and the fight was on.

Noah slammed Greg in the stomach with his head, driving him against the bar.

Barstools skittered and fell.

Stefano jabbed at Eli.

Eli ducked.

Stefano connected with Eli's forehead.

Both men staggered back; Stefano gripped his fist, Eli his head.

Then Eli rammed Stefano with his shoulder and they smacked the wall.

Everywhere in the bar, fights broke out. It was

a riot. A horse-ridin', saddle-leather, no-bullshit John Wayne movie. Exactly what the Di Lucas had been looking for.

Primo rolled on Rafe, used his weight to pin him to the floor, and proceeded to pulverize him with his fists. Not that Rafe didn't know a few moves that would have taken him out, but this was a friendly fight. That would be cheating.

Rafe thought he was dead until one of the bar customers flew through the air propelled by a punch, landed on Primo's kidneys, and knocked him off Rafe. While the big guy was gasping, Rafe evened the score with a series of well-placed punches that broke Primo's nose and bloodied his lip.

It couldn't last, of course. Primo had him pound for pound, muscle for muscle, and pretty soon Primo picked Rafe up and held him against the wall.

Rafe braced for the impact.

Primo looked at him, his big brown puppy-dog eyes kind. "Hey, man, sorry about your grandmother."

"Yeah, thanks," Rafe answered, and kicked him in the 'nads.

Primo threw him across the room into the middle of another fight.

Rafe landed hard.

A knife flashed.

In one smooth move, Rafe flipped the guy and

removed the blade from his hand. Standing, he held it aloft and shouted, "Next knife I see, I'll use it to cut out your heart."

Eli and Stefano stopped fighting, picked up the slasher, and threw him out the window.

Glass shattered, spraying the parking lot.

The guy landed on a car; the alarm went off.

Rafe threw the knife toward the bar. It stuck in the wall next to the cash register.

Someone hit him with an uppercut to the chin.

And the brawls started again.

In about two minutes, the floor was slippery with blood, sweat, and snot.

In about five minutes, Rafe's ears were ringing.

No, wait. Those were sirens.

The cops were coming.

The evening had been, altogether, very satisfying.

Chapter 19

I can't believe I'm bailing my grown children out of jail." Mrs. Arianna Marino, as broad as she was tall, stood haranguing her sons as she signed the papers to free them. "Primo, do you know what your papa's going to say when he finds out you broke your nose again after he paid to get it fixed last time?"

Primo cowered away from Mrs. Marino's wagging finger.

Stefano and Greg eased out of her line of sight.

"And you." She fixed her dark eyes and her loathing on Rafe and his brothers. "Why are you three standing there smirking? You think you're anything but three overgrown thugs who come out and pick a fight while your poor grandmother is suffering in the hospital?"

Brooke stood at the counter in the police station, dressed in a black sweat suit, nodding her head in agreement as she signed papers to free the Di Luca brothers.

Mrs. Marino continued. "Poor Sarah Di Luca, attacked and beaten by a gangster! Then her own grandsons, who she raised out of the graciousness of her heart and by the sweat of her brow, dishonor her by getting drunk and looking for trouble. And finding it! Coming to my bar and picking a fight with my boys. Wait until I tell her what you've done. Just wait!"

Noah slid Brooke out of his way and smiled winsomely at Mrs. Marino. "Please don't do that. Nonna's still weak from the attack."

Rafe remembered that Noah had always been Mrs. Marino's favorite Di Luca. Then—

Mrs. Marino slapped Noah upside the head, right on the raised black-and-blue lump he'd earned when he tried to take out the bar with his skull.

He fell to his knees, groaning.

"You should have thought of that sooner!" she snarled.

Brooke laughed out loud, then returned to filling out the paperwork.

Rafe, in the wrong time zone and fortified with wine and whiskey, reached out to twirl Brooke's dark hair around his finger.

She slapped his hand away.

He tried again. "Pretty," he said, fascinated by the brown luster.

She turned on him, and for a moment, her expression mirrored Mrs. Marino's frustration and anger. "Look! Today, you act all concerned about me and how I'm doing too much for your grandmother and at the resort, and I finally get to bed at a decent hour—and, buster, I was asleep—and you call me to spring you out of jail. And look at you! Split lip. Bruised throat. An ear half torn off. And for what? A fun little brawl?"

Rafe scratched his head. He had a goose egg back there, too, but he wasn't going to tell her that. "It's not that bad."

"It's not like any of us need hospitalization," Stefano said.

Mrs. Marino cracked him across the brow.

Brooke continued. "Do you really think I'm going to cuddle with you now? Now? When you're all bloody and disgusting, and you stink of liquor and God knows what else? I don't think so!"

Rafe knew he should shut up, but he couldn't stop himself. "Sometimes a fight is fun. If you ever hit someone, you'd know what I mean."

Brooke made a fist and slammed him in the solar plexus, right at the base of his breastbone.

The force of the blow sent him staggering backward.

"You're right." She smiled tightly. "That was very satisfying." With a flip of her hair, she turned back to the papers on the counter before her and continued to fill them out.

Eli caught Rafe's arm and supported him while he gasped for air. "Be glad she didn't use her foot. She teaches the kickboxing class with Jenna Campbell twice a week."

"She is a good girl, Rafe Di Luca, and you don't deserve her. So leave her alone!" Mrs. Marino spun around, a dynamo who controlled her family with doses of terror, and half the town with well-applied blackmail. "Sheriff DuPey!"

Bryan DuPey, medium height, wiry, with thinning brown hair and bloodshot eyes, removed his hat. "Yes, ma'am?"

"Why are you letting these Di Luca boys go? You know they started the fight!"

Slowly, patiently, he replied, "No, ma'am, I don't know that. Accounts are conflicting."

Mrs. Marino advanced on him. "They were in my tavern!"

"True. But that does not mean they started the fight. It just means they were thirsty."

Rafe began to have a previously unforeseen appreciation for DuPey's imperturbability.

"Who's going to pay the damages?" Mrs. Marino asked.

"We'll pay half," Eli said.

"You'll pay all!" Mrs. Marino insisted.

Rafe didn't know what made him do it. He'd had a few sips of wine and a couple of shots. So he wasn't drunk. Maybe just a little too relaxed . . . "The whole bar isn't worth a hundred dollars," he mumbled.

Mrs. Marino's head came up. She fixed him in her pitiless gaze. While everyone scurried out of her way, she scowled and rolled toward him like a tank, and the only thing that saved him was his long legs and quick stride as he leaped like a gazelle out the door and into the cool night air.

So at one in the morning, he found himself alone, sitting on the steps of the police station, listening to the distant music from a downtown bar, and looking up at the stars.

Most of the time he survived on the edge of ugly: ugly men, ugly politics, ugly tempers. Men willing to kill and torture for money or cruel ideals or fun. Tonight had been a good night, a night to get back in touch with his brothers, with his roots: to remember that people lived to dance, to drink, to laugh and talk and fight and *be*.

Now as he waited for Brooke and his brothers, and planned evasive action if Mrs. Marino came out first, he pulled his cell and took a look.

No word from his men in Kyrgyzstan in the Kokshaal-Too Mountains. No word about the downed helicopter pilot and whether they'd broken her out yet.

God. He hadn't wanted to leave. He'd left his best men there, but no matter what, the chances of success were fifty-fifty. Sitting here, he knew he'd made the right decision. He had a responsibility to his grandmother, to the woman who had raised him.

At the same time . . . Nonna had raised him to do the right thing, to fight injustice, and to save the innocents.

How could he live with himself if Captain Stephanie Spence died in captivity?

Mrs. Marino stomped out, her sons and nephew

in tow. Stopping, she waggled that admonishing finger at him. "You! You go take care of your grandmother, you ungrateful wretch. Grow up, get married, have babies to make your Nonna happy. Behave like a man instead of a spoiled boy."

He stood. "Yes, ma'am. Thank you for the advice."

Primo grinned at him and pantomimed a chicken.

"Primo!" Mrs. Marino snapped. "I changed your diaper. I can still spank your behind." She headed for her car, the Marino boys trailing behind like dejected ducklings.

Brooke came out next.

He took a step toward her.

She said, "Come near me and I'm leaving for Sweden tomorrow!"

He didn't even know what that meant but he stepped back.

She stormed down the stairs.

Noah and Eli came out next, and seeing her striding down the street, Eli called, "Hey, Brooke! Can we get a ride?"

She turned to face them. "For all I care, you Di Lucas can sleep in the street!"

The brothers watched her walk away.

"What's she sore about?" Noah asked plaintively.

DuPey spoke from the door. "Come on. I'll take you boys back to the resort."

"Great." Rafe recognized an interview opportunity when he saw one. "We'll buy you a drink."

DuPey came into the bar in the resort, accepted a glass of wine, and took a couple of sips before he said, "I've got to go. It doesn't do for the chief of police to spend too much time in a bar, no matter how upscale." He glanced at his watch. "Even if I am officially off duty."

Rafe pushed back his chair. "I'll walk out with you."

The two men strode out onto the street.

DuPey's police cruiser was parked around the corner in the public lot; Rafe supposed it didn't do for the chief of police to park in front of a bar, either. But the car sat under a streetlamp, and although the lot was full, no one was parked beside the cruiser.

Rafe supposed most people hesitated to get too close to an officer's car.

DuPey pulled out his keys. "So what can I do for you?"

No point in beating around the bush. "Do you know if Brooke Petersson is lying about shooting that attacker?"

"What makes you think that?" DuPey slowly walked around the vehicle.

Rafe recognized the move. DuPey was looking for signs that someone had tampered with the cruiser. Yes. The little town of Bella Terra was growing up, and not always in a good way. He followed DuPey, performing a second visual inspection. The cruiser looked a little battered on the underside from driving around vineyards, but other than that, fine. "I questioned her about it. No one kills a man for the first time and speaks of it so calmly. Not unless she's a psychopath, and I can say with some assurance that she's not."

"No. I wouldn't call Brooke a psychopath." DuPey finished his inspection, remotely unlocked the car, and suggested, "Maybe she's told the story so many times it has lost its meaning for her."

"What the hell!" Rafe had heard that careful tone before. He knew what it meant. "You know she's lying!"

DuPey faced him, exasperation in every line of his body. "The trouble with talking to you, Rafe, besides the fact that you think you're smarter than everyone else, is that you're trained to read people."

"It's one of those job requirements that helps me live a little longer." Rafe considered all the angles and could come up with no good reason why the sheriff should shield Brooke from her actions. "So why are you covering for her?"

For the first time, DuPey looked Rafe in the eyes. "I pay my debts. She did a favor for me once. I owed her."

Now they were getting to the core of the truth. "What did she do?"

DuPey stood there, tossing his keys from hand to hand, eyeing Rafe and making his decision. Finally he asked, "Do you remember my old man? Police Chief DuPey?"

"Are you kidding? He hated me. He used to terrorize me." When Rafe had heard the son of a bitch died of a heart attack, he had rejoiced.

"He used to terrorize me, too. I was the son of Bella Terra's chief of police. No matter what I did, it was never good enough." DuPey leaned against the hood, relaxed and resigned now that he'd decided to tell the story. "So, you know, I acted out."

"I don't remember that."

"You were hot shit. You weren't paying any attention to me or any of the lower classmen. But trust me, sophomore year, I was stealing cars."

"Wow." Rafe leaned beside DuPey. "That is acting out."

"I had to do something. I couldn't just cower. I couldn't stand myself. I knew how to pick a lot of old car locks—Dad had the picks—and even better, I knew stupid people left their keys in the ignitions. So I hung around the convenience stores and the grocery store, waited until some woman walked in to grab something and left her car running."

Remembering the big, fat-bellied, mean-ass

175

cop who had been DuPey's father, Rafe said admiringly, "I didn't know you had it in you."

"I wouldn't have had anything in me if I'd gotten caught." DuPey exhaled, long and slow. "I would have had the crap beaten out of me by my father, and by the time I got out of prison, I would have been a hundred and fifty years old."

"C'mon. Car theft isn't good news, but not even your father would have had that much influence on a jury. You would have gotten one hundred years, tops." Rafe tried to inject some humor, but he suspected he was failing miserably.

"He wouldn't have had to do much. Not when you added kidnapping to the charge."

Chapter 20

Kidnapping." Had DuPey kidnapped Brooke? No, she would have told Rafe. In those days, she told him everything. "What did you get up to?" Rafe asked.

"It was just after dark, about nine o'clock on a Saturday night. This girl, couldn't have been more than twenty, drove up to the twenty-four-hour In and Out convenience store, hopped out of her car, left the motor running." DuPey barked his account as if he still felt the pain and humiliation. "I pulled a woman's stocking over my face, got in the car, drove off, got two blocks, heard a noise in the backseat, looked in the rearview mirror . . . and there was a baby's car seat."

"Oh, my God." Rafe broke into a cold sweat thinking about it.

"Yeah. There was this little boy, maybe a year old, with big brown eyes and curly dark hair, and he looked at me like he didn't know what to think. I pulled into the Safeway parking lot and bailed out. But I couldn't leave that kid, and I couldn't walk away. Or run away, either."

Rafe got a sick feeling in his gut. "This is where Brooke comes in."

"She was going to the store to get milk for her mother. I called her over. She sort of figured it out, figured me out, right away." DuPey wiped his sweaty forehead with the flat of his palm. "Remember that line of trees that used to be beside the parking lot? She pushed me that direction, told me to hide, told me she'd take care of it."

"And she did." When DuPey didn't answer right away, Rafe began to dread the rest of the story.

"She opened the back door and reached in to get the baby. She was talking to me, telling me she was going to take him inside the store and say he was in a car and she didn't know where his parents were." DuPey passed his hand across his eyes. "The sirens blared. The searchlights blazed. My father and his men had tracked the car and they nailed her as the thief. They pulled her out of the car, pushed her to the pavement, held her there, and searched her."

"You didn't come out of the bushes?"

DuPey shook his head.

Whatever sympathy Rafe had felt for DuPey evaporated in a burst of anger. "What then?"

"The mother showed up from the convenience store and screamed at Brooke, tried to attack her. My father cuffed Brooke's hands behind her back, held her down with his foot on her neck. She wasn't fighting, but he was always that kind of guy. Really brave when he was picking on women and children."

Rafe breathed hard, trying to subdue his fury.

"I would like to think that I would have managed to stop cringing before he shoved her into the patrol car. But luckily for her, and for me, the manager of the convenience store showed up." DuPey tried to smile, didn't quite make it. "He'd seen the guy who stole the car. It was definitely a man, about twenty-five, about six feet tall with a beard."

"You were six feet tall?"

"Yes. I took after my father."

"You had a beard?"

"I could barely grow five hairs on my whole face. I believe the manager saw the stocking on my face and, in the crummy lights in their parking lot, he thought that was a beard. He was so adamant, my father had to let Brooke up. He took the cuffs off, asked her how old she was, asked her who her parents were. I know him; when she told him she had a single mother, and that mother wasn't from one of the founding families, he was relieved. He gave her a lecture about coming out at night. She asked if she could get the milk for her mother." DuPey laughed, a bitter burst of amusement. "I never saw my father look as discomfited as he did then. He tried to give her money for the milk. She backed away like he was offering her a bribe." He laughed again, still bitter. "Which he was, of course. The old bastard. She had a bruise on her cheek."

A vision of the youthful Brooke's scraped, black-and-blue face flashed across Rafe's mind. "I remember that! She told me she fell down." So much for his youthful conceit—she hadn't told him everything.

"Yeah, she did." DuPey folded his arms across his chest. "Are you going to kick my ass? I won't fight you if you do. I deserve it. Even after all this time, I deserve it."

"You sure as hell do. Your father never found out it was you?"

"I'm still alive, aren't I?"

Rafe considered curing that. "This story—this is why you let Brooke tell you a lie during your investigation?"

DuPey turned on Rafe in temper, then regained control. "Let me speculate here. The perp came at one of the women who works for Brooke with a knife. The woman, whoever she was, shot and killed him. I'm going to guess the woman has a criminal record? She had some sob story, because Brooke runs to type. She rescues poor pathetic losers like me. And you."

Rafe considered objecting. Decided against it.

DuPey was looking smarter all the time.

DuPey continued. "So when Brooke arrived on the scene, she sent the woman away, wiped down the pistol, put her own fingerprints on the weapon, and claimed responsibility for the crime."

"And you let her take responsibility?" That was what stuck in Rafe's craw.

"It was what she wanted."

"Because you owed her?"

"Hey. At least I paid her back." DuPey leveled an accusatory stare at Rafe. "Which is more than I can say for some people."

Rafe watched him get in his police cruiser and drive away, and wondered whether Brooke had told DuPey all that had happened between the two of them. But no, he knew she hadn't; whatever DuPey knew, or thought he knew, was gossip and speculation. Damned good speculation; like Rafe, DuPey was good at reading body language. He knew guilt when he saw it, and Rafe was guilty about the way he'd treated Brooke. But she was better off without him. Wasn't she?

Wasn't she?

Chapter 21

Sometimes it was easier to beg forgiveness than ask permission.

Better still if I don't get caught.

The resort's security room was at the end of a hall behind an anonymous door on the main floor of the main building. The lock was a good one, electronic and expertly installed, but Rafe had the gizmo to sneak through the program undetected. In less than five seconds, he was inside.

The door shut behind him with a satisfyingly solid sound. Good: It was soundproofed.

This security room was really more of a walk-in closet, five by eight, with a pressed-concrete floor. An old table retrieved from a guest room held the computer, converted from some other use to act as the server. Cables snaked from the plug-ins to the back of the computer, to the monitor, to the keyboard and mouse.

Rafe seated himself in the stained office chair, pulled his laptop and cable out of his briefcase. Following the written instructions from his own personal hacker, he plugged his laptop into the security server, typed in Darren's access code, and when Darren's youthful, pimply face popped up on the screen, he said, "You're connected."

Darren glanced at Rafe, did a double take, and

stared. "Man, what did you do to yourself?" Darren's voice echoed in the bare room.

"Shh!"

Darren paid no attention. "You look like you went nine rounds with a grizzly bear. Man." He grinned. "I thought you were the hawt king of self-defense."

Rafe gritted his teeth. This was the trouble with hiring a seventeen-year-old. He had no sense of what was appropriate, and no volume control. "I went out last night and had some fun." Rafe refrained from touching his swollen ear, his split lip. "Can you access the program without a password?"

"Wow. Your idea of fun doesn't mesh with mine." Darren was typing while he talked. "And sure. I'll get through the firewall. It's not like this server is highly protected, like a financial computer or something. It's more on the level of the U.S. government. What did your grandmother say about your bruises?"

Rafe started to ask how Darren knew he'd been to visit his grandmother, then decided against it. When the kid got interested, he knew everything, and the newly uncovered concept that his loner boss had a personal life seemed to fascinate him.

"My grandmother looked at me and laughed."

"Really? So Nonna is cool?"

"She's very cool. She made us—my brothers and me—have a picture taken with her, because she said that way everyone would have to believe she'd been in a bar fight. Although perhaps she was subtly saying we were stupid to go looking for the kind of injury that put her in the hospital. . . ." Come to think of it, that was exactly what she was saying. "Her doctor came in about then and we had to leave." So whatever she had wanted to tell him and his brothers had had to be postponed. Too bad, because Nonna clearly thought they needed to know, but she'd waved them away and told them it was old news and could wait one more day. "About that password—if you want, I can guess a few things Noah might have used. His birthday, his dog's name, the usual."

"No, no big deal. I'm in."

The kid was a genius. Geeky and literally living in his parents' basement, but definitely a genius.

"Downloading." Darren grinned. "Your brother bought this program from a vendor who customized it for the hotel. Want to have some fun? We could have every occupied guest room call for K-Y jelly right now."

"It's my family's resort. I own some portion of it. So no." But an amusing idea. "Just download the program, put me on as an administrator, and add it to my hard drive."

Darren sighed. "You old guys are so boring."

"I know. Sucks to be you." Rafe thought it

184

sucked to be an old guy, too. This morning when he got up (late), he had discovered his hip had a bruise on it so deep and painful, a mountain of ice wouldn't have helped. Vaguely he remembered being thrown into the corner of one of the Beaver Inn's fine tables; at the time he hadn't noticed. Now . . . he noticed.

"So are you going back to the hospital after they move your grandmother into rehab?"

"How do you . . . ? Been hacking into hospital records?"

"I thought you'd like to stay on top of stuff."

"They're moving Nonna into rehab?" Good to know.

"Because of the concussion, they don't want her on her feet unless she's supported. But because of her broken arm, she can't use a walker unless she has training." As he talked, Darren never stopped typing.

"Haven't you heard? We're hiring a nurse."

Darren ignored the sarcasm, or maybe he heard it so often he didn't notice. "Apparently the doc has been a friend of your family for a long time, and he says Nonna's going to hate having someone wait on her and she'll try to get up on her own and fall, and maybe break her other arm or a hip. So they need to train her to take care of herself, ASAP. Plus they're going to make sure Bao and this new nurse are trained, too."

"Hm." Rafe tapped his fingers on the desk,

leaned back in the stained desk chair—and discovered one wheel had a glitch. He caught himself before he fell backward, muttered, "Noah, you cheap bastard," righted himself, and said, "Darren, when you get done, would you run a profile for me?"

"Sure. On who?"

"The new nurse. Olivia somebody."

"Olivia Kelly. I did. Good nurse. No complaints. No criminal record. Want me to dig deeper?"

"No." Because he really was becoming a suspicious bastard. "That's all I wanted to know."

Once Darren had downloaded the security program to Rafe's computer, Rafe would be able to study the resort's layout, view the videos, and check for any anomalies. Because in his experience, common criminals weren't any too smart, and if Nonna's attacker was on-site, Rafe intended to pick him out of the crowd. And punish him in ways DuPey would never approve.

"Man, you look grim." Darren had stopped typing and was staring at Rafe in fascination. "I'd hate to get on your bad side."

"Then hurry up," Rafe told him.

Darren went back to work.

Rafe checked his cell.

Still nothing from Kyrgyzstan.

He wanted a progress report, damn it. This

silence was ominous, and there were only a few reasons for it.

The satellite transmitters were down.

His men were fleeing with the helicopter pilot, Captain Stephanie Spence, and were afraid to give up their position.

Or they were all dead.

Rafe pinched the bridge of his nose—and winced.

Yeah, Primo had landed a few punches there, too.

Out of habit, he checked the desk drawer for any kind of information: passwords scribbled on a sticky note were not out of the ordinary.

Nothing, not even a Gideon Bible.

He looked under the desk, but under there it was merely cables and tape. He ran his fingers behind the computer—

And behind him, the soundproofed door opened.

Chapter 22

Damn. Noah had caught him.

Rafe swung around in the chair and met not Noah's gaze, but that girl's. The blonde. With the tits. The one he'd gone to high school with. And groped in the library. Gemma. No, Gloria. No . . . Jenna.

Yeah. Jenna. Jenna Campbell. That was her name.

"Whoa."

Rafe heard Darren's heedless, whispered exclamation, and rolled the chair in front of his computer to block Jenna's view of the gawking teenage geek. With a push of the key, Rafe muted the speakers and took Darren off the screen.

"Hi!" She recovered fast, and smiled her cheerleader smile. "I didn't expect to see you here."

"No?" He lifted his eyebrows. Had she seen him breaking in and followed him with the intent of seeing whether she could wrestle him to the floor?

But no. He'd been in here ten minutes. And either her surprise was real, or she was wasting herself working at a spa. She should be an actress.

So why was she here?

Jenna started chatting like a hostess with a

reluctant guest. "I come in here when it gets to be too much at the spa. You know, when everyone is talking at me and nagging me for towels and two of the nail girls call in sick and . . . Oh." She peered at him from large, guilty, fear-ridden eyes. "You won't tell Noah I came in here, will you?"

"I don't know." She looked so worried he didn't hesitate to attack and see whether she turned tail and ran. "How did you get in?"

" 'Cause I'm the manager of the spa, I've got a master." She showed him her key card.

"The master doesn't work for that door." He'd checked.

She looked shocked. "Mine does!"

Okay. Picking the lock hadn't been easy, he hadn't heard her working it, and she had the key in her hand, so yeah, it wasn't out of the realm of probability that her key had been programmed incorrectly.

"So, why did you come here?" he asked.

"I told you." She fussed with her hair, then reached down and unbuttoned the third button of her golf shirt.

The webcam was still on, and Rafe could almost hear Darren groan with lust.

"They're driving me crazy at the spa. I come in and play a little FarmVille, center myself again, and then go back into the fray." She did that little dip like a *Let's Make a Deal* spokesmodel.

"Really?" She was playing a game on Facebook on the computer that ran the resort's security cameras? And no one had caught on? Ever?

Stranger things had happened, he supposed. But he was curious to see whether she accessed the Internet through some kind of glitch in their program, or if she had to work the system. He stood and rolled the chair in front of the keyboard. "Who am I to stop you?"

"So you're not going to tell on me?" She seated herself and tugged her shirt down to display yet more cleavage.

Rafe hoped Darren's fiery passion didn't fry the cables.

Jenna looked up at Rafe. "What are you doing in here?"

Ah. Her little brain had jumped through the guilt hoop and had moved on to the possibility of blackmail. "I'm checking the resort's security program."

"Is there something wrong with it?" She widened her eyes.

"Not that I know of. Why? Have you had any problems in the spa?"

"No . . . well, yes. Some of the girls steal the toilet paper from the storage closet. Can you make them stop?"

He rubbed the bruises on his ribs. "No. Toilet paper has a way of disappearing, and there's nothing any security man can do about it. Now, if the girls were stealing something important, like the hot stones for the massages, I might be able to help you."

Jenna laughed, a low, musical chime, and put her hand on his thigh. "I wish you could help me."

"I can." Leaning over, he pulled the keyboard closer to her. "I don't know much about Facebook games. Do you need the mouse, too?" He dislodged her hand, walked around to the other side of her, and handed her the mouse.

She rotated her shoulders—an expensive stripper would be proud of the way those breasts swirled. Then, taking the mouse, she slowly moved it up and down on the pad.

Subtle she was not.

Taking the keyboard in her lap, she typed at an astonishing speed. Facebook flashed onto the monitor, then disappeared, then appeared again. "Oh. You make me so nervous." She made a brokenhearted sound. "I can't do this while you're watching me."

"I'm sorry. I won't watch anymore."

She pushed another couple of keys, then shook her head. "No, I can't do this while you're here. Anyway, I should go back to the spa. I've got an appointment with Mr. Edward Doherty. He likes me to give him his massage. He's a boob man." Leaning forward, she adjusted her breasts, and when she glanced up and caught Rafe watching—like he could look away—she trailed her hand down his hip and thigh. "I am awfully good on a massage table. Why don't you make an appointment and try me out?"

He stepped back to give her room to stand. "As soon as I have a free minute, I'll do that."

She sauntered toward the door. Opening it, she looked back at him. "I bet you'll make time pretty soon."

He smiled back, and when she'd shut the door behind her, he said, "I'll bet I won't."

Behind him, his computer blared, "Why not?"

Obviously, Darren could control the volume on Rafe's laptop from his end.

"I don't do sluts," Rafe said. Brooke had taught him what a quality woman meant.

"Do you have every hot chick in the world after your ass?" Darren shouted. "And how do I get in on this action?"

"I guess you make an appointment for a massage." Rafe made a note to place microphones in the massage rooms. If Jenna really was "good on the massage table," and if word got out that the masseuses at Bella Terra resort were prostituting themselves, the resort and the spa would have a public relations nightmare unlike any since a similar scandal in the seventies. *Ugh.*

"I live in Indiana!" Darren said.

"That's a long way to come for an easy piece of pussy."

"Jenna? You mean Jenna? She's not easy. Is she?" Darren sounded bewildered and hurt.

"What did you think that was all about?" Rafe looked at Darren's crestfallen face.

Oh, no. The kid was a virgin.

"Yes, she's easy," Rafe said brutally. "She's always been easy. And she only does it with guys who have money or influence."

Rafe could almost hear Darren's heart breaking. "But she's so pretty!"

"She's a mercenary." His grandmother had used a harsher term about Jenna. "Now—what was she doing on the computer? I saw Facebook flash up on the monitor."

"Um. Yeah. Uh . . ."

"You didn't check her keystrokes?"

"I can go back and pick up her keystrokes." Darren sounded less ardent and more intent. "Yeah. She was on Facebook. Yeah, she plays the games. Yeah, her profile picture is hawt."

"But was that all she did on the computer?"

"There were a couple of extra keystrokes, but she types one hundred and thirty-five words a minute. When she's that fast, she's going to make some mistakes."

"Follow the stray keystrokes and make sure she didn't mess with anything." Because the way Jenna fawned on him made Rafe suspect ulterior motives. Not that that was necessarily true—he'd had women fawning on him all his life. But she was so sleazy about it he wanted her to be guilty.

Darren was still as whirly eyed and infatuated as a cartoon character. "I videoed almost every bit of that luscious body from the time she walked in to the time she walked out."

Forbiddingly, Rafe asked, "Did you place the Bella Terra security program on my computer?"

"Yes, sir!" Darren gave him a military salute.

"Good. I'll let you know when I need you again. In the meantime, try not to get your ass arrested. I don't want to go looking for a new hacker."

"They're not going to catch me. I do a good background check before I ever take a job, and I don't take stupid chances."

Rafe thought about Jenna and her advances, about his responsibilities to his grandmother, about Noah's resentment and Eli's aloof anxiety. About the story DuPey had told him about Brooke, his admission that he knew Brooke had lied about the murder she was supposed to have committed . . . about how Brooke had moved on with her life, and didn't need Rafe to complete her. "You're a smart guy," he said to Darren. "Never, ever take stupid chances. Stupidity hardly ever pays off."

Chapter 23

It had been one of those days.

In the hotel business, they happened frequently. A guest's kids had put the plug in the tub, plugged the overflow drain, turned on the water, and left it running. The parents had been apologetic, but that didn't solve the problem of an overflow so huge it ran out of the bathroom, soaked the bedroom carpet, leaked through the light fixtures into the room below, soaked the bed and carpet, and finally brought down the ceiling to ruin that guest's clothing and suitcases. With two suites out of commission, rooms had to be juggled, tempers soothed, insurance adjusters called.

Brooke had been up late the last couple of nights: posting bail for the Di Luca boys, then handling a crisis with a grown man who had picked up a garter snake out of the flower beds to show his kids and been bitten. He'd been surprised and indignant. She'd considered it proof that all men were stupid, although perhaps seeing the bruised, beaming Di Lucas around the resort had had something to do with her mind-set. She was tired, she was cross, she had about one nerve left, and everyone was standing on it. So when she took the elevator down to the lobby from the soppy mess that was the lower guest room, and her pager went off and the cell rang at the same time, she glanced at the cell—it was Rafe—and decided to deal with the pager instead.

The page was Madelyn's; it said, *Lost diamond. Honeymoon Cottage, Millionaire's Row.*

Surely to God finding a lost diamond would be easier than talking to Rafe about . . . whatever it was he wanted to talk about. He was so . . . intense. When he looked at her, he stared as if all of her secrets had been stripped away, and next up—her clothes.

Worse, every time she saw him, she was glad. Pleased by the way he moved, by his dark hair and blue eyes. Pleased to hear his voice and know he was near. That pleasure was nothing but a hangover from her high school infatuation, and she scoffed at herself every time. Nevertheless, when he walked by, her heart trilled.

Sweden was looking better all the time.

Brooke started toward Millionaire's Row.

But her rotten luck held—she met Rafe on his way in.

Heart trill.

"You didn't answer your phone." The muscles beneath the T-shirt were sculpted, as if he'd been to the gym this morning.

She brushed her bangs off her forehead. Summer's heat had arrived early: good for business, tough when a woman wore a black suit as part of her professional image. "Dandy to see you, too."

He didn't get the hint. "Why didn't you tell me there's a motorcycle on the property?"

"A motorcycle?" She tried to think. Tried to think of something besides how good he looked in faded jeans and a clean T-shirt. No wonder Jenna Campbell had started following him around.

Not that Brooke cared. "On the property? Where . . . ? Oh."

"Oh?" Rafe gave that Gerard Butler mocking half sneer. Maybe because it hurt to give a whole smile.

Amazing how quickly Brooke's pleasure turned to irritation. "It didn't occur to me. Because the motorcycle—it's Noah's."

"Noah's?" Obviously, she'd startled him. "What does Noah have a motorcycle for?"

"To try to smash his brains all over the pavement. I don't know!" She took a breath. "Because when he goes up to the vineyards, he likes to ride with Eli. But Noah is more than a little protective of his toy. The motorcycle's in a locked garage with security sensors. That can't be the motorcycle that went up to Nonna's. . . . Wait." She stared at him more closely. "How did you find out about it?"

"I was looking for a motorcycle and I broke into the garage."

She looked at her pager. "The alarm didn't go off."

"The alarm wasn't set."

"If Noah hadn't set the alarm, the backup would have notified us."

"That alarm system is only going to keep out casual thieves. Apparently someone with the know-how tinkered with the alarm."

She stopped and stared at him, at his fading bruises and his hard, cold eyes. "Or someone had the code."

"Or someone had the code," he agreed.

"That is the motorcycle Nonna's attacker used to get to the home ranch?"

"That's it."

You're sure? But she didn't ask. Because of course he was sure. "Have you told Noah?"

"No. No one saw me go in. No one saw me come out. We're going to keep it that way."

"Right. Because whoever it was might come back to use it again." She felt foolish for admitting it, but she had to say, "I know how to ride a motorcycle."

"I remember."

She'd made him teach her in high school. "So I'm a suspect."

"You never weren't a suspect." His hair looked damp, as if he'd recently showered. He smelled good, too, like the resort's orange spice soap.

Sweden. Sweden. Sweden.

Maybe Norway.

Or maybe she should just concentrate on how much he annoyed her. "Why tell me about the motorcycle, then?"

"I wanted to know why you hadn't told me about it when it strengthens the case against you."

Her pager buzzed. She glanced down. Madelyn again, a little more frantic. "Look. I don't have time for this now. I'll talk to you later, but you know, if you're determined to distrust me, there's not a lot I can do about it." Once again she headed toward the Honeymoon Cottage, leaving Rafe staring after her.

Madelyn stood on the threshold, looking concerned and frazzled.

Brooke caught her arm. "Have you been inside?"

"No."

"Not at all?"

"No."

"Exactly right." Brooke stepped into the room. "Mrs. McClaron? What's happened?"

"Brooke. Brooke! Thank heavens you came." Linda McClaron crawled out from under the bed, stood, and rushed to Brooke's side. "I lost my ring!"

Another hotel nightmare—a guest accusing the maid of stealing valuables. But Mrs. McClaron was one of their regulars, a beautiful woman, a trophy wife, not too bright and never organized, but always kind. Madelyn said she hadn't gone in—and the security video would confirm that. Perhaps they'd make it out of this mess without a huge public relations fuss and a massive insurance investigation. "Did you have it in the room safe?" Brooke asked Mrs. McClaron.

"No, when I came in last night, I put it on the nightstand and now I can't find it! I called the maid in to help me look, but she said that's against hotel policy and called you."

Brooke relaxed infinitesimally. "Good. That's exactly what she should have done."

"The thing is . . . I was a little sick last night, too much to drink, you know, and I'm afraid I might have knocked the ring into the trash can and then . . . Early this morning, there was a garbage cart outside the room. I took the liner out of the trash can and put it into the cart to get rid of it and I . . . That ring cost a lot of money! It's a pink diamond, a whole carat! Did you know pink diamonds are the most precious diamonds in the world? Or the second-most precious." She chewed her lip. "I can't remember. But expensive! And pink is my favorite color. I really, really wanted that ring, and Mike bought it for me only last week. He says I'm too careless and a ditz. If he finds out—"

"Have you checked your purse?"

"Yes."

"Did you have pockets in what you wore last night?"

"I checked them. And I've been under the bed three times, and moved the end table and looked under the lamp and pulled out the drawers and dumped them."

"I see that." Mentally, Brooke made a note to tell Ebrillwen to schedule extra time to clean the room.

"Please, Brooke, please, won't you send someone after that cart?" The poor woman was trembling and tearful.

"What time was it when you put the bag into the cart?"

"About seven this morning." Linda McClaron sat down heavily on the bed. "I can't tell Mike. I just can't. He never relaxes, he always works, and on this trip, we've been having such a good time. If I've lost that ring, he'll be so angry."

It was almost noon. "The bag's in the Dumpster now. I'll go after it myself."

"You can't do that—go through all the garbage. That's horrible!" To Mrs. McClaron's credit, she realized the sacrifice involved.

"It's not quite as bad as you might think. This isn't the first time something like this has happened, so we require our waste handlers to mark the bags according to where they picked up the trash." Although they weren't always conscientious about that. "So I only have to find the one bag for this section and search it. Don't worry; if the ring is there, I'll find it. Besides— the Dumpster is emptied every other day. And today's the day. It has to be done, and it has to be done now."

"Oh, my God." Mrs. McClaron put her fists to her mouth. Then she grabbed Brooke and shook her. "Hurry. Go!"

"Don't panic. The garbage truck comes about four." Brooke took her by the shoulders and turned her to face the room. "In the meantime, you keep looking."

"I've already looked everywhere I can think of!"

"Then look where you haven't thought of."

"Right." Mrs. McClaron nodded and knit her brow. "Where I haven't thought of . . ."

"Come on," Brooke said to Madelyn. "Let's go see what we can do."

Chapter 24

Armed with her oldest tennis shoes, latex gloves and a step stool, Brooke and Madelyn walked down the path to the enclosed garbage area, alone on a service road away from the public areas.

As Madelyn unlocked the tall wooden gate, she said, "I'll climb into the Dumpster."

"I'll do it."

"Please, Ms. Petersson, you've done so much for me—"

"No. I don't ask my staff to do things I won't do. And it's not the first time I've had to go Dumpster diving." Not that Brooke liked Dumpster diving, but Madelyn had towering self-esteem issues, and anyway, after the week Brooke had had dealing with Sarah's mugging, the time at the hospital, the investigation, and Rafe, a little ripping and tearing through bags of garbage had a disgusting appeal. For sure it sounded better than going another round with Rafe the cold-eyed investigator–slash–former passionate lover.

They stepped inside the enclosure. The every-other-day pickup kept the stench from overwhelming any guests who got lost back on the resort acreage. But in here, Brooke was aware that all morning, the sun had beaten on the pavement and the tall wooden walls, warming the Dumpster and curing the garbage to a smell between overripe pineapple and rotting flesh. Knowing the amount of fruit discarded from the continental breakfast, and the fight the gardeners waged against the gophers, she supposed there was plenty of both.

The two women looked at each other in unspoken dread; then together they lifted the metal lid and rested it against the wall.

A swarm of flies wafted up, buoyed on the stench of human refuse.

Brooke set the step stool and climbed up.

The Dumpster was full of large white garbage bags, filled from the guest rooms and tossed in by the waste handlers. From experience, Brooke knew the contents were personal and frequently revolting. Pulling on her latex gloves, she reached in and tugged at the first bag. "I'll lower the bags down to you. Holler when you see the right one come through."

"Yes, Miss Petersson."

She lifted the first one.

Flies buzzed with glee. The odor of rotting everything grew stronger. And within five minutes, Brooke was glad she worked out at the resort gym. The bags were heavy; lifting them up and over the edge used her biceps, her pecs, her abs. Her weight-class instructor would be proud.

On the other hand, doing this work while holding her breath . . . well, that wasn't actually a good idea, since she might pass out into the Dumpster—horrifying thought.

When she got to the point that she couldn't reach any more bags, she paused, wiped her forehead on her sleeve, and looked inquiringly down at Madelyn.

The maid was flushed red with exertion and she'd set her mouth against the revulsion.

Brooke could only imagine she looked the same. "Nothing from Millionaire's Row?"

"Nothing. Why don't we trade places?"

"Don't tempt me," Brooke muttered, then, louder, "Why is it never the first bag?"

"Murphy's Law."

"Why does Murphy's Law always apply to the hotel business?"

Madelyn didn't answer; apparently she could spot a rhetorical question when she heard one.

"If you'll come up the steps, I'll shift the bags at the back to the front. You lower them to the ground. If we don't find the right bag there—"

"God couldn't be so cruel," Madelyn said fervently.

"—I'll start on the second layer." Swinging her leg over the edge, Brooke climbed in. Like rolling seas of garbage, the slick bags shifted under her weight. She balanced and finally bent to the first twist tie. She tugged at the bulging plastic bag.

The bottom broke.

Trash spilled everywhere.

The flies circled gleefully.

Brooke stood there, holding an empty white plastic bag aloft like some mockery of the Statue of Liberty. "Crap!"

"Among other things." Madelyn prepared to step in and help.

Then . . . then a glint of gold caught Brooke's eye. Dropping the bag, she gave a crow of delight, leaned over, grabbed for it. Her gloved fingers sank into something rotten, slimy, disgusting. Still holding on to the ring—it was a ring, wasn't it?—she stumbled backward.

Several things happened at once.

Her foot sank into something squishy and released a smell like rotting sewage.

She realized the glittering thing was attached to a chain, that chain was attached to a neck, that neck was attached to a head, a corpse's head, round and rotten.

Lifted by her grip on the chain, the body rose out of the loose garbage, its skin sagging, its face covered with soil, eaten by worms, swarming with flies.

Brooke stared into the eye sockets, into one man's lifeless eyeballs.

Madelyn screamed.

The chain broke.

Still clutching the gold, Brooke fell backward onto a trash bag.

The body sank down.

In horror, in panic, she scrambled up and over the edge of the Dumpster.

She fell. Hit the hot asphalt. Knocked the air out of her lungs. As soon as she regained her breath, she began screaming again—when had she started?—while Madelyn knelt beside her, babbling questions about *was she all right?*

Then, before Brooke could comprehend, Madelyn got up and ran away.

Brooke didn't blame her. Brooke's foot was covered with . . . *Oh, God. Oh, God. OhGodohGod.*

Her hand, too. Sure. She had on a glove. Who cared? This was . . . She couldn't stop shuddering. Dropping the chain, she ripped the glove off and threw it toward the Dumpster. Some of the flies followed as if it were bait, but most of them . . . most of them hovered around Brooke, and when she looked down at herself, she rolled onto her hands and knees and vomited.

Then Madelyn was back, lugging a housekeeping bucket. Taking Brooke's hand, she plunged it into the soapy water and scrubbed at it with her own. "We'll get it off you, Miss Petersson," she said. "We'll get you clean."

Out of control with anguish and revulsion, Brooke said, "My foot's worse. And my pants."

Madelyn helped her up.

Brooke plunged her foot into the water.

Madelyn reached in and unlaced her shoe and tugged it off, then peeled away Brooke's sock. As the water turned a slimy brownish black, Brooke unfastened her pants, peeled them off, and threw them toward the Dumpster, too.

Madelyn scrubbed at Brooke's foot with her bare hands.

"Thank you," Brooke found herself saying over and over. "Thank you. I couldn't do this by myself."

"I owe you," Madelyn said fiercely. "You've done for me, and I owe you. Sit down there on the bench and I'll get you clean water."

"All right." Brooke sank down on the bench. The plastic was hot under her panties, but she didn't care. She was cold. Bone cold.

Because when she dropped the chain and cross, she had recognized them. She knew what they meant.

She knew who was in that Dumpster.

Chapter 25

All her life, regardless of the circumstances, Sarah had tried to maintain a cheerful nature. But she did not like rehab.

Every day it was the same thing.

First thing in the morning, she visited the psychologist, a young lady from Boston, who always gave her three words to remember for later. Then the young lady asked Sarah questions: her name, the date, her address, the names of her relatives. At the end of the session, she asked Sarah to repeat the three words back.

Every day Sarah did as required. Sure, the routine was silly and boring, and it made Sarah impatient, but she was eighty and she'd been hit on the head. So she answered and remembered because she understood the reasons behind it.

She was not quite so complacent about the physical rehab. The things they made her do hurt. More than once they made her cry.

More important—as she healed, she grew homesick. She wanted to sit on her porch. She wanted to look out over Bella Valley. She wanted to watch the vines and the orchards grow verdant in the heat. Most of all, she wanted to be alone, to never listen to a television blaring some stupid reality show or hear another person's voice.

She wanted silence. She wanted peace. She wanted her own house and her own bed.

Not too much longer, the health care professionals promised her. Once she could walk two lengths of the hospital corridor with her walker, they would send her home.

She didn't need a walker, she told them. She could walk just fine.

But what with the concussion and the broken arm, they wanted her steady on her feet. They didn't want her to fall and hit her head again.

So everyone agreed on that one thing.

She wouldn't go home alone—she was to have a nurse, Olivia.

As Sarah made her way down the corridor toward the patients' lounge, Olivia walked beside her.

Sarah liked Olivia. Olivia was young and pretty, wide-eyed and interested. In fact, Olivia reminded Sarah of her younger self.

And although Sarah couldn't see her, she knew Bao observed from the nurses' station.

When Sarah first met her, she thought Bao was a caregiver of some kind. Then, as Olivia took over, Sarah realized that Bao worked for Rafe. Sarah was no fool. Bao must be her bodyguard. So Bao would go home with Sarah, too.

That was all right. Sarah was resigned to having protection. The attack on her had scared the whole family. Her, too. She didn't like being frightened to be completely alone . . . yet she was.

Sarah concentrated on moving the walker in a straight line, not easy when one arm was in a cast. The wheels creaked. The farther she went, the more the end of the corridor seemed to move away. Sarah was so involved in getting to the lounge, she didn't notice the man who stepped in front of her.

"Sarah!" he said.

She recognized that voice. She looked up hard and fast.

Joseph Bianchin stood there, Old World Italian, handsome even at eighty-one. He had a full head of white, curly hair, thin lips, and strong white teeth. His bright brown eyes sparkled with pleasure.

The pleasure of seeing her?

She knew better. What did he want? "Joseph, I never expected to see you here."

"Nor I you." He reached for her hand.

"I can't shake hands. With the cast on my arm, it's all I can do to use the walker." She took care to sound politely apologetic. Actually, for the first time, she had found a reason to be glad for the broken bones.

"Let's sit down and talk," he said, all geniality and deception, and indicated the plastic chairs that lined the long, sterile corridor. "After all, such old friends deserve a few moments alone."

Sarah glanced at Olivia.

How odd. The young nurse stared at Joseph as if she had never seen a man of his stature, as if he were the reincarnation of a god.

Sarah glanced at Bao.

The Vietnamese girl was beaming. Why not? Since she'd come to help Sarah, Sarah had received visits from her grandsons and from Brooke, and from her girlfriends in her bridge group, and calls from her sisters-in-law. But no men had come a-courting, certainly not an eighty-one-year-old with a military bearing and a charming nature.

Joseph used the charm as a mask, but how was Bao to know that?

The girls hung back to give them privacy, and although Sarah felt the chill of his presence, she knew herself to be safe.

Surrounded by patients and nurses, and in the bright light of day, Joseph would take care to conceal his true nature—but Sarah never doubted that he was here for a reason.

She made her way to one of the chairs, and with excessive precision—it would not do to show any weakness to him—she seated herself. "What brought you to the rehab wing of our hospital?"

"I had a knee replacement last year. That's the reason I carry this." After sitting down, he lifted a walking cane, fitted with a cold-eyed, sharp-beaked rosewood eagle for a handle and carved with savagely painted faces up and down the shaft.

"How very appropriate," she murmured.

He continued. "Every six months I come in for a tune-up." His tone changed, became less gracious and more contemptuous. "Of course, I had my work done in San Francisco. The doctors there are so much more skilled than those here in Bella Terra."

Sarah saw heads turn up and down the corridor. "Say that a little louder, Joseph. Not all the caregivers heard you."

His eyes narrowed, and he looked suddenly like the cruel eagle on his cane. "Do you really imagine I care what these people think?"

"No, I don't imagine that at all." Did he really imagine that when the time came for them to subject him to an examination, he wouldn't be poked and prodded a little more vigorously than necessary?

"That's always been the problem with you, Sarah. You court other people's good opinions regardless of whether those people are important."

"All people are important in their own way."

"In their own minds, more like." He snorted. "You should have accepted my marriage proposal. You should have wed me. I would have raised you above your common station."

"I would have hated that," she said mildly. She would have hated him, she meant.

He comprehended, and his face grew cold and still. "I'm healthier than Anthony, stronger—still alive when he's been in the grave for more than ten years. If you had married me, you wouldn't have to spend your twilight years alone."

"As you are doing?" She could be cruel, too.

"Once you refused my suit, no other woman would do."

"Once you wreaked your havoc, no other woman would have you."

"That is not true. Once I made my money, women flocked to me."

He wasn't bragging, she knew. He had had his women. And if she had wedded him, he would still have indulged. "You should have married one of them."

"I didn't want them. I only wanted you. I would have given you more than one son."

She told the story everyone believed to be the truth. "I couldn't have more than one son."

"I don't believe you. After Anthony suffered that bout of typhus, he couldn't give you more sons. Or daughters." He leaned forward, locked gazes with her. "Think how happy you would have been with a dozen children to call your own."

How skillful Joseph was—had always been—at placing the knife in her heart. Yet she had her weapons, too, although usually she was loath to use them. "It was not the typhus that destroyed Anthony's health, Joseph. You know that. The placement of that gunshot was no accident."

"If you'd married me, no one would have been hurt." Being Joseph, he truly believed himself blameless.

"If I'd married you, my children would have been your children. I never wished to bring monsters into the world."

His teeth snapped together.

For the first time, Olivia looked with concern between her patient and the visitor. Bao noticed something was wrong, too, and started toward them.

"My monsters, as you call them, would have protected you from attack." Again Joseph used his knowledge of Sarah, of her life, of her loves to wound her. "Your son and your grandsons failed miserably in that regard."

Sarah was tired of dancing around the truth, of retreating as Joseph attacked. Now she leaned toward him and asked fiercely, "How is it possible that a man who professes to love me should send someone to attack me?"

"I didn't send someone to attack you."

"You sent someone to rob me and in the process I was hurt. What's the difference, Joseph?" Sarah lifted her cast. "This is your fault."

He lowered his voice. "I sent someone to retrieve what is mine. It is a matter of honor."

"Honor? No." Sarah waved Bao away. "With you, it's the same thing it always is—a matter of money. Somehow, some way, you intend to make a profit."

He gave up all pretense of friendliness. "Perhaps you're right. In that case, you'd be wise to give up that which I desire."

"Why do you want it?"

"You know why." But his gaze fell away from hers.

"Why now?" That was the real question. What had started this battle again now?

Bao and Olivia huddled together, talking rapidly, unsure whether to defy Sarah and come to her rescue or let this sharp and unexpected quarrel continue.

Sarah continued speaking to Joseph. "It was not given to you. It was never meant to be yours. It is not your birthright."

He clenched his bony, gnarled hand into a fist in his lap. "It should have been!"

Sarah had thought this battle had died with Anthony. Now she saw that Joseph would commit any atrocity to get his way. Only one thing would stop him—and she knew that thing was impossible. "Believe me or not. I don't know where it is."

Throwing back his head, Joseph laughed aloud,

and the sound was not that of the noble eagle, but the croaking of the raven. "No. No. I don't believe that at all." Catching her hand, he squeezed her fingers until her knuckles ached. "Give it up! This is a battle between the Bianchins and the Di Lucas. The blood that flows in your veins is not Di Luca blood. Fight, and you'll find me an inimitable enemy."

"I can't give you what I don't have." She took a breath. "But regardless, I would not surrender an ounce of what is Anthony's inheritance."

The two of them stared at each other, hostility crackling between them.

He began to bend her fingers back, his intent clear. If he couldn't force her to his will, he would break her another way.

Bao had started toward them.

Then from down the hallway, Francesca's voice called, "Sarah, darling, who is that simply delicious man you're sitting with? You must introduce me so I can steal him from you!" She arrived without apparent hurry, but she was at Sarah's side before she was through speaking.

Joseph let Sarah go. He got slowly to his feet, dazzled by Francesca's beauty as men would always be.

Francesca smiled at him, extended her hand, allowed him to kiss it. "Any friend of Sarah's is a friend of mine."

Francesca kept her gaze on Joseph as he

introduced himself, but Sarah knew she had been rescued from her own foolish pride . . . and Joseph's cruelty.

Flexing her fingers, she watched Francesca charm him, and then started the slow walk back toward her room to call her sisters-in-law and get their advice.

Chapter 26

Rafe sat reviewing the police report on Nonna's attack and comparing it to the security report from the resort.

In the past four days, he'd progressed not at all in the pursuit of Nonna's attacker, had begun to entertain the suspicion that DuPey was right: that the mugger had been nothing but a drifter who'd come into town and out again. And if that was the truth, what purpose did Rafe have in Bella Valley?

Eli had his vineyards.

Noah had his resort.

Nonna enjoyed Rafe's company, but she had recovered from the concussion with no ill effects and her rehab was going well. She didn't need him here.

And Brooke . . . Brooke had her place, too. She was busy with the hotel, keeping the guests happy, answering questions, leading her kickboxing class.

Taking his cell phone out of his pocket, he looked at it, willed it to ring.

He'd heard nothing from his team in Kyrgyzstan, and every minute without word meant another hope lost. If he were there, halfway around the world, he'd be with them. Perhaps he would have made the difference

219

between life and death . . . or perhaps not.

With a sigh, he put the phone back, and inevitably, his mind returned to Brooke.

Whenever he saw her, she was cool and distant, and he . . . he was not cool.

He was horny.

He wasn't proud of it. He supposed, in a perfect world, with his grandmother in rehab and his security team lost in the wilds with an ever-decreasing chance of survival, he should be above such crude lusts.

Didn't work that way. Never had. Not around Brooke.

When he met her in the lobby or saw her on the paths, he never had a doubt about who commanded his body. Every time, the little general stood up and saluted.

Then he remembered what DuPey had told him: that she allowed herself to be almost arrested, to be bullied by DuPey's father; that she had been willing to sacrifice herself out of kindness for a friend, and that made Rafe wonder exactly what role he had played in her life.

If he had been forced to put his thoughts into words—and thank God he hadn't—he would have said they were star-crossed lovers.

But in high school, had he been like DuPey? A project, someone wounded by life, someone to be saved?

When he came back from Afghanistan, had she

viewed him as a lamb to be nurtured and returned to the flock? Had she treated him so gently, given him what he so desperately needed out of pity?

He could not stand the idea.

He needed to leave, to go back to work, to be in Kyrgyzstan on the front line.

His cell vibrated against his leg. He snatched it out of his pocket and looked at the ID.

Not Kyrgyzstan, but a call from Brooke . . . who didn't want or need him and possibly never had.

He almost didn't answer, but maybe she had information about who'd ridden that motorcycle up to Nonna's house.

It wasn't Brooke at all, but a small, trembling female voice. "Hi." She stopped.

"Hi!" he said encouragingly. Who was this? Had Brooke lost her cell phone? Was someone's kid playing with it?

"Hi," the girl repeated. "I'm one of the maids here at Bella Terra. Brooke told me to call you and ask you come to the garbage area for Millionaire's Row."

The garbage area. "What's wrong?"

"Come now." She hung up.

Astonished, he looked at the phone. Brooke had sent him a message like that? Through one of the maids? Really?

Why? Why hadn't Brooke called him herself? Had she been hurt?

221

No, the maid would have called the EMTs.

He brought up the map of Bella Terra Resort, found the garbage area, realized it was off the beaten path.

Had she been ambushed? Like Nonna? Was she being held hostage?

To some people, notably Noah, that idea might seem absurd. Yet violence, normally so far from Bella Valley, had arrived, and with a few quick adjustments, a loaded pistol, an extra knife, Rafe transformed himself into a warrior, prepared to rescue Brooke . . . or be attacked. He staked out his route, moved quickly and quietly, and when he neared the garbage enclosure, he loosened the pistol in his holster and checked the position of the knife under his jacket.

The maid—pale faced, blue eyed, tattooed, and with a shaved head—popped out of the open gate to the Dumpster area.

He remembered her from his first day here. She'd been cleaning in the lobby.

When she saw him, her relief was pathetic, transparent and frantic. "Mr. Di Luca! Thank God you're here. Miss Petersson . . . she needs to shower, and we'll have to call the police, but she insisted on talking to you first."

This garbled message didn't erase his suspicions, but it did change them. "She needs to shower?" Was this girl crazy?

The maid paid no attention to his

bewilderment, but pushed him around the corner.

Brooke was upright and half-naked on a plastic chair, thin and pale and desperate. A red, rough scrape covered her icy white cheek, and her expression . . .

He was on his knees beside her before she realized he was there. "Brooke?" he called her name softly. "What happened?"

Her eyes shifted, vaguely out of focus. Her gaze sharpened. "Rafe? Oh, good. Do you remember the gardener I told you knew something about the attack on Sarah? Luis Hernández? The one who disappeared?"

"Yes."

"I found his cross. He's in the Dumpster."

Rafe looked around at the small, close, desolate area. "Why were you in the Dumpster?"

Brooke cradled one hand in her lap. The other one she held out as if it were alien to her. "Um . . ." She had to think. "One of our guests has lost her ring. We were looking for it. I saw the glint of jewelry, grabbed it, and he—" She closed her eyes and lowered her head.

The maid made an incoherent sound of anguish. She flung her hand over her eyes as if she couldn't bear the memory of what she'd seen.

He assessed the maid's incoherence and Brooke's near nudity differently. "Brooke, I'm glad you called me first."

"It's something to do with the attack on Nonna, isn't it?" Brooke asked. "That's why I called you. You knew it wasn't a vagrant. You knew."

"I suspected," he amended. "Let me call DuPey and get him on his way; then I'll ask you a few questions." And get her something for the scrape on her face, and some cool water to drink, her and the maid.

"That's good." Brooke nodded. "I knew you would know what to do."

Rafe ran his hand over her hair, then rose and walked out the gate and made his call. After a moment's hesitation, he called Noah.

His brother hung up before Rafe had finished the first sentence.

Noah was on his way.

Glancing back inside, Rafe saw the maid kneeling beside Brooke, helping her wash her hand in the bucket. The two women had just been through hell together.

The maid looked pale, too, and slightly sweaty.

These women were in shock.

Walking back in, he asked the maid, "Who are you?"

"Madelyn."

He remembered the name . . . Ebrillwen had spoken about her, and not in a complimentary manner.

But what mattered now was how Madelyn cared for Brooke. With his hand under

Madelyn's elbow, he lifted her to her feet. In a slow, clear voice, he instructed, "The spa is close. Go there. Get two bottles of water, and get Brooke a robe."

Madelyn's eyes focused, and she nodded as if glad to have something to do.

He continued. "If they give you any trouble, tell them—"

Madelyn's face grew cold. "They won't give me any trouble." She looked back at Brooke, and her expression trembled on the edge of pain. "She can't seem to wash enough. If you would help her—"

"Yes." He understood. He knew.

He'd seen what Brooke had seen, suffered as Brooke had suffered.

In this, at least, no one could help her more.

Chapter 27

Madelyn sped out of the enclosure.

Rafe walked over to Brooke, knelt in front of her. He moved the bucket aside, dried her hand on his T-shirt. "Sweetheart."

Slowly she lifted her head, opened her eyes, stared at him as if she'd never seen him before.

He pulled her off the chair and into his arms, then sat against the wall, holding her tight. Rocking her in his arms, he murmured words of comfort, and when Madelyn came back with the robe, he helped Brooke stand and huddle into it.

He knew what she was doing: acting on instinct, hiding herself as if she were dirty.

He opened the water bottles for them—the plastic twist tops were tight and Madelyn was now trembling so hard he was afraid she'd fall down. As the sirens started in the distance, he coaxed them both to drink.

In a slow, calm voice he said, "You two are going to have to talk to Sheriff DuPey about what happened. Can you do that?"

Both women stared at him as if he were speaking a foreign language, and nodded as if they were numb.

He hoped the numbness would last through their questioning.

Two police cars pulled up in front of the gate

and blocked the road, sirens blaring, lights flashing. Two officers got out of one car and cordoned off the area with yellow crime scene tape. DuPey came through the gate looking grim and competent. Another guy dressed in jeans, a button-down shirt, spotless running shoes, and carrying two heavy leather bags, followed.

As Rafe went to meet them, Noah pulled up in one of the resort's golf carts and arrived at a run.

DuPey introduced the guy in the button-down shirt as the coroner, then asked, "What happened?"

Rafe told them what he knew.

Noah informed them that the trash collectors were due soon.

The coroner, grim and efficient, shed his leather bags and pulled on his latex gloves. He placed the step stool and climbed into the Dumpster.

DuPey went to the two women, speaking softly, asking his questions.

Rafe watched, but he knew the women's breakdowns were inevitable. The question was how soon.

"Rafe!" Noah snapped.

Rafe glanced at his brother. "What?"

Noah's green eyes were hot with irritation. "I'm trying to get this straight in my mind. The gardener who disappeared right after the attack on Nonna is in the Dumpster. He's dead and has been dead for a while."

"I'd guess someone killed him after he spoke to Brooke," Rafe said, "when his behavior made her realize something was wrong at Nonna's."

Brooke was, as expected, replying to DuPey's questions straightforwardly, putting her distress aside for the necessary investigation.

Madelyn took her cue from Brooke, talking, gesturing, responding in a manner meant to move the investigation along.

"Is he the one who attacked Nonna?" Noah asked.

"It's possible, but in all probability this is a murder. So someone else is involved. He didn't jump in that Dumpster by himself."

"Right." Noah nodded. "Someone hid the body, then brought it here when the trash collectors were due, figuring it would get dumped and he'd be off the hook."

"Or she," Rafe reminded him. "We don't know it's a guy."

"And this person has to have access to the Dumpster area and know the pickup schedule, which means he—or she—works here." Noah's eyes got angrier.

"It's not out of the realm of possibility that someone outside of your organization could get through the gate, but given the situation, I'd say you're correct."

Noah stepped up to Rafe and stood before him, toe-to-toe. In a low, forceful voice, he said, "I'm going to tell you this one time, and one time only."

"What?" His brother was being weird.

"About the attack on Nonna being premeditated—you were right."

This place smelled like rotting garbage and decaying flesh. Rafe itched to take Brooke away to safety. And although he didn't like it, this investigation would change Bella Terra forever.

But he couldn't help grinning at Noah's reluctant admission. Wrapping his arm around Noah's neck, he pulled his younger brother close enough that their foreheads touched. "I thought you knew—I'm always right."

"Oh, I know." Noah bonked their foreheads together hard enough to hurt. "But I don't have to like it."

They broke apart, rubbing their foreheads and grinning.

Then Noah's smile faded. "Oh, no. Look who just came through the gate. It's her."

Ebrillwen Jones had arrived, head up, shoulders back.

The two officers who had been guarding the compound followed in her wake, trying to eject her.

The head of housekeeping imperiously ignored them. Her cool gaze swept the area and she made her assessment. In a voice so severe and formally

British it frosted the air, she said, "What is going on here, Madelyn?"

Madelyn looked at her boss's stern countenance. Her composure faded. Her face worked as she fought the sudden onset of tears.

"Here we go." Rafe started toward the women.

Ebrillwen stiff-armed him, pushed him aside, and marched over to DuPey. "This young woman is one of my maids, and her dereliction of duty has thrown my schedule completely off. If she's not under arrest, and if you're done questioning her, I'll take her to my office and settle this matter of her neglect of her duties."

DuPey straightened, put his hands on his belt, and tried to stare down Ebrillwen. "Ma'am, I really don't think she has had a lot of choice about her activities this afternoon. Perhaps you could dial it back a few notches."

"I'll take your opinion under advisement." Ebrillwen's tone made it clear she considered his advice an impertinence. "I will, of course, be responsible for my employee's continued presence on the premises."

Brooke stood. She scrutinized Ebrillwen, then spoke quietly to Madelyn, who wiped her face on the hem of her own shirt and nodded.

Ebrillwen pointed to Madelyn, then indicated the gate.

Madelyn walked through it, and the two women disappeared down the path.

"I don't know why Brooke wants to employ that woman. She's the most frightening piece of work I've ever seen," Noah said.

"I guess." Rafe looked toward the spot where the head of housekeeping and her employee had disappeared, then back at Brooke.

Madelyn had been protective of Brooke, and in equal measure, Brooke had been protective of Madelyn. Yet she'd let Madelyn go to an apparent reprimand and possible dismissal without argument. Which meant she knew something not immediately apparent to DuPey, Noah, and Rafe; Ebrillwen was in fact rescuing Madelyn from continued interrogation.

Ebrillwen was right: Madelyn had been through enough.

So had Brooke.

From within the Dumpster, the coroner called, "I've found him!"

Brooke flinched at the reminder of what was in the Dumpster.

"I'm taking Brooke away. Give me your cart key," Rafe said to Noah.

Noah delivered at once.

"And make sure we can get into her cottage."

Noah got out his cell phone and made the call.

Going to Brooke's side, Rafe wrapped his arm around her and told DuPey, "I'm taking Brooke home now. If you have any more questions, she'll be available tomorrow."

Obviously torn, DuPey looked between Brooke and the Dumpster.

The coroner called again.

"All right, later," DuPey said, and, grabbing the digital camera, he headed up the ladder.

Noah walked with Rafe and Brooke through the gate, past the police officers, past the gawking gardeners and the spa employees and the maids and the tourists. While Rafe climbed behind the wheel of the golf cart, Noah helped Brooke into the seat. After a glance at her frozen expression, Noah turned to the crowd and shouted, "Any of my employees who don't have anything to do except stand around are going to find themselves looking for jobs."

Rafe recognized some of the ones who left: Jenna Campbell; Zachary Adams; the barkeep, Tom Chan; and Trent, the handsome young waiter. He recognized the ones who stayed, too: Victor Ruíz, who pushed forward to speak to Noah, gesturing toward Brooke with frowning concern, and a glamorous redhead disguised with large sunglasses and a scarf tied over her hair.

All of them were suspects now.

Although he supposed he couldn't in all good sense suspect his own mother.

He started the golf cart up the path, maneuvered his way through the guests who lingered and gossiped; then, as the way cleared, he sped up. As they drove past the pool area, they met Josh Hoffman carrying a white plastic garbage bag.

Rafe slowed. "Where are you going?"

The young gardener indicated the bag. "I've got a bunch more gopher bodies to dump."

Brooke whimpered and put her head down on her knees.

"What's going on?" Josh looked between the two of them.

"If you're going to the Dumpster, you'll find out soon enough." Rafe stabilized Brooke with his hand on her back, then zipped past Josh and brought the cart up to full speed. As they turned onto the path that led to Brooke's cottage, he told her, "The air will make you feel better."

"Right." She eased herself up again, but kept her eyes closed.

As they neared her cottage, they met a beautiful, curvaceous blonde running up the path. As soon as she saw Brooke, she called, "You're so wonderful! So wonderful. You told me to look where I hadn't thought of!"

Brooke opened her eyes. She gestured to Rafe.

He stopped the cart.

Impervious to their tension, the blonde bubbled over with joy. "In my evening purse, the one I didn't carry last night. When I got back to the room, I must have stuck it in there to keep it safe. Look, Brooke, look." She waved a sparkling piece of jewelry. "I found my ring!"

Chapter 28

Rafe stopped in front of Brooke's cottage. "Stay there," he told her.

She made no objection, didn't suggest she could take care of herself or that what had happened today didn't matter.

It did matter. A man she had known and liked was dead. She'd lifted him out of the garbage. She'd stared him in the eyes. She'd stepped into his decaying body . . . and nothing she ever did would erase that memory.

Now all she wanted was to get into her cottage and be alone to curl into the fetal position and try to forget.

Gathering her willpower, she prepared to move . . . and Rafe stepped up to her side, reached into the cart, lifted and carried her to her front door. "It's open," he said.

She looked at him in disbelief.

"I spoke to Noah. Just turn the handle and we're in."

She did it. She turned the handle.

He carried her over the threshold, through the front room, and into the bathroom. He put her down, stripped her out of the spa robe. Reaching into the gray tiled shower, he turned on the faucet. As soon as the water started steaming, he pushed her in and shut the door after her.

She stood there in her shirt and bra and panties, alone and desolate, happy to be in the warm water, yet knowing she had never been so isolated in her life.

People had stared at her. The guests. Zachary and his gardeners. Jenna and her manicurists and her masseuses. Brooke was a freak, a woman who had raised the dead.

Wrapping her arms around her waist, she let the shower massager pound the tense muscles of her shoulders and her neck. Her legs trembled; she could have sat on the blue tile seat, probably should have, but she didn't have the strength or the will to move.

Then the door opened.

Rafe stepped into the shower, big, naked, intent—but not aroused. That was all too obvious.

She shouldn't have cared. After what had happened, it shouldn't have been a matter of importance that this man who had always desired her now did not. Yet that meant nothing; she did care, and Rafe's physical indifference to her raised her misery to a new level.

He unbuttoned her shirt, slid it off, and tossed it over the glass door. It made a soppy *thwap* as it hit the tile floor. He reached for her shoulders, turned her back to him, unsnapped her bra, and slid her panties down her legs.

Now she was naked, too.

Still nothing sexual in his touch.

Of course not. Who would want her now? She'd brought a dead man up out of the garbage. She'd stepped into his rotting body.

But right from the first time she'd seen him, Rafe had been her friend. He proved it now, staying with her, turning her to face him, taking the soap in his hands and creating a lather, then washing her face and turning her into the downpour to wash it off. He scrubbed her neck and ears, her shoulders and arms, her hands. Taking the handheld down, he turned the dial to "pulse" and rinsed her with a spray so vigorous it felt as if he were peeling her skin off.

Gradually, she relaxed.

This was exactly what she needed.

Taking her nail brush, he cleaned her right hand again, lightly on the skin, then briskly under her fingernails.

He used the massage spray once more.

He washed her chest, her breasts, her belly. He turned her and soaped her back, between her legs, down to her feet. Then again he used the brush on her foot, scrubbing her, rinsing her with the handheld, and washing her again.

Funny. She would have thought nothing could ever make her clean again, and yet . . . Rafe understood how she felt. He knew what to do. She didn't think there was another man who would come into the shower and help her without flinching in revulsion.

He knelt at her feet. Looked up at her. "Better?" he asked.

She looked down at the suds swirling around the drain. Disappearing. She gazed at her hand, at her foot, the skin pink from a thorough scrubbing.

Fragments of thought drifted her way.

So many times on the news the reporters spoke of the discovery of a body. The story always spoke of the one who was fallen, of the deceased's family, of the manner and motive of the death. On the TV shows, the story was always about solving the crime. No one ever spoke of the shock and terror of the one who found the corpse. "Is everyone traumatized by the sight of death, or am I overreacting?" She looked down at Rafe, his blue eyes kind, his hair glistening and curly, his skin so beautifully tanned, the water dampening it to a warm sheen. . . .

"No," he said. "You're not overreacting."

"How do you stand it?" Her voice rasped as if the tears waited just beyond reach. "How do you bear the memories of people you've seen die? Of people who are rotting in their graves? Do you see them every time you close your eyes?"

"Sometimes I see them. The people I've killed." He stroked her hip and her thigh, not sexually, but tenderly, reassuring her that she was not alone. "More often, I see my friends who have died at my side. They haunt me. Sometimes in my mind, I hear the whisper of their voices. Sometimes at night, I can't sleep for recalling the good times . . . and the bad. Sometimes in a flash I see my friends as they were in death—and you know the kind of deaths I mean. I told you once."

"I remember." She remembered, too, feeling sympathy for his pain. But never had she imagined she would experience those emotions firsthand.

She didn't want to experience those emotions firsthand.

She wanted time to reverse. She wanted to be the woman she had been this morning when the worst of her concerns were a missing diamond and an annoying and too attractive ex-boyfriend.

She gave a single sob, loud and unrestrained.

But the tears weren't here yet. It was still all horror and fear and disbelief and sorrow.

He continued to kneel, continued to speak. "The nightmares come and go, but they never completely vanish. Still, I ask myself—would I want them to? Would I want to be so inured to ugly death that I no longer shudder in fear and unwilling sympathy? I've met people who no longer notice death, who no longer grieve their friends and their families, and to reach that place, they live in the lowest circles of hell." In a slow, deep, familiar voice, Rafe was informing her of matters she had never comprehended. "Thank

God for the nightmares, Brooke, and know that tomorrow you'll feel the sunshine on your skin."

The warm water misted her face, wet her hair, sluiced down her naked body. The moist, bitter-orange-soap-scented air filled her lungs.

Rafe was right. She was alive—but still grieving. Still chased by relentless memories. Still seeing Luis and his eyes, so wide and reproachful in death . . .

Something had to be done.

And she knew only one guaranteed solution.

She was an adult. She full well understood the consequences when she asked, "Can you make me forget?"

Chapter 29

Oh, yes. I can do that." Rafe looked up at Brooke, his eyes serious and intent, his erection stirring.

Reassuring to know she could still move this man to passion.

Pushing his fingers into the small ruffle of hair over her nether lips, he wordlessly sought permission to touch, to taste. "If you're sure that's what you want."

"Forgetfulness is exactly what I want." Arms straight, palms flat, she leaned back against the cool tile and let it support her. Sliding her legs apart, she braced herself and waited . . . waited for the oblivion she knew he could give her.

Leaning into her, he took a long, hedonistic breath. "The scent of you . . . You are pure woman, seductive, generous, a nurturing earth mother and a cruel seductress all at the same time."

It was a sorcerer's trick to make her sound so desirable . . . but it was a trick she could live with.

His tongue flicked out. He struck like a snake, getting his first sample of the world between her legs. "I love to taste you." His whisper was hoarse, low, warm, secretive, taking her away, back to another time when he first taught her how a skilled man could make a woman sing out her pleasure. "When you come, it's like honey on my tongue."

"I can't come. Not yet. If I let myself go—"

"You'll scream. You'll cry. You'll curse the fate that brought you to that Dumpster at that moment. I know. So let me enjoy myself and you can simply stand there and endure." His tongue rasped against her again. "You can do that, can't you?"

"You're so full of shit," she muttered. And he was, because he knew perfectly well she would do more than endure.

As he licked her, sucked her, used his tongue and lips and teeth to explore her, her mind emptied, her thoughts vanished, and she was all sensation and growing lust. Her knees trembled under his assault; she wondered if she would ignominiously collapse onto the floor of the shower and sprawl there with her legs apart while he had his way with her.

At this moment, that sounded good.

But he pulled away, a move that made her whimper in distress. With his hands on her hips, he moved her to the tile seat. "Here." He stood, helped her sit; then, with one knee beside her hip, he leaned over. Their lips met. He opened her mouth and with his tongue, that talented, versatile tongue, he kissed her.

That kiss was a blatant imitation of intercourse;

he thrust in and out, heating her from the inside out. The friction was good. The taste of him was better. When he wrapped his hands around her neck and fed her memories of their first kiss, she discovered she harbored no thought at all.

He sank into the kiss as if that encounter expressed his every wish for the two of them. . . .

It did not express her every wish. She leaned back, braced one foot against the tile wall, and lifted her hips, wantonly offering herself to him.

He seemed oblivious, using his fingers to massage the tight muscles behind her neck until she groaned with the delight of relaxation . . . and need.

Tilting her head back, he used his teeth against her throat, nipping in short, almost painful bites that made her jump and open her eyes.

He smiled down at her, then bent down and lightly kissed first one of her nipples, then the other.

He had always loved her breasts, been fascinated by her cleavage, by the weight and the shape and the way she moved and moaned when he touched her.

But contrary to her expectations, he moved on, kissing the pale, soft skin on the insides of her elbows, then the sensitive skin on the insides of her thighs. He used a finger to lightly slide down to her ass, and when she whimpered, he used the flat of his thumb against her clit.

Then . . . then he kissed her ear and lightly bit her lobe.

She didn't know what to expect. She didn't know where he would be next. She knew he wanted her—that was obvious—but how and where? The questions occupied her mind, confused her, entranced her.

It seemed as if he were trying to keep her off balance.

It was working.

He sprawled onto the tile floor, leaned on his elbows, spread his legs, and indicated his erection. "What would you like now?" he asked.

She remained on the seat, looking down at him.

He wasn't the young man he had been when she first loved him, nor the wounded warrior who had disrupted her plans for marriage. He was a man, tough, mature, uncompromising.

For all the good it did her, she loved him in all his incarnations.

She loved him now for his generosity.

Slipping off the seat and into the shower's spray, she prowled up his body, stroking his feet, his calves, his thighs, his hips. The tiles were smooth beneath her knees. Wrapping her hands around his erection, she held him and kissed the silky head of his penis. In slow increments she took him into her mouth, and oh, God, he was delicious, decadent, like ice cream on a hot day. He groaned, deep and desperate, and the sound made her feel in control again. In control and at the same time wild and free, without a care except to feed the urges of her body.

He made her feel like the woman he claimed she was, earth mother and seductress all at once.

Releasing him, she used her tongue on his belly, his chest. She kissed the red scar that sliced up his arm and over his elbow.

The water rained down on them, dripping in her eyes, around her neck, dribbling down her breastbone, between her legs.

Strong, unyielding, all man, he trembled in her power.

Putting her knee between his legs, she massaged his balls with her thigh and kissed his lips with her mouth. She thought of nothing except herself and the warrior beneath her. Then, like an electric shock to her brain, her eyes sprang open and she expected to see . . . death staring her in the face.

But it was Rafe, alive and seething. At her? No, perhaps not. But at the memory that ripped her from the sensual cocoon he had so expertly spun around her. "You will not!" he said.

So swiftly she never saw him move, Rafe flipped her onto her back. "You're here. Now. With me." He wrapped his arm behind her head and kissed her, hard. He moved his chest against her breasts, chafing her nipples with his rough, curling hair. He pushed her legs apart with his thighs, pressed his dick the first inch inside her.

He intruded on her body. He intruded on her mind. He dominated her.

And she welcomed him, wrapping her legs around his hips, hooking her feet around the small of his back.

This was living. This was being. This was celebration.

He rocked inside her, barely inside her, the breadth of him pulling at her clit, making her swell, turning her wanton.

She clawed at his shoulders.

His carefully proscribed rocking motion became a fast jab of need that hurt and exalted.

Her cry of surprise must have yanked him out of his fervor, for suddenly he was out of her and on his feet, towering over her as he grabbed her massage oil from the shelf—when had he put it there?—and rubbed it on.

Still in a fury, he pulled her to her feet and shoved her spine against the wall. "Spread your legs," he said, but he didn't wait for her to comply. He pushed them apart, then bent until he could fit his body to hers. He pushed. He slipped inside her, the lubrication easing the way, then thrust, fast, hard . . . but again an inch. Or four. Not even halfway.

He was dividing her, but barely, and all the while, deep inside, her need was growing.

She grasped his hips and tried to force him to fill her.

He laughed and pulled out. "Not yet," he said. "You're not ready yet."

Grabbing a handful of his hair, she pulled his face close to hers and glared. "I know when I am ready!"

He shook her off, spun her around, and bent her over the seat. With his hand on her neck, he held her down. Using two fingers of his other hand, he pressed inside her. "Does that satisfy you?"

"No!" She tried to fight him, and summarily discovered an unassailable truth.

He was bigger than her. He was stronger than her. He was a warrior, and he controlled her easily. "Come anyway," he said, and all of a sudden he was on his knees behind her, shoving his tongue inside her, using his fingers to create friction against her clit.

At his command, she came, bucking against his grip, her whole body in spasm, and behind her closed eyes, she saw gold and yellow fireworks, felt the explosions slide up her nerves, her spinal column, and take over her brain.

When she calmed, when she was shuddering and sighing, he stood. Holding her hips, he eased inside her.

She'd forgotten how large he was, how bold. She came again, a long, brutal flow of unimaginable passion. Opening her legs wide, she pressed back toward him, trying to impale herself completely, to bring on the ultimate orgasm that would finish her.

He had other plans.

He pushed her thighs together, tightening her body's hold on his cock. Then, at the deepest point of her, he pressed and flexed, so deep inside she writhed and whimpered—and came some more.

Would she even recognize the ultimate orgasm when it came? Or would this go on forever, an ever-increasing storm of sensation?

He flexed and flexed, and when she flexed back, he whispered, "That's right. That's good." He rewarded her with another slow thrust of his cock, and another, and another, until she was sobbing with the release that took her and the release that was still building.

He pulled out too soon, and not soon enough.

Her legs were trembling. She was glad he was finished. Yet she was still reaching for that ultimate orgasm, and she wished . . . wished . . .

He gently pushed her onto the seat and looked into her wide, amazed eyes. "How much hot water do we have?" he asked.

"What?" What kind of question was that?

"How much hot water do we have?" he repeated.

"Um . . ." She shook her head in confusion,

tried to think. "There's no tank. It's an on-demand water heater. It never empties."

"That's good. I'd hate to run out." He pulled her off the seat, onto the tiled floor, and eased her onto her back. He kissed her breast, then took her nipple into his mouth and suckled.

She arched her back, and sensation streaked up every nerve on the surface of her body. "What are you doing?"

He pressed his erection between her legs and swiftly, smoothly filled her. "You didn't imagine we were finished, did you?"

Chapter 30

That evening, by ten o'clock, Brooke was finally asleep, sprawled naked on her bed, exhausted by the traumatic events of the day and by the nonstop sex Rafe had used to put a halt to her thoughts. Tenderly he tucked her under the covers. Leaving the bedside light on, he went in search of his pants—his cell phone was in his pocket—and checked for messages.

Nothing from Kyrgyzstan.

Yet almost as good—a text from DuPey. The sheriff wanted to talk to Rafe. To fill him in, he said.

Thank God. Rafe was afraid he'd have to pry details out of DuPey—or direct Darren to hack into the sheriff's department computer. But as soon as he called, DuPey said, "I'm on the grounds. I'll be there in five minutes." Rafe heard a man's voice, and DuPey added, "*We'll* be there in five minutes."

Rafe made an educated guess. "Noah's with you?"

"He seems to think he ought to know what's going on," DuPey answered.

Rafe heard Noah shout, "On my own property, damn it!"

Rafe laughed and hung up. He glanced into the bedroom at the still-sleeping Brooke, then slipped into the bathroom and dressed.

He hoped DuPey was keeping him in the loop not because he was going to ask Rafe where he'd been last night when the body had been dumped, but because he wanted advice. Sure, Rafe knew he was a suspect—they were all suspects—but DuPey was turning out to be a better sheriff than Rafe ever imagined. The son of a bitch had no experience with this type of crime, but he had either done some study or had a knack, because he was learning fast.

Rafe walked outside, carefully shut the screen door to keep out the insects, and stood waiting on Brooke's tiny front porch. From here he could see the subtle lighting that illuminated the winding path, and the artfully placed plants and trees that created the illusion the cottage was located in the country. Yet downtown Bella Terra was close; faintly Rafe heard music from the bars on the main street, and lights from the lobby washed the light of the stars from the sky. Rafe recognized Bella Terra for what it was: a beautiful location, a clever fantasy, and one of the cornerstones of his family's fortune. Noah held the reins, and he fiercely protected his property. Of course he wanted to know everything about DuPey's investigation.

When DuPey and Noah drove up in one of the resort's golf carts, Rafe walked out to the white picket fence.

"How's Brooke doing?" Noah looked as if it had

been a long, exhausting, far-too-revealing day.

Rafe turned his head and listened. He heard no sound from the cottage. "Asleep."

"If she has nightmares, we can get a doctor in here to give her a sleeping pill. Or an antianxiety drug," Noah said.

Did Noah consider Brooke his to protect?

Perhaps. But from the interaction Rafe had observed, Noah's attitude originated in his protectiveness for the property he tended. Brooke was an important part of that property.

"All drugs do is postpone the inevitable." Rafe knew what he was talking about here. "Don't worry. I'll help her get through this."

"That's exactly what I'm afraid of." Noah stepped through the gate into the yard. "Who's going to help her get over you? Who's going to be at her side when you get called to one of your save-the-world projects?"

Rafe wanted to say the rest of the world didn't matter, but it wasn't true. His firm had calls coming in every day, and every day he dispatched security assignments to movie stars, athletes, the wealthy, and those who had something to hide. He had individuals and teams trained to handle every crisis. Right now, he had a squad somewhere in Kyrgyzstan, dead or dying or holed up in a cave and freezing to death . . . and God only knew whether they'd completed their mission.

So he did want to save the world. And his grandmother. And he wanted to be here with Brooke.

He couldn't have it all. He knew he couldn't. But his gut burned, and when he glared at Noah, Noah nodded. "Yeah. You owe her more than the occasional drive-by fucking, don't you?"

"I pay my debts," Rafe said.

Like a laconic Old West sheriff, DuPey leaned against the fence and watched the interplay between the brothers.

His attitude royally annoyed Rafe—because after all, DuPey had admitted he'd let Brooke get away with murder. Or rather, he'd let someone get away with murder and let Brooke take the blame . . . or the credit. Rafe snapped, "Can we agree the attack on Nonna and the body in the Dumpster are somehow linked?"

"Why?" Noah asked. "How?"

Rafe filled them in. "According to Brooke, she was first on the scene when Nonna was attacked because she spoke to Luis Hernández. He gave off enough guilty vibes to send her flying up to the home ranch. When she went looking for him later, he was gone, and she figured he'd run away to avoid being questioned."

DuPey's eyes narrowed. "Whoever did attack her thought Hernández knew too much and eliminated him."

"Yes, fine," Noah said impatiently. "So now we know why Hernández was killed. But what's the motive for the attack on Nonna?"

"I don't have enough facts. I can't as yet discern a pattern." Rafe looked between DuPey and Noah. "The question is—was the killing Brooke committed also somehow connected?"

As if that were a new thought, DuPey jerked slightly.

"Two bodies and an attack, all in the space of a month and all somehow related to the Di Lucas," Rafe reminded him.

"Might be coincidence," DuPey said.

"If Brooke didn't actually pull the trigger on that gun, who did?" Rafe asked.

"Do you really think Brooke Petersson would protect a ruthless murderer?" DuPey shot back.

Now Noah watched the interplay. "Wait. Brooke didn't kill that guy?"

DuPey turned to him. "As far as I know, there is no reason to doubt Brooke's account of the incident. Just because she reacted to the sight of a rotting body with horror and took the shooting in stride is no reason to believe she's a conspirator."

"I don't think that." As far as Rafe was concerned, Brooke had proved her innocence . . . and besides, he hadn't really thought she'd done it in the first place. Suspecting everyone was part of his job, and suspecting her . . . Well, when he first arrived, keeping a wall between them had seemed like a good idea.

They'd effectively demolished that wall today. "I do want to know who actually shot Cruz Flores. It might matter."

"Yeah." DuPey sighed. "It might. Do you want to talk to her about it?"

"No. Right now, she's feeling safe with me, and after today, that's important. You give it a shot, see what you can get her to say." Rafe had made his point. Now he asked, "What have you found out while I was otherwise occupied?"

DuPey gave his report with stoic unflappability. "The body has been tentatively identified as Luis Hernández."

"Who IDed him?" Rafe looked at Noah. "Did you?"

"He was one of my gardeners. Brooke knew him, not me." Noah shook his head. "Zachary gave an ID based on the clothes and jewelry."

"His mother's on her way. We'll get DNA and a positive ID, but I'd bet that it's Hernández. The coroner confirmed that the body had been buried for some time, at least a week, and then dug up and deposited in the Dumpster." DuPey's hangdog face never changed expression, but Rafe thought he was pleased with the results of his investigation. "I say the body was buried somewhere close."

"Because otherwise, why bring it back here?" Rafe looked between the two men. "But why not leave the body where it was?"

"It's spring," Noah reminded him. "The vintners are plowing around the vines."

"Right." Rafe followed the logic to the next fact. "The killer figured the body would come to light. He was better off if everyone thought Hernández had merely quit."

"The good news is"—DuPey didn't quite grin, but he looked damned pleased—"all the vineyards test their soils all the time for information on the best nutrients to use to maximize the grape yield."

This was better news than Rafe could have anticipated. "So you should be able to figure out where the body was buried by testing the dirt clinging to the flesh."

"Exactly," DuPey said.

Rafe knew how difficult it was to haul a body, especially a decomposing body. "So possibly the vineyard on resort grounds."

"Probably." Noah sounded disgusted and perturbed. "This is bad for business. I've already got guests checking out because they're freaked by—"

"Shh!" Rafe held up his hand and looked toward the house. He heard it again, a call muffled by fear and distance, and plunged toward the cottage.

As he ran, he heard DuPey say, "I dunno, Noah. I'd say he's going to pay his debt one way or the other."

Chapter 31

Brooke was sitting up, eyes wide, covers pulled up to her chest.

Rafe walked into the room, making enough noise to alert her to his presence, making sure nothing seemed weird or supernatural. "Hey, there, Brooke." He kept his voice low and soothing. "You're awake. Do you need to go to the bathroom? How about a drink of water?"

She watched him suspiciously, as if she'd never seen him before.

Going to the bed, he presented his palm.

He had hoped to ground her with his touch, to take her away from the shadows of night and death and bring her back to the mundane and bearable.

She considered him, then placed her hand in his.

And when her fingers wrapped trustingly around his, he found her touch worked on him, too, that she took him away from his worries about his team and the mysteries that haunted his visit to Bella Terra and pulled him into some kind of normal all-American middle-class life.

Some people would call that life a nightmare.

He knew better. That life was everything a weary, disillusioned warrior could ever desire.

He helped her into her bathrobe—he'd found it, a short blue silk robe, hanging on a hook on the back of the door—then escorted her to the bathroom. He asked if she needed help, and when she shook her head, he left her alone and went into the kitchen.

When she came out, he had food on a tray beside the bed: artfully arranged appetizers, fruits and vegetables cut into bite-size pieces, finger foods and dips. "The chef sent these over from the restaurant kitchen with a note hoping that you're doing well."

"He's a good guy." She looked shaky, but her voice sounded surprisingly natural, and she seated herself on the bed and looked over the food with mild interest.

"After a day like today, you need some fuel." He kept chatting, treating the afternoon's events casually, then moving on. Pointing to the radish roses, he said, "Check that out. How do they make them look like that?"

"More important, why do they make them look like that?" A smile played at the edges of her lips. "I've always thought a vegetable that masquerades as a flower is faking it."

"Here. Let me put it out of its misery." He popped the radish into his mouth.

She chuckled and spread a cracker with pimento cheese. As she ate, he continued the smooth, bland, nonthreatening conversation until she abruptly leaned against the pillow and said, "That's enough."

"Sure." He handed her an open bottle of water. Picking up the tray, he headed back toward the kitchen.

"Rafe!" she called, stopped him in the doorway. "Is Madelyn okay?"

"I haven't checked." He'd been busy with other things. With her.

She reached for the phone. "I'll find out."

While he put the food in the fridge, he listened to her speaking to someone on the other end, and when silence fell, he went back in the bedroom and found her sitting on the bed, staring at the half-empty bottle in her hand.

"Everything okay with Madelyn?" he asked.

"I talked to Ebrillwen. She took Madelyn home and is staying with her and her daughter."

"Madelyn has a daughter?" That surprised him. Madelyn, with her tats and her shaved head, looked too young and tough to have a kid, especially a daughter.

A daughter . . .

"Nice girl. She's been through a lot lately, too." Brooke's voice shook.

He scrutinized her. The color rose and fell in her face, and her eyes were haunted. Not too much longer, and the memories would overwhelm her and she would be lost to the storm of emotion.

Then she took a long breath and was calm once more.

Yes, a storm of emotion hung ominously on the horizon. But not yet. Not yet.

"Ready for bed?" he asked, and kicked off his shoes and peeled off his shirt.

As he unbuckled his belt and dropped his pants, her eyes grew wide and startled.

"How do you do that?" She stared at the erection that lifted his boxers. "You've been hard half the day, and here you are again."

"Happens every time I'm near you."

She pulled a long, disbelieving face.

"You're thinking you haven't seen me walking around with the little general standing at attention. There's a reason for that."

"Do tell."

"Since I got home, I've spent so much time in the shower trying to get rid of my permanent hard-on, my toes are wrinkled and pruney."

Brooke gave a spurt of laughter. "You mean you've been—"

"Slapping the salami? Yeah." He grinned at her. "Why do you think I have such a firm handshake?"

She laughed harder. And harder.

Abruptly the laughter turned to tears.

He reached for her, pulled her into his arms, and she cried until she had sobbed herself into exhaustion.

Chapter 32

When the sun came in the window, Brooke woke.

There was no comfortable, fuzzy moment of amnesia, no leisurely stretching or moment of sexual satisfaction. Instead, she remembered immediately: the Dumpster, the body, Rafe, DuPey, the shower, the sex, the laughter, the tears. Everything that had happened yesterday was branded into her mind, now an integral part of her character. But although the sorrow and horror still weighed on her, she was at peace. A little sore between the legs, but at peace.

Yesterday and last night, Rafe had helped her. He had washed her, distracted her, fed her, entertained her . . . held her while she cried and while she slept.

This morning, the monsters were gone. Maybe they would return; probably she'd have night-mares; certainly for all her life she would recall looking into a corpse's eyes and knowing he had once been a man she had known and liked.

But she was herself once more . . . and she was, perhaps, a little more in love with Rafe than she ever had been before.

Rising, she used the bathroom, then donned her robe and wandered out to the kitchen, following the smell of bacon.

The front door was open, letting in the fresh morning air. The screen door was shut, closing out the bugs. Rafe stood before the stovetop, barefoot, bare-chested, clad in a pair of jeans and a leather belt. When she stepped into the kitchen, he never turned his head, but he called, "Bacon and eggs, because you need protein to get you through. Today's going to suck, what with DuPey bugging you for details and everyone asking if you're all right."

He was right. It was going to suck. "Protein sounds good." She eased herself onto her stool at the breakfast bar.

"One egg or two?"

"One. You want me to make the toast?"

"I want you to sit right there and let me wait on you." He shot her a laughing glance. "Enjoy it. If you're lucky, it'll only happen once."

"Because a day like yesterday will only happen once, you mean?"

"Right." He put the plate in front of her. Cantaloupe, crisp bacon, wheat toast, marmalade, *two* eggs.

"High-handed," she said mildly.

"Orange juice?" he asked.

"Milk."

"You bet."

A glass of skim appeared at two o'clock on her place mat. "Thank you." She ate with appetite, not like last night, when she had nibbled, feeding an unsteady stomach. Today she ate with the full knowledge that she couldn't change the past and today was going to be, as Rafe predicted, difficult.

Glancing up, she watched Rafe pull on a clean black T-shirt. "Where'd you get that?"

"Before daybreak this morning, I took the walk of shame to my cottage and picked up a different outfit." He leaned on the counter and grinned at her. "I figured you wouldn't want me traipsing out of here dressed in the same stuff I wore yesterday. Might sorta make people think something went on here last night."

"What did happen here last night?"

"We found each other again."

She put down her fork. She reached across the counter, grabbed his shirt, and pulled him close. "Sometimes I remember why I like you."

His blue eyes turned a dark, greedy gray. "Why do you?"

"You're not always a jerk."

"Damned with faint praise."

"Sometimes you're pretty smart."

"Your flattery stings like a slap to the face."

"You want flattery? You're great in bed and you have moments of thoughtfulness."

"I'm great in bed because you're between the sheets." His voice was a solemn breath.

To be so close to him, to know what he'd done for her, how he'd understood and cared for her . . .

The two of them shared so much history. She breathed in the scent of his soap, watched his lips grow closer, and today, this moment, felt like sex and love and two souls in union.

With a thunk, the front screen door snapped open.

The two of them jumped and swung to face the newcomer.

Kathy Petersson, her mom, dark haired, blue eyed, leaned on her walker and glared coldly. "I came by because I was worried about you, Brooke, but I see I needn't have bothered."

Brooke suffered a moment of disorientation. She had been here before. They had all been here before. In high school. In college.

How did it always come back to this?

Brooke let go of Rafe's shirt, and of the moment.

Rafe straightened.

Brooke felt herself redden.

No one else on earth could have made her feel guilty. But her mother could, and did.

Brooke cleared her throat. "Mom! Did you hear about—"

"The murder? On the news this morning. Yes." Kathy pushed her walker into the cottage. "I knew Rafe would be at the crime scene. I didn't expect him to be in your kitchen after being so clearly in your bedroom."

Brooke expected Rafe to say something. Help her out. Explain.

But he stood and watched her mother move slowly into the living room in seeming astonishment, as if he didn't understand why she was perturbed.

Brooke tried to think of the best way to explain. "Rafe stayed with me last night."

"Obviously," Kathy said forbiddingly.

Brooke was an adult. She had had sex. So what?

Why was she feeling obliged to explain?

Oh, yeah. Because this was her mother. And although they lived their own lives, the two of them had been and always would be family.

"Rafe is here because he understood the kind of trauma I went through." Taking her fork, Brooke poked him in the arm to make him talk.

He jumped. "I do understand Brooke's trauma. So do you, Mrs. Petersson. I guess I should have thought to call you."

If this wasn't such a desperately embarrassing and significant moment, Brooke would have grinned. He sounded as he'd sounded when they were in high school: nervous, tentative, hopeful.

Her mom wasn't buying any of it. "That would have been pleasant."

He continued. "But I had to help Brooke through the trauma because . . . well, because after all the times she helped me, I owed her. And I wanted to pay my debt."

Chapter 33

Rafe didn't understand what happened next. But he knew that Brooke went from happy to angry.

He knew Mrs. Petersson went from angry to amused.

Somehow—he didn't understand how or why—he had totally screwed up.

"What?" Brooke slid off the stool. "What? You helped me last night because you owed me?"

"Yeah. I owed you. You helped me through my trauma. You know." He lowered his voice, speaking only to her. "After I came back from Afghanistan."

She stood straight. She looked at him as if she'd never really seen him before.

Red alert! Red alert! She was furious. She was hurt. He tried to think what he'd said wrong. He started backtracking. "Not that what I did for you could ever compare to what you did for me. You saved my life, my mental health. If it hadn't been for you, I would have been sidelined by the military and been forced back into civilian life."

Mrs. Petersson crowed with laughter.

Oh, God. Brooke had her hand on her chest as if her heart hurt. He hadn't fixed anything. But he still didn't know what he'd said in the first place and why she wasn't responding to his explanations.

"So you stayed with me last night because I helped you when you came back from Afghanistan?" Brooke's voice rose.

It was like she was rearranging the words, but saying the same thing, trying to grasp his meaning.

Maybe she was angry that he hadn't mentioned how much he'd enjoyed the night with her. That made sense. No woman wanted to think of herself as a pity fuck. "I was selfish, too. I wanted to help you, but I also wanted to have . . ." He glanced at Mrs. Petersson.

Mrs. Petersson crossed her arms, tilted her head, and stared.

He tried again. "That is, I always feel a strong desire to hold you and . . ."

Brooke watched him unsmilingly.

He faltered.

Her house phone rang, loud and shrill.

He jumped.

Brooke walked over, very controlled, and answered it. She listened for a moment and said, "Give me fifteen minutes. I'll be there." Hanging up, she looked at Rafe. "Better put on your shoes."

"Why?"

"You're going to get a call."

Everything she said sounded ominous to Rafe.

"Another murder?" Mrs. Petersson asked.

"No. Someone trashed the Luna Grande Lounge." Brooke's face was troubled. "There's definitely some kind of vendetta against the Di Lucas."

"Italians never forget a grudge," Mrs. Petersson said.

Brooke looked at Rafe. "Some of the rest of us remember, too." She walked into the bedroom and shut the door. Shut him out.

He swung on Mrs. Petersson. "What's wrong with you?"

She looked startled. "I don't think you're the right man for my daughter."

"No. I mean . . . you use a walker. First time I've seen that, and you're hardly old enough. So—what's wrong with you?"

She straightened her bent shoulders. "Speaking as someone who is allowed to hang a disabled parking placard on my rearview mirror, I'd like to remind you there's nothing wrong with me. I am just fine."

"You're right. I apologize for my ham-handedness." At least this time he comprehended how he'd been insensitive.

She inclined her head. "However, I have a disease called rheumatoid arthritis that inhibits my movement."

Even with the evidence before his eyes, the diagnosis took him by surprise. "How? When?"

"There's no consensus on the cause of RA. When I was thirty-five, I was in the first stages. The Air Force gave me the ugly verdict and honorably discharged me. Once I told Ken, he couldn't wait to inform me he had another wife, younger, prettier, in good health. So I did my research, moved to Bella Terra. . . ." Mrs. Petersson walked to the breakfast bar, sat carefully on one of the counter stools, and gestured toward the closed bedroom door. "And here we are."

He rubbed his hand on his face, trying to adjust his thinking.

When he was a teenager, Mrs. Petersson had been part inspiration, part personal terror.

She had been the kind of person he'd wanted to be: independent, tough-minded, a military leader, with high expectations for her daughter and, by extension, for him, expectations they had done everything in their powers to fulfill. She had encouraged him in his aspirations of courage and heroism. In all his life, he had never imagined this woman would be assaulted by a foe as insidious as rheumatoid arthritis. Thank God she was the fighter that she was. Thank God she had Brooke living close. . . . "Your symptoms weren't obvious for years."

"The medications and my exercises kept me functioning at a high level."

"When did Brooke discover you had RA?"

Mrs. Petersson set her chin. "Her senior year of college."

"After I came home from Afghanistan?"

"That's when I told her, yes."

The bedroom door opened. Brooke came out dressed for work in a black skirt and white shirt, with a black linen blazer tossed over her arm. She glanced at him. "Better get those shoes on." Going to Mrs. Petersson, she kissed her cheek. "Mom, I've got to go. Business. But really, thank you for coming; I'm all right. And I'll be better when this is all over."

Mrs. Petersson kissed her back, frowning. "Okay, honey, but be careful. There's a killer out there."

"I am careful, I am capable, and I can fight. You taught me all that." Brooke turned to face Rafe. "And no matter what, I know I've got Rafe watching my back." She wasn't warm and sweet, as she had been earlier. Her eyes were steely, challenging him.

Yet her words warmed him. She knew he would keep her safe. He nodded, once, briefly.

She walked out, letting the screen door slam.

Her interruption gave him time to process the information Mrs. Petersson had revealed, and now he asked, "Did Brooke want to come after me when I left?"

"She had one semester before she graduated from college with a degree that would give her endless employment possibilities. She was engaged to another man, a good man. I wanted her to be happy." Mrs. Petersson hadn't answered his question—which was an answer in itself.

"You didn't believe she could be happy with me—"

"I didn't want her to commit to a man as screwed-up as you were!"

"So you deliberately used your illness to make her guilty, to make sure she returned to Bella Terra."

"She felt sorry for you."

"No." He slashed the air with his hand. "Brooke's not stupid. If all she felt for me was pity, she would have dragged me to a psychiatrist."

Her slight incline of the head might have been an acknowledgment. "Look. I'm a military strategist. I scrutinized the situation, weighed your disastrous history together, and recalled my own observations of servicemen suffering from PTSD. Brooke is my only child. I would do anything to protect her and her happiness."

"Yes. I see that." In a cold part of his mind, he admired Mrs. Petersson's strategy. But the cold part wasn't ruling him now. He was furious and insulted. "You talked to me. You told me to leave. You said I was too screwed-up to be any good to her."

"Perhaps I was wrong to interfere, but allow me to point out—you let me make that decision for you, and you never tried to come back for her." She challenged him with her gaze and her strength of mind. "You didn't care. Not enough."

He wanted to argue. Argue that she was unfair, that he'd been ill and trusted her insight. But damn it. If not for her interference, who knew what might have happened!

His phone rang.

He groped for his pocket and answered it.

"Come to the Luna Grande," Eli's terse voice instructed.

Here was the call Brooke had predicted.

"I have to go." Rafe sat down and laced up his running shoes. Picking up his jacket, he slid it on and felt the reassuring weight of the knife in his sleeve.

How odd to feel the need for protection in Bella Terra.

"All right. I understand where you're coming from." Although he didn't like it. "I'm a man. Why did I let you steer the course of my life—and Brooke's? But I assure you, I've never done anything to deliberately hurt Brooke, and I never will."

"You've never used malice, you mean. But deliberately . . . yes, you have. You two have been in love and out of love, but how would you even know if the same things are important to both of you? What kind of relationship do you have that you don't talk to her about your job? About what matters to you? About your plans?"

"Fair enough. I'll take all your points under advisement. Now take mine under advisement. I've dealt with my PTSD. It changed me, true—in the end, it made me a better man, and one able to help Brooke in her hour of need. It's time for some honesty between Brooke and me, and for you"—he pointed his finger at Mrs. Petersson—"to back. Off." He didn't wait for her to argue. He didn't have the time and he didn't have the patience. Instead he walked out the door and into the warm spring morning.

No matter what he told himself about making love to Brooke to divert her, it had been no struggle at all to fulfill his duty. This morning, his body was satisfied as it had not been for years. . . . No. As it had never been before. So he had to ask himself—this time, even if she was better off without him, would he be willing to walk away from Brooke? Would he be able?

Chapter 34

Rafe saw Zachary and Josh huddled together in a flower bed and talking furiously.

As Rafe walked past, they fell silent.

He walked past the spa and he caught a glimpse of Madelyn and Jenna in the reception area, talking and shaking their heads.

When they saw him, they looked away.

Outside the lobby, a city police officer stood guard over the entrance while Victor spoke sternly to the young waiter—what was his name?—Trent.

When the two spotted Rafe, they stepped back to let him pass, as if he were a condemned man walking his last mile.

What had happened? What was so terrible that it compounded last night's discovery of a body in the Dumpster?

When Rafe stepped into the lobby, he at once recognized the scale of this new disaster. He could smell it, the rich, pungent, fruity odor of spilled wine . . . a lot of spilled wine. No wonder he'd been called. No wonder Eli had sounded angry and brokenhearted.

The officer guarding the entry to the wine bar stepped back to let him in, but Rafe halted in the doorway, unable to take in the scope of the destruction.

High on the wall, the glass doors that protected the most expensive wines hung open. The slots where the wine should be were empty—and red splattered the bar, the windows, the chairs, the far wall.

The bottles, all of the bottles, had been dropped from the top of the ladder, two stories up.

Glass littered the brushed concrete floor, crunching under Rafe's shoes as he walked forward to meet the little group that stood huddled together, eyes wide, staring at the carnage.

DuPey was on the phone, speaking in the hushed tones one used at a funeral.

Tom Chan stood wiping his eyes on a bar towel.

Ebrillwen walked in circles, surveying the mess and shaking her head.

Noah and Brooke watched Eli, who knelt behind the bar, picking up the chunks of glass held together by wine labels, looking at each one, then putting it down.

When Rafe caught his breath, he asked, "What in the hell happened?"

DuPey got off the phone and answered, "Last night, after the bar closed, someone came in and . . ." He waved a hand.

"How?" Rafe asked. "Whoever it was should have tripped the sensors."

Ebrillwen had left the room and came back

with a squeegee at the end of a broom handle in her hand and Madelyn carrying a basket of cleaning supplies.

Brooke went over to hold a low-voiced conference with Madelyn. The maid nodded and spoke, then went to work wiping down the furniture.

Brooke patted her on the shoulder and came back to stand close enough to listen.

"No alarm," DuPey assured him.

"Then who?" Rafe persisted. "What do the security cameras show?"

Noah joined them. "They show Victor going into the bar and never coming out."

Rafe turned on him. "That's impossible. He has to have come out."

"This morning, he's the one who called in the damage," Noah said.

"Does he have an alibi?" Rafe looked between the two men.

Brooke answered, "He says no."

"He says no?" Rafe remembered the policeman hovering near Victor and the entrance, not guarding the door, as Rafe had assumed, but Victor. "You don't believe him?"

"He's lying," Brooke said. "I'd swear it. Protecting someone or something."

Rafe lifted his brows at DuPey.

"I tend to think she's right." DuPey spread his hands. "But if he won't talk, I'm going to have to take him into custody."

From behind the bar, they heard Eli snarl, "Son of a bitch!" He stood, looked at his wine-stained palm, then carefully withdrew a long glass shard. A new, thicker red oozed up. "Chan, hand me a bar towel."

Chan did. "Eli, if you don't stop, you're going to need a transfusion."

Ebrillwen started to squeegee the broken bottles and the wine.

Eli looked up, and in his brown eyes Rafe saw pure, utter rage.

Ebrillwen backed off, went to Madelyn's side, and started using the towels to wipe down the windows.

With his gaze still on his older brother, Rafe asked, "What do the cameras inside the bar show?"

"They show the bottles hurtling to the floor," DuPey told Rafe, "but they're pointed the wrong direction to identify who's doing the damage."

"No." Incredulous, Rafe pulled out his cell. "Not even possible. None of this is possible. Let me get my nerd on the phone and get to the bottom of this." He dialed Darren and put him on the speaker.

Darren's sleepy face popped onto the screen. "Hey, man, is this important? Because I'm on an Art of Vampire gaming marathon, and after thirty-two grueling hours, I'm about to drive a stake through the master vampire's heart."

"Let me show you something." Rafe pointed his on-phone video camera at the wreckage and panned from one end to the other.

He turned the camera back at himself.

Darren sat with his mouth hanging open. "What the hell . . . ? What? That's the wine bar at the resort? No." He started typing as fast as he could. "That's impossible. No alarm. What happened?"

"You tell me."

"I don't know." He scratched his head, bent back to the task. A blast of screaming came from his speakers.

Everyone jumped.

"What was that?" Rafe asked.

"Master vampire just ripped my throat out," Darren said absently. Then, "Right there. There's a glitch. Why didn't I see that before? There's a glitch in the program. This is . . ."

Victor walked into the wine bar, his suit pristine, his demeanor calm, every inch of him the perfect concierge. He pulled out a chair, frowned, used his handkerchief to wipe it off, then took a seat and waited—waited to be arrested.

The mystery deepened. "How soon can you figure this out?" Rafe asked Darren.

Eli paced toward him.

"I don't know." Darren shook his head as he stammered and typed. "It's been sabotaged.

Sabotaged. Shit! But I don't know by who. Usually I recognize the, um, signature."

"Signature?" Eli asked.

Darren replied, "All hackers have their own way of doing things. I may not know who the person is behind the hacking—obviously, we protect our identities—but usually I recognize the way any specific hacker works. As far as I can tell, this is a new entry into the field. Happens sometimes. But damn, he's good."

"How soon can you figure it out?" Rafe repeated.

"The hack is moving away from me when I get close." The kid suddenly looked more than his seventeen years. "This is my fault. I should have seen it. Twenty-four hours or less, I promise."

"Make sure that it is twenty-four hours or less." Rafe clicked off.

Eli stood directly in front of him. In a low voice that vibrated with emotion, he said, "It's not that kid's fault."

"No, it's mine."

"You're right. It is. Listen to me, Rafe. I hoped you'd find Nonna's attacker, but I was like everybody else. I thought it was a vagrant, and I figured as long as you were here for Nonna, that was all that mattered." The bar towel wrapped his palm, and Eli had a look on his face Rafe had never seen before: bitterness, grief, and hopelessness. "Then you started sticking your nose into the security of the resort, acting like the big man on campus. When Noah was pissed, I stood up for you. I figured you'd tweak the security, make it better, and you'd feel like you were accomplishing something."

Right now, Rafe didn't feel like he'd accomplished anything. He felt small and incompetent.

Eli rolled on. "We get a body in the Dumpster—one of our gardeners—poor son of a bitch. Okay, he was killed before you got here. But he was placed in that Dumpster after you arrived. Half the guests checked out. Noah's profits for the quarter are totally screwed. Which sucks for everyone all around. And me—I'm still standing up for you. I'm saying, 'Look, Rafe was right; it wasn't a vagrant. Better to know and catch the bad guy.' That's because I still imagine you've got a handle on the security." He waved a hand at the wall. "Then this happens. This . . . carnage. I picked out those top-end bottles myself. Do you have any idea the value of the wine that was destroyed here?"

"Hey, Eli, calm down." Noah put his hand on Eli's arm.

Eli slammed him against the bar. "You little shit. Don't patronize me."

Abruptly the atmosphere in the bar went from uncomfortable to shocked; Rafe had never seen

Eli as wild and angry as he was now. "Eli," he said quietly. "It's me you're mad at."

Eli slowly let go of Noah's collar, but nothing about him was contrite. He glowered at Noah, then turned back to Rafe, and as if he'd never been interrupted, he went back to his tirade. "Some of the bottles on that wall were one-of-a-kind bottles. Thousands of dollars apiece. Thousands. Owning those bottles . . . that's like owning history. Or, let me make it clearer for you—it's like owning an antique car. Our insurance won't pay for their destruction." He closed his eyes as if in pain.

One thing became clear to Rafe: Eli wasn't being an artist. He was crushed by not only the aesthetic values; the financial loss also weighed on him.

"One-of-a-kind bottles. Do you understand what that means?" Eli opened his eyes and his gaze drilled Rafe. "It means we have a Chateau St. Neuf 1943, bottled at great risk during World War II, that has disappeared off the face of the earth. It means we have an Alessandrine Côté 1891, bottled in New York State—have you heard of her, Rafe? Possibly the greatest female vintner this country has ever seen, the only female vintner of the nineteenth century, and it was her last bottle. Her last bottle. We had a bottle created during Prohibition by Massimo, right here in Bella Terra, circa 1933. Gone. Gone forever. If I had sold those bottles at auction, prices could have gone over fifty thousand apiece."

The price of the wine made Rafe want to gag. The loss of his brother's goodwill made him want to grovel. "Eli . . ."

But Eli wasn't finished. "I didn't take those bottles to auction. I knew that sitting in our wine wall, they made us a place of pilgrimage for the great wine connoisseurs of the world." He paced away, then paced back. "Those bottles are gone now, irrevocably destroyed, and the tragedy is— they were never tasted. Wines that old might have been—probably would have been—nothing but vinegar. They might also have been ambrosia. But we'll never know. No one will ever know." Eli poked his finger into Rafe's chest. "Let me make this clear. I want whoever did this punished. I want him in jail. I want him dead. And I expect you, Rafe, to do what everyone thought you were doing, and protect this resort from any further deprecations. Do you understand me?"

"Yes, Eli." It was the only answer Rafe could give.

"Good." Eli took a long breath. "I'm leaving for San Francisco. I'm going to attend the winemaker's dinner. I'm going to receive my awards, accept my accolades, knowing all the while that everyone in that mammoth dining hall is not envying me, not cheering me, but pitying me. And when I come back, this had all better be cleared up, because it's springtime, I have vines to tend, and I don't have time for this kind of horseshit!"

"I'll take care of it, Eli," Rafe promised.

"See that you do." Eli stalked out of the bar.

DuPey wandered over to Victor and spoke quietly.

Noah and Brooke moved to join Rafe.

"I've never seen him like that," Noah said.

"I've never heard him use that many words in a month," Brooke said.

"I've never been so firmly put in my place before," Rafe said.

"Why'd you let him do it?" Noah looked at Rafe differently than he ever had looked at him before—with less hostility and more appreciation.

"He's my older brother. And he was right. If I was going to stick my nose into Bella Terra's business, security should have been improved." Rafe considered Noah and Brooke. "I think it's time I took Nonna for a drive. Maybe take her home for a few hours. Either of you want to go with me?"

"What?" Noah stared at him as if he'd taken leave of his senses. "Now, when you're supposed to be cleaning up security?"

Of all the people here, Brooke understood what

had happened. She had been Rafe's lover. She knew Noah and Eli. She worked at the resort and she understood what the wines meant to the family. And she had witnessed every minute of the scene between Rafe and Eli. Turning to Noah, she explained, "The security problem is handled. Rafe's got his hacker on that. His point is—Nonna wasn't rambling when she said all that stuff at the hospital. She knows something, and we need to know what it is."

Chapter 35

By ten o'clock in the morning, Rafe was driving the road to the home ranch, Brooke was scrunched into the backseat of the Mustang, and Sarah sat in the front seat, looking relaxed for the first time since the attack.

Checking her out of the hospital, even temporarily, had been a profound hassle that ended in Rafe's firmly announcing rehab could wait and Brooke's asking softly whether a patient suffering from depression could perform up to her potential.

Sarah had done her part by looking pitiful.

As soon as they got her in the car, she grinned at them. "You're the best two children in the world."

"We brought lunch, too." Brooke indicated the picnic basket beside her.

"Thank heavens." Sarah patted her stomach. "It's not that the food in the hospital is *awful*. But it all starts tasting the way it smells . . . like antiseptic."

They drove up to the house. Rafe put the car in park.

Sarah looked at the house, just stared, her face so poignant that Brooke came to a hard and ugly realization.

Sarah didn't complain. She always kept up a

cheerful facade. But she was depressed. The hospital, the injuries, the rehab: They had oppressed Sarah's spirit. Brooke wished she had realized what Rafe had known: that Sarah needed to get away.

Rafe helped Sarah up the porch steps to her rocking chair. "Noah wanted to come, too," Rafe told her.

"Next time," Sarah replied.

"Something's come up at the resort," Rafe continued.

"Shh." Sarah put her finger to her lips.

Brooke started to lay out the lunch on the table.

Sarah shook her head. "Not yet, dear. Let me sit here for a few minutes and simply . . . be quiet."

Rafe and Brooke exchanged glances.

"Okay, Nonna." Brooke seated herself in the porch swing.

Rafe, always an opportunist, seated himself beside her.

Brooke didn't want to sit with him—Mr. I Slept with You Because I Owed You—but she didn't want to make a scene, either. He wasn't worth it. A scene would upset Nonna.

With his foot against the floor, he pushed them slowly, back and forth.

The silence, the warm breeze, the sense of being above the day-to-day troubles of the resort . . . they brought the peace that Sarah sought. And they worked on Brooke, too. Her anxiety slipped away and she was doing nothing but breathing, relaxing, being.

This was why she loved to visit Sarah. Here Brooke left responsibility behind. She didn't think; she didn't worry. . . .

Sometimes she dreamed, but a woman could be forgiven her dreams.

She looked at Rafe, motionless, watching the valley with the sad intensity of a man saying good-bye.

Perhaps it was time this woman changed her dreams. Maybe it was time she dreamed of Sweden and a new life.

Sarah sighed. "Thank you, children. This was exactly what I needed." She looked at them. "Now—why did you bring me up here? It wasn't merely a kind thought on my behalf. I hear things, even at the hospital."

Rafe grimaced. "We never could put anything past you, Nonna."

"What happened at the resort that Noah couldn't come with you?" Sarah asked. "Has it got to do with the wine?"

Rafe and Brooke simultaneously turned their heads to stare at Sarah.

"Oh, no." She thumped the back of her head softly against the rocking chair. "I wish your grandfather hadn't been so stubborn. I wish we'd ended this years ago. To have this shadow hanging over the family now, after so many years . . ."

Brooke leaped to her feet and unpacked the lunch, spreading it on the table where they could all share the cheeses, the salamis, the breads, and the dried fruits.

Rafe eased out of the swing and opened the two bottles of wine Chef had packed, poured a barbera for himself and Nonna, and a riesling for Brooke. He handed out the glasses and prompted, "What shadow?"

"The story starts with Massimo Bruno." Nonna accepted a plate from Brooke.

"Massimo . . ." Rafe's eyes grew narrow. "He was a winemaker."

"That's right. And a good man." Sarah shrugged a little. "Or at least, my father said he was. My mother said nothing, but she said it very loudly."

"What did you think of him, Nonna?" Brooke asked.

"He disappeared before I was born," Sarah said.

Brooke blinked at Sarah.

"Oh, yes. The story is an old one. But almost from the beginning, I was afraid it would never be over until all of us were dead."

"Go on, Nonna." Rafe placed slices of cocktail rye on his plate and, using five different cheese-and-meat combinations, made himself a series of sandwiches. He took almost all the chocolate-dipped apricots, perching them around the edge of his plate, and went to sit facing his grandmother with his back against the main porch post.

His appetite wasn't affected by the morning's tragedy or any emotional angst.

Brooke bit into a prosciutto-wrapped cantaloupe. She was *so* glad for him.

Sarah considered him fondly. But what grandmother wouldn't?

Last night, for Brooke, he had been all temptation and seduction, a man in charge of his sexuality . . . and Brooke's. Today the sunshine stroked the strong angles of his face, illuminated the dark fringe of eyelashes, and brightened the intense blue of his eyes. It sparked off his dark hair and rested lightly on his broad shoulders. The sunshine and the fresh air, the boyish pose and the manly self-assurance . . . literally and figuratively, what a package.

Brooke supposed she shouldn't be thinking about sex when sitting at Rafe's grandmother's house. But last night was so near: the passion, the exploration, the heated press of skin against skin. Even with what had come afterward, the memories connected her to the past, like pearls on a string of time.

Nonna ate a few bites, then put her plate on the table. Taking her napkin, she used it to dust her fingers, then twisted it tellingly in her lap. "In the nineteenth century, among the Italian families who settled Bella Terra, the Di Lucas and Bianchins were the most successful. Successful in the Old Country. Successful here, battling for land, money, and influence."

"What about the Marinos?" Brooke asked.

Sarah grinned. "The Marinos were from the south. Rude, loud, pushy thugs. My mother was a Marino."

Rafe sat up straight. "Nonna! I didn't know that."

Sarah laughed at him. "Why do you think you head over to the Beaver Inn every time you need to blow off some steam? You're like a salmon swimming back to your spawning ground."

"That's barbaric." Rafe ate another sandwich.

Oh, good. Not even unwanted family revelations affected his appetite.

"Why aren't they part of the family at Christmas?" Brooke asked.

Sarah's amusement disappeared. "My grandfather disowned me when I married Anthony. But disowning doesn't change the bloodline, does it? Give them another hundred years. The Marinos will go into politics, take over the West Coast, and own Bella Terra."

"God forbid!" Rafe said.

"Don't kid yourself, Raffaello. They have an energy and a drive that only people fighting their way up from the bottom can have." Sarah rocked, her eyes distant.

Rafe paused in the middle of eating his minisandwiches and ate a chocolate-covered apricot.

Brooke pushed the swing with her toe and wondered if he was afraid he'd get too full, what with that bread, cheese, and meat.

Sarah's smile faded, and she returned to her story. "In the early twentieth century, all the Italian families in Bella Terra raised grapes and made wine. When Prohibition came along—I think it went into effect in 1920—the Bianchins converted their lands to orchards, and their prosperity was undiminished. The Di Lucas refused to replace their vines and chose instead to build their hotel business. Ultimately it was a good decision—the old vines grow the best grapes—but with the Depression overlapping Prohibition, the family took a hard hit." She looked at the two of them. "I got all this from my mother-in-law, rest her soul. She did love to gossip."

"Thank heavens, because the only family history I've ever heard you talk about is the cheerful, we're-all-in-this-together stuff," Rafe said.

"I hoped we wouldn't have to worry about the rest of this. What's happened is probably punishment for my hopes, because the only way this trouble would not have reared its ugly head again was if Joseph Bianchin had died." Sarah looked across the valley, her eyes narrowed against the sun. "But only the good die young."

Chapter 36

What has Massimo Bruno to do with any of this?" That salami-and-cheese sandwich was actually looking pretty good to Brooke.

"Oh. Massimo." Sarah smiled painfully. "He is the pivot on which the whole story spins. Massimo was from the Old Country. He was a little old man, kindly and generous, who bought grapes from various families and made highly regarded wines. He was also a thief and a racketeer who disappeared for weeks at a time." Sarah considered Rafe and Brooke. "At least, according to my mother, this was the case. As I said, I wasn't born yet. One fateful year, that was 1930, on the same day, the Di Lucas and the Bianchins each had a son."

"Anthony Di Luca," Rafe named his grandfather.

"And Joseph Bianchin." Brooke tried not to eat salami and cheese, of course. They were so fatty and cholesterol-laden . . . and so tasty, especially on rye with tapenade. And as concierge, she should avoid anything so garlicky in the best interests of the guests.

"Exactly," Sarah said. "The oldest sons of each family. On the birth of any son in the valley, Massimo traditionally gave a bottle of homemade fine wine to the families, to be laid down and decanted when the young man turned twenty-one. Massimo's skill as a vintner was revered. To be presented with a bottle of wine of his making was an honor. The families were grateful."

Every word Sarah spoke punctuated Brooke's knowledge that she had landed among people connected by histories to the past. Even their tragedies reflected their traditions.

Sarah continued. "That year, as Massimo made his wine, the revenuers broke into his cellar and discovered the alcohol."

"During Prohibition, a household was allowed to make enough grape juice for their personal consumption. I'm going to guess he'd made more than that?" Brooke stood, walked over to Rafe's plate, and took the coveted sandwich. She took a bite. It was wonderful. "And perhaps he had allowed his grape juice to ferment?"

Sarah ignored the byplay. "Exactly. The revenuers used their axes and destroyed his barrels. And although Massimo preferred the Bianchin family, he gave the last bottle of wine he ever made to the Di Lucas for their son Anthony, my Anthony, saying he had been born first by a few hours. To the Bianchins, for their son Joseph, he gave a silver rattle. It was a triumph for the Di Lucas, a blow to the Bianchins. Not long after, Massimo disappeared."

"Really? He was never seen again?" Brooke took another bite. Yes, the sandwich had been made just the way she liked it. She grinned at Rafe, walked back and sat down, and devoured it.

When she looked up, he grinned back at her.

He knew how much she loved salami and cheese. He'd flaunted those sandwiches. He'd suckered her.

"My mother believed he was one of the thieves who were shot stealing a Monet in Belgium." Sarah shrugged. "Maybe so. Maybe not. I don't know."

Rafe had suckered Brooke, and why?

Because after last night, he was concerned about her getting enough to eat. Which was sort of sweet. Not that he didn't polish off the other four sandwiches and the apricots. "What happened to the bottle of wine?" he asked.

Of course. Brooke caught her breath. She'd allowed herself to be distracted by the story. Well, by the story and the food. But it was the wine that should have her attention.

Sarah told them, "Twenty-one years later, the Di Luca family celebrated Anthony's birthday and his wedding day—"

"And yours," Brooke said.

"Yes, my wedding day, too. Anthony and I were married with a full Mass in the church, and came back for the reception right here in the front yard." Sarah waved her hand toward the lawn. "Anthony's father built a dance floor on the lawn. We had a band. Everyone in the valley was invited. Everyone brought a dish. Everyone except the Bianchins."

"They weren't invited, or they didn't bring a dish?" Rafe asked.

"We invited them. They didn't come. We roasted a lamb and a steer. When night fell, we had Chinese lanterns strung from the trees. The night was clear and warm, and it was beautiful, so beautiful. Even now, I remember . . ." Sarah sighed nostalgically. "For the highlight of the evening, we were going to open Massimo's wine, but before we could, the Bianchins attacked with guns, knives, and sledgehammers. My God." Sarah held her fists close to her chest, old grief contorting her face. "Men shouted. Women screamed. Everyone ran. The Bianchins smashed everything. All the wine. All the gifts. They upended the tables. My mother screamed at Joseph's father. He slapped her face. Joseph tried to take me. Anthony fought and they shot him in the hip."

Brooke remembered Anthony, a quiet man who could fix anything, who raised his grandsons and treated his wife with respect, who walked with a limp and in his last year remembered none of them.

"After the blood was running, the tables

295

overturned, the feast ruined . . . the Bianchins ran away. The cowards left my wedding celebration in shambles, for they believed they had smashed the bottle of wine Massimo had given, and they knew they had killed Anthony."

Rafe leaned forward. "Was this never reported to the police? Were the Bianchins never indicted for it?"

Sarah chuckled. "Of course. There was jail time served. A little. But the Bianchins had money and they knew how to buy a judge and keep him bought—and they did."

Brooke sat, hand suspended in midair. "It's like the California Mafia."

Sarah sobered. "Not quite so bad, but you have to understand, our parents learned their lessons during Prohibition when corruption was rampant in the police force. *They* didn't trust revenuers. *We* didn't trust cops. Because even in the fifties, no one liked foreigners."

"The family had been in the U.S. for sixty years," Rafe said.

"We spoke Italian," Sarah said matter-of-factly. "We were Catholic. We drank wine."

"Horrors," Brooke said.

"We were different," Sarah insisted.

"What about Nonno?" Rafe asked. "He didn't die, obviously."

"We thought he was going to, but he recovered." Sarah smiled slightly. "And I had a son exactly nine months after my wedding day."

Brooke thought that through. "Nonna, if I assume you didn't celebrate your wedding night at the hospital—"

Sarah smiled slightly. "Let's just say Anthony was practiced at climbing in my bedroom window at my father's house."

Sarah had just confessed to premarital sex. *Wow*. Brooke wanted to give her a high five.

But Rafe looked as if he'd been slapped in the face with a fish, horrified by the idea of his grandfather and grandmother's passion.

Brooke exchanged a grin with Sarah, then asked primly, "What happened to Massimo's wine?"

"We kept the bottle." Sarah ate a dried apricot wrapped in a thin slice of caprino cheese. "Anthony let it be known it hadn't been destroyed. I didn't blame him. He was angry. He was in pain. He wanted to smear the Bianchins' noses in the fact that they had failed. Me, I thought a little smearing was fine, but after a while, it became obsession. Every Christmas, I tried to convince Anthony to drink it. On his birthdays, on my birthdays . . . He refused. I said it was going to turn to vinegar. What was the point of having a bottle of vinegar? But he said it was fitting that the wine the Bianchins coveted should be sour. We hid the bottle in the cellar, and Anthony loved knowing that Joseph and the

Bianchins still lusted after that bottle." Sarah clutched the arms of her chair.

"So you've still got it?" Brooke was in awe.

"Not . . . exactly." Sarah picked up a cracker, then put it down. "You know, as Anthony aged, he became senile. Dementia, the doctors called it. I took care of him, kept him here until the end."

"That was good of you, Nonna," Rafe said.

"Good of me? No. I loved him," she said simply. "After he was gone, on his birthday, I thought . . . well, I thought I'd take the bottle to the cemetery and share it with him at last. But when I went down to the cellar, it was gone."

"Gone? Really?" Rafe sounded as if he didn't know whether to believe her.

"We kept the bottle down by the floor in a hole in the concrete wall. It was gone. In its place was a note in Anthony's handwriting saying, 'Upstairs.' "

"What does that mean?" Rafe sounded confused.

In exasperation, Sarah said, "I don't know, dear. Your grandfather had dementia. You tell me."

"Upstairs in the house?" Rafe asked.

Sarah answered, "I looked."

"At one of your neighbors'?" Brooke asked.

"Anthony would never have trusted anyone else with the bottle," Sarah said.

"In the shed?" Rafe shook his head and answered himself. "If such an old, fragile wine were still drinkable, the changes in temperature would certainly ruin it. Although perhaps the dementia confused Nonno enough that—"

"I cleaned out the shed," Sarah told him. "There's nothing there. I've cleaned every nook and cranny inside the house. Nothing."

Brooke looked toward the house, remembered the candles on the dining table that had been so carefully lifted from the bottles. . . . "This is just weird."

"You believe Joseph Bianchin sent someone to get the bottle from you?" Rafe asked.

"Who else?" Sarah asked.

"Today I learned from Eli the worth of a rare bottle of wine." Rafe still looked faintly stunned at the realization. "Joseph Bianchin may not be our only suspect."

"He as good as admitted his guilt to me." Sarah looked from Rafe to Brooke. "He came to the hospital. To threaten me."

Rafe's blue eyes grew heated. "That son of a bitch. If he weren't so old, I'd teach him manners."

"You can't teach a jackal manners," Sarah said.

Brooke thought it was time to get them back on track. "Don't worry, Nonna. Rafe will trace the crime back to him."

"For all the years of his life, Joseph has

covered his tracks." Sarah leaned forward. "But if you could find out why now, perhaps the rest will be revealed."

"Yes, knowing why now might help us solve this case. I'll put my hacker boy on the case." As he did so often and so compulsively, Rafe checked his phone, then hefted himself up off the porch. "I can't stand it anymore. I'm going to go tap on the walls in the cellar."

Sarah laughed. "Of course you are. Have fun!" She watched him fondly as he headed into the house. Maneuvering carefully, she rose from the rocking chair and walked over to sit on the swing. Looking into Brooke's eyes, she said, "Dear, I wish you'd give that boy another chance."

Chapter 37

H ow many chances should he have?" Brooke asked. "He's never gotten it right."

Sarah counted on the five fingers of her left hand, then lifted her cast and continued to count the fingers that stuck out from the plaster.

Brooke watched, and when Sarah held up nine fingers, she asked, "What does that mean?"

"It means I was married to Anthony for almost fifty years, and he messed up nine times. Nine major times, I mean." Sarah chortled. "Minor stuff, he was good for nine times a day."

"Like grandfather, like grandson."

Sarah continued. "I'm a good Catholic girl. I would never have divorced him. But every once in a while I wanted to, so badly, and once I actually threw him out of the house. Told him I was done with him and he should go stay at the resort."

Brooke couldn't imagine seeing Nonna that mad. "What did he do?"

"Said he was tired of taking care of our grandsons. Said our son should take care of his sons. Said we deserved to have a few years alone together before it was too late. I told him he was a fool to think those boys could survive any more anguish in their young lives, that when the boys were grown, we would have all the time alone together we wanted." She took a breath, then released it heavily. "It turned out I was wrong and he was right. I've always wondered if he recognized the signs of his own impending dementia."

Brooke ached for Sarah's pain. "I am sorry. But what choice did you have?"

"Exactly. Even if I knew what would happen, I wouldn't change my decision. So. In fifty years, I forgave a man major missteps nine times. By the way, that time I threw Anthony out and told him to go stay at the resort? He slept in the car. It was cold that night, too. Damned old fool. I wish I had him back"—her voice shook with sudden emotion—"so he could do something else stupid and unforgivable and I had to forgive him again."

Brooke put her arms around Sarah.

Sarah put her good arm around Brooke. "If you like each other, you can always find your way back to love, even if you have to march through hell to reach the path." Giving Brooke an extra squeeze, she said, "Now I'm going to go lie down on my own bed in my own bedroom until it's time to leave."

Brooke stood and helped Sarah stand, then watched her walk to the entrance. There she softly stroked the doorsill as if seeking welcome from an old friend, then made her way into the house.

Troubled, Brooke followed and lingered until she was sure Sarah had everything she needed.

Brooke wandered down the hall to the kitchen and stood listening at the door of the cellar. The light was on, and she could hear Rafe tapping on the walls.

Good. He was occupied.

The story that Nonna told explained so much about the recent days: the attack on Nonna, the murder of Luis Hernández . . . and maybe a couple of other things. Pulling her phone from her shirt pocket, she looked through her contacts until she found one very special name, one she had hoped never to call.

But this was an emergency.

He picked up on the first ring, and his voice, tinged with a French accent, was warm and welcoming. "Brooke! *Chérie!* When I gave you my private number, I never dared hope you would actually call."

"Gagnon, I've been waiting all my life to call you." Contacting the most charismatic con man she had ever met seemed a precarious move at best; she knew better than to think any favor he did for her would not require a favor in return.

He laughed. "Why don't I believe you?"

"I don't know. I never lie."

"Only in the pursuit of courtesy." The man possessed charm all the way to his toenails.

Maybe Brooke's mother had a point. Maybe

Brooke should forget Rafe, give Gagnon a whirl, go to Scandinavia, be a wild woman.

But the fact of the matter was . . . Rafe was dangerous. She knew that. She'd never doubted that. But she also knew he would never do anything criminal. She didn't know that about Gagnon. In fact, she thought . . . well, she thought any woman who trusted Gagnon could land in prison or worse.

Which did not eliminate Sweden. She could still go there.

Gagnon got down to business. "What can I do for you?"

"We've got a situation in Bella Valley that I think might be bigger than I'd imagined."

"Tell me all about it," he invited.

She did, and when she had finished, he said, "This is truly fascinating. Let me check on it and I'll get back to you before your evening is over."

"Thank you, Gagnon. When you visit the resort again, I promise you a very special bottle of wine to express my gratitude." Hopefully that wouldn't get her into too much trouble.

"Only if you'll share it with me."

"I will, indeed." Sharing a bottle of wine with Gagnon would fulfill every woman's fantasy. The trouble with Gagnon, as far as Brooke was concerned, was simply that he was too handsome, too clever, too lacking in integrity, and, when it came to women, too inconsistent.

"I look forward to it, *chérie*. And, *chérie*—I want to enjoy that wine with you, so until this murderer is caught, you be very, very careful."

"I will."

He hung up without another word.

Now Brooke walked to the dining room. Once there, she again went to the table and arranged the wine bottles before her. One by one, she lifted the candles out, turned the bottles over, and shook them. They were empty.

All the while Brooke thought about her mother and how she wanted Brooke to leave Bella Terra and the memories of Rafe, and how Sarah wanted Brooke to give Rafe another chance.

What about Rafe—what did he want?

For that matter, what did Brooke want?

Looking across, she saw a memory leaning against the wall.

Rafe. Not Rafe as he was now, but the blurry outline of Rafe as he had been at Christmas her senior year of college.

Brooke had come home to cold weather and rumors that Rafe had been a prisoner of war, and when she asked her mother about it, Kathy looked her in the eyes and said, "I didn't think the story was important enough to disturb your studies. Besides, you're engaged to another man." Her mother's voice warmed. "I can't wait to meet Dylan."

"You'll like him." By that, Brooke meant he

was the polar opposite of her father: scholarly, unadventurous, as faithful as an old dog.

Brooke refrained from asking anything else about Rafe. After all, he didn't matter to her anymore.

As always, Brooke and her mom headed up to Nonna's on Christmas Eve. Every previous year, she'd come home, celebrated with her mom, visited her friends, and whenever she saw Rafe, she had pretended that he didn't matter to her.

Every year, it became more and more true.

He helped, of course. His military haircut, his ramrod posture, reminded her of her father, and that was enough to put a distance between them. Then she took care never to be alone with him, and in that, her mother helped. Whenever Kathy saw Rafe Di Luca, she managed to get between him and Brooke.

Every year on Christmas night, Brooke and her mom always went up to Nonna's to pay their respects—as Kathy said, Sarah had been unfailingly kind to them.

The home ranch was always full of visitors and family; Brooke and her mom always ate too much of Nonna's cooking, drank a mug of mulled wine, exclaimed about the decorations on the tree, and talked to Eli and Noah. Brooke carefully kept her conversations with Rafe to a casual, "Hi, how are you?"

That year, as usual, the warmth of the house

enfolded them. Someone thrust food and drink into their hands. They made their way into the gaily decorated dining room to greet Sarah. Brooke remembered thinking that Sarah was showing her age and maybe the strain of raising her grandsons.

Then Brooke came face-to-face with Rafe . . . and everything else faded away.

He stood unmoving, his back to the wall. He wore jeans and a short-sleeved blue T-shirt that hung on his spare frame. He was so still, only his eyes moving, flickering as he observed everyone in the room. Scrutinized them as if trying to decide which of them would be the first to try to kill him. The room was full, but around him a small space had formed, as if he gave off a force field to hold them away . . . or as if whatever had happened to him was contagious and everyone was afraid to get close for fear they'd catch it.

Brooke looked from him to Nonna.

Nonna met her gaze and her eyes filled with tears.

Brooke looked back at Rafe, only to discover he was staring at her with such a world of pain and longing. . . .

Brooke's mother stepped between them. "Honey, try this. It's Sarah's fruitcake and you know how much you love it."

Brooke stared at her, uncomprehending. Then her brain snapped back to normal; she smiled into her mother's worried face and said, "Thank you, Mom. It smells great!" Taking the cake, she ate a few bites, and tried the cookies and the prosciutto and the marinated artichokes. She drank wine and sang Christmas carols by the piano. She showed off her engagement ring to her cadre of envious school friends, and only once looked toward Rafe, when she saw Eli approach his brother and speak to him, and the two left the room together. Nothing about Brooke's behavior indicated she had a thought other than enjoying her last Christmas in Bella Valley without the man she would marry in the spring.

But when she got home, she lay on the bed, feeling alone as she had never been in her whole life.

She hurt. She waited.

And she listened.

Two hours later, when the spray of gravel hit her window, she was up and leaning out, offering her hand to Rafe. "Come in," she said.

"I can't."

She didn't know why he couldn't, but his voice was so flat and dead, she believed him. So she wiggled through the window in her flannel Christmas pajamas and fell into his waiting arms.

Chapter 38

R afe held Brooke tightly as he carried her to the alley and into the shadows where he'd parked Nonna's Mustang. She stretched down, opened the passenger door, and he put her in. She watched him walk around to the driver's side, a shadow stealing through the dark night. The car door opened softly, the lock almost muted by his care. He slid in and started the engine. And he drove. He drove for an hour, up into the foothills, then higher into the mountains, foot on the accelerator as if he were trying to escape something. To escape himself.

Finally, at three o'clock in the morning, she put her hand on his arm. "Stop and tell me about it."

He pulled off the paved highway onto a small, rutted dirt road that went nowhere. When they broke out of the trees and into a mountain meadow, and the Mustang's front wheels sank into the mud, he stopped the car.

They sat looking at the stars—so many stars, a hundred million stars in a clear black sky—and he began to talk.

"Eight of us. We were supposed to blow up the rebels' munitions storage, the biggest in the Afghan mountains. It took us weeks to get into position. We went in at precisely the right time. Everything went perfectly. . . . There's a saying in the military: *If your attack is going too well, you're walking into an ambush. We were. They caught us. Put us in cages where we could see the ammunition we were supposed to destroy. Held us for ransom. I knew that wouldn't work— the U.S. military doesn't ransom their people."* His voice was flat and hard and very quiet, as if even in this isolated spot, he feared being overheard. *"They knew it wouldn't work, either, but they also knew they could make us give video confessions, and those confessions would play on the Internet and the media would give them attention."*

"I didn't see any videos online." During the fall semester, she had been studying hard, but she had glanced at the headlines occasionally. She would have noticed Rafe's face.

"Because we beat one another up."

"What?" She had meant to keep her voice gentle and without inflection, but that surprised her.

"They wanted to show us freely confessing we were spies, so we punched one another enough to cause some ugly bruises. Pissed them off, so they stopped feeding us or giving us water, which pretty much worked to make us willing to do anything they wanted." Rafe seemed to think that would surprise her, so he added, *"Yeah, really. Without water, I'd do almost anything. But bodies don't heal without hydration, so it was a*

stupid move on their parts. We lost one guy then and there, Walter Davis from North Bend, Indiana. He got an infection and died. I think he died because he hated being underground all the time."

"They kept you underground?"

"In the caves, yeah. We lost Harou Yoshida from Honolulu, Hawaii, and Madison Dominguez from San Diego, California, because those two motherfuckers, you know, wouldn't shut up." Rafe's voice almost smiled. "They were always ragging on the guards about their hygiene and whether they . . . Well, those two guys were gross. Funny gross. Fuck, man. Those guys. There was nothing they wouldn't say."

Rafe had never sworn like that. Not in front of Brooke. But she didn't think he'd even noticed. "How did you lose them?"

Abruptly grim, Rafe said, "The guards got mad and shot them. Left them there. That's when the rest of us got sick. You know, you can't leave two bodies rotting in the cages with living human beings without some horrible disease popping up. When the guards finally came to haul the bodies away, we were all so sick, dysentery, I think. We were dead men. None of us were going to last another hour. So they walked in, put down their rifles, threw a tarp over the bodies, and started to drag them away. If I'd, um . . ." He stopped and rolled down the window, thrust his

311

head and shoulders out, and breathed deeply, trembling.

It was a cold night. The heat generated by the car was gone. Steam had crept up the windows, enclosing them in the small interior of the Mustang.

And he was hanging out, gasping for breath.

Now she understood why he couldn't come inside her bedroom. He didn't want to be inside anywhere.

She didn't blame him.

She pulled her legs up on the seat, tucked the hems of her pajama pants over her bare toes, hugged herself to create warmth, and watched him until he shook like a dog and pulled his head in.

"Sorry." He sounded more like Rafe than he had all night. "Just had a moment. I shouldn't be filling you in on all the details, anyway. They're disgusting and uncivilized. Nobody wants to know. They just want me to get better."

So many things she could say. So many approaches she could take.

She settled on breaking the tension. "Let's have some respect. I'm not that civilized."

"Really? You're not?" He sounded wryly polite.

"When there's a thunderstorm, I go out and walk in the rain without an umbrella. I could be dead in an instant, but I defy the lightning!"

"Whoa."

"Exactly. Politically correct I am not. One time when I was eight, I threw the cat into the sprinkler."

"You're out of control." He gave her a proper amount of awe.

"Yes, I am. Best of all, in my freshman year at college, we had a hard freeze and my whole dormitory went out and jumped in the fountain."

"Did you have your clothes on?" He sounded stiff and perturbed.

"My sweat suit!"

He cackled. There was no other word for it. He definitely cackled. "I am now fully respectful of your feral side."

"That's right, ba-bee." She was cold enough to shiver in little shudders.

He noticed at last, and rolled up the window. "Wait a minute." He got out, went around and opened the trunk, and came back with the ragged quilt Nonna kept in the back. For picnics, she always said, but long ago, in high school, Brooke and Rafe had more than once made love under its protection.

He got back in and held it close to his chest. "Give me a minute; I'll warm it for you."

Brooke knew she would give him as many minutes as he needed. She'd stay here all night if he wanted her to, and with the front wheels stuck in the mud, they might be here part of the day, too.

She spared a thought for her mother's frustration; then he wrapped her in the blanket and she forgot her mother. Offering him a corner, she asked, "Don't you want to share?"

"I don't feel the cold," he said. "In the caves . . . it was hot down there."

"All right." Her shivering was easing. "So anyway, tell me the rest of the story. The guards were dragging out the bodies and you—"

"If I'd been somewhere where I wasn't lying on the ground in my own feces, I don't think I would have been able to get up. All I can recall is this upswell of vomit and anger. I leaped up and grabbed the rifle. I remember the looks on their faces when they heard the round go into the chamber and turned and saw me on my feet—it was pure I'm-going-to-hell terror. Don't kid yourself, Brooke. I'm not a good person. I was glad they were shitting themselves."

"Did you shoot them?"

"I shot them both."

She looked down into the dim reaches of the car, thinking that someone like her—a female college student with no experience with violence—shouldn't be so ferociously joyful about his brutality.

But she couldn't lie. "I'm glad, too. What did you do next?"

"First, I grabbed their canteens and drank their water. Wrong! Because the shot echoed all

over that cave and every damned insurgent heard it. But I was crazed. The second thing I did was what we'd been sent to do. I set a charge under the munitions."

Her eyes opened wide. She stared through the dark at his faint silhouette. "But . . . you were in there. Weren't you likely to blow yourself up?"

"Like I said. Crazed. Then I went back into the cages, grabbed our commander, and dragged him out. He was dead."

"What was his name?" She asked because saying the names seemed to mean something to him.

He hesitated, then said, "He was Colonel Federico Martínez from San Antonio, Texas."

"A good commander?"

"The best." Rafe's voice grew thick with emotion. He controlled it and continued. "Next I dragged out Alex White from Boston, Massachusetts, and Isaac Berkowitz from New York, New York."

"Wasn't anybody shooting at you or anything?"

"They kept running at us, shooting like crazy. Then when I screamed like a madman and pointed at the charge under the ammunition, they would run. And scream like little girls. I liked that part."

Screaming seemed like a good idea to Brooke. "How did you get out?"

"I wasn't thinking right—you had that figured out, didn't you?"

She nodded. Her sense of dread was growing.

"The good part of that is that I didn't set the charge right, so when it blew, it blew part of the munitions out the front of the cave. Took out every one of their men, all their computers, all their weapons, all their tactical plans. I don't know all it took, but it left the way free for me to carry out Berkowitz and White." Rafe rubbed his forehead with the back of his hand. "Too bad we'd been in there a couple of months, so it was winter outside. I dumped them in the snow and went back to finish the job. I'll bet ninety percent of the munitions were left, and when they blew, the whole hillside lifted and settled, and the caves, miles of them, collapsed."

"But you were outside in the snow with nothing." She was telling him something he knew, but still, she couldn't comprehend the magnitude of his insanity.

"Took our troops about two hours to come in with helicopters to clean out any remaining nests of insurgents." Rafe's voice strengthened. "I managed to get their attention. White died. Berkowitz and I survived."

"How's Berkowitz?"

"Better than me." Rafe's voice grew hushed again. "But that's not saying much. I just . . . I can't sleep. If I sleep, I see them. The guards. My friends. The bodies. I can't stay inside long. If I do, I start clawing at the walls. Sometimes I jump up in a panic because I need to blow up those munitions. And I remember those guards I shot, and I'm so glad. So glad."

Brooke had taken a psychology class her freshman year of college. She was so not qualified to deal with this. On the other hand, she knew without a doubt that no one understood him more. "Rafe. You did survive. You completed your mission. And you brought back a man alive who counted himself as dead. More important"—she got up on her knees, and although he was nothing more than a dim outline, she faced him—"you saved yourself. Right now, that might not feel like anything important to you, but to your grandmother and your brothers, and maybe even your father and mother . . . they want you here to talk to, to eat with, to laugh with—"

"What about you?"

Leaning forward, she cupped his chin. "I couldn't live in a world without you."

Chapter 39

*T*he blanket slithered to the floor.

Rafe plunged his fingers into Brooke's hair, pulled her mouth to his, and kissed her, and she tasted his despair, his anguish, his need. She wanted to cry for him. She wanted to live for him, and make him live for her.

She got up on her knees and leaned into him, across the emergency brake that dug into her thigh, her chest against his.

He slid his hands down her back, under her elastic waistband, and pushed her flannel pajamas off her butt. She struggled to kick them off her legs and suck his tongue into her mouth at the same time.

His palms rode up and down her thighs. He made groaning sounds deep in his throat.

She pushed his T-shirt up, unbuckled his belt, unzipped his pants.

Now he was fighting his way out from under the steering wheel. He tore his mouth from hers, pushed his seat all the way back, leaned across her and down, and pushed her seat back—and when he came up, she'd managed to unbutton her top and he got a faceful of her breasts.

She didn't know how he did it, got from his side of the car to her, but suddenly his pants were down around his knees and he was on top of her.

Then he was inside her, desperate for her, filling her while she cried with the joy of knowing he was here and alive.

Placing her feet on the dash, she lifted herself into his thrusts, over and over, dragging him back to life, forcing him to be with her in this moment.

He kissed her, over and over, her cheeks, her lips, the top of her head. His tears dripped on her as he began to thrust faster and faster, as his climax neared, as the reality of breath and love and freedom burgeoned in him, in them, overwhelming them both.

Then he came. She came.

And for a few precious minutes, he was her love once more.

The next night, Brooke went out the window.

The night after, Rafe came in the bedroom.

The night after that, Kathy Petersson caught them doing the wild thing.

The next day, Rafe left Bella Valley without a word, returning to the psychiatry hospital for treatment, breaking Brooke's heart again.

She ended her engagement anyway.

She waited for Rafe to come and get her.

That never happened.

She considered going to get him.

But this time, he was the one who had left her. He had gone back to the military. That was a message, wasn't it? A message she should heed?

Rafe's ghost face faded off Nonna's dining room wall. Brooke came back to the present; the memories still made her feel weepy and foolish.

How many times would he get it wrong?

How many times would she?

At the sound of footsteps behind her, she jumped.

"Hey, have you found anything?" Rafe put his hands on her arms, rubbed them up and down. "I didn't. Nothing in the cellar."

"I was playing with these bottles, trying to think where your grandfather would put Massimo's wine." Brooke looked around the dining room. "This house is so simple, yet it's been added onto how many times? Over how many years? Plus, Nonno was a builder and an electrician. Massimo's wine could be anywhere in here."

"Nonno ran the resort until the dementia took him and Noah got the job. The bottle could be in the wine cellar down at the resort, too."

"Oh, God." She turned to face him. "This is the biggest mess I could possibly imagine."

Rafe pulled his phone out of his pocket and looked, then shook it as if trying to jiggle out a message. "No, there are bigger messes."

She would start feeling sentimental about him; then he would annoy her like this. "You check that phone every fifteen minutes. What are you waiting to hear?"

"Nothing you need to be anxious about."

Secretive. No communication skills. What was she thinking, feeling maudlin about Rafe? "I don't need to be anxious because I wouldn't understand your concerns? Or because I wouldn't give a shit? Or because—"

"This isn't a concern. This is a problem. Okay, listen." He lowered his voice. "I left my team in Kyrgyzstan dealing with a kidnapping, and I haven't heard from them since shortly after I got here. I'm worried."

He seemed suddenly to get that he should talk to her, and she wondered what had turned on the light in his head. "You think something has gone wrong?"

"It's mountainous. It's still winter there. The territory is hostile. We were rescuing an American pilot, a female. I wish I were there. I have to be here. I'm not doing that well handling this situation."

"I'm sorry. I didn't realize . . . All this time, you've been worried about your team? And the mission?"

"I work the case I'm on, and in this instance, my case is finding Nonna's attacker—and the mystery keeps growing. But yes, I am concerned. They're good people. They've been with me a long time. And the pilot—I promised to do everything I could to get her out. I simply wish I could be there personally." He took a breath. "Now, tell me, how are *you* doing?"

She had wanted to know what was on his mind, and knowing made her realize the heroic man he had become . . . and how little she knew about him. "I'm fine." She was. Because of him, she'd eaten well. Because of the situation in the wine bar, she had things on her mind other than yesterday's rotting body.

"Did Hernández's body yesterday remind you of the man you shot and killed a month ago?"

"No!" What kind of question was that? "Why would you think such a thing? No."

"Seeing death of any kind is usually a big deal for a civilian. Shooting someone is usually a big deal for a civilian. It seems as if you should feel some connection between the two bodies."

Brooke caught her breath. "Is there a connection?"

"You tell me."

Amazing how he could in the space of a hundred heartbeats take her from heated reminiscences to massive indignation to inglorious rage. "I know nothing about who attacked Nonna. I wish I did."

"Before DuPey took Victor away, I snatched a minute and talked to DuPey. He said they'd done the preliminaries on Hernández. The gardener was strangled with a wire around his throat."

Brooke put a hand to her unexpectedly vulnerable-feeling neck.

"No fingerprints and no murder weapon were anywhere to be found. You have to be strong and fast to pull off that kind of murder."

"I would imagine."

"Or maybe the killer took the victim completely by surprise."

Brooke recalled Hernández's plain, simple face, and knew that was exactly what had happened.

Rafe continued. "We know, because the killer has hacked into the resort's security, that he's smart. We're all in danger, but because of Hernández's connection to you, I'm afraid you, especially, are a target."

Perhaps Rafe wasn't trying to make her angry. Maybe he was trying to make her think. "I have racked my brain, but I don't even remember what exactly Hernández said that made me think Nonna was in danger. I simply recall that blind panic that had me driving up there, all the while thinking I was making a fool of myself over nothing. If I'd paid attention to my instincts and called nine-one-one, they would have beaten me up there and Nonna would have been rescued that much sooner."

"Some people have good instincts. I suspect you're one of them. So if you remember anything about Hernández, who he hung out with, anything he said previous to the day he disappeared, I need to know." Rafe grasped her arms. "Listen, about this morning when I said what I said."

She frowned at him. He'd changed the subject . . . sort of.

"At your house. The thing that made you mad. I didn't mean it."

Instantly suspicious, she asked, "What did you say that made me mad?"

His eyes widened. He looked to the side as if seeking escape.

"What didn't you mean?" She pressed him harder.

He struggled to speak.

"You don't know, do you?" Her phone rang. She pulled it out of her shirt pocket. "You haven't got a clue what you said, Rafe. You have never had a clue. You are faking it." Snapping her phone open, she said, "Hello!"

A man's voice said, "Could I speak to Rafe Di Luca, please?"

Holding the phone away, she looked at the number. Strange area code. Putting it back to her ear, she asked, "Who is this?"

"I'm Darren. I'm Rafe's hacker. I really need to speak to him."

Was Rafe invading every part of her life? "Rafe has a phone. You could call *him*."

"It's not that easy, Miss Petersson. If you'd let me talk to him, I'd be grateful and humble."

She snorted, and handed her phone to Rafe.

"Did you give him my number? Because I do not appreciate this."

Frowning, Rafe took her phone and put it to his ear. "Yeah?" He listened for a moment, then turned and walked into the hallway and back toward the kitchen. Brooke could hear his voice fading in the distance.

And she started counting the number of chances she'd given him, and wondered if Sarah was right.

Chapter 40

Holding Brooke's phone, Rafe walked out into Nonna's backyard and stood under the immense sweep of the live oak, flush with new leaves. He knew this place so well—the grass that thinned under the trees, the sagging shed some Di Luca had built so long ago, the tall swing Nonno had built for his son. Yet today the familiar felt different. Today he felt surrounded, scrutinized, paranoid. Paranoid in Nonna's backyard.

Damn it.

The guard stationed at the house stepped out from behind the shed. "Um, sir?" Young and gauche, he flushed under Rafe's gaze. "Everything okay, sir? Can I help with anything?"

Rafe stared at him.

Had the background check on Alden been thorough enough? Was Alden what he purported to be? Or was he a spy?

Alden flushed again. "Sir?"

Surely the kid couldn't fake those blushes. And right now, Rafe knew he would be suspicious of anyone who guarded Nonna's house.

Rafe waved him away, and Alden once more slipped out of sight.

Rafe spoke into the phone. "I don't understand, Darren. How did my phone get hacked?"

With the patience of a young man for an old duffer, Darren said, "Your phone is a computer, as powerful as I could make it. The hacker, whoever he is, controls the Wi-Fi for the resort. He accessed your phone and, hey! Now it's his."

The implications tumbled through Rafe's brain. "He's been listening in on my phone calls. He knows about you."

"He already knew about me, recognized my pattern of hacking."

"The way you expected to know his—and didn't?"

"Exactly. He's studied me, really nailed me. If he hadn't, I would have caught him by now. But as a hacker, I'm anonymous. No one really knows who I am. Taking control of your phone gave him a lot of information he didn't have before. He knows exactly who I am, where I live, what my phone number is. There's blackmail material there."

"You've had threats?"

"Nope. He's playing me." Darren sounded trapped. "My parents will be seriously unhappy if they find out what I've been doing."

"If it becomes necessary, I'll help with your parents."

"You don't know my parents. They're not going to listen to some guy they've never met just because he's a hotshot security agent."

"Yeah." Rafe stroked his chin and thought of

how Nonno and Nonna would have responded if he'd gotten up to something even vaguely illegal. "I'll help if I can, and I promise to keep you out of jail. That was the deal when I signed you, right?"

"Right." Darren took a long breath. "Thanks."

With his Kyrgyzstan team in mind, Rafe asked, "Has the mystery hacker been intercepting my calls?"

"Listening for sure. Intercepting? I don't think so. I think he'd rather just listen. He's learning a lot that way."

"Hm." Having the resort's computer hacked presented too many dangers in a situation changing too rapidly, and Rafe had control over none of it. "Does the hacker know that you know about my phone?"

"He might suspect, but nothing I've done has alerted him."

"Very good." Rafe almost purred with delight.

When Rafe said nothing more, Darren continued. "I've got a friend, Cepheus, who just started working at the resort. He's got a computer for you. It's small. It's in a case made for an e-reader. You can make phone calls on it. It won't be fun—it'll be clumsy—but it's possible. It's set up the way I want it, impregnable and, since I've uploaded a program that's keeping the hacker busy, undetectable. I want you to keep it on you all the time. The GPS will keep track of you and

I'll call you on Brooke's phone or Noah's phone or whoever's phone is nearby."

"Right." Rafe's mind had shuffled through the scenarios, and now he saw an opportunity to end this thing quickly. "Darren. Is there any way you can bring up the map of the wine cellar under the main hotel building? Could you do it without the mystery hacker knowing that you're doing it?"

"Sure. I've got my friend Scuffy running the occasional block for me. I think MH—"

"Mystery hacker?"

"Right. I think MH knows Scuffy is there, but he hasn't been able to catch him. What do you need?"

"In the wine cellar that's under the main building, there are a lot of corridors."

A moment of silence, then—"Whoa. Yeah. Here's the map. What crazy dude built this?"

"A lot of people. The main cellar was built when the original hotel went up. The halls started winding around as they added on upstairs."

"What's this room? It's reinforced like a bunker." Darren sounded curious, then excited. "Oh, man, is this a *bomb shelter?*"

"A fallout shelter, really, built by my grandfather in the late nineteen fifties during the height of the Cold War."

"To protect against nuclear radiation. I know. How cool. I didn't know anyone had a . . . a fallout shelter anymore." Darren's enthusiasm was almost palpable.

"We Di Lucas are lucky in a lot of ways," Rafe said drily. "Are there surveillance cameras in there?"

"None."

Perfect. "Is the television feed coming out of there still live?"

"A television feed. In a fallout shelter. *Really?*"

"They had televisions in those days," Rafe assured him.

"I know. With three whole channels." Darren's voice smirked.

"You're a spoiled brat," Rafe said mildly. "The TV cable went to the antenna on the roof, right? Although who they thought would be broadcasting if the atomic bomb dropped, I don't know."

Darren got serious again. "Okay, I can't tell if the feed is live. I'd have to have something that worked on both ends of the cable to tell. And if there's a TV in that fallout shelter, it's no longer functioning."

"Probably the tubes are dead."

"Sure." Darren obviously didn't have a clue.

"Where does the wire go up?" Rafe tried to remember the way the shelter sat in relationship to the rooms above. "Up the wall in the fallout shelter and into the . . . ?"

"Into the main electrical center."

"Perfect." Rafe's luck had turned. "I can tap into that easily enough."

Darren's voice grew speculative. "Is that why the electrical center is there? Because the shelter is below?"

"More likely the shelter is there because the electrical center was above." For the first time in this crappy investigation, Rafe had caught a break—and his plan could work.

Still eager, Darren said, "The whole basement is cool. You could hide a body down there."

"You could hide a lot of things down there." Which was why the location was ideal. "I want you to check for something else."

"Sure. I've got the map right here." Darren's enthusiasm was contagious.

Rafe felt his hopes rising. "Most of the corridors terminate in a bare wall, but the one with the fallout shelter on one extremity terminates with a locked door on the other."

"Right. Behind that is a big square room." Darren was typing. "I'm giving Scuffy the heads-up."

"That room," Rafe said, "is where the family hid their wines during Prohibition."

"Cool." Darren sounded pleased to know that the Di Lucas, too, had flouted the law.

"I need to know if there are security cameras in that area, and if they're compromised."

"All the cameras are compromised. But wait a

second; I'm having Scuffy check—yes! You've got a nice array there. He's sending me the feed, and if I'm looking at the right place, there are wine racks but not many bottles stashed there. Mostly there are some really big-ass old wine barrels. I mean really big."

"That's the place." Rafe went to sit on the back porch steps. "Are there microphones in there?"

"No. No microphones down below at all."

"Better and better. That's what I needed. Thanks, Darren." Rafe started to hang up, then remembered and asked, "Have you had any luck regaining control of the security program?"

"I've got twenty-four hours," Darren reminded him.

"Don't worry. We'll wrap this up tonight." Rafe hung up, dug out his own phone, and called Noah. "Hey, bro."

"Bro?" Noah snorted. "Since when do you call me—"

"I'm worried about that special bottle we were talking about." Rafe figured Noah was going to catch on fast. "Is it still in the same place?"

"That special bottle . . ." Rafe heard the moment Noah snapped to attention. "As far as I know, it is. You worried about it? You think they found it?"

This conversation should command MH's attention. Rafe hoped his eyes were bugging out of his ugly, treacherous head.

"I'm up at Nonna's now," Rafe said. "I'm coming down, and we need to check on it."

"Right. I'll meet you in the lobby."

"I'll be there right away." Rafe hung up, satisfied for the first time in days.

Eli had demanded the situation be fixed by the time he came back.

Rafe had the matter well in hand.

He entered the kitchen, calling for Nonna and Brooke.

Brooke rushed down the hall toward him, her finger on her lips. "She's asleep."

In dismay, he said, "I've got to go back."

"More problems?" Brooke's blue eyes grew wide.

"The problems we have are enough, don't you think?" It wasn't an answer.

But she didn't notice. "Is there anything I can help with?"

God forbid. "Not this time, Brooke. As Eli pointed out, I made the mess. I had better clean it up." He touched her cheek with his fingertip. When this was over, the two of them were going to have a long talk about the past, the present, the future. . . . The thought of long talks, especially with Brooke, made him queasy. But not talking damned sure wasn't working either, and Mrs. Petersson's biting criticism echoed in his mind.

What kind of relationship do you have that you

don't talk to her about your job? About what matters to you? About your plans?

So he'd bite the bullet and have a conversation . . . later.

For now, he needed to tell her one important fact. "The reason Darren called on your phone is because mine has been hacked."

"What?" She glared at him as if she blamed him. "Hacked? How?"

"The same way the security cameras were hacked. So listen carefully. If you need me in the next few hours, I'm meeting with Noah. Call him—and be careful what you say."

"Right. Sure. Because your phone is hacked." She sounded incredulous.

"Exactly. I'm going to send Bao out here to join you." He made the call on her phone. "If you see a guy lurking outside, it's the guard I set on the house. His name's Alden. He's got brown hair and he looks like he had a good time at the beach, because he's got one hell of a sunburn. Until Bao arrives, if you see anyone else— *anyone else*—hanging around, you call nine-one-one and scream your head off."

"I will," she promised.

"If at any point in the rest of the day you're in trouble or think you're in trouble or smell trouble, call nine-one-one."

"And scream my head off?"

"Yes."

She glanced toward the bedroom where Nonna was sleeping. "Rafe, you're scaring me. I mean . . . scaring me more."

"I don't think you need to be scared. I think you need to be cautious." He pulled the keys out of his pocket. "Hang on. In the next few hours there'll be some big changes and this will all be over." He gestured toward the front door. "When Nonna wakes up, get a car from the resort."

"I'll make sure she gets back to rehab . . . although not on time for her next session. I'll call them and cancel all her appointments." Brooke removed her phone from his hand.

"Okay." Pulling her toward him, he held her tightly, relishing her warm vitality. "I don't want to lose you now." Letting her go, he walked out to the Mustang and drove away.

Chapter 41

When Rafe got back to Bella Terra Resort, he went first to his cottage and picked up the tools he needed, then to the electrical room where he located the antenna cable coming up from the fallout shelter. With a flashlight held between his teeth, he cut the power to the main building—alarms sounded everywhere—and with a few quick slashes he cut and spliced a transmitter onto the cable. He flipped the power back on and scooted out before the on-site electricians arrived to check out the problem.

He hoped to hell the outage had done something awful to Mystery Hacker. Given him a shock to the ass if nothing else.

In the lobby, Rafe found Noah behind the concierge desk, showing someone Rafe did not recognize the tourist maps and literature.

Glancing up, Noah made eye contact with Rafe and gestured him over. He spoke to the concierge-in-training for a few more minutes, then told the well-groomed young man, "If you have any questions, Robert, you can ask the desk staff. They know the drill, too."

"Thank you, Mr. Di Luca. I'll do that."

"Hang on a minute, Rafe. Let me give the floor

manager a heads-up that I'm leaving Robert on his own." Noah walked away.

Robert turned to Rafe. "Excuse me, are you Rafe Di Luca?"

"Yes."

"Someone left this for you." Robert handed him a black, scuffed, padded flat case zipped on two sides.

Rafe eyed it in puzzlement.

"I think it's an e-reader," Robert said.

"Oh!" Rafe considered Robert.

This young man looked as if he were in college . . . a church college. He wore a dark suit, white shirt, and blue tie, his hair was cut conservatively, and his blue eyes were calm and focused.

"What's your name again?" Rafe asked.

"You might know me as Cepheus." Robert didn't blink. "I hope you enjoy using the e-reader. I certainly enjoy mine. I especially like viewing mystery-feed video on it."

Robert was Cepheus? He didn't even wear glasses, and he had a tan, so obviously he spent time outside in the sun.

Wow. A hacker who didn't live in his parents' basement. Who knew?

Noah rejoined Rafe and grimly said, "So many guests have checked out, it's a good time to train a new concierge—especially with Victor sitting in jail."

Rafe led the way out of the lobby and down the hall toward Noah's office. "Victor hasn't confessed, has he?" Rafe asked.

"No, he says he left the bar about fifteen minutes after he went in, but he has no alibi. Nobody believes he did it, though."

Remembering the distinguished South American, knowing the trust Brooke had put in him, Rafe didn't believe it, either. "If he had, it would be damned stupid to be the one to report the damage."

"Right. But why not tell us where he was and what he was doing?"

"I don't know. It would save everyone a lot of trouble. But nothing about this case has been easy." Rafe checked his old phone, then unzipped the e-reader case and checked the new one. *C'mon, Team Kyrgyzstan.*

Noah smirked at Rafe. "So, *bro,* what are we doing?"

"Remember when the three of us were kids and played hide-and-seek in the wine cellar?"

"Yeah." Noah sounded cautious.

"Remember when you hid in the big old wine barrel and we couldn't find you, so we turned off the lights and locked the door?"

"Remember? How could I forget? You little assholes. I'm still scarred."

"You were always dumping us to go look up some little girl's dress. We thought you had sneaked away again."

"Finding the light switch was the best moment of my life."

"The best moment? Even including getting laid the first time?"

"Well . . . maybe not the best moment." Noah opened the door to his office, then blocked the entrance. "Are you just tormenting me, or we headed anywhere with this?"

"Tormenting you for sure. But get the keys and come with me. We're going down." Rafe pointed toward the floor.

"The basement? Really?" Noah looked Rafe over, noting the dark sports coat and pressed blue shirt. "You're kind of snazzy for a visit to the underworld."

"After last night, I've taken to carrying a gun all the time, and I like that holster hidden. Plus, this jacket is tailor-made for me, with a few extra pockets for the equipment I have stashed."

"You are looking a little lumpy." Noah dug in his desk drawer and extricated a large, old-fashioned iron key. "But I thought you'd just eaten too many of Chef's desserts."

"That, too." The thought of finally gaining control of this situation made Rafe happy as he had never imagined. "It's about to get very interesting around here."

The two brothers went into the closet that hid the door to the basement. They thrust the key into the massive old lock and worked for ten minutes before they got it to turn. Light spilled down the stairs only a little way as the two brothers descended gingerly into the cool cellar. Noah groped for the light switch.

When he flipped it, dimly illuminating the hotel's underbelly, Rafe whistled in amazement. "It hasn't changed a bit." The place smelled earthy, like a tomb, and on the ceiling a series of bare bulbs reached into the darkness in two directions along the echoing length of corridor lined with dusty wine racks and the occasional discarded piece of furniture.

"You ought to clean this up," Rafe said.

"No way. If I told Ebrillwen what was down here, she'd have her maids scrubbing the concrete floors once a week."

"We'll deal with the fallout shelter first," Rafe decided and turned left.

"Haven't been in there for years." Noah's lip curled in disgust. "It's like a moment of ugly panic frozen in time."

"Glad to hear I'm not the only one who thinks so."

They walked the hundred feet to an ironclad door, pushed it open and hit the light switch.

The room looked exactly as it had in nineteen fifty-nine, with bunk beds, shelves filled with canned goods, a table covered with a red-checked tablecloth, and a television console wider and taller than the screen it housed.

Noah indicated the three bright orange chairs grouped around the TV. "A lot of Naugas died to make that furniture." When Rafe just stared at him, he said, "You know? Because they're upholstered in Naugahyde?"

"Bad joke." Rafe looked around. "But my hacker was right. There are no cameras in here."

"I didn't see the need," Noah said.

"Good man." Going to the TV, Rafe unhooked the antenna cable, pulled the length of it toward the door, and when he knew for sure he had a clear line of sight to the other end of the corridor, he spliced a receiver onto that end.

Noah watched with fascination. "Why are we down here?"

"We're setting a trap." Rafe dusted his fingers, stowed his tools, checked the alignment on the receiver once more. Looking at his brother, he said, "We're going to get the bastard."

"How?"

"Watch and learn, little brother."

"God, you're obnoxious," Noah said with fraternal loathing.

Rafe grinned—obnoxiously—and led the way out of the fallout shelter. When Noah turned off the light, Rafe glanced back to see if the receiver was visible to the casual eye.

It was not.

"If we set the bait correctly," Rafe said, "our man will be so anxious to get his hands on his reward he won't check to see what we did in there."

"What did we do in there?" Noah asked.

"I worked my video magic. Listen, when we're in the corridor, we're being watched, so keep that in mind." As they walked, Rafe noted the locations of the cameras, and noted that they smoothly followed them as they passed.

Noah glanced at the cameras, too. "Do you know who's watching us?"

"Not yet. That's what we're here to find out. Be calm. Talk casually." Rafe was glad to have Noah with him. His little brother had kept a cool head through this whole ordeal. "Do you keep wine down here anymore?"

"Okay . . . the wine. For the most part, the bottles down here are so old they're not viable. Or they're empty. If Eli wants to experiment with a different grape or use the old barrels to create a different flavor, we'll store them down here. We started that after one of the winery employees messed up and added a barrel of carignan to Eli's zin bottling. God, what a mess that was! I haven't seen Eli that mad since . . . Well, he was madder this morning." Noah stopped and faced Rafe. "I've never seen him lose it like that."

"I'm honored to be the cause of Eli's biggest shit-fit." In fact, Eli had always been such a good, steady guy, facing his own problems without complaint and helping Rafe and Noah through theirs, that every time Rafe thought of Eli's frank assessment of his competence, he felt worse.

"I don't know. He's always quiet, but ever since Nonna was attacked—well, actually, I noticed a little before that—he's been positively withdrawn."

"Woman problems?"

"Just because *you've* got woman problems, Rafe, doesn't mean the rest of the world does."

Rafe started walking again.

Noah caught up with him. "No, I don't know what Eli's problem is."

"Did you ask?"

"Nonna did. Eli said he was fine and nothing was wrong."

"Right."

The two brothers walked companionably to the door leading to that last room in the depths.

Noah put the key in the lock. "You found out what Nonna knows, didn't you?"

"Yeah, I did." While Noah struggled to turn the key, Rafe told him the history of Massimo's wine and Joseph Bianchin's grudge—when Noah realized Bianchin had been behind the attack on Nonna, Noah broke his promise to be cool, but Rafe figured it was okay. All the MH could see was Noah doing what looked like a native dance across hot coals.

When Noah finished his fit of temper, Rafe

surreptitiously showed him the old, skunked bottle of wine he'd brought from Nonna's cellar and hidden in the inside lower pocket of his jacket, as well as the miniature satellite network cameras he'd retrieved from his room. "I'm going to put the bottle in the barrel, without the MH seeing me; then you're going to pull it out and show it to me as if you'd just retrieved it. We're going to grin and celebrate. Then you're going to make a fool of yourself. Pretend to drink it, almost drop it . . . I don't care what you do, but keep those cameras and whoever is watching focused on you."

"I can make a fool of myself," Noah assured him.

"I know it."

Noah punched him on the arm.

Rafe punched Noah back.

"What are you going to do?" Noah asked.

"I'm going to place my cameras around the room, and these cameras will record who comes to retrieve this very special bottle of wine. They'll send the signal to the transmitter I'll place at the back of the room. That'll transmit to the receiver in the fallout shelter, which will send the signal up the antenna wire to the secure transmitter above. Since the entire system bypasses Bella Terra's security system, the video will go to my nonhacked computer and we'll catch our perp."

"And beat him up?" Noah asked hopefully.

"Well. If he were to struggle when he was arrested, he might be accidentally injured." Rafe and Noah exchanged retaliatory smiles. "The good thing about these cameras is that placement is simple and fast—pull off the protective strip and place the adhesive wherever I want. So . . . I'll place a few, come over and argue with you, place a few, come back and put the bottle back in the barrel and give you a lock to put on it. . . ."

"Got it." Noah turned the handle and they were in.

Rafe scrutinized the area. "There are more barrels than I remember."

"We haven't changed it a bit."

"The lighting sucks."

"Well, pardon me."

"No, that's good. He won't see the cameras, but we'll see him."

Noah headed toward the biggest barrel, six feet around, eight feet long, and resting sideways on a stand. "This is it." A small trapdoor had been cut into the flat side facing the entrance.

Rafe swung it open and the odor of old wine-permeated wood wafted out. "Wow. After all these years."

"I smelled like that for days after I crawled in here."

"Really? I thought you smelled like flop sweat."

"Little assholes," Noah muttered again.

Rafe slipped the bottle into the barrel. "Okay, now pull it out like it's been there all along."

Noah reached in and brought out the bottle.

The two brothers looked at it in assumed awe.

Noah's awe actually consisted of, "You substituted that cheap skunky cabernet that bimbo girlfriend of Pop's brought Nonna for Christmas? What was that girl's name?"

"Don't you remember? Tab-ith-a." Rafe pronounced it exactly as she had.

"She thought the joke label was so funny."

"So the bottle's finally good for something." Rafe wandered toward one of the smaller barrels, stripped the protective strip off the first camera, stuck it slightly behind the iron hoop, and pointed it toward Noah.

Noah held the bottle up to the light to read the label. "Château de Wretched. You think the perp's not going to notice that?"

"I doubt it. He'll be excited about the prospect of making his fortune. He'll look at the year—"

Noah glanced at the bottle. "Which is, by the way, 11935."

"—think it's some weird notation Massimo did, and make a run for it." Rafe stuck a camera into one of the wine slots.

Noah lifted the bottle and pretended to drink, then performed a pratfall so realistic Rafe leaped toward him to catch the wine. When Noah came up grinning, Rafe wanted to strangle him. "Damn it! You scared the hell out of me. If you'd dropped that bottle, this plan would be worthless."

Noah burst into laughter. "Remember when Chevy Chase came home with Dad and taught me to fall?"

Rafe's heart beat hard and fast. "Forget it. *SNL* doesn't want you."

"I don't know. If I can scare the hell out of you, I'm doing something right." Noah pretended to drink again, then to spit it on the floor.

Rafe palmed one of the tiny cameras and handed it to Noah. "When you put the bottle back, lean all the way in and stick this inside pointing right at the opening."

"Aren't you afraid the perp'll see it when he reaches for the bottle?"

"I'm afraid this is a stupid plan and probably won't put the guy in jail unless we can prove he hacked your security and murdered Luis Hernández, but at least we'll know his identity." Rafe watched Noah lean in and replace the bottle. "I've got more than broken wine bottles to worry about. That bastard hurt my grandmother . . . and he's stalking Brooke. I'm going to take him out."

Chapter 42

The car returned Nonna, Bao and Brooke to the hospital. Bao stood guard while the driver helped put Nonna in a wheelchair.

"I'll be about a half hour," Brooke told him.

"I won't keep her any longer than necessary, young man," Nonna told him.

He smiled at her—who could resist her charm?—and touched his cap. "Take your time, Mrs. Di Luca. I've got instructions to drive you wherever you need to go. Miss Petersson, when you're ready, give me a call and I'll pick you up at the entrance."

The check-in took only a few minutes, and after looking at Nonna's cheerful face, none of the nurses said a word of reproach. Brooke gave Nonna a good-bye kiss, nodded to Bao, and headed toward the hospital lobby. And her phone rang. She pulled it from her pocket and looked.

Private caller. She answered.

Gagnon's warm, French-accented voice purred in her ear. "*Chérie*, it is I, Gagnon. I've done as you asked and you were absolutely right."

"I love to hear that I'm right . . . except in this instance."

"An anonymous buyer has placed a standing order for Massimo's wines: He wants them by any means. The reward is substantial, and there's buzz among the community that a bottle exists in your little town, one that could bring the discoverer untold wealth."

"Oh, no." Would Nonna ever be able to live alone, in safety, again?

"Word is that a person of power is handling the matter—"

Brooke stopped by the elevators. "Joseph Bianchin."

"Do you know that? Because no one has any information on where the matter originates."

"I don't *know*. But my suspicions are justified." She started toward the lobby and out the door.

"Interesting." His voice lingered over the word.

"What else?" The air was fresh, sunshine bright and warm.

"A couple of men who tried to interrupt the acquisition process have been killed already."

"Luis Hernández."

"Yes."

"And Cruz Flores."

"Yes."

Brooke leaned against the rough stucco wall, warm from the sun, but the cold struck clear to her bones. She breathed deeply, trying to ease the constriction in her chest.

Gagnon sounded concerned, almost as if he

knew she felt faint. "If the current operators don't get the job done soon, there's going to be a rush on Bella Valley."

"So the people who are working it now have the incentive to be ruthless killers." She already knew that. She really did. But saying it made it so much more real.

"They do indeed." Gagnon's voice became very, very serious. "Be very careful, *ma chérie*. You are in the center of a firestorm. You know too much, and I am not happy with what's happening in Bella Terra."

"I can't run away."

"I know that."

"I can't abandon my mother or Nonna."

"Your character is too strong for fear."

She laughed. "Not true. I'm terrified."

"Not terrified enough."

"I do know how to protect myself. When I was a kid, my mother made sure I took self-defense, and I teach kickboxing here at the resort." With a smile, Brooke said, "I'm a killing machine."

Gagnon did not sound amused. "It is one thing to know how to hurt another person. It is another to be willing to actually do it. Sadly, you seem to me to be a gentle soul who avoids violence. . . . Remember, *ma chérie*, in a choice between you and the other guy, it's better to cry over their spilled blood than to have your mother weep over your casket."

"Wow. Thanks for that uplifting lecture."

"*Chérie* . . ."

At that warning tone in his voice, she got serious in a hurry. "I know. I understand. Strike first, apologize later. I will remember."

"I should take you away from there right now."

His words struck a chill that went clear to her bones. "Gagnon, I adore you. But I would take that very badly."

"Ah, but you would be alive."

A few more comments and they hung up, leaving Brooke with the feeling that Gagnon was sincerely worried about her and her safety. How uncomfortable was that, knowing a man she suspected of being an international criminal thought her life was in danger?

Recalling the corpse that had risen like a horror show from the Dumpster, she felt sick all over again. And this time, Rafe wasn't there to love her out of her fear. She knew, too, that he would soon solve the trouble that stalked Bella Terra and once again disappear from her life.

Her mother was right: Brooke would need a real change to distract her from the violence and the murders . . . and her own loneliness.

But right now, not even Sweden sounded good.

The driver must have seen her standing there, for he drove up and hopped out. He opened the door for her, and only when she started to slide in did he see her face, for he asked, "Are you all right?"

"I'm fine, thank you."

He shut the door and came around to the driver's seat. As he put the car in motion, he said, "It's the hospital, isn't it? The hospital is a trial for most people."

"No, it's not the hospital."

He glanced in the rearview mirror and met her eyes. "You found the gardener's body. That must have been tough."

Bella Terra always ran a background check on their drivers. But right now, after lifting Hernández from among the garbage last night, and with Rafe's warnings ringing in her head and Gagnon's alarm, she looked at the pleasant-looking, formally dressed gentleman and wondered whether he was going to drive her to some secluded place and murder her.

He didn't.

But right now, everyone looked like a suspect.

When they pulled into the resort's parking lot, she thanked him profusely, then walked swiftly along the paths toward her cottage, avoiding the guests, the employees, and any potential muggers lurking in the bushes. With a sigh of relief, she let herself into her home. She locked the door and set the dead bolt . . . not that she wasn't good about locking her doors. Any single woman with the slightest shred of a brain took that precaution, but—

An African-American man, tall and broad, with long hair and colorful tattoos, stepped out of her kitchen.

She screamed.

Chapter 43

Zachary held up his hands. "Please, Miss Petersson, I'm sorry. I'm sorry! I wasn't trying to scare you, but I wanted to talk and I didn't want to do it where, you know, people could see us."

Brooke put her hand on her racing heart. "Zachary, if I had a gun on me, you'd be dead right now." Then she cursed herself for admitting she wasn't carrying a gun. Because she liked Zachary, and admired the drive that had taken the big man from a Southern prison to the head of gardening at a California resort. But she'd seen that body in the Dumpster close up—and Luis Hernández had been one of Zachary's employees.

He seemed to read her mind, though, because he stayed where he was, kept his hands in the air, and waited for her to decide whether to scream again and run.

That helped. "How did you get in?"

"I have access to the resort master key."

"Right. What's up?" she asked.

Zachary sighed. "I've got to talk to someone. I thought you'd be the most likely to listen."

"You know something about Luis's murder?" She told herself she wasn't scared. But she didn't walk any closer.

And he didn't lower his hands. "I don't know anything. That's part of the problem. Please understand; I know I'm not one to point fingers. I've made my mistakes, and they were big ones. But I've been getting bad vibes from one of my guys, and when that body turned up in the Dumpster . . ." He waggled his giant head. "I wasn't going to say anything. He's supposed to leave as soon as he gets the money for college. Except I think that he's planning on getting a lot of money and not going back to college, and I think he needs to go to prison. Or rather, back to prison."

Brooke's heart sank. "Are you talking about Josh Hoffman?" Bright, handsome, hometown Josh, who always talked about going to college.

"Yes, ma'am. He's got . . . problems. You know how he volunteers to catch those gophers? That's because he likes to pull their legs off and watch 'em try to run away."

Brooke shuddered and wrapped her arms around herself.

"Yes, ma'am, that's gross." Zachary's slow, Southern-accented voice rumbled with distaste. "I knew guys like that in prison, and they were always in there for torture or rape or murder, usually all three."

She took a long breath. "Why haven't you said something to somebody?"

"First—it's not against the law to torture

gophers. There's lots of folks with lawns who think gophers deserve to die."

"But they kill them. They don't torment them."

"Yes, ma'am. As far as I'm concerned, that is a big difference." Zachary was still immobile, his hands in the air. "Then there's the other thing. This is America. It's a great country. I recognize that in any other country in the world I couldn't have changed my life. But still, a black former convict is going to think twice before he accuses a handsome college-bound white boy of bad things, especially without proof."

He had a point, a good one. "You said Josh had been in prison?"

"Some foreign prison in Asia. He's got a tattoo on his shoulder that I've seen on other convicts. I don't know what it says, but I'm pretty sure it's not 'Welcome to Macy's.' "

The two of them looked at each other, making judgments and decisions.

Brooke nodded. "Thanks for telling me. I'll pass this on right away."

"If you can, you'll keep my name out of it? Because even if he has nothing to do with the goings-on here at Bella Terra, that young man Josh is not someone I want to get cross of."

"I promise." If Zachary was right, they had found not only their hacker, but also their murderer, and as Brooke remembered Josh's height and strength, she realized she should avoid him at all costs.

"Now, Miss Brooke," Zachary said, "I'm going to keep my hands up over my head and head toward your back door. Hopefully no one will see me and we'll both come out of this without anyone noticing we had a conversation."

"Yes. Thank you." She watched him back toward the kitchen and open the door.

"Listen to me. I'm going to secure this"—he twisted the lock on the doorknob—"but as soon as I'm out of here, I want you to use the dead bolt. I'm sure Mr. Rafe has told you you're in danger, and I'd feel guilty if you disappeared like poor Luis."

"I'll shoot that dead bolt," she said.

Zachary shut the door behind him.

She darted across the kitchen and flipped the dead bolt, then leaned against the wall, her heart racing.

She knew what to do now.

Grabbing her cell, she started to call Noah—but if Rafe's phone was compromised, possibly hers was, also. And maybe Noah's. She couldn't call nine-one-one yet, not without involving Zachary. But the house phones—they were busy all the time with calls from the guests. The murderer didn't have time to listen to every line, and Brooke could call from the lobby.

So she did. She walked to the lobby and called Noah on the house phone, and when he didn't pick up, she left a message. Then she went in search of Madelyn.

She had questions to ask, private questions that could change both their lives . . . again.

A dozen twelve-inch monitors alternated views of the corridors and pathways of the resort, and on one, Josh Hoffman watched Brooke head into the main building and pick up the phone in the lobby. He almost didn't listen in, because on the big monitor he was watching the Di Luca brothers exult over their bottle of wine, and that was pretty damned entertaining. But Brooke had proved both a great distraction for Rafe, and a troublesome problem for Josh. So he groped for the phone and heard Brooke say something that got his attention.

"Noah, I need to talk to Rafe." She hesitated. "It's about one of the gardeners."

Josh leaned forward.

She continued. "I'm going to find Madelyn— I've had a thought. You can try my cell, but it occurred to me it might be, um, bugged. . . ." She trailed off as if uncertain.

Josh jerked. Had they discovered Rafe's phone had been hacked?

Brooke continued. "No matter what, I'm not leaving the grounds, so come find me."

Josh put down the phone. He looked back at the monitor.

Noah wouldn't be receiving that call. Not while he was underground. And Rafe wouldn't be picking up the message from his girlfriend. If Josh had anything to say about it, he would never talk to her again.

Chapter 44

Brooke poked her head into Housekeeping. Ebrillwen stood with a clipboard resting on one arm and a pencil in her hand, making an inventory of cleaning supplies. "Ebrillwen, where do you have Madelyn working?"

Ebrillwen looked over the top of her black-framed reading glasses. "In the bar. I wanted to keep her close today in case she had problems after yesterday's Dumpster incident."

"That's very thoughtful of you." Although "thoughtful" was not the term Brooke usually associated with Ebrillwen.

"It's simply good management," Ebrillwen said frostily.

"Of course." Brooke subdued a smile. "Could I speak with her?"

Ebrillwen sighed. "Yes, although this continued disruption of service is playing hell with my schedule."

"I know," Brooke said in apology. "I wouldn't ask if it weren't important."

Ebrillwen put her clipboard on her desk, slipped the pencil behind her ear, and clicked into her pager. "I have summoned her. Would your desire to speak with Madelyn have anything to do with what happened with her husband?"

Brooke widened her eyes, all innocence and

wonder—and at the same time, she was horrified at the turn of the conversation. "Husband? Madelyn is married?"

"Her husband." Ebrillwen enunciated each word. "The criminal now deceased—Cruz Flores."

Brooke thought hard and fast.

Either Ebrillwen managed to figure out the whole situation by herself, or Madelyn had spilled her guts. And while Brooke had the greatest respect for Ebrillwen's acuity, Brooke had even more respect for Ebrillwen's ability to interrogate any subject until she cracked—Madelyn being the subject in this case. "Madelyn told you she had been married to Cruz Flores?"

"She told me everything. She married Flores out of a misguided desire to get him his green card—"

"And because she was pregnant," Brooke said.

"Once he had his green card, it quickly became clear to her he was a thug and a drug dealer and would eventually kill her and her daughter." Ebrillwen spoke confidently. "When he almost did, she disappeared off the face of the earth. She's been safe at Bella Terra."

"At the time, I didn't know what her problem was." Madelyn's skittishness had broken Brooke's heart. "I only knew she was frightened."

"Like the animal he was, he tracked her here,

stalked her for a while, scared her enough that she got a gun . . . and when he trapped her while she was cleaning a hotel room, she shot him."

Every detail was correct. Madelyn really had spilled her guts.

Brooke saw no point in lying to Ebrillwen—but she would like to put the facts to her in such a way that Ebrillwen would understand and condone what she had done. "If the cops had investigated Madelyn for murder, they would have discovered she was working under an alias, they would have treated her as if she were the criminal, and they would have taken her little girl away from her. Neither Madelyn nor her daughter deserved that, and I knew if I said I'd killed Flores, I could get out of the charge without jail time."

Ebrillwen folded her arms over her chest. "I told her she should tell the police the truth."

"Good God!" Here was trouble. "Why?"

"While I respect your desire to do the right thing for Madelyn, you didn't take into account all the consequences of these actions. She has parents, parents of strong and proper morals who disowned her when she married Flores. She wants to see them. She wants her daughter to meet them. She can't explain to them that she's assumed an alias." Ebrillwen's own strict moral code was evident in the starch of her words.

"I didn't know. She didn't tell me. There wasn't time."

"After the shooting, you mean? Yes, I understand; you had to make quick decisions without knowing all the facts." Ebrillwen's comment was kind, but she continued speaking of Madelyn, making it clear she had thoroughly discussed the situation with the young woman. "Once Madelyn has achieved contact with her parents, she wants to go back to school, to get a different job, become a teacher or a counselor. For all that, she needs to assume her real identity."

Brooke stopped protesting. "Yes, she does."

"There'll be trouble . . . for you both," Ebrillwen warned.

"Yeah, thanks." But Brooke wasn't really angry.

"In the end, while the police will have to slap both of your hands for falsifying the events, they can hardly prosecute Madelyn for the killing any more than they did you. Especially since it was, as you both claimed, self-defense. In the end, she'll come out without undue distress."

"Yes. Good point." With wry amusement, Brooke realized it would be as Ebrillwen declared, because Ebrillwen had declared it. "I still want to talk to her, though, because at the time, she didn't know how Cruz had tracked her from L.A."

Ebrillwen looked at her pager and frowned. "Where is that girl?"

An ugly thought occurred to Brooke. "Rafe's phone has been hacked. Perhaps your pager has been compromised, too?"

"Come on, then. Briskly." Ebrillwen headed out the door, Brooke on her heels. "What do you hope to discover from her?"

"Before the police arrived, Madelyn went through Flores's pockets, said she wanted any money he had on him. Said he owed it to her daughter." Brooke hadn't argued. She figured it was true.

Ebrillwen nodded. "So she told me."

"She took everything he had on him. I want to know if she found anything more than money on him—a letter or a notice offering a reward for retrieving an object of value for an unknown buyer."

Ebrillwen stopped. She turned on her heel. Her horror was palpable. "You think he was here for some reason other than the fact that he tracked Madelyn down?"

"I think it's a strong possibility." Had Flores been the first man Bianchin had brought in to retrieve Massimo's bottle of wine? Had he accidentally set up the tragic reunion between Flores and Madelyn, and then had to hire someone else, someone local? Had he hired Josh Hoffman?

Chapter 45

In the wine bar, the glass doors that protected the wines still hung open, some with broken hinges. Plastic garbage cans filled with glass shards lined the walls of the bar. Most of the wine had been mopped up, but the fruity, aged oak odor still permeated the air.

A gloomy Tom Chan worked behind the bar, doing an inventory of the bottles left intact.

Madelyn was not here.

"Mr. Chan, where is my housekeeper?" Ebrillwen asked.

"She left about an hour ago." He sighed heavily as he wiped off a bottle of wine.

"She left?" Ebrillwen was clearly horrified. "Where did she go?"

"I don't know." Tom read the label; then through tearful eyes, he looked at Brooke. "At least the bastard missed the 1968 Mosberger cabernet."

"How did she leave?" Brooke felt bad for Tom, but there was more at stake here than the fate of his bar.

"She walked out." He placed the wine on the bar with the lineup of other stained and battered bottles, then reached for another.

"Did she say anything?" Ebrillwen asked.

"I'm not her boss!" he said in exasperation.

With frosty disdain, Ebrillwen said, "No, Mr. Chan, I am, and I'm trying to ascertain why my employee abandoned her post."

Tom was a sweet guy, in no way able to stand against a hard-ass like Ebrillwen. Meekly he said, "She was sort of muttering to herself about a man. . . . Spotted somebody out the window, I think, because she jumped up all of a sudden and left."

Ebrillwen looked directly at Brooke. "That is not like the girl. She is supremely responsible."

Brooke's niggle of panic was growing. "Do you think she's gone to check on her daughter?"

"Her daughter is in school. We dropped her off on the way to work this morning."

"Do you think she went to the police?" Brooke asked.

"She was by no means convinced she should do so. She was, as you said, frightened she would lose her child." Ebrillwen drew herself up. "Besides, surely she would have done so in her off-hours."

"Right. Try paging her again."

"I've paged her twice." But Ebrillwen did it again.

Tom Chan now watched them with concern. "You ladies are sure worried about one housekeeper."

A movement outside the windows caught Brooke's gaze.

Josh walked through the lush garden outside the wine bar, looked inside, and smiled broadly at Brooke—and winked.

Every nerve in Brooke's body tightened in fear. "Did you see that?"

"That very handsome young man?" Ebrillwen looked down her nose at Brooke as if suspecting her of lascivious thoughts. "Yes, he works here."

"I suspect he killed Luis Hernández." As Brooke said the words out loud, she realized she believed Zachary. Something about Josh was just . . . off, like spoiled meat or old milk. "If he has Madelyn somewhere . . ."

Ebrillwen's alabaster complexion became ashen. "Why would he do that? Why?"

"Because if it's true"—the memory of that smile and wink sent a chill down Brooke's spine—"if Flores came because he was working a job and Madelyn has the papers to prove there is a job, Madelyn is a threat."

"To Josh?"

"To the man who hired him."

Tom picked up the house phone. "I'm calling the police."

"I'm going after him." Ebrillwen strode out the door.

Brooke started after her.

Tom Chan grabbed her arm. "I usually keep a pistol behind the bar. Of course, it disappeared when the bar was vandalized. But listen, if you suspect this guy, don't chase him without a weapon. Take this." He ripped the foil off a scuffed bottle of champagne and handed it to her.

He was crazy. Tom Chan was crazy.

"It'll work," he assured her. "Take the wire off from around the cork, shake it up, aim it, and pull the cork. Even if you don't pull the cork, it'll pop on its own within a few minutes. Delayed release. A time bomb."

"Right. Thank you." She ran after Ebrillwen.

"Plus you can carry that and none of the guests will think a thing about it," he called after her. Then he said, "Oh, hell," and limped toward Noah's office.

Chapter 46

Noah and Rafe relaxed in Noah's office. Rafe's new, secure computer was propped up against the lamp, and both men watched the feed from the wine cellar and talked desultorily.

"When do you figure he's going in?" Noah stretched back in his office chair behind his desk and hooked his hands behind his head.

"Soon." Jacket off, Rafe leaned against the two-drawer file cabinet. "The way these things usually work is—the thief has so much time to acquire the merchandise before he's done."

"Done how? They kill him?"

Rafe laughed. "Wishful thinking. You've been watching too many movies."

"This guy already killed at least one person and attacked Nonna. It's more than just wishful thinking." Noah's smile was bright, toothy . . . vengeful. "It's preplanning."

Rafe's amusement faded. "It's a policy in my company that we try not to get ourselves arrested when we apprehend a perp. I do think this guy is getting anxious—the escalating violence means he's desperate. Why else would you do things guaranteed to call attention to yourself?"

"Desperate equals sloppy?"

"In this case, it does. Assuming Bianchin is behind all this, he's ordered a pickup, not a hit."

Rafe paused, then added, "But he's not too picky about how the job is done."

Noah seemed fascinated by the details. "How do you know he didn't order a hit?"

"I don't, but murder entails prison time, and I'm guessing he's smart enough to avoid committing himself to violent intentions. The people causing the problems usually make sure there's a lot of distance between them and the crime. They aren't the ones who get caught, and if they do, they don't get prosecuted for the worst charge." *Damn it.*

"I could kill the old fart myself." Noah's voice came from deep in his chest, the growl of a fighter who had seen his grandmother injured and his business hurt by the malice of one selfish man.

Ten minutes passed in silence.

"This is boring," Noah said.

"Mind-numbing," Rafe agreed. "And you thought I had a glamorous job."

"Another dream crushed." Noah turned to the computer on his desk. "If you'll watch the monitor for a while, I'll do some of my glamorous job—accounting."

"Our lives are the envy of millions," Rafe said drily. Picking up the computer, he wandered toward one of the chairs and sat. He perched the computer on his knee, halved the screen, and brought up a game of solitaire.

Five games in, he still hadn't won and the cellar remained stubbornly empty. The afternoon was getting late, and for the first time he wondered whether the perp was suspicious. Had he seen Rafe remove the bottle from under his coat? Had he noticed Rafe place his cameras? Or his transmitters? That would thoroughly suck.

A faint knock sounded at the door.

Rafe flipped the cellar to full screen, stood, and looked out the peephole. "Uh-oh."

"Who is it?" Noah asked.

Taking a long breath, Rafe opened the door. "Hi, Mom. What's up?"

Francesca burst into the room with all the exuberance and emotion of the Italian drama queen that she was. "Rafe! Is it true? Have the wicked *polizia* dragged Victor to prison?"

Oh, God. What role was she performing now?

With great care, he placed his monitor on Noah's desk. "I wouldn't call DuPey wicked, but yes, Victor's in custody."

Noah stood. "Won't you take a seat, Francesca?"

"Ah, Noah, good afternoon." She smiled at him with all the pleasure she always showed for Rafe's family. "Thank you, but I cannot sit. Not while this injustice continues. Victor is not guilty of any misdeed!"

Not now, Mom, I'm really busy. But Rafe couldn't say that—not if she knew something

371

that would spring Victor from jail. "Probably he's not, but he can't provide an alibi."

"I can provide the alibi." She struck a pose. "He was with me!"

Victor and his mother? Rafe wanted to slam his head against the wall—or hers. "Another affair?"

"No. No!" Her nostrils flared in disdain. "I would not sleep with that man if he begged me on bended knees. But he was with me."

Rafe looked at his brother for help.

Noah grinned, sat back down, and settled in to enjoy the show.

"Really?" Rafe glanced at the monitor.

It wouldn't save him. Still nothing moved in the cellar.

He returned his attention to his mother. "I mean, really? Because if you're on some imaginary mission to save some guy who's been respectful to you—"

"No!"

"Or who you slept with—"

"No!" She stomped her foot. "I tell you, I do not like him at all."

"You don't like a handsome, courteous gentleman who admires you?" Rafe had more than a little trouble believing that.

Her mouth turned down, not in the attractive pout she had perfected, but in a thin, petulant line. "He does not admire me."

The brothers exchanged raised-eyebrow glances.

"What did he do?" Rafe asked.

She didn't answer.

"What did you do?" Noah asked.

Francesca turned on him. "Nothing! I did nothing! A little light flirtation, that is all."

"I'm confused." Noah sat forward, glanced at the monitor, then stared compellingly at Francesca. "Why should you be angry with Victor if you indulged in a little flirtation with him?"

"Not with Victor! I flirted with that young waiter, the handsome one. The one who works the lobby and bar. Tall, blond, firm buttocks—"

Rafe covered his eyes with his hand.

"Trent?" Noah suggested.

"Yes. Trent." Francesca's voice turned sultry. "He worships me. But I wouldn't have slept with him!"

This was getting more and more odd.

Apparently Noah decided Rafe needed help, because he took over the questioning. "What does Victor have to do with Trent?"

"It was late. The boy and I were teasing. The wine bar was closed." She frowned at him. "Noah, the bars close too early here."

"I have nothing to do with that, Francesca." Noah's scrutiny wandered to the monitor, then returned to the conversation. "The state of California regulates the hours."

"Preposterous!" she said.

"Victor, Mom," Rafe prompted.

"Victor arrived in a huff! He spoke rudely to the boy of whom I am very fond—"

"What's his name?" Rafe asked.

She hesitated. "Trevor."

Noah cackled.

"How fond can you be of him, Mom? You can't even remember his name." Rafe glanced at the monitor again. Still clear.

"That is of no consequence! He was sweet to me! And Victor sent him away." She threw her hands into the air. "Then he . . . he escorted me back to my cottage."

Noah leaned into the keyboard and started typing, his gaze fixed on the screen.

"Mom, did he hurt you?" Rafe asked.

"No. He is not that kind of man." Francesca sounded huffy on Victor's behalf.

"Can you see them on the security tapes?" Rafe asked Noah.

"I'm looking. Yes!" Noah pointed at the screen. "There's a shot of them on the path to her cottage, and the timeline is right."

Rafe looked. "Okay, so Victor and Mom were out the door of the Luna Grande after the feed to the cameras was cut. That's why we never saw him exit the bar. When did Victor leave her cottage?"

"Looks like about four in the morning."

"He shouted at me!" Francesca was clearly

affronted and astonished they were not outraged on her behalf.

Noah was jumping from one time frame to another, one camera to another. "Victor went straight to his room and didn't come out for two hours, right before he reported the vandalism."

"So Victor's off the hook," Rafe said with satisfaction.

Francesca tugged at Rafe's arm. "No, he is not, because in my cottage, he said rude things to me."

Rafe was liking Victor more and more all the time.

"I can't imagine any man saying rude things to you," Noah said. When Rafe glared, Noah shrugged. "Really. Have you looked at her?"

"I know." She took a deep breath. "It is outrageous." But her voice shook, she sank onto a chair in front of Noah's desk, and a tear dripped down her cheek.

At his mother's sniffling, Rafe's liking for Victor faded. "What did he say?"

"He said . . . he said I should not waste my time chasing after children." A sob hiccupped out of her. "That sleeping with a little boy would not recapture my own youth."

"Ouch," Noah said.

"He said a beautiful woman deserved more than . . . than vapid posturing men who want only to u-use me for my money and influence in the movie business." Her shoulders shook as she tried to suppress her tears. "He said . . . he said I do not need any man, that I should be . . . should b-be strong by myself. Only th-then could I meet a man who was my . . . my . . . my . . . equal."

Noah passed Rafe the box of Kleenex.

Rafe offered the box to his mother. "I've been saying that for years."

She pulled out a handful of tissues and blew her nose. "But you are my son. Of course you must say nice things to me about how strong I am. But it's not true!" She tossed the wad of tissue at the trash can. "The body is no longer firm, the skin is not smooth and beautiful anymore, and I still have no one to love me with the passion and the fire I desire!"

For once, she wasn't speaking for effect or providing a spectacle. She really meant what she said, and Rafe knelt in front of her and smiled. "Mom, you don't need anybody else. You're pretty damned cool all by yourself."

"Do you think so?" She got more tissue and blew again.

"Who was the young girl who fought her way up from the streets of Naples to become Italy's biggest film star?" he asked. "Who picked her own scripts and put her name on the top of the credits? Mom, you don't give yourself enough respect."

"I'm a big fan of yours, Francesca," Noah said.

"On-screen, you always play the kind of strong woman I admire."

"Don't play me, Noah Di Luca," she retorted. "I know the truth. Most men like stupid, clinging women."

Noah nodded. "Sad but true."

"Yes, there are very few men whose egos are sturdy enough to stand up to a strong woman, but we are the only ones worth having," Rafe said.

"You!" Francesca threw the box of tissues at him, but she laughed. "So I must grow old alone?"

Rafe got serious in a hurry. "Surely that's better than being humiliated by men like your former husband."

"Yes . . ." She dabbed at her red nose, and stood. "Victor is innocent of this vandalism, but he would not say that he had been with me because he didn't want anyone to know we had been together in a cottage. He is an old-fashioned gentleman, and he didn't want false rumors that said we had been lovers."

"Why didn't you tell the truth as soon as you heard?" Rafe asked.

Her gaze fell. "Because I didn't want people to know I had been scolded like a wayward child."

Noah nodded. "I can see it would rankle."

"So, Rafe, will you tell your *polizia* that Victor is innocent?" she asked.

"It would be better if you did that, as your first

act of independence." Rafe waited to see how she would respond.

She thought, then said slowly, "I could do that."

Rafe opened the door. "Perhaps you could arrange for the car to bring Victor back so he knows who sprang him from jail?"

"He doesn't deserve such a courtesy!" She tossed her hair again and strode out.

The storm was over. Francesca was back in fine form—but perhaps between Victor, Noah, and Rafe they'd given her food for thought.

Rafe sure hoped so.

As he shut the door, Noah leaped to his feet. "Rafe! We missed it! He's in!"

Rafe swung away from the door. "Who is it?"

"Blond. Tall. He's turning so I can see his face. . . ." Noah pointed at the monitor. "Josh Hoffman. Josh Hoffman! I gave that little shit a donation for his college fund!"

"Focus, Noah. Let me make sure we're recording." Rafe walked to the desk. The record light was on.

Then, for the first time since it had been hacked, his cell phone rang. Suspiciously, he pulled it from his pocket.

The number was from overseas. From Kyrgyzstan. He answered, put the phone to his ear, and shouted, "Where the hell have you been?"

His team leader shouted back, "In hell, but you know what Winston Churchill said—if you're going through hell, keep going. We brought her out. She's alive and well!"

Rafe crowed with laughter and relief.

His team was out of the mountains and safe, their mission accomplished, the helicopter pilot safe in their hands.

He was looking at the hacker—they'd caught him red-handed.

Success. Success all around. Success at last.

"Congratulations, Ellis!" he said into the phone. "Listen. I'm working a situation, but do whatever is necessary, call in any reinforcements to get out of the country and onto a U.S. military base. I'll meet you there and—"

Somebody knocked furiously on the office door.

He and Noah looked at each other.

"Just get out," he said to Ellis. "Okay?"

"Affirmative." His team leader hung up.

Whoever it was started hammering with a fist.

Rafe hurried to the door and yanked it open.

Ebrillwen stumbled in, her perfect hair mussed, her cool eyes wild. "I can't go down there. Come on. Come on! I can't go down there."

Tom Chan limped up behind her. "We've got a mess on our hands, man."

"Calm down," Rafe said, although his own heart started a fast, powerful beat. "What's wrong?"

"She sent me to get you." Ebrillwen had her hand on her chest. "It's Josh. He's going down into the cellar—"

"It's okay. We're taping him," Rafe told her.

"Son of a bitch!" Noah shouted. "Brooke's in the cellar. She followed him down!"

Chapter 47

Heart racing, hand clutching the bottle of champagne, Brooke stood outside the last cellar door, at the end of the long, gloomy corridor. She'd followed Josh from a distance, taking care to stay back, to move soundlessly, to be one with the shadows.

She thought she'd succeeded. He seemed oblivious to her presence.

Now she peered inside the murky room, trying to remain as still as possible, to see what—or who—was in there. All Brooke could recall was Zachary telling her that Josh liked to pull the legs off the gophers.

Why hadn't Madelyn come when Ebrillwen paged her?

Did Josh have her trapped down here?

Oh, God. Brooke wished Ebrillwen were here with her. But Ebrillwen had taken one look at the stairs leading down to the cellar and backed up, shaking her head.

Brooke had discovered Ebrillwen's phobia—going underground.

Nothing had shaken her refusal, and Brooke didn't have time to persuade her. Didn't really want to worry about someone so out of her mind with fear that she would give them away.

But Brooke didn't want to be alone.

Ebrillwen wasn't the only one who, just on principle, didn't like basements. Brooke didn't like them, either, and more than that, she didn't want the responsibility for Madelyn's rescue to be hers and hers alone. Because the cellars smelled like a tomb, looked like a tomb. And Brooke was afraid that for Madelyn, this was a tomb.

Brooke had sent Ebrillwen to get Rafe. The housekeeper could handle that—and hopefully, she had.

Josh walked from an unseen corner to the huge barrel that stood on its side on a stand. He worked eagerly to open the trapdoor at the end. He pulled out a bottle of wine, glanced at the label, and laughed.

The wine? Massimo's wine? Was that why he was down here? Had he found it?

Because Brooke wasn't willing to risk her life for a bottle of wine, no matter how valuable.

She started to ease back—and jumped when he said loudly, "See? I told you this was where I'd find gold."

He turned and looked toward the corner closest to the door, out of Brooke's line of sight.

Oh, no.

Madelyn was there. Or at least, someone was.

He walked toward the person, saying, "I know, you don't care, but I'm going to make a fortune . . . and you're going to stay here forever and ever." He disappeared from Brooke's view . . . and grew silent.

Brooke needed Rafe. He'd save Josh's prisoner.

Ebrillwen had promised to send him.

Brooke would leave, go meet him, give him all the details.

But first, she could do this one thing. A distraction that might save the prisoner's life.

Brooke twisted the wire off the champagne. Shook it up. She put it on the floor and prepared to run.

And Josh leaped from behind the door, grabbed her arm, and slammed her forehead against the wall.

She screamed in surprise and pain.

He laughed, twisted her wrist high behind her back, and marched her inside the cellar room. "You are so fucking stupid." He spoke into her ear. "I knew you were there all the time. I heard your message to your boyfriend. Man, as soon as I heard my name, I knew it was time to set a trap. And you fell for it! So fucking stupid."

Her eyes were swelling. Her nose was bleeding. "Didn't think you could monitor all the phone calls."

"Shut up." He yanked her arm tighter.

Would he dislocate her shoulder? Rip it off?

He steered her toward the darkest corner. "You know everybody. Everybody trusts you. And you're big, wonderful Rafe Di Luca's girlfriend. We were listening to your calls 'specially."

He was right. She had been stupid.

But that champagne bottle . . . it was still on the floor, waiting to blow. Thank God for Chan's suggestion. Perhaps the distraction would be enough.

No . . . the distraction *would* be enough. She would make it enough.

"If I turn off the lights and lock you in here, it's going to be a long time before anyone finds you." Josh giggled. "You'd probably run in circles for hours, bang on the door, and cry like a baby. So it would be a kindness if I break both your legs first. Right?" She felt his lips move against her ear.

"No."

He bit the shell of her ear. Broke the skin.

She screamed again.

"Right?" He jerked on her arm, twisted her elbow, bringing the pain in her shoulder to an exquisite agony.

Tears poured down her face.

A voice spoke from the door. Rafe's voice. "Let her go."

Josh and Brooke both jumped.

Josh released her. He spun her around, pulled her back against him.

Rafe's face swam before Brooke's blurry gaze. *Thank God. Oh, thank God.*

Josh jammed something small and cold against her forehead. "I'll kill her," he said.

A gun.

Of course. What else? He had a gun.

"And add murder to your crimes?" Rafe's voice was warmly reasonable. Even better, he held a pistol pointed in their direction. "That would be stupid. Josh, you're not stupid."

The bottle Brooke had placed by the doorway. Champagne. Why wouldn't it blow?

"What difference does one more body make? You know I killed Hernández." Josh's voice lost its manic edge, became petulant and whiny.

"There's only one way out of this cellar. You can't escape. You know you can't." Now Rafe sounded harder, more authoritative. "Give up."

"I'll use her to get me out." Josh squeezed her throat with the bar of his arm. "You'll do anything for her. I know you will."

Champagne. Was it not going to work?

"Yes, I'll do anything to save Brooke," Rafe said.

"Good to hear," she croaked.

He paid no attention. "But law enforcement has been called. Do you imagine—"

Boom! The detonation from the corridor was small but loud.

Rafe started.

Josh recoiled.

Brooke rammed her elbow into Josh's ribs,

stomped on his toe, spun, and dropped to the floor.

Shots blasted, echoed, died.

Josh shrieked and fell backward.

She crawled, desperately, blindly, wanting away from him.

Voices shouted.

Lights flashed on, bright lights. Spotlights on Josh's writhing form.

Someone swooped her up—Rafe, it was Rafe; she knew it was Rafe—and ran down the long, dim corridor toward the hotel level.

She was safe now. She knew she was safe.

And she passed out.

"It's only minor injuries when they happen to someone else." Nonna leaned over Brooke's hospital bed and smiled into Brooke's right eye.

The other eye was swollen shut.

Her nose hurt.

Her shoulder ached.

Her head . . . her head throbbed with the beat of a thousand arrhythmic drums.

"They're keeping her overnight because they're worried about a concussion." Her mother's voice spoke from off to Brooke's left. "And because she's in shock."

"Rafe?" Brooke mumbled. They were keeping her all night. She was in the hospital. The doctors must have ordered drugs, because she could hardly talk. And she was so tired.

"Rafe's fine," Nonna said proudly. "Not a scratch on him."

"Madelyn's fine, too," her mother said. "Rafe said you thought Josh had captured her, but she apparently saw DuPey on the hotel grounds, decided to tell the truth about the Flores murder and to do it before she lost her nerve, and while you were searching for her in the cellar, she was in police custody."

"She wasn't hurt at all?" Somewhere in the deep reaches of her mind, Brooke was glad. So glad.

"She really is fine. Josh Hoffman wasn't so lucky." Her mother's voice again, rich with satisfaction. "Rafe's shot went through his spleen. They operated, saved his life, but he'll be lucky if he ever walks again."

Where's Rafe?

"Who would have thought that fool was smart enough to fool my grandson and paralyze the hotel's security system?" Nonna asked.

"Not me," her mother said.

Not me, either, Brooke wanted to say. But her mouth wouldn't work, and somehow both of her eyes were closed.

Someone patted her hand, and Nonna said, "Go to sleep, dear. Sleep is the best thing for you now."

Chapter 48

When Kayla Garcia pushed Brooke's wheelchair out the hospital doors, Brooke smiled with relief and delight.

Victor was waiting to drive her to Bella Terra. Victor, dapper and handsome, looking none the worse for his experience with an American jail.

"I'm so glad to see you," she said.

"And I to see you." He helped her out of her wheelchair into the backseat, gave her a bottle of cold water to drink, an ice pack for her forehead, and a broad-brimmed hat. He went around to the driver's seat, buckled himself in, and said, "I'll have you back to Bella Terra in fifteen minutes. Noah's waiting to take you to your cottage. I know that's where you want to be. Only in your own home can you truly recuperate."

"Thank you, Victor. You're very sweet." She smiled and refrained from asking the one question that haunted her—*Where's Rafe?*

Other than a big, ugly headache, Brooke didn't remember much about her hospital stay. But she did clearly remember Nonna assuring her, *Rafe's fine. Not a scratch on him.*

Even under the influence of major meds, Brooke had been delighted and relieved.

Now . . . not so much, especially since from the moment he'd dropped her at the emergency room, she hadn't heard his voice. Which meant . . . which meant he was busy with other things. Important things.

Clearly, she was not an important thing.

Victor put the car in gear and glanced in the mirror. "Everyone at Bella Terra wanted to line up to welcome you back, but I told them you wouldn't be well enough to handle it. I did discourage them, although I fear you'll still have to run a small gauntlet. Noah has promised them that as soon as you're healed, we'll have a party in your honor."

"Everyone is very sweet." She was tired. And lonely. In pain. And depressed.

"Everyone knows the whole story now. Noah told us—"

Noah. Not Rafe.

"—about how Josh hacked into the computers and that's why he was able to commit those crimes without being caught. He was insane, I think. What did he have to gain?"

Obviously Noah hadn't told everyone about Massimo's bottle of wine. Wise man. All the horrible things that had happened—Hernández's murder, the destruction of the wine bar, yesterday's horror in the cellar—were the fault of that damned bottle. The bottle, and Joseph Bianchin. "So as soon as DuPey discovered Josh was behind the crimes, he let you out of jail?" she asked Victor.

He didn't smile. Not quite. But he seemed warmly pleased when he said, "Actually, Miss Francesca Pastore came to the jail and testified as to my whereabouts that evening. I was not in the bar, as I had previously claimed, but with her." He lifted one finger off the wheel. "Although not in any biblical sense. We were simply talking."

"Of course." Brooke didn't quite smile, either.

"I am telling the truth," Victor said.

In deference to his dignity, she banished every remnant of her amusement. "Of course," she said again, very seriously.

"Miss Pastore is the one who sent you the hat. She said you'd like to protect your injuries from the sun."

"She's very thoughtful." Although what Brooke really wanted was to hide her misery behind a pair of sunglasses. But with the bridge of her nose so swollen, that wasn't possible. Not that it mattered who saw her.

Rafe wasn't here.

Victor drove the car up to Bella Terra's main entrance, and as he had predicted, the staff awaited her arrival.

Ebrillwen, looking a little less haughty since her refusal to accompany Brooke underground.

Madelyn, apparently out on bail and looking tremulously happy.

Zachary and a cadre of his gardeners, smiling broadly.

Tom Chan, leaning on his cane, frowning at Brooke's red, puffy features.

Brooke donned the hat and stepped out of the car, feeling less like a heroine and more like a fool for love—again.

The little crowd didn't seem to care. They broke into applause.

She waved formally, little flips of the hand like the queen of England, and as they chuckled, Victor helped her climb into the waiting golf cart beside Noah.

She relaxed against the seat, her body sore and bruised, her spirit . . . just as bruised. She wanted to get away, as Victor said, to get home. There she could hide like a wounded animal, lick her wounds, prepare herself to face the world . . . alone again.

"Stop!" Francesca called.

Brooke sighed.

Stepping close, Francesca took Brooke's chin in gentle hands. She removed the hat, turned Brooke's face toward the sun and examined her, then pronounced, "You'll heal well. No permanent damage."

Oh, yeah? Too bad I got entangled with your son again. But all Brooke said was, "Thank you, Francesca. That's a comfort to know."

Francesca's blue eyes shone with compassion.

That woman knew exactly the desolation Brooke suffered.

But Brooke couldn't handle kindness right now; she was about one stiff upper lip from bursting into tears. With another regal wave, she told Noah, "Let's go."

Noah drove toward her cottage. He seemed oblivious to her distress as he filled her in on their preparations. "Chef has stocked your refrigerator. Your mother's coming in this afternoon to check on you. You'll be safe, of course, now that Josh is in the hospital and under guard."

"Unless Joseph Bianchin has hired more thugs."

Noah's reassuring expression grew grim. "On my rather strong suggestion, Bianchin has left the area, at least temporarily. We'll hear about it if he returns. He has also assured me the problems are over."

Brooke didn't quite know what to think. "What did you say to him?"

Noah cast her a glance quite unlike the genial resort host she thought she knew. "I suggested that Nonna was beloved by ninety percent of this town, and if it became common knowledge that he had hurt her, he'd be hard-pressed to buy a tank of gas or get a tooth filled." While Brooke digested Noah's unexpected show of muscle, Noah added, "He's got other homes in other locations. Let him go elsewhere to live and die— preferably die, and preferably soon."

"Yes. I wish he would die, and this stupid Italian feud with him. All this fuss about a bottle of wine . . . Did you ask him why now?"

"He said family honor, and that Massimo's bottle was his birthright." Noah shook his head. "Yes, you're right. Stupid Italian feud—but we're known for them, aren't we?"

"All right. Thank you. I feel safe." She didn't think twice before adding, "At least until I leave."

Noah pulled up in front of her cottage and turned to face her. "Until you leave? Are you going on vacation?"

"No, this is my official two weeks' notice." She took the plunge, cut the ties, shook the dust from her shoes. "I'm quitting and moving to Sweden."

"Sweden? You've got a job in Sweden?" Noah's astonishment was both satisfying and irritating.

"Am I really so boring that you have to act like a single act of spontaneity means I've lost my mind?" she snapped.

He hesitated.

"Never mind. Don't answer that." She took a breath. "I don't have a job yet, but I will have." Of that she had no doubt.

"But why . . . ?"

"Why am I leaving? Or why Sweden?"

She had seldom seen Noah floundering, but he was floundering now. "Yes. Both."

"Except for college, I've lived in Bella Terra since I was eleven." She had been safe. Secure. "It's time I explored the world." The safety had been an illusion. She knew that now. And it was time she lived like a single woman, free of responsibilities. "And as for Sweden—it's different from here. I like that."

"Very different." Noah seemed to be picking his words. "You'll need more than one coat."

"I like to shop."

Finally Noah got around to asking the question he'd clearly wanted to ask right away. "What does Rafe say about this?"

"I really don't know; nor do I care." Although she didn't realize it, her eyes were flashing.

Undeterred, Noah pressed on. "Does he even know?"

"You mean, did I tell him before he left for his next job?" She flounced out of the golf cart. "No. I was unconscious. Now if you'll excuse me, I need to go pack." She didn't look around as Noah drove away.

Let him go off and call Rafe and tell him good old reliable Brooke was leaving.

Rafe wouldn't care.

No one was irreplaceable. She knew it. She knew that in two weeks she'd be gone, and in another two weeks Victor would have successfully stepped into her shoes and no one would even care or remember.

She stomped up the porch stairs.

Wrong thing to do. The painkillers weren't quite good enough, because her muscles and joints hurt, the trip from the hospital to her cottage had wearied her, and she wanted a nap.

She fit the key card in the lock, turned the knob, and as she opened the door, Jenna ran up the path, bounded onto the porch and trilled, "Brooke! My gosh, I'm so glad you're back in one piece!"

Brooke turned to face her former classmate and the current Bella Terra spa manager.

They were about the same height, the same weight. They were both in great shape, were both successful women.

But Jenna was blond, curvaceous, with boobs so pointy no guy in the world ever noticed her face. She used her sexuality like a weapon, and even now she made Brooke feel like a troll.

Here was yet another reason to be glad she was leaving. If she had to face another day being the dark-haired bitch boss to Jenna's blond perkiness, she would throw up.

"What can I do for you?" Brooke was pleased to note that she sounded none too welcoming.

Jenna lifted a bottle of champagne. "I came to help you celebrate your victory over that big, bad Josh Hoffman." She widened her blue eyes. "Who knew he was such a felon?"

"Really. Who knew," Brooke said flatly. "I

appreciate the gesture, but I'm on pain meds. I can't drink."

"It's okay!" Jenna pushed past Brooke and into the house. "I can!"

"Of course you can. And really, what else matters?" Brooke followed her in and let the door slam behind her. "I'm busy right now, packing." Might as well give Jenna first shot at the gossip. After all, no one would enjoy it more. "I just gave Noah my two weeks' notice. If you hurry, you could be the first one to apply for my job." *That* should send Jenna rushing out the door.

Brooke headed for the bedroom.

"I don't think I could get it." Jenna didn't sound nearly as animated as she had been, and the champagne gave a solid thump as she placed it on the coffee table. "You see, you're not the only one who's leaving."

That stopped Brooke in her tracks. She turned on her heel. "You're leaving Bella Terra? Why?"

"Because if I stay"—Jenna stood tall, her fists on her hips—"the police will arrest me."

Brooke stared at that cold, angry, resentful face—and she got it. She got it, but she didn't, couldn't believe it.

"Don't you want to know why they're going to arrest me?" Jenna mocked.

Brooke sorted through the facts she knew. "For hacking into Bella Terra's security system?"

396

Because no one had believed Josh had the brains to do that, and in school, Jenna had always been great at logic and math—and computers. "As an accessory to murder?" Because Josh might have wielded the actual garrote, but Jenna was cunning, intelligent, and ruthless. "For trying to steal a valuable bottle of wine and for trying to kill me?"

"Josh tried to kill you." Jenna smiled with frank gratification, pulled a tiny pistol from her pocket, and pointed it at Brooke. "I'm the one who's actually going to do it."

Chapter 49

Rafe got back to Bella Valley and went right to the hospital, only to be told Brooke had checked out less than an hour before.

Good. That meant her injuries weren't serious enough to require further treatment. Yet he knew she'd still be bruised and shaken.

In fact, he was depending on it, since he had no doubts she'd be angry and hurt that he'd left her at the hospital without a word. This way, she couldn't run away when he locked the two of them in her cottage so they could have a conversation about their past, their present, and their future. He'd put it off long enough, and when he'd seen her yesterday, bleeding and in the hands of a killer . . . he shuddered.

Yes, he wanted to talk to Brooke in her own cottage without the medical staff coming in and out, her mother glaring, and his grandmother hovering, prompting him to get it right at last.

He would get it right. This time he would.

As he pulled into the Bella Terra parking lot, his cell phone, his wonderful, unhacked cell phone, rang. He picked up and grinned at the youthful, worried face that popped up on the monitor. "Darren, my man, we got our perp."

"You got the killer?" Darren's hair looked as if he'd been pulling at it.

"Yesterday." Rafe got out of the car. "Sorry I didn't call sooner, but another job came through and it involved military security clearance, so I've been in the cone of silence for twenty-four hours. I'm now thoroughly debriefed."

"Thank God you got that bitch." On-screen, Darren actually did pull his hair. "I was sweating bullets here, trying to figure out how to tell you I'd screwed up."

"I wouldn't say you'd screwed up." The path toward Brooke's cottage wound through artful plantings. So Rafe cut across the lawns.

He needed to see Brooke now.

"I would. The thing was, she kept coming back into the security room, and she'd sit there in the chair with the webcam pointed right at her, and she'd fluff her tits. And it's not like I can't see that every day on some porn site, but this was like . . . She didn't know I was there so it was . . . Oh, geez, this is so embarrassing." Darren was babbling, making no sense. "It was, like, naughtier than porn and at the same time cleaner, if you know what I mean."

Rafe had been without sleep for thirty hours. On the plane back from Washington, he had been totally focused on what he should say to Brooke. Right now, he felt fuzzy brained and stupid; he knew Darren was telling him something important, but he wasn't catching on. "Jenna, you mean? Jenna Campbell? She came into the security room some more. To play games?"

"She was playing games, all right. She was playing me big-time. She knew I was there all along, probably saw me on the computer that first time she walked in." Darren sounded disgusted and his face was bright red. "So she'd fiddle with her boobs, and while I was drooling, she'd substitute a whole new security program that muffled the alarms wherever she wanted."

"How could she do that? She'd have to be an expert computer programmer."

"An expert with a gambling habit."

Darren wasn't making any sense. "How is that possible?"

"I know. She's a girl! A girl! Girls don't hack. Most of them don't know how to save a file."

"You have a lot to learn," Rafe mumbled.

"I never suspected her. God, Rafe, I apologize. I never suspected her at all. But I've been checking her records all night. She got kicked out of college because she was so into gaming—playing them, developing them—she cut classes. The only reason she was there for two semesters was because she went into the college computer and changed her grades in the system. She wasn't as good then as she is now, so they caught her. She still games, still cheats, too, and when those guys finally traced the money, she was totally screwed. If she doesn't pay them back, she's dead." Darren rubbed his forehead. "But you got her. Okay. As long as she didn't kill anyone else."

Rafe stopped walking. "What in the hell are you talking about? Jenna Campbell isn't the one we trapped. We trapped Josh Hoffman."

"The gardener?" Darren sounded absolutely incredulous. "He's nobody. I mean, he's vicious and everything, but he's dumber than a board."

"So you're saying Jenna Campbell—"

"Jenna Campbell is the brains behind the whole operation."

Rafe heard a gunshot.

He threw the phone to the ground and started running.

Wood and Sheetrock sprayed Brooke as she dived low toward Jenna. She landed on the area rug and skidded into Jenna's legs, taking her down like a bowling pin. Brooke heard a second blast of the pistol, the crash of the table, and the explosion as a lightbulb blew, and she kept rolling. She came to her feet, saw Jenna flat on her back, and kicked the pistol out of her hand. "What the hell's the matter with you?" Brooke shouted. "Did you let Josh talk you into doing this? Hurting Sarah Di Luca? Killing Hernández? Destroying the wine wall?"

Jenna grabbed Brooke's foot and pulled it out

401

from under her. Fortunately the pistol was still out of her reach.

On the way down, the back of Brooke's head slammed the end table. Black spots swam before her eyes.

Jenna jumped on her. Took her by her throat. Squeezed as hard as she could. "You stupid bitch. Josh! Josh is nobody. A good fuck. So what? I did it all. I did."

Brooke grabbed handfuls of Jenna's hair and pulled. Hard.

Jenna screamed like a scalded cat and clawed at Brooke's face—her tender, swollen face.

Brooke yanked her head back. Catching one wrist, she twisted, knocking Jenna off and yanking her arm up and behind her back. Placing one foot on her spine, Brooke considered whether a good hard yank would dislocate Jenna's shoulder.

After all, Jenna deserved a little pain. Because Brooke still ached from Josh's attack.

But she didn't want Jenna screaming. Not yet. "What's wrong with you? What are you whining about? Ever since I hired you, you've undermined me. Been a handful of thorns."

"Working for you. God, there is no justice. I'm smarter than you. Prettier than you. Even in high school, you didn't realize what I could have done—changed your grades, given you a prison record, or falsified your medical records." Jenna laughed hoarsely. "In fact, I did. According to your doctor, when you were sixteen, you had the clap."

Outrage made Brooke see red. "I was a virgin!"

"Yeah, but no one would ever believe it." Jenna's voice turned ugly again. "I could have brought you down anytime. Should have, but I wanted to see you suffer."

Incredulous, Brooke asked, "Suffer why? Why? As far back as I can remember, you always had everything. You were popular. You were a cheerleader. You were the head of the class. You made me miserable in high school."

"I didn't have everything. You had him." Was that bitter envy in Jenna's voice?

Brooke's raging headache eased. "Him? Rafe?"

"I had him. I kissed him." Jenna lifted her head, looked sideways at Brooke. "You didn't know that, did you? He didn't confess what we did in the library, did he? He was so horny because you—"

Brooke yanked on Jenna's arm.

Jenna flung herself sideways, knocking Brooke onto one knee. Grabbing Brooke's sore shoulder, she slammed her face-first to the floor. "Kiss your ass good-bye!"

Chapter 50

Rafe raced up onto the porch, let himself into Brooke's cottage—and stopped short.

A bruised and bloody Brooke Petersson knelt on Jenna Campbell's back, holding her wrist twisted in a very simple, very controlling karate move. She looked up at him and with a cool that would have made any one of his operatives proud, said, "Rafe, good timing. Could you take over for me? I need to get a towel—my nose is bleeding again."

"Of course." He walked over, his heart hammering, sweat trickling down his spine.

Brooke transferred Jenna's wrist to him. "I know one thing—if I wasn't buzzed on pain pills, I'd be out cold." On that preternaturally calm pronouncement, she staggered into the kitchen.

Jenna turned her head. "The bitch is crazy," she whispered. "She attacked me. Let's sneak out of here before she gets her gun and kills us both."

"I don't think so." He smiled evilly down into her face. "I've talked to Darren."

"Darren? Who's Darren?" She fluttered her lashes and pretended ignorance.

"The foolish boy hacker you seduced."

Brooke wandered back in, a dish towel pressed to her face. "Look at this mess," she muttered.

He looked around. End table knocked over.

Area rug crooked. Lamp on the floor, shade broken, bulb shattered. "Yeah, you women had quite a fight. Sorry I missed it."

"She attacked me." Jenna tried to struggle.

He tightened his grip a little bit.

She stilled.

"I know about your gambling debts." He was talking to fill Brooke in . . . and to push Jenna a little farther toward the edge. "I know that the collection agency is after your blood, and if you don't pay them back, they'll kill you."

As Jenna realized she was well and truly trapped, her color changed from pale to red and back again. "Now I've got the wine psycho after me, too. I don't even know who he is, but he said he'd kill me if I didn't deliver that wine. Because of you two, I've got nothing!"

Jenna was blaming them for her addiction, her stupidity, for the consequences she would face. Rafe couldn't believe her gall.

"I don't know." Brooke sounded nasal, and her eyes drooped. "I think you'll have three meals a day and a very nice exercise yard in the correctional facility."

"You stupid cow," Jenna hissed. "I won't live through the correctional facility. The collection agency will take me out."

"You should have thought of that sooner." Brooke flinched as the door swung all the way open, then relaxed as her mother banged her walker into the screen door. "Hi, Mom." She wavered where she stood.

Rafe wanted to hurry to her side.

But she paid him no attention. If he didn't know better, he would say she had a grudge against him.

Yeah. Probably she did.

"Would you call the police?" she asked her mother. "I'm going to go lie down with this ice on my face."

Kathy Petersson entered and took in the chaos with her typical unflappable demeanor. Pushing her walker ahead of her, she went to the phone. "You bet, honey."

When Brooke woke up in her own bed in her own bedroom, it was dark, she was cold, she was hungry, and she had to pee.

She flipped on the light. She changed into her nightgown and put on her robe. She took care of matters in the bathroom. She headed toward the kitchen and heated up lasagna and made a salad. Taking it into the living room, she put it on a tray and curled up on the couch.

There. She'd fixed all her immediate worries.

Well . . . except she was alone, too, and that problem wasn't easily cured.

A woman, after being battered two days in a row, would think that someone would hang around. Her mother. Rafe . . .

If she felt better, she'd start packing for Sweden. Instead, she ate heartily—the lasagna was good!—found Masterpiece Theatre's *Jane Eyre* on her DVR—it was sweepingly romantic and Toby Stephens was hot—and settled down for an evening alone—one of far, far too many.

Maybe her mother was right. Maybe she should put the moves on one of the guests at the hotel. She was pretty sure Gagnon would oblige her. Although—she maneuvered around until she could look into the round, gold-framed mirror on her wall—perhaps for her already battered ego's sake, she should wait until the swelling had disappeared and the bruising faded a little more.

Tonight, she'd spend a lovely three hours with Mr. Rochester.

She was cuddled onto the couch, comfortable, full, and warm, watching him beg Jane to stay with him, when someone tapped on her door. Before she could stir, someone swung it open, easily and without undue effort.

Rafe walked in carrying a bag from the restaurant.

"Come on in." She was pleased to realize she felt well enough to be sarcastic.

He didn't notice. Or he didn't care. "Hey," he said softly. "How are you feeling?"

"I'm okay." *Great.* He was going to be solicitous.

Too late, buster! She refused to forget that he'd

scooted out of town as soon as he dropped her at the hospital.

He examined her. "You look better. Bruised, but not so exhausted."

"Ice and sleep. Lots of it."

He'd disappeared while she was in the hospital . . . but he had come back, and if she was going to be logical, she would correctly remember he had arrived in time to handle the Jenna situation, and for that she was glad. She didn't know what she would have done if he hadn't appeared when he did. She hadn't had many more rounds with Jenna left in her.

And he looked tired, a man who'd had too much work and too little sleep for too long.

"Did you hear from your team in Kyrgyzstan?" she asked.

"You remembered!" He looked touchingly pleased. "Yes, they're out, everybody's safe, and if I tell you anything more, I'll have to kill you."

She laughed unwillingly, and just as unwillingly examined him as closely as he examined her.

His hair was damp. He was wearing a black tee that cut a line across his sculpted biceps, and a pair of black jeans that hugged his . . . Brooke brushed her hand across her eyes.

Obviously, she had been enjoying Mr. Rochester's seduction a little too much, because, well, not that Rafe didn't always look good, but right now, he looked delicious.

She needed to remember who he was, who she was, and act sensibly.

Sitting up, she tugged the belt of her robe tight and pushed her hair out of her eyes. "What have you got?"

"Dessert. I figured with your pain pills, you couldn't have a glass of wine, so I'd bring an offering of chocolate, fruit, and cream to the kick-ass goddess."

Rafe had a way about him. With any other man, Brooke would call it flattery. But Rafe had that admiring gleam in his eye, and that both warmed her and made her explain, "Jenna and I spar during kickboxing. We're pretty evenly matched, but today she really, really made me mad. She never had a chance."

"Remind me not to make you mad." He headed into the kitchen, disappeared from sight. Brooke could hear plates and silverware rattling as he called, "I had to go down to visit with DuPey, fill him in on developments, have him fill me in. He said the soil tests were done on Hernández. Josh and Jenna buried the body right here among Eli's vines—"

Knowing Rafe as she did, she felt free to interrupt. "When Eli finds out, there'll be two more bodies buried there."

Rafe stuck his head out of the kitchen and

looked at her quizzically. "I said exactly the same thing." He disappeared again. "If you hadn't gotten into that Dumpster, chances are no one would ever have found Hernández's body."

"Lucky me."

"DuPey wanted to talk to you. I told him he could have you tomorrow. Nonna called Eli and gave him the deets about Massimo's bottle of wine. He was flabbergasted, and I think he's forgiven me for letting Josh take out his wall of wine, although it's a huge loss for the winery." Rafe came back out with a single dinner plate, two forks, and a six-layer chocolate cake with chocolate frosting, decorated with berries and grapes, and served with decorative whipped cream on the side. He took her dinner plate and put it on the table, pulled up a chair, and sat facing her, knees touching. "Chef said this was your favorite."

"I love it, but I don't eat it!" He looked confused, so she explained. "I mean, not on a regular basis. The calorie count is about a million."

"There has been nothing regular about this last month." He offered her a bite of cake.

He was right. The scent of chocolate rose heady and rich in her nostrils. There'd been nothing regular about the last month.

So she took the cake in her mouth. The texture was porous and hearty; the thick frosting melted sweet and dark in her mouth. She closed her eyes to fully savor the flavor, and when she opened them, Rafe was staring at her, fork suspended in midair . . . and he wasn't thinking about the month's events.

He was thinking sex, deep and carnal.

She was not. She had control. She was absolutely not thinking about sex. She was thinking about the day's events. "Thank you for covering for me. I don't think I could have gone down to the police station and given any kind of coherent report."

"I, um . . ." Rafe put the fork onto the plate. It rattled against the china. "DuPey was sadly disappointed to discover both criminals were not only lethal, but local. He's looking at Bella Valley in a whole new way." Taking a glob of whipped cream on his finger, he held it to her lips.

What was he trying to pull here?

When she stared at him, eyes narrowed, he touched it to her lips. "Eat it. It's melting."

She took his hand, held it still, and licked the whipped cream off. Somehow his finger found its way into her mouth, and that made the whole experience suggestive and—she pushed his hand away and took a long, slow, deep breath—erotic.

She was involved with him again. She didn't want to be, but she was, the two of them tangled up in love and struggling to get away.

At least, she was struggling to get away.

He was plucking red, round grapes off the stem and offering them to her one by one.

She chewed the fruit; it was slick and sweet against her tongue. She swallowed and said, "Rafe, I've got to tell you something."

"About Sweden?" A smile quirked his mouth.

She leaned back in a huff. "Noah has a big mouth."

"He's my brother. His loyalty is to the family." Rafe smeared a strawberry through the frosting and offered it to her.

The scent of ripe red fruit teased her, and when she took a bite, she moaned with pleasure.

Rafe froze, his expression that of a man tied to a stake with the flames licking his legs.

Good. She was right: He was tangled, too. She relaxed, satisfied and feeling as if she had won at least one battle in this war of love.

Then Rafe said, "You could have Noah's total loyalty, too. All you have to do is marry me."

Chapter 51

Brooke slowly and deliberately chewed and swallowed. Contemplated Rafe and his sneak-attack dessert, and tried to decide whether he was serious. "Marry you? Because I beat up Jenna Campbell? You know, guys who get turned on by girls fighting are pathetic."

"Nothing about Jenna Campbell turns me on. Only you turn me on. I love you. Always have. Always will. And I want to marry you." He sounded, looked sincere, leaving her to wonder whether he'd reached into his past and called upon his acting ability, or if he meant what he said. And if he did . . . why now?

"It's never worked out before, you and me," she said. "And I'm going to Sweden."

"Okay."

He yielded so easily, she was suspicious.

Rightly so, for he put a dab of chocolate on her lower lip. Leaned into her . . . and licked it off.

The scent of chocolate and Rafe. The heat of his body. The texture of his tongue. Suspicion skidded away to be replaced by . . . lust. Hot, grand, burgeoning lust.

"What do you think?" he whispered against her mouth.

"Huh?"

"Will you marry me?"

He was irritating her. Talking to her and distracting her at the same time. "I told you—I'm going to Sweden."

"I like Sweden."

She put her hand flat on his chest and shoved him away. "You can't be serious."

He slid his arm around her shoulders, pushed her back against the pillows, tilted her head back, and smudged chocolate into the hollow of her throat. With his lips and tongue, he cleaned it off, slowly, thoroughly, his chest rubbing hers, his breath sweeping her skin. . . . "I have offices all over the world. I can work anywhere," he murmured.

She struggled to figure out what he was talking about. "I don't need you."

"I know. But *I* need *you*—desperately." He dropped his head onto the pillow beside hers and looked at her. "I can't keep living like this, Brooke, leaving you here, wandering the world alone, getting in tough spots and resolving to come back and get you, then not doing it because I know you're happy in Bella Valley. Because you're comfortable in Bella Valley. This time, you were in danger right here. You were almost killed—twice."

The cake was fun. The whipped cream was cute. The strawberries and grapes were silly. But he was serious, his blue eyes almost gray with earnestness.

"I'm fine." She smoothed his hair back from his forehead. "You don't need to propose marriage because you got a little scared."

Typical Rafe, he paid no attention to her. "While you're with me, I'll keep you safe. And when the kids start coming, we'll come back so Nonna and your mom can enjoy them."

Kids. He was ahead of her there.

That reminded her . . . "My mom said . . . she cursed me, actually, put a mom-curse on me. She said she hoped the next time I had sex, the condom would break."

"Did she?" A smile played around his mouth.

"The next time I had sex, we didn't even use a condom."

"I didn't have one on me." Because they were in the shower, he meant. "And I bet your mom didn't want the next time to be with me."

"That's the trouble with curses. You have to be really specific."

"You could be pregnant." When he saw the way Brooke was watching him, he tried to tone down his exultant expression. "I swear I didn't do it on purpose. I wasn't thinking. I was *feeling,* and what I felt in that shower was the desperate desire to make you happy."

She believed him. He had been desperate. So had she, desperate with grief and horror and needing an affirmation of life.

He continued. "If you're going to have a

415

baby . . . that would be wonderful. We'd be great parents. We've both seen how not to raise children, and we've both seen how to. And we're smart people with a lot of love to give."

"You've thought this through."

"A thousand times."

He made her want to laugh—except really, nothing had changed. "Why should I marry you, Rafe? What possible reason do I have for marrying you?" She put her finger in his face. "And don't you dare say because I might be pregnant."

"Of course not! You should marry me because you love me."

"Yes, that hasn't changed."

"And I love you."

"I believe you." All the warmth was fading. "But that doesn't change anything, either."

"I believe in the sanctity of marriage." A funny thing to hear Rafe say, but clearly he meant it. "I watched my father and my mother fight and separate and get divorced and I swore I wouldn't do that. Because if I got married, I wanted to stay married forever. You and me—the first couple of times around, probably we couldn't have made a marriage work. We loved each other, but we didn't talk about what we wanted in life, about our goals. If we had, we would have known we wanted different things in life. That would have saved a lot of heartache."

She swallowed, almost in tears with the memories and the hopelessness.

"No, don't cry for us. Now we're older, smarter, more mature. This time I know that when we get married, it will be forever. Our lives don't have to be all what I want or all what you want. I want to share your life, whatever life you choose, wherever you choose to have it, and have you share mine. I always liked to listen to you—now I've figured out I need to talk to you, too." He smiled, a sudden beam of light. "For instance, right now—I'm doing a pretty good job, aren't I?"

"You are." She smoothed his hair again. She had always loved his hair, the way it held the warmth from his body, the way it sprang back against her touch. "I'll tell you what we're going to do. I'll go to Sweden. You go off to wherever you need to go next. And we'll think about this. After the excitement of Jenna's little stunt has faded, my swelling has gone down, and you're not worried about me anymore, we'll talk about marriage again."

"So you aren't intrinsically opposed to marriage to me?"

"No. But I think we should wait to make sure—"

"That I'm not having a weird fit?" A grin flitted around his mouth. "A return of PTSD?"

"When you talk this much, I do worry."

He hid his face against her head, but his laughter was a rumble in her ear and against her chest. "It just so happens the next place I need to go is Sweden." Leaning back, he pushed his fingers into her hair and held her for his kiss, long and slow, deep and wet. "Darling, I'm a grown man. I don't propose marriage because I'm feeling wobbly. I propose because I know what I want."

Now she was feeling wobbly. "I still think a waiting period would be good."

"Sure. We'll wait as long as you want."

"Really?" He had given up very easily.

"Sure."

So she was right. This marriage proposal was nothing more than a knee-jerk reaction to the recent danger.

Good thing she'd been wary and insisted on caution.

She sighed deeply. If only she didn't love him quite so much . . .

Sitting up, he slathered frosting on his finger and put it to her mouth. He smiled as she licked it, as the rich frosting slid down her throat, warming her like dark, sumptuous lava.

She had him figured out now. "You're seducing me with chocolate. You think you can feed me a strawberry, then have your way with me!"

He looked down at her.

Her robe had fallen open; her bent knee revealed her long, naked thigh.

"Don't be ridiculous." He smoothed his palm up her leg, baring her to her waist.

"It's not going to work," she said. "I'm not so easily swayed." She hoped.

Because he wore that expression again, the one that made her heart beat more quickly, made her want to shift and moan. That particular look of his made chocolate superfluous.

Hooking his arm under her knee, he spread her legs, and, taking one of the grapes, he slid it inside her.

She gasped, which was silly, and asked, "What are you doing?" Which was sillier.

Leaning down, he used his tongue to manipulate the grape in and out, up and down. . . . It was slick and cool, then slick and warm. Then it seemed to disappear completely, and there were only his lips, suckling softly on her clit until she had come more times than she could count.

When he lifted his head, he murmured, "Negotiating."

"What?" What was he talking about?

"I told you we'd wait as long as you want to get married." He picked up a red, ripe strawberry, placing it on the concave part of her stomach, and smiled at her. "I'm negotiating the waiting period."

By morning, the cake was gone. The strawberries were gone. The whipped cream was gone.

And they were in Reno being married by a justice of the peace.

Chapter 52

Eli spoke to his friends and relatives—he knew or was related to almost everyone in the giant ballroom. He complimented the women dressed in fringe and feathers, teased the men in double-breasted suits with spats and gangster hats. He listened as voices rose and laughter grew boisterous, sure signs that the wine tasting was successful. He looked appropriately modest as his compatriots congratulated him on the rare and coveted ninety-five rating on his Teardrop Aglianico. He ignored the subtle hints and blatant demands for information on the unrest at Bella Terra and the loss of so much fine wine.

The carnage in Bella Terra's bar was no one's damned business except his. His and his brothers', but because of the wine . . . mostly his.

In a few minutes the charity auction would start, and, lubricated by alcohol, the guests would bid exorbitantly on posh wine dinners and long wine weekends, raising money to send low-income kids to college. The winemakers' committee would congratulate themselves, announce the totals; then everyone would troop into dinner.

And at some point that elderly Italian guy who looked like the Godfather would corner him and make him an offer he couldn't refuse.

He didn't know who the guy was, or why he was studying Eli, or what offer he would make, but this kind of thing had happened before. So many people wanted to partner with an upcoming winemaker to market him and his product, or to show him how to increase his yields, or to export him under a different label. . . . In his time, Eli had heard it all.

Never had he been forced to take the offer. He wasn't likely to start now.

Usually Eli enjoyed these functions, but this time . . . this time he wanted nothing so much as to escape, to be alone and try to figure out how in the hell he'd managed to get himself into this mess and how he was going to get himself out. Sure, he could talk to his family, tell them what had happened, and they'd pull together to solve his problem.

But it was his problem, his responsibility, and after all that had happened in his childhood, he had sworn never to depend on another person. Never. Not even his grandmother, not even his brothers. Anguish always followed.

Normally he would have ignored the vibration of his phone, but so desperate was he to escape, he pulled it out of his pocket to look.

A text from Rafe.

Congratulate me. Married today.

Eli stared, then broke into a smile. "Excuse

me," he said to the flirtatious, nubile, clearly available lady at his side. "I've got to call my brother." He strode out of the ballroom into the large, almost empty antechamber, picked a quiet corner, and dialed Rafe. When Rafe answered, Eli turned his shoulder to the room and asked, "Has poor Brooke sobered up enough yet to realize what a mistake she's made?"

Rafe sounded relaxed and happier than Eli had ever heard him. "I'll have you know she was totally sober when she said 'I do.' "

"But the pain pills helped!" Brooke yelled toward the phone.

Eli snorted. "I knew there had to be a reason why a sensible girl like Brooke would marry a *sfigato* like you. Well, congratulations! I'm glad someone managed to get something good out of the trouble at Bella Terra."

"You sound bitter, brother. Wanna tell me about it?" Rafe's voice had changed, become thoughtful and probing.

Eli should have remembered that both Rafe and Brooke had majored in perspicacity. "Nothing I can't handle." Firmly, he turned the subject to Rafe's impending problems. "Running off to get married! You two are in so much trouble with Nonna."

"And my mom and Brooke's mom." Now Rafe didn't sound quite so pleased with himself.

"What did Nonna say when you told her?"

"She had just got home from the hospital," Rafe said.

"They released her?" For one blessed moment, every muscle in Eli's tense body relaxed.

"She has to return to rehab every other day, but yeah, she's out." Rafe sounded as pleased as Eli felt. "She said congratulations to us and asked when we were planning our real wedding."

For the first time in weeks, Eli laughed out loud.

Rafe continued. "So tomorrow I'm driving Brooke back to Bella Terra to face Nonna, my mom, and Kathy."

"Kathy Petersson hates your guts!" Thoroughly enjoying himself, Eli leaned against the table piled with brochures from all the wineries represented inside. "What did she say?"

"She said if I didn't take care of her little girl, she'd shoot me and no one would ever find the body."

Eli laughed again, then sobered. "Wait. She could probably do that."

"I intend to take care of Brooke, anyway," Rafe said. "I would die for this woman."

"I know you would." Eli bitterly envied his brother. At the same time, he couldn't help it, but he thought him a fool.

Brooke must have taken the phone away from Rafe, because her voice was suddenly right in Eli's ear. "You know Nonna, Mom, and

Francesca are going to want a big wedding at the resort." Unlike Rafe, she sounded sullen. "I hate big weddings. I wanted to go to Sweden!"

Rafe retrieved his phone, and Eli heard him saying in a soothing tone, "We'll go to Sweden. Those women don't need us to plan a wedding. In fact, I'm pretty sure we'll be in the way."

Eli removed his black fedora, dropped it on the table, and pushed his fingers through his hair. "Listen, yesterday, Nonna told me the details about Massimo's bottle. Has anybody ever figured out why Bianchin suddenly decided he had to have it? Is he dying or something?"

"We don't know why, and frankly, if he's dying, he can't go fast enough. But it doesn't matter. I've been through Nonna's cellar and it's not in there, and she swears Nonno hid it before he died."

"I want that damned bottle of wine. It's ours, our inheritance. I want to pour it, taste it, flaunt our glasses in front of Joseph Bianchin, and make damned good and sure it doesn't cause us any more trouble." He hunched his shoulders as he remembered the wreckage of the Luna Grande, of his grandmother, battered and bruised in her hospital bed. Even the memory gave him the shivers.

"Amen, brother." Rafe sounded as riled as Eli felt.

No, wait. That prickling along his spine was caused by more than a memory. Someone was watching him. He glanced around the room.

The elderly man had stepped through the doorway of the ballroom and once again stood watching him, the sort of summing-up of one acute businessman for another.

It felt odd to be scrutinized so closely, so knowingly. Did Eli have this all wrong? Was this guy some old friend of the family? Was he from Eli's desolate past? "Rafe, I've got to go. Good for you on catching the villain, and even better on catching Brooke. You don't deserve her."

"I know it." Once again Rafe showed his knowledge of Eli and his reactions. "You sound stressed again. You okay? Need backup? I could get someone there in less than fifteen minutes."

The Italian was maybe sixty, with iron gray hair, sagging jowls, a droopy nose, and, by God, he was no more than five feet, six inches tall, with a dockworker's figure. But those eyes . . . He was shrewd. Yes, Eli's first reading of him was correct. This man was the Godfather incarnate.

"I don't think I'm in danger, but I am going to get off the phone." He straightened away from the table. "Congrats, Rafe. Condolences to Brooke. I'll see you back at Bella Terra before you leave, right?"

"Right." It was Brooke on the phone again.

"You be careful, Eli. I've never had a brother before, and I don't want to lose you now."

"No chance of that," Eli said, and hung up. To the Godfather, he said, "Can I help you?"

The man walked up and offered his hand. "Tamosso Conte. I am glad to meet you, Eli Di Luca." Conte spoke English with a decidedly Italian accent and the harsh notes of the city in his voice.

Eli shook his hand solemnly. "You're from Rome?"

"Milan. I'm in leather goods."

Sure. And Eli was in fruit production. "I hope you're enjoying your visit to the United States."

"It is always a pleasure to visit. I'm here on behalf of my daughter—she's half American and amazingly independent."

"American girls are like that."

"Yes." Conte put down his wineglass and reached into his pocket.

Not that Eli was worried he was going to pull out a gun, but it was a relief when he brought forth his wallet.

Conte pulled out a worn picture of a young woman seated at a desk, smiling brilliantly at the camera. "Pretty, isn't she?"

Eli barely glanced at her. "Very pretty." As tattered as the photo was, she was probably ten years older and twenty pounds heavier.

Conte beamed. "I worry about her. . . . She's an

author, you know? She wrote a mystery, hit the *New York Times* first time out."

"You must be very proud." Obviously he was. Not many men showed off photos of their adult daughters at the drop of a hat.

"Proud? Yes, but concerned." Conte gazed at the picture as if he couldn't get over the fact he even had a daughter; then he tucked it back in his wallet. "A girl like that, she doesn't need a man, or so she thinks. A father worries."

"I can see that you would." Eli had no idea where this was going, but he knew he didn't give a damn about this man's kid. Not when he was drowning in his own problems.

Conte got down to business. "Listen. You and me, we can do each other favors. Solve each other's dilemmas."

Ah, here it came. The ridiculous offer. And who knew? From this guy, maybe a threat. "What dilemmas are those?"

"Mine—I want grandchildren while I'm young enough to enjoy them. You"—Conte stepped in front of Eli and stared into his eyes—"you want enough money so that you don't lose your family's winery."

Eli stepped back fast and hard, and slammed his hip into the corner of a table. It hurt. He knew it did. But right now, he couldn't feel it. "What are you talking about?"

"You know what I'm talking about." Conte's

eyes were dark, determined, pitiless. "You were busy growing grapes, making wines, getting awards. You left the business in the hands of a dear old friend. He embezzled how many millions of dollars and fled to South America, leaving you in . . . How do Americans say it? Shit shape?"

"Close enough." No one knew. No one. How did Conte find out?

The very available lady who had been hoping for so much in the ballroom stepped out, spotted Eli and started over. She was weaving. She was smiling. She got within five steps of them and the sense of crisis between the two men stopped her in her tracks. Her eyes grew large and frightened; she swerved away and walked out the door as if she'd always been headed for the restrooms.

Conte waited until she was gone; then he continued. "You might have been able to sell some of those valuable bottles of wine from your bar in your resort. But the vandal destroyed them."

Eli spoke between his teeth. "Did you have a hand in that?"

"No. That was luck for me."

Eli stared, trying to see the truth about Conte.

Conte stared back, inviting him to read his character. "I am always lucky, Eli Di Luca. It is something to remember."

Eli wanted to bring this guy down. "My family is not without resources. I can ask my brothers for help."

"But you won't. The winery and everything concerning it is your responsibility."

How did the old man know *that?* Eli never told anyone his feelings.

As if he'd asked, Conte said, "I went looking for a good Italian boy to wed my daughter. Your name came up. I studied you. I know more about you than you know about yourself."

"No." About that, Eli was certain. "You don't."

"I know you've been trying to figure a way out of this mess, but you don't know what you're going to do." Conte spoke the classic line: "So—I'll make you an offer."

"At least I knew that was coming." An odd relief, to guess right about at least one thing.

"I help you. You help me," Conte said.

Eli wet his lips. "What kind of deal are you offering? Because I'm not putting the winery up as collateral—"

Conte chuckled. "No, you have the wrong impression. Deliberately? Or because you're an American and really don't understand? I don't know, but I don't want your winery." As if it were nothing, he waved off the one thing that Eli loved with all his heart. "I told you—it's about my daughter. I want her to wed. I want her to have children. If she had been raised like a proper Italian girl, I would tell her who to marry. But her mother raised her to be an independent woman. An American woman. So she has to fall in love. I want this to happen soon." The man whom Eli had marked as being shrewd, shallow, driven by greed, suddenly became a man overwhelmed by the need for family, for affection.

"I get all that." Eli had caught the drift of the proposal, but he really needed this spelled out. "What has this to do with me?"

The shrewd businessman returned. "It's easy. We sign a contract. The terms are clear. You court my daughter. You convince her she loves you. You wed her. And in return, I solve all your financial problems, the winery is on its feet again, and you are in complete control."

"About the wedding—you're joking." Conte had to be joking.

"Not at all." Conte pulled out the photo and again waved it at Eli. "I'm proposing what the English call a marriage of convenience."

Center Point Publishing

600 Brooks Road ● PO Box 1
Thorndike ME 04986-0001 USA

(207) 568-3717

US & Canada:
1 800 929-9108
www.centerpointlargeprint.com